BLACK MIRROR: A CAIT REAGAN NOVEL

AOIBH WOOD

For any woman who has felt beaten down by a system rigged
to her detriment.

And for Emma, the guiding star of my writing.

THE BOSTON PRETERNATURAL
INVESTIGATIONS SERIES

BLOOD RITUALS
BLACK MIRROR
GREEN RATH
DARK SISTERS (COMING 2024)

PROLOGUE

The doorbell rang, and I extricated myself from the hug. "I'll get it."

I strode to the door and opened it, wiping the tears of laughter from my eyes. Outside stood a tall man in his late forties with dark hair and a fairly long, unkempt beard. He wore a brown wool trench coat with fraying sleeves and held out an envelope. "Cait Reagan?" His voice sounded familiar, but I couldn't place it immediately.

"Yes?"

He looked like a guy serving court papers. I'd been through this before, so I took the envelope and held out my hand for the pen to sign. My tongue flicked out, catching the scent of stale cigarettes, alcohol, and greasy cheeseburger on his breath. His body odor suggested he hadn't bathed in a while, regardless of how much Old Spice he slathered on. I glanced down at the envelope; it was blank.

"Die, you vampire bitch!" He shouted, and before I could do more than look up, he blasted me in the chest, point-blank, with a shotgun he'd pulled from under his coat. I fell backward to the hard floor, feeling the wind knocked out.

"F-f-fuck," I stuttered and gasped, tasting blood and feeling a warm line trickle down my cheek. No matter how hard I tried to suck in a breath, I couldn't get air. Panic set in. My vision tunneled at the edges. Tires squealed somewhere. I looked left. Then right. My hands clawed at the marble.

Liz appeared over me. "Cait, darling! Hold on. I got you. Just hold on, baby."

"Mama, stay with us." It was Katie's voice, but my vision was spotty, and I couldn't see her. Liz sliced open her throat, and cold drops of her blood fell into my mouth and across my cheeks, but I couldn't swallow.

I coughed. Blood spattered back over Liz's face. I tried to speak, but nothing came out. I squeezed at Liz's hand as a tear rolled down my cheek, and I realized this was it. *Who would take care of them all if I wasn't there?*

Time seemed to slow down as the pain finally burst through the shock, and my body convulsed just once. I flicked my eyes back and forth through my blurry vision, and I tried to gulp once, then twice. Then the pain fell away.

Liz and Katie said something else, but their voices were just faint echoes as the blackness swallowed me.

CHAPTER ONE

Friday, December 10th

One month before my murder. . .

"That's one of Schmidt's vampires, alright. I think her name is Cynthia. I don't know her last name, though." Cold and milky, Cynthia's sightless eyes stared at me from her decapitated head. Her mouth was drawn back in a feral snarl of defiance, fangs bared and frozen in time—her final moment.

Heavy steel chains wrapped Cynthia's headless corpse, binding it to the only piece of furniture in the room, a ponderous, garage-built wooden table constructed of heavy four-by-fours and solid oak. Apart from the table and the dead vampire's discarded clothing lying on the floor, the cellar was largely empty. A rusted-out water heater lay propped up against one wall. Dust-covered ductwork spidered about the ceiling, dangling like fat silver tentacles over an open spot where the furnace once stood.

I glanced back at the body and noted that the chain attached to Cynthia's left arm was broken; one of the links had shattered. She'd put up a struggle. I paused to take a breath, trying to control my emotions. I imagined poor Cynthia, strapped to the table, terrified and near helpless, desperately trying to free herself as her captors brought down the final stroke. The thought took me down a dark well of memory where I sat hunched in the corner of my cell as vampiric blood-lust wracked my nerves and senses and metal spikes bound a cuff through my forearm. I shivered and squeezed my eyes shut, pushing the flashback slowly aside.

I snatched out one of my numerous handkerchiefs to wipe away a few burning tears. *No one deserves this,* I thought, with a sniff.

Carol knelt with me, snapping a few shots of Cynthia's head. "What is it?"

"Sorry, I can't help it. I was just imagining how frightened she must have been." I sniffed again and wiped my nose.

Carol nodded solemnly. "It happens to us all at some point. Did you know her well?"

I shook my head. "Not really. I met her once. Nastasia held a meeting of all local vampires two weeks ago. Cynthia was there. She seemed nice and pretty down to earth."

Carol looked at me as one might look at a traffic accident, with a mixture of horror and morbid curiosity. There might have even been a bit of disappointment in there somewhere, too. "What were you doing at a vampire meeting?"

I sighed at her accusatory tone. "Mandatory attendance. Nastasia still considers me a vampire, despite being cured. Not going isn't an option for me."

Carol twisted her mouth and pursed her lips. "Since when have you been afraid of a vampire?"

I didn't answer. Instead, I looked away, focusing back on the work. Fear wasn't the reason I kept going to the meetings.

Carol fished through Cynthia's discarded blazer, pulling something out of the inside breast pocket. "And here it is."

She handed me a business card of expensive thick stock, solid black on one side. I flipped it with a gloved hand, revealing a solid yellow field emblazoned with a highly stylized platinum lion's head and a diagonal stripe of gold and silver leaf. It looked for all the world like a family crest. The lion's head and the foil stripe looked like real precious metals. It was identical to the one we'd found on a dead vampire two weeks ago. I had suspected it was the killer's calling card, but this confirmed it. Calling cards were bad news. It meant the killers wouldn't stop. This was just the beginning. I bagged it and took it to the evidence tech outside, returning a moment later.

I looked back at Cynthia's corpse again. *Why hadn't she been staked? Why take the risk?* During the day, I could see that, but at night, I'd have kept her immobilized. A simple reason came to mind immediately. The bad guys had lost track of time. Easy to do in a basement.

Carol moved to the table, taking more photos and drawing me out of my musings. "Nastasia is the pretty one, right?"

I scoffed. "God, I should never have mentioned that."

"But you did!" Carol declared in unabashed amusement.

I sighed and rubbed my nose on my wrist to ward off a sneeze from the dust. "Yes, Carol, Nastasia's beautiful. I mean, attractive doesn't begin to describe her. But she's also ruthless with a capital R, bordering on evil. Not to mention she gives off a serious domme vibe."

Carol chuckled. "Maybe Doyle could date her. She's got a thing for pushy, bad girls."

Doyle bounced down the stairs, her auburn ponytail swishing wildly from side to side. She carried a portable fingerprint scanner and her kit. "Date who?"

"Nevermind," I dismissed, not wanting to give Doyle any ideas, but Carol fucked up that plan when she said, "A smoking hot brunette vampire who likes torture." I rolled my eyes. Carol just couldn't keep her mouth shut sometimes.

Doyle's face tilted in an odd bemusement, then slowly, the corners of her mouth erupted into a wicked grin, and she looked at me. "Ooh, does she have a number?" I was pretty sure she was trying to sound sultry, but it just came out cute.

I chuckled and shook my head emphatically. "No, Doyle. Just no. I like you in one piece." Doyle was young and friendly, but she had an oddly intense, almost sociopathic approach to her job, unaffected by the daily horrors we saw. It was sometimes unnerving how dispassionate she was. She was also into vampires with an almost compulsive obsession. After I'd been turned, she'd been pretty googly-eyed about it. She never asked me to bite her, but I thought that was more a matter of her nerve than her desire. So rather than argue with her, I changed the subject. "Anyway, where have you been? You're late."

"Sorry. I was out for dinner and had to go home to change."

Carol gave her a suggestive look. "Anyone that we know?"

I looked at Carol and sighed. "Come on, Carol, leave the poor girl alone."

Doyle's expression twisted in mock irritation. "It's fine, Cait. For your information, I was alone. I take myself on a date at least once a month."

Carol barked a laugh. "That's sad."

"It's not sad. It's self-care." Doyle said, pressing a finger from the corpse to the AFIS reader.

Now I couldn't resist. "It's sad."

Doyle turned on me playfully, hands on her hips. "Well, if it's so sad, why don't you do something about it?"

"She's got you there." Carol enjoyed fucking with us way too much.

I glanced up at Doyle's face, noting her raised eyebrows as she waited for an answer. I flushed. "How did this get to be about me? Besides, I have Liz and Katie to take care of. I don't have time to date."

Carol scoffed. "You're kidding. You can't be talking about the crazy blond vampire that locked you up in a dungeon."

I grimaced, and not that I shamed anyone's shade of kink, but I just knew Doyle would twist that all kinds of pervy.

She didn't disappoint, opening her mouth in mock surprise. "Why, Cait, I didn't know you were into that. Do you like restraints or cuffs? You look like a cuffs girl to me."

I turned about six shades of crimson and began to sputter like a cornered teenager with a crush. Christ, she hit close to home. "Really? Honestly? It's not like that. Liz is sweet."

"Oh, I bet she is!" Doyle said, making me laugh and flush even deeper.

"Oh, come on. I don't mean it like that. Nothing is going on; we're just roommates. She's helping me take care of Katie and my mom."

I thought that would shut them up, but Carol had to dive in for the kill, turning snide. "Katie wouldn't be a vampire if it weren't for Liz, so she doesn't get points for that."

I shot Carol an irritated glare and snapped. "You know what, Carol? You don't know what the fuck you're talking about. So please do me a favor and shut up about it. I don't talk to you about Janelle or how much you can't stand her parents or make jibes at her dad's stone age political views."

Carol snapped her jaws shut and screwed up her face. "Sorry, I didn't realize—"

"Didn't realize what?"

"I didn't realize how close you two were," Carol answered sheepishly. "I'm sorry."

I blew out an exasperated breath. "I just said it's not like that. We've become friends, that's all."

Doyle whistled loudly, grabbing our attention, and turned back to her camera with a 'don't get your panties in a wad' expression. Carol glanced away, studiously examining the table. Then she tried to make nice, changing the subject abruptly.

"How's your mom doing?"

My mood dropped even lower, along with my stomach. The aftermath of opening the black gate had left her neurologically devastated. She'd never be the woman who raised me again. "Yeah, Ma's not so good. We took her back to the rehab center, but she's deteriorating. They have no idea why. And before you say anything else, that wasn't Liz's fault, so lay off."

Carol squinted in irritation. "I wasn't going to say a word. I'm sorry to hear about your mother."

Doyle, being Doyle, walked over and wrapped me in a hug. "I'm sorry, Cait. I was only teasing. If you need anything, you know where to find me."

"Thanks, Doyle, that means a lot." I drew back quickly, afraid I'd start crying, and no one needed to see that on the job. Also, I felt a disconcerting shudder and the rush of skin prickling.

Doyle stopped as she moved around the table, pulling on a pair of magnifying glasses. She examined the stump of the neck and then ran a gloved finger over a groove in the table aligned with it. "This cut is straight and clean. Looks like they used an ax?"

I looked up. "An ax?"

"See the shape of the cut." She re-traced the groove in the table. "It had a wide, curved head."

"Like a headsman's ax?" Carol asked, moving over to examine it with us. "That's weird."

I snorted humorlessly. "Dead vampire Carol. Of course it's weird." I filed that information away, though. These guys had been pretty well prepared.

We finished our walk of the crime scene, seeing several cigarette butts and some footprints, but not much else. I kept smelling something in the air that was bugging me. "Speaking of axes, there's a whiff of men's cologne in here. It's faint under the blood and the cigarette smoke, but it's there."

"You smell cologne?" Doyle raised an eyebrow. "I don't smell anything."

I flicked out my forked tongue at her.

Doyle pressed her lips together, suppressing what looked like a grin, and hurriedly looked away. "Do you smell anything else?"

I smirked at Doyle's discomfort. "Let's see." I tasted the air once more. "You had fish for dinner and something with garlic. Carol had West Indian stewed chicken for dinner with her mom's—"

"Oh!" Carol had removed her glove and touched the table, then she turned pale and wobbled a bit, beginning to stumble.

I rushed over and caught her arm before she fell. "You okay?"

"Umm, yeah, I think so. I had a horrific vision of the victim growling at me and biting a man's hand. He was wearing a blue dress shirt, I think." When she looked back up at me, her expression turned horrified. She shook her head.

"Are you sure you're okay?"

"I don't know," Carol whispered, placing both hands on the table, then jerking them back with a jaw-rattling shiver. "I don't feel so good."

We were done walking the scene anyway, so I led Carol out of the cellar and into the bitter winter air, Doyle in tow.

As soon as we got topside, the AFIS machine connected. Moments later, it gave an annoying chime that was supposed to be more pleasant than a beep. It wasn't. Doyle read the results. "Our vic is Cynthia Ann Wilson of Colorado Springs, Colorado. No warrants."

I rubbed my hands together, trying to warm them up before donning my winter gloves. "You know there are some advantages to being cursed with un-life."

"Let me guess. You couldn't feel the cold?" Doyle said.

I sniffed my suddenly runny nose. "You got it. Honestly, though, it wasn't that I couldn't feel it. It just wasn't uncomfortable. I was aware of the temperature, like an itch or a mild breeze. It's not unpleasant, just there. I'd fuck someone for some of that right now."

"That'd be nice," Doyle commented, and the corners of her mouth crooked up. Then she added quickly, "Not feeling the cold, I mean. Though—"

Carol barked a laugh and shook her head with the amusement of someone who thought the two of us were acting like children, which was appropriate because we were. Then she said, "You know, Cait, you say fuck a lot."

I pulled up my hood. "Yeah, blame my da. I mean Mike. He said it so often; it was my first word."

Carol snorted at that as she pulled on a pair of leather gloves she had fished out of her long wool trench. "You know, that coat makes you look like an albino Wookie."

"Oh, fuck you, Washington," I shot back lightheartedly. "It was all I could find on short notice. My old winter coat had a hole in it."

"The word you're looking for is Yeti, Carol," Doyle said with a laugh. Then she abruptly switched subjects, catching me off guard. "You talk to your sister yet?"

I frowned and nodded. "We've had a couple of brief calls. I think we're both just trying to figure out how to talk to each other after so long. It's awkward as fuck, right now."

I hoped Doyle didn't ask anything further. It was a sore

enough subject. But she just gave me a sympathetic smile, and I caught something in her expression, like she could relate. Then she gestured to the evidence collection bags. "I'm going to load this stuff up. You guys head on back, and I'll meet you there."

I watched her walk away, privately admiring her figure. Doyle was adorable in a too-young-for-me kind of way. Or at least that's what I told myself, though deep down, I was much more afraid of my shit getting all over her life. My association with vampires and werewolves had a way of fucking up a person's existence.

"Anyway, enough about me, how have you been, Carol? Still having those dreams?"

Carol stared into space, and I asked her again, waving a hand in front of her face when she didn't answer. "Yoo-hoo, anyone there?"

Carol blinked and looked at me.

"I asked if you're still having those dreams?"

Carol blinked again as if coming back from somewhere far away. "Sorry, I—" She paused for a moment and rubbed at the corner of her eye, blinking rapidly, and continued. "Sometimes. But I'm finally sleeping again."

"Still the same dream?"

"Yeah, pretty much. I'm looking through this black mirror, a small thing, round. Inside, I see a woman on top of a mountain overlooking a dark volcanic landscape. It's all surrounded by a wall of black fog, like the eye of a hurricane—you know?—swirling around. And the woman, she's absolutely stunning. She has silver hair, like real silver, not gray, and her skin shimmers. But there's this fine black dust. It swarms around her in clumps like angry bees. The worst of it is her eyes."

"How so?"

Carol twisted her mouth, thinking. "Her expression is hateful and angry, but her eyes are terrified and pleading, and I get this sense of something immense, like she's about to explode. But the hate isn't directed at me. It's like she's trapped. In one dream, she was pleading with me. She just kept saying, 'please help me.' The shit is so creepy and horrifying that I wake up in a cold sweat."

"I don't suppose you've been trapped under the old Schmidt place on Humboldt."

Carol rolled her eyes. "No, Cait. Some weird parasite hasn't infected me. These are more like visions than dreams, though. My mom says they're gifts from Ori."

"I'm sorry. I don't know what that means."

"It's kind of like your divine self, I think. I don't understand it all, either. My mother's never discussed it before now. It was more my grandmother's beliefs than hers."

I slipped off my booties and handed them to one of the techs. Then, turning back to Carol, I said, in all seriousness, "I think you should keep a journal. Your mother probably isn't far off."

She nodded. "Do you mind driving back to HQ? I'm not feeling spectacular right now."

"Sure."

For most of the ride back, Carol stared out the window, lost in thought, but when I jerked the wheel to avoid a monstrous pothole as I pulled onto Amory Street, she asked, "Cait? Are you sick?"

I glanced over at her. "No, I'm fine. Why?"

"When I stumbled in the cellar, after whatever that was, I looked up at you, and for just a second, you looked all sickly and pale, like you were starving or something."

I didn't answer her for a moment, half listening to the callouts coming over the radio. Another 'full note' was called, but squad five picked it up. "Carol, you're scaring me," I said finally. "What's going on?"

Carol didn't answer me, instead looking out the window for quite a while, waiting long minutes before she spoke again. "Can I ask you something?"

"Sure, go for it."

"Why are you living with vampires, especially the one who helped fuck up your mom?" Her tone sounded accusatory, and I bristled at the question.

An odd spike of rage plowed into my consciousness, and I found myself gripping the wheel tightly. Carol was seriously pissing me off tonight. I drew a breath in through my nose and tried to remember that she meant well, so after I'd calmed, I answered as impassively as possible. "I turned Katie. I made her what she is. I couldn't very well dump her on Liz and make her do it."

"Why not? Didn't you say she was working with the guys responsible for what happened?"

I sighed. "Because, Carol, I love Katie. Yeah, it was shitty what they did to her, and no, I wasn't completely to blame. But if I don't care for Katie, who will? Her parents don't care about her, and they certainly couldn't help her now, even if they did." I glanced at Carol, turning short with her. "Now, did you really want to know the answer to your question, or were you just asking so you could argue with me?"

"No. I'm sorry. I do want to understand."

"Look, you remember how devastated I was after Marcella split? Liz offered to help. And it's nice having someone to talk to who can understand what I've been through. It doesn't hurt that she's funding Mom's rehab. I couldn't afford it on my own."

"And she did all this out of the goodness of her heart?"

"No, Carol. I'm pretty sure she felt guilty for what happened to us. She's trying to make it right."

"But—" Carol started, but I cut her off.

"Carol, look. I get it. You don't like vampires, and I know nothing I say will satisfy you. So, please, for the last time, put your petty bigotry aside and let it go. And if you can't do that, then, out of respect for our friendship, I'd ask you to leave it alone."

Carol's jaw worked for a moment. "Sure, Cait. I'm sorry. It's just the way I was raised. I blame my mother. She does it to me all the time, sticking her nose in just far enough to give me advice and then bitch me out when I don't take it. I'll try to keep out of it."

"Carol, we've been good friends for years, so I'll tell you this. I feel at home with Liz and Katie. It's almost like having my own family. And I need that, especially right now."

Carol nodded, then whispered, "I'm not a bigot." I didn't

respond, and by the time I worked up the nerve to tell her what I thought about that, we'd arrived back at HQ, so I let it go.

Returning to my desk, I pulled out my phone and called Liz. She picked up on the first ring. "Hey, pretty lady, how's work?"

I laughed. "Long and painful, hot stuff. How's our kid?"

She giggled back at me. "She's fine, working on her handwriting at the moment, and her vocabulary is improving almost hourly. Out of nowhere, she used the word 'contemplate' in context. We haven't even studied that word, and I don't think I've ever said it in front of her."

"Wow. That's crazy." Just six weeks before, Katie had no language skills of any kind. Her progress was terrific, but underneath that was a lingering worry. While I was almost dead certain her memories were all but gone, I was scared she'd get them back. Would she still love us as she did now?

"Yeah. That's what I thought, too. So, do you know when you'll be home?"

I looked at my watch. "Around midnight."

"Excellent. I made dinner. I'll finish cooking it when you get home unless you've already eaten."

I snorted cynically at the ridiculous idea. "Of course, I haven't eaten, but you didn't have to cook for me. I can take care of myself, Liz."

"Why do we have this same conversation every day? I like to cook for you. I haven't had anyone to cook for in at least fifty years, and I'd forgotten how much I enjoy it. I used to be a chef—"

"In a restaurant in Paris," I finished with a bit of snark, rolling my eyes. "That's like the thousandth time you've told me. And before you ask, yes, I love your cooking, but I feel guilty about you cooking all the time, while the best I can do is score you a bag of blood once in a while."

"Well, Cait, someone needs to look out for you."

I smiled at that, then paused for a moment, remembering why I called and trying to figure out how to break the news about Cynthia.

"Cait? You still there?"

"Um, yeah, sorry. So there's no good way to tell you this. Someone killed Cynthia Wilson."

The line went quiet for a moment then Liz came back, voice low. "Same as Merano?"

Carol and I had worked another homicide right after I'd come off vacation, a guy named Dwight Merano. Like Cynthia, the guy had been strapped to a table and decapitated, though they'd staked him first. According to Liz, it was no real loss to the vampire community; he was a total douchebag. Maybe I should have felt something for the guy, but I didn't. Cynthia was a different story.

"Yeah. Same calling card and everything, though, Cynthia wasn't staked. I'm sorry. I don't suppose you have any ideas."

"Vampire hunters," Liz responded without hesitation. "Whoever it is, they've managed to kill two of us with no mistakes. I don't have to tell you how much I don't like being on the back foot like this."

"No, you don't." I was starting to worry about Liz and Katie. I could care less about Nastasia, but she was keeping everyone else in line right now. We had other baby vamps roaming the streets of Boston, and so far, we hadn't had a lick of trouble from them. I wanted to keep it that way. If something happened to Nastasia, it wouldn't take long before all holy hell broke loose, and one of them did something stupid.

Liz sighed. "Alright, I'll call a meeting tonight, so you may want to come up the back stairs when you get home."

I chewed my bottom lip, trying to decide how to respond. "Liz, honey? I know it's Marcella's house, and you have authority there, but I'm not going to skulk into my own home like some kid avoiding their parents."

Liz attempted to be conciliatory. "It's okay, Cait. I just thought it would be easier for you. I know you don't fancy a run-in with Nastasia."

"No, I don't, but, as I said, I'm not going to creep into my own home like a criminal. I'm sure I can keep the rabble in line. Half of them still think I can kill them with a word like I did Schmidt."

Liz chuckled. "That's what I love about you. You take no shit. I'll see you tonight."

"Okay. Later. I—" I paused. I had been about to say, 'I love you.' Fuck, that would have been awkward. "I'll see you soon."

"Take your time, love. We'll be fine. Just don't forget about the Finchers tomorrow." She hung up.

CHAPTER TWO

"Oh, look, darling, your little pet is home," Nastasia practically spat, stepping in front of me as I walked toward the kitchen from the garage stairwell. She wore an outfit of black, patent leather stiletto heels and a red party dress that should have looked sleazy, but her natural poise and grace, not to mention her killer legs and gorgeous body, made it seem almost elegant. But it wasn't her physique that always stopped me. It was her eyes, dark and alluring. They were enough to turn even a straight woman's head, and her red-lipped, supremely kissable mouth revealed a string of pearl-white teeth in every wicked smile that made her more beautiful than anyone should be. I hated her for that and how she strutted around like the queen of all creation. But, God, she was nice to look at. As we say in Boston, a total smoke show.

Reminding myself I'd just been insulted by said smoke show, I stepped up to her, hands on my hips, and shot her a v-sign. "I'm not her fucking pet. You know, at eight hundred years old, you should have better manners, grandma." It was the wrong thing to say, and I knew I'd pay for it, but fuck it. I needed to keep some dignity in my own home.

Nastasia jammed me into the wall faster than I could follow.

God, they were all much faster and stronger now that the gate was open.

"And you should have some respect, little girl," she hissed, then licked my cheek in a slow wet stroke. My body betrayed me with a brief shudder of excitement. "God, you taste so good for a vampire, all shivery and pent-up."

"I'm not a vampire anymore, Nastasia, but if I were, I would have your ass for this," I grunted out as I struggled to get free. The threat was beyond idle. Even as a vampire, I'd been no match for her.

Liz set a hand on Nastasia's shoulder. "Nas, let her go, please."

She shoved Liz away roughly with one hand, sending Liz to her rump and sliding across the marble floor. "Hush, child. Cait and I are chatting."

Distracted, Nastasia had loosened her grip, so I took the opportunity to jam my right arm down on her elbow and twist around, tossing her over my shoulder. Then I yanked my weapon and jumped on Nastasia's chest, pointing the gun under her chin in one fluid movement.

"Fuck you," I snarled. "Now I'm gonna—"

I froze as anxiety flooded my chest, sending ice water into my veins. My heart pounded in my throat, and a fear-stinking sweat broke across my body. I couldn't pull the trigger as hard as I tried. My finger just wouldn't move, and my weapon hand started to tremble with the effort.

"Damnit," I swore, my voice almost a whimper.

Nastasia knocked me off with an easy slap like swatting an insect and jerked me back up to the wall, pinning me again. "Oh, you shouldn't have done that, Cait," she cooed. "I like it when you struggle."

She donned an evil smile full of vicious delight, and I fell neatly into her eyes, glowing like amber in the scintillating light of the chandelier. There was no tell-tale brush of mind or crashing of will. The fight just left me like someone yanked a plug, and my weapon clattered to the floor. I found myself wondering why I'd even struggled to begin with. I slid one hand around her waist and the other up her right leg, lifting the edge of her short dress as it traveled.

My breathing grew heavy, and my eyelids drooped. I bit my

bottom lip in anticipation as I relaxed in Nastasia's arms, waiting to service her needs, whatever they might be. God, I wanted this. No. I needed this. I needed her. I only wanted to fuck her, then and there, on the floor. I'd do anything for her.

"See there. That's so much better, isn't it?" Nastasia leaned into me, inhaling deeply as she nuzzled into my throat, pushing my hair away from my neck and speaking in low, seductive tones. "You are still a vampire, Cait. I don't know exactly what's happened to you, but I have a theory, and I'm certain you are far from cured. But that's okay, my darling. I'm going to fix this right now."

My body shuddered with a heady mixture of terror and need. I closed my eyes, turned my head, and lifted my chin in further invitation. "Oh, God, please do it," I pleaded in a hoarse whisper and moaned whorishly as she ran her fangs across the soft skin above my pulse, trailed by her wet, deliciously soft tongue. I wrapped my arms around her, bunching up her dress, pulling her closer as she opened her mouth wide, preparing to take my throat.

A blur of movement, faster than I could follow, tore Nastasia from my arms as Katie slammed her to the opposite wall, cracking the plaster in a rain of powdery bits.

"Leave Mama alone," Katie snarled.

Nastasia didn't struggle, though she could have easily knocked Katie aside. Instead, she smiled impishly and chuckled. "Mama? That's just adorable. Can I keep her, Cait?"

"Stop!" Liz shouted, and I felt the rush of her power wash over us, making me tremble and squeeze my eyes shut. I blinked a few times as the sudden sexual urge and pulse-pounding fear evaporated. Katie and Nastasia both froze for a moment. Nastasia recovered quickly, looking at Liz as if she'd just been yelled at by a cranky toddler—unhurt and unimpressed.

Moments later, Liz released Katie, who in turn released Nastasia slowly and moved to stand between us. If the situation hadn't been so dire, it would have been funny how Katie took a power stance, her hands on her hips and her legs shoulder-width apart like a superhero.

I did my best to shake off the lingering flush of arousal and pulled my daughter close, kissing her on the forehead. "It's okay, sweetie. We've got this. Go back to the kitchen." Katie did as I asked, shooting Nastasia a hateful glance and two fingers over her shoulder for good measure. *Now I wonder where she learned to do that.*

Nastasia moved almost, but not quite, nose-to-nose with me. Liz took a half step forward, but Nastasia held up a dismissive hand. "I am leaving, Elizabeth." She looked into my eyes in a way she hadn't before, almost questioning, and a small 'v' of interest or puzzlement formed in the crease between her eyebrows. "I misjudged you, I think." She gave me a crooked grin. "And I like the kid."

I tried to glare at her, but the cold hand of fear still wrapped my heart in an icy grip, so it probably didn't look very threatening. "After what you and Schmidt did to her, if you ever touch her again, I'll kill you."

Nastasia raised one incredulous eyebrow, and her voice rose in pitch with indignation. "Did to her? You must be joking. You did this to Katie, not me." Burning guilt fluttered through my stomach, but I stomped on it, even as each of Nastasia's words blew her deliciously cool, blood-laden breath onto my face, bringing with it an intoxicating mix of dread and intense desire. Then she lowered her voice to a whisper. As if Katie wouldn't hear anything she said at this distance. "Besides, my darling, her parents didn't give a fuck about her, and you know it. She's much better off. Now," she straightened her dress, brushed a hand through her hair to push the mussed-up mass back into place, and brushed off her ass, "I was just on my way out."

I wasn't done yet, and even though I knew to argue more bordered on recklessly dangerous, I seemed to love grabbing the hot stove and holding on for dear life. "Don't ever talk about Katie again, you trollop. Next time, I'm sure you and Liz can discuss things at a bar or all-night coffee house—or brothel."

Nastasia turned back with a wicked smile and winked at me. The abject terror returned, so powerful it almost buckled my knees, and I had to grab the railing with a white-knuckled grip to steady myself. Then she laughed her velvety laugh, scooped her purse and coat from the stairs, and headed out the door. Liz and I followed and watched her continue laughing down the street.

"I hate that bitch," I said after she was gone.

Liz snorted and looked at me skeptically. "So you keep telling me."

I don't like Nastasia, I thought. *But, fuuuck. What is it about her that has me tied in knots? It's not like she's the first pretty girl with an attitude I've ever met.*

Of course, I didn't voice any of that. Instead, I just said, "What?" and gave her my most impressive gaze of irritation.

"You know." She closed the front door and locked the deadbolt.

I bent over and put my hands on my knees as my head spun a little. Nastasia had put the whammy on me, and I'd felt none of the tell-tale signs I usually did, no brush of the mind, no weird sense of clouded thoughts, nothing. One instant, I'd been enraged and feeling pretty much murderous, and the next, I wanted to be her wanton whore.

I flushed, silently admitting to myself that I had relished that loss of control. It was so easy, like submitting to a raging torrent of water after swimming against it to exhaustion. Even the fear she'd laid on me had a heady quality, and I shivered again with an almost addiction-like reminiscence. That was swept aside, though, by a more sobering thought. *What if she caught me alone?* My heart palpitated at the idea, even as a naughty little part of me anticipated the possibilities.

Liz chuckled briefly at my predicament, then came to check me over, practically feeling me up. "Wait, are you alright?"

"Yeah, I'm fine," I said, trying to keep my voice steady and shooing her hands away. Not that I wanted to. Hell, after that particular confrontation, I wanted to rip Elizabeth's clothes off, throw her on the sitting room sofa, and have my way with her. *God, what is wrong with me?*

She continued to fuss. "Nothing broken?"

"No."

"Then why are you doubled over like that?" She asked, now crossing her arms and giving me a skeptical stare.

I stood up immediately, drawing a deep breath and blowing it out to calm my nerves, though it did nothing for my shaking hands. "She scares me, Liz. She can glamour me without me even knowing it. What else can she do?"

"She's an elder, like Marcella. They're always more powerful than the rest of us in one way or another." At my bemused expression, Liz continued. "Marcella didn't do you any favors by leaving. She should have at least taught you more."

"In her defense, there wasn't much time for education. Everything happened so fast. I was turned, then cured days later, and she left."

"Fair enough," Liz said and beckoned me to follow her into the kitchen.

Katie was sitting in one of the chairs, attempting to work out a math problem involving the volume of concrete needed for the deck of a round pool, an algebra problem, which meant I'd be useless. I looked at it anyway, trying to figure out how to help, when I noticed her hands, usually in constant motion with one thing or another, were deathly still. She looked up at us with unabashed and unmistakable hatred, fangs still bared, and a chilling quality in her eyes that took me aback.

"What is it?" I asked as I sat beside her, carefully taking her hand and stroking it tenderly with my thumb.

"Can I kill her? I've been watching her like you told me, mama. She leads with her left and always leaves an opening when she strikes. I could easily get a stake in under her left arm. After that, I'm sure the cleaver would do the job."

I blanched in shock. "No, you can't kill her! We don't kill unless we have no other choice, period, especially other vampires. That's the rule. You know that."

"Besides, Katie, mama's got the hots for Nastasia," Liz teased, making me flush, and my heart fluttered again. *Fuck.*

Katie looked at me with open disgust. "Eww, mama. Nastasia? Really? I know she's pretty, but she's such a skeeze."

I shot Liz an indignant glare. I couldn't believe she called me out like that. "Really, Liz? No, Katie. I do not have the hots for Nastasia. Don't listen to your Aunt. And where did you even learn a word like skeeze? We don't call people that."

Katie ignored the question. Instead, she put her ear to my chest, right over my rebelliously speeding heart. "Uh-huh. Right," she said skeptically and gave a little girl laugh that was both cute and terrifying all at once.

"I'm still coming down from the adrenaline rush, that's all." Katie didn't say anything else, but I could tell she didn't believe me. Hell, I wouldn't have either. *Fucking vampire senses.*

"I'm glad you're still down here, Katie," Liz said. "So you can hear what I have to tell your mother."

I took the word in stride, but it was the first time that Liz had called me Katie's mother. She usually just said Cait. Sometimes she'd say mama, re-affirming our relationship for Katie's sake. But this was different—and new. And if I was honest, heartwarming. And it almost made up for calling me out like that.

"Vampires didn't just spring from nothing," Liz said as she gently pulled the math book away from Katie and closed it. "There is a being that Marcella and Nastasia call the 'Dark Goddess.' She created the first of us, and not all at once. None of us know exactly who she is or where she came from. But she's been walking the earth for millennia. Of course, no one has seen her in over four hundred years, so she may be gone or dead for all we know."

Interesting, I thought. I'd always figured vampires came from some devilish pact, like in movies. It never occurred to me that we—or rather they—were created by a goddess.

"The first generation of vampires," Liz continued, "the ones we call The Elders, consists of four: Marcella, Nastasia, Hideyoshi Ito, whom you have not met, and the one they call 'The Queen.' None of us has ever met 'The Queen,' so we know almost nothing about her. Marcella only knows about her from a reference she found somewhere on an inscription. She may even be dead. We simply don't know. What you need to know about The Elders is that each is blessed with a gift. Nastasia's is glamour, as you've seen, Cait. Marcella can command other vampires. Having been turned by her, I share something of that ability."

"Ugh," Katie mumbled in annoyance. "We're aware." Liz had used it on Katie a few times to end an argument or get her to clean her room. I could understand her frustration. Unfortunately, despite being cured, it worked on me, too. Liz hadn't used it on me but once, but it still rankled me. I was convinced I shouldn't have to deal with it anymore. It seemed rude and unfair somehow.

"Hideyoshi is nearly unkillable. He's no stronger than I am, but I have watched him calmly walk over, pick his head up off the floor, and place it back on his shoulders."

"Wow, that's cool," Katie said, now totally into the conversation. "How would you kill him then?"

Liz frowned at the question but answered anyway. "The last time we discussed it, I think we all agreed that cremation would do it. But none of us wants to try it. And why would we? Hideyoshi tends to keep to himself. He bothers no one and keeps a low profile. None of us has even spoken to him in a couple of centuries. All I know is that he lives in Tokyo. Marcella has his address somewhere. They talk occasionally."

"What was Schmidt's gift?" I asked.

"Being a smarmy git," Liz sneered. "He wasn't an elder. He was our money man. He kept us flush with cash and ensured our larger endeavors were kept quiet. He had a real knack for money laundering. If I recall correctly, he was turned sometime in the sixteen-hundreds by some effete, foppish Spaniard named Ferdinand or Fernando or something. He was on the council because he was ruthless and held the purse strings, nothing more."

Though we could probably use Schmidt's expertise now, I was more than delighted that I'd killed him. Well, I'd made Blackman kill him. Watching his disembodied head fall to the ground in the gate chamber had been highly satisfying after what had happened to Katie and me. He'd been an arrogant prick anyway. Before I could comment, I noticed a delightful smell. "Wait, what's cooking?" I asked, looking sidelong at Liz.

Liz smiled mysteriously. "Are you hungry?"

I took in a deep breath, my frayed nerves finally feeling steady. It'd probably be a while before my hands stopped shaking, but I pushed the thought aside. "Yes. I am."

Liz pulled a beautifully presented chicken friand with mushroom sauce and a side of roasted potatoes from the microwave and set it in front of me at the table. I didn't stand on ceremony and began to dig in like a ground pounder. I was absolutely starving. "Oh, my God, this is so good, Liz. You didn't have to do this, but I'm glad you did."

"I helped!" Katie exclaimed, jumping up and heading to the refrigerator.

"Uh uh," Liz scolded as Katie opened the Traulsen. "No more blood. You've had plenty. It's expensive, and you don't need it right now. You fed yesterday."

Katie's face screwed up in teenage irritation, but she closed the refrigerator and went over to stand by the center island, watching me eat. "Is it delicious?"

"It's wonderful, mo chroi. Would you like a taste?"

She stuck out her tongue. "Blech, no thanks. I'm just glad you like it. It was Aunt Liz's idea," Katie continued. "She said you'd be coming home tired, and we should do something nice for you. I rolled out the puff pastry. It was fun!"

I looked at Liz, who had picked up the unfinished Sunday crossword puzzle from the table, pretending to be engrossed in it. "What's a five-letter name for blabbermouth?" She asked, looking up at Katie.

Katie crossed her arms and scuffed the floor with a toe. "Sorry, Aunt Liz. At least I didn't tell—" Katie clapped a hand over her mouth, eyes wide.

I looked at Katie out of the corner of my eye, holding a mass of chicken filling over my plate. "Tell me what?"

Liz looked up. "Cait, darling, what is a five-letter word for dummy?"

I didn't even look at her. "Dummy is five letters, Liz."

"And so it is." Liz filled another entry and looked pointedly at Katie, who just stood there, a shit-eating grin on her face.

Both of them were acting genuinely peculiar. Katie was practically hiding behind the center island, looking fit to burst, and the corners of Liz's mouth had quirked up into a sharp grin.

My fork clattered to the plate. "Okay, you two, what is going on here?"

Liz looked up again from the crossword. "Katie, would you please excuse us?"

Katie squealed and ran upstairs.

"Where is she going?"

Liz didn't answer, sitting there quietly, but there was a sudden nervousness to her demeanor, and she was toying with her hair in a way I'd never seen before. Hair that had been cut and styled, I suddenly noticed. *When had she done that?*

I squinted at her suspiciously. "Elizabeth Abigail Charlotte Medlyn, what are you up to?"

Liz cracked a smile at the use of her full name, almost laughing as I squirmed in anticipation and a giddy sort of annoyance. "Absolutely nothing, Cait. Now, eat your dinner."

I finished eating. I hoped that Liz wasn't going to come onto me again. It wasn't that she wasn't attractive or even that I wasn't interested. Frankly, Liz was beautiful. She was statuesque, blond, and fit, with fabulous emerald green eyes, a small-ish nose, and a dazzling smile. We were even, it seemed, emotionally compatible. Our relationship didn't have the fiery passion that Marcella and I had shared, probably because neither Liz nor I would let it. Ours was more of a sense of belonging together, a burgeoning friendship that we knew would likely become stronger over time. That wasn't usually a bad thing, per se. But if Liz and I became physically involved, I knew I'd fall head over heels, and I didn't want that right now. I'd been with only one woman and wanted to enjoy life for a bit.

Not that Liz was anything like Marcella. Liz was sweet and kind in a way that vampires weren't supposed to be. Marcella had been kind, but it had been a front for her insane manipulations. Nastasia didn't know what the word 'kind' meant. She was just an evil creature through and through, a smoking hot evil creature with doe-like brown eyes, luscious, kissable lips, full, round breasts, and legs that I'd kill for, but evil nonetheless.

As soon as I was done with my food, Liz took my plate to the sink and washed it, leaving it to dry along with the silverware. For the first time since I walked in, I realized the kitchen was spotless and cleaned within an inch of its life.

"Did you clean?" I asked.

"Well, someone has to since I had to let Robert go." She took my hand and led me from the table to the sitting room doors. Katie came racing down the stairs.

"Is it time?" Katie said, a wide grin on her face, showing a disturbing amount of fang. I needed to talk to her about getting in the habit of putting those away.

"Time for what?" I asked cautiously. "Okay, now. What is going on, ladies?"

Liz smiled broadly and pulled open the sitting room doors. I gasped. A roaring fire burned in the fireplace, and the furniture had been re-arranged with the sofa pushed to the far wall. Centered between the windows opposite the fireplace stood a large, beautifully decorated Christmas tree. Crystal stars and glass globes adorned the branches. Silken and velvet ribbons wrapped the entire tree, and strange lights winked about within its depths. It took me a moment to realize they weren't electric lights.

"What are those," I asked in awe, indicating the lights.

Liz smiled warmly. "Fairy glamour. I had Ionia make them." Ionia was the dryad I'd met my first time visiting camp two with Marcella. I flushed a bit at the memory. The blinking lights flitted through the tree from branch to branch, sometimes perching on the ornaments or sliding around the ribbons. It was, literally, magical to behold.

Beneath the tree sat two presents immaculately wrapped in green and red plaid wrapping paper adorned with silver holly leaves and finished with shiny silver bows. Next to them sat a box wrapped in mangled green paper, topped by an oversized stick-on blue bow, and covered in scotch tape.

"I wrapped that one," Katie said, pointing to the green box.

"Is it for me?" I asked, and Katie nodded.

"I love it," I said with a laugh.

Sitting on the end table was a fat mug and a ceramic teapot. The sweet aroma of apple cider and cinnamon wafted through the air.

I looked at Liz. "So this is the big surprise?" I couldn't help my shit-eating grin.

"Yes," Liz replied. "I hope you like it. It's only two weeks to Christmas, you know. And it has been an exceptionally long time since I've had anyone to celebrate it with."

I looked up at her, feeling all mushy inside. "It's wonderful. No one has decorated for Christmas for me since my da died." I leaned up on my toes and kissed her on the cheek. "Seriously, Liz, Thank you. It means so much."

Liz quirked a grin and stepped to the sofa, pouring me a mug of apple cider.

I giggled at the irony of her handing me the vampire bedhead mug that read, 'I'm not a morning person.'

"So, now what?" I asked, standing there sipping the cider. It was a crappy store brand, but it still did the trick and wasn't any less appreciated.

Liz pulled a throw blanket from the sofa and sat on the floor, leaning against the couch. Katie moved over and sat down next to her. "Come sit down, mama. I want to read you a story."

I smirked. So that's what the big production was about. Katie wanted to show how well she was learning to read. I smiled, proud of her beyond measure, and sat down between them.

Katie pulled up one of my favorite creepy-ass childhood books, *A Christmas Carol* by Dickens, and began to read, somewhat haltingly, from the first page.

CHAPTER THREE

Katie finished reading, closed the book, and looked at us expectantly.

"That was lovely, Katie," I cooed, beaming with pride as she turned to me. "You're getting so good." Then she hugged me tightly, and I grunted. "Easy, girl. Too tight. Too tight."

She loosed her grip and turned to Liz. "How did I do?"

Liz smiled in that soft way she always did when she was proud of Katie, motherly and sweet. "Mama was right. It was lovely."

"Great, can I go watch TV now?"

I laughed loudly. *Typical teenager,* I thought. "Sure, kid."

Katie bounced out of the room, her sneakers padding their way up the main stairs.

I turned to Liz and was shocked to find tears limning her eyes, golden by the light of the fire. She sniffed and brushed them away, blinking rapidly.

"Thinking about your girls?" I asked and gently placed a hand on her knee.

She closed her eyes for a moment, gathering herself, then spoke. "Yes. I still miss them. God, it never gets any easier. Raising Katie has been wonderful, but sometimes—oh—" She broke off.

"I'm sorry, Liz. It didn't even occur to me—"

"No, it's not your fault. She needs us. It just gets hard sometimes."

"I mean that I'm sorry I don't ask how you're doing more often. I'm always so wrapped up in myself."

Liz's mouth crooked up in a half smile. "Cait, stop. It's okay. You've never raised a child, so how could you know what this might bring back for me?"

She placed a cool hand on my cheek and looked into my eyes. I thought she would say something else, but she only sat like that, and I felt a little uncomfortable, maybe even a little confused. I didn't know what to say or do next. I found myself wondering if I should kiss her. Hesitantly, I pulled away and stood.

"I'm, uh, gonna go get some wine."

Liz nodded and turned her head back to the fire. Her eyes were sad, and she looked a little bit lost. As if she were feeling things she couldn't comprehend. It was an expression I'd had on my face plenty of late, and I empathized as I wandered to the kitchen, returning only a moment later with a nearly full bottle of Cabernet I'd left sitting on the counter from a few nights before and a wine glass.

"Here, let me," Liz said, taking the wine bottle and glass from my hand and pouring.

"Hey, I'm not a hooligan. I can pour a glass of wine. You should know I'm a faerie princess."

Liz raised an eyebrow and handed back my glass. "Really? A faerie princess. How exactly does that work?"

"It's an old story my mameó used to tell us. It's bittersweet but totally true."

Liz looked at me skeptically while I took a heavy drink from my glass. "Okay, this I have to hear. Go on. No, wait." She left the room and came back with a wine glass full of blood and a half-empty unit of the stuff. "Sorry, I decided you shouldn't drink alone."

I raised my glass, and she clinked hers with mine. Then my thoughts stalled for a second as gooseflesh popped across my body from smelling the blood. I couldn't wait until that stopped happening.

"Okay," I began. "So, it's an old legend in my family. Mameó, my grandmother, used to tell the story that her grandmother was one of the old Irish goddesses. It's actually a bittersweet story."

"I thought you said it was a true story." Liz shifted slightly, moving and turning so she could face me.

"It is!" I said with a bit of a twinkle in my eye. "Mameó said so! Don't be arguin' with me mameó now."

Liz held up her hand defensively. "I'm sorry. Mameó. Right. No arguing."

I donned Mameó's Mayo accent as I told the story. "Right, now, my great-great-grandda, Collin Ó Néill, was a Ferrier by trade. He often shoed horses for the local landlord and made a decent livin'. One night, while assisting in the foaling of one of the landlord's mares, he was visited by a crow. Being a good Irishman, he knew better than to shoo the crow away. It would lead to bad luck, you see." I paused, dropping the accent for a moment, and said scandalously, "Mind you, if it weren't for bad luck back then, the Irish would've had no luck at all."

Liz smirked, then snorted in amusement. "I always wondered about that phrase, 'the luck of the Irish.' In my experience, especially before Irish independence, good fortune was not what I'd have thought of as an Irish trait."

"I know, right?" I said, then picked up the accent again. "Anyway, he left the crow alone. And it watched over the birth of the foal. Unfortunately, the colt was born poorly, and both the mare and the foal died. The landlord blamed Collin and kicked him off his land.

"That evening, Collin walked out his door with only the clothes on his back. As he crossed the Lough Mask bridge between Galway and Mayo, he saw her on the far side, the most stunningly beautiful woman he'd ever seen. She had raven hair and pale skin the color of winter snow. He said her eyes were black as night, and she captured his heart. She was washin' blood from the clothes of the landlord. She told him that her name was Badb, named for the Irish goddess, and that Collin should go home. Everything would be grand.

"Collin told her that he'd been kicked off his land, but she said, 'Nonetheless, return home, and all will be well.' Collin, curious, did as she asked, finding that the landlord had died that very morning without telling anyone about Collin's eviction. So, Collin stayed.

"Two nights later, during a horrible storm, Badb came to his home begging for a place to wait for the night. Collin, grateful for her advice, agreed. One night turned into two, then to a month, and a month into nine, after which she gave birth to my great-grandmother. You see, they'd fallen in love, he with her and her with him. And though she was supposed to stay but one night, she found she couldn't leave him, having fallen in love at first sight.

"Now, it is said that she loved him enough for a lifetime in those nine months. But needs must be as they are, and a few days after my great-grandmother was born, Badb disappeared mysteriously. Collin searched the countryside for her to no avail. There were whispers that she was fae-folk, the Sidhe, you know? But they were only whispers. Eventually, Collin gave up his search. But he never forgot her, and he spoke of her constantly.

"Almost twenty years went by, and Collin did his best to raise his daughter, but he was heartbroken and taken with depression and drink. One summer, after a hard day of shoeing horses in Galway and a hard night at the pub in Tourmakeady, Collin saw her again. She hadn't aged a day, and this time she was washing clothes on the Mayo County side of the bridge. The clothes she washed, stained with blood, were Collin's very own."

"And what happened?" Liz asked, sounding intrigued.

"'Oh, Collin,' she said. 'I'm so sorry. I love you, but I have no choice but to be what I am. I will come for you when 'tis all done.' The next night, Collin died trying to break up a drunken brawl. One of his best friends slugged him, and Collin hit his head on the hearth in the pub, breaking his neck. A crow could be seen calling on the window sill of his home the very time it happened, the home he shared with his daughter, Cáitlín, for whom I'm named. Mameó believed that his soul was taken to Tir Nan Óg, the land of the ever-living, where he shares many a night with his love. And that is the story of Collin Ó Néill and Badb." I raised my glass with a flourish.

Liz gave me a crooked, knowing smile. "And if Mameó says it, it must be true."

It was my turn to laugh. "Indeed," I said. "So, faerie princess." I held my arms out in mock grandeur. "So, now, it's your turn. Tell me a story. You've lived for three hundred years. I want to hear something good."

She snorted. "I'm not as good of a storyteller, but let me think."

"You said you were with Marcella for fifty years. What was that like?" I prompted.

"Oh, goodness." She chuckled a bit in reminiscence. "It might be better to tell you about just after. It's much more interesting."

I nodded in agreement. "Fair enough."

"Marcella and I had a huge fight. It was something that had become all too common after fifty years together. We fought over everything, women, money. You name it. We even had a knock-down drag-out, teeth and all, over place settings at a party we'd arranged but hadn't even attended. I mean, bloody childish things, really."

I grunted in agreement. "I'm guessing you were just sick of each other."

Surprisingly, Liz shook her head. "It wasn't that. We loved each other, but it had been three of us for thirty years, not just two."

"Three?"

"Yes. Marcella, me, and Marguerite."

I raised a solicitous eyebrow, eager for this tidbit of salacious info. "And who, pray tell, is Marguerite?"

"A vampire we met in Paris in 1670. Marguerite was the glue that held us together. Marcella and I are more alike than we are different, and that often led to poor choices, which, in turn, led to stubborn arguments, as I said. Marguerite smoothed everything out. To this day, I'm not sure why it worked. But when she was around, Marcella and I just didn't fight."

I looked at my wine glass, which was now getting perilously close to empty, and went to refill it. "So what happened to her?"

Liz's eyes turned a little watery as she went on. "She died in a house fire in Marseille. It started in the kitchen after breakfast, and the house was ablaze in minutes. Marcella and I escaped, but Marguerite insisted on saving one of the servants' children. She was selfless like that. Marguerite became trapped when the second floor collapsed. None of them made it out."

I handed Liz a box of tissues we kept sitting on the wet bar.

"Thank you." She wiped her eyes. "Goodness, I haven't thought about Marguerite in a hundred years at least."

"So when she died, that was it, then?"

"Yes. Marcella and I first blamed ourselves for Marguerite's death. Then we started blaming each other. Then we started fighting. Finally, one day, in a rage, she told me I was a common strumpet and that I should have died with my children."

I was appalled. "Jesus. I didn't think she had that in her."

"She was just angry and hurt. We both were. I said a fair number of unkind things myself that night. It wasn't one-sided. In any event, she left, and I was stuck in France by myself. So I decided to get as far away as possible."

I nodded. "Where did you go?"

"I traveled around Northern Africa for a while, but on a whim in the early seventeen hundreds, I decided to spend some time in the Caribbean, so I boarded a ship for Jamaica. I never made it."

"What happened?" Now I was interested. "Pirates?" I'd gobbled up *Black Sails*, so it didn't take much for me to imagine a grand pirate adventure.

"Precisely. My ship was attacked, and while I survived, obviously," she paused to take a sip from her glass, then continued, "I was taken hostage. I could have easily escaped, but where was I to go? I was on a ship in the middle of the Atlantic, so I used my glamour to keep the men off me until we made port in Nassau."

My eyes went wide in awe. "Holy shit. You were in Nassau during the Pirate Republic. Oh my God, Liz. What was it like? That sounds like an amazing adventure."

"Oh, yes," she laughed in derision. "A glorious adventure in endless sunlight, rampant misogyny, and the subtle nuances of human body odor."

"You're killing it, Medlyn," I protested loudly and pouted at her. I looked at the wine bottle, which was pretty much empty, then I held up a finger. "Hang on, pause that while I get another bottle and go to the loo." I stood and tottered a bit. *How much have I had to drink?* I wondered. *Fuck it. I deserve to take a break and cut loose.* I made a wobbly beeline for the bathroom to pee and then grabbed a fresh bottle from the kitchen.

When I returned, Liz looked up at me, shook her head, and laughed, then said, "Another bottle? Okay. So, as I was saying, Nassau was both wonderful and terrible. Every day brought something interesting. But it was the ocean I loved."

I kicked off my shoes and socks and poured myself another glass of wine, setting the bottle on the mantle while she went on. I was only half listening, anyway. Instead, I watched her, marveling at her eyes. Why was it always the eyes for me? Liz's eyes were a dark, lustrous green that no one should be allowed to have. Marcella had said my eyes were the green of life. If that was so, then Liz's were the sparkling green of a goddess. *Marcella,* I thought. *Now, she has amazing eyes, ice-blue and captivating. God, I miss her.*

"Cait? Are you okay?"

I looked up. I was lying on the floor with my head in Liz's lap, and she was looking down at me, her forehead puckered with worry.

"What did I do?" I whispered as fat tears fell from the corners of my eyes onto Liz's leg.

Liz smiled a sympathetic smile. "Nothing, love. You didn't do anything."

"But—" I sat up and poured another glass. "Why?"

Liz did something that I didn't expect; she pulled me bodily into her lap, wrapping her arms around me.

I looked at her face, so close to mine. "Um, Liz, what are you doing?"

"I'm holding my friend, Cait. You're drunk, and you're slushy and sad." Liz gazed down at me, and the firelight caught her eyes. In my alcohol-induced haze, I couldn't understand what I was feeling. Marcella had cradled me just like this through so much, but it was Liz I remembered at that moment.

I had just returned here to Marcella's home. Liz had caught me as I fell into the elevator. She'd endured me tearing into her flesh in a futile attempt to get at her blood. Then, as I'd been so broken, screaming my anguish to the universe, Liz had come over and run a hand through my hair in sympathy. She hadn't even known me then, not really. *'Not too different than I was at first,'* she had said.

Without thought, I reached up and pulled Liz to me, pressing my lips to hers. For a moment, she returned the kiss. Then she placed a hand on my chest. "No, Cait."

"But why?" I whispered. "When we first moved in together, you were so forward and sexy and pushy. I thought you wanted me."

"That was before," she said softly. "Now it's different."

"I love you," I whispered.

"You're drunk," Liz whispered back with a chuckle.

And that broke me. I burst into tears, pulling myself into her. "Why doesn't anyone love me anymore?" I sobbed.

She chuckled at my childish outburst. "Oh, Cait, I love you plenty. But I'm not going to do this. Not now. Not when you're like this."

Not now. Not like this. Those had been Marcella's words to me when I'd been so broken, so alone, just like I felt right now. So, I curled up into Liz's arms and turned loose my grief over Marcella. I'd been immortal, in love, and almost happy. Then it had all gone horribly wrong, and now I didn't know who I was anymore.

CHAPTER FOUR

The next day at work was hellish, saddled as I was with a raging red-wine hangover. *You should stick to white, Cait.*

The tannins in red made my head feel like it was being laid into by howitzers every time I moved. And somewhere during the previous night, I was pretty sure I'd licked the floor of a taxi cab. I had woken mortified, remembering the night before, or at least most of it. Liz had been gracious, carrying me up to bed and shushing me in my booze-sodden misery, but God, I felt stupid. What was worse were the feelings it stirred in me.

Liz had tried to take some of the weight and difficulty from my shoulders, but she'd only added to it. I wrestled now with even more conflicted feelings, feelings I didn't want to admit. Getting drunk had only stolen my inhibitions. I wasn't just lonely, which I'm sure Liz thought was the case last night. I liked her. I was attracted to her, and not just physically. And what was there not to like? Even though Liz had worked with Schmidt, she genuinely cared for me. We shared the bond of parenting a child. A weird child, sure, but still. Liz was beautiful, tall, and oddly sweet for a vampire. She respected me even though I was an absolute mess. The whole affair left me confused and unable to concentrate.

The resulting dawdling, coffee drinking, procrastinating, and noodling over my personal feelings meant it took two hours for me to wrap up paperwork that should have taken thirty minutes. My obsessing over my muddled emotions was interrupted almost as soon as I'd finished.

"Hey, Reagan, someone wants to see you," Detective Freyer said, and there was a touch of amusement in his voice.

I ceased typing but didn't look up as my thumb hovered over the spacebar. An alarm bell sounded in my head, and a chill of anticipation and dread rippled through me as I remembered what day it was. I looked up slowly.

Towering over me, all six-foot-two of her, was the woman I'd once called the Red-Haired Goddess Extraordinaire, Morgan Kennedy. "Oh, my God!" I whispered. My heart skipped a beat, and a cold sweat broke out on my palms, making them all clammy.

Morgan's eyes crinkled with a crooked smile stretched from ear to ear. "Hey there, Kitty Cait."

I had planned several times over the last few weeks how I'd react when I saw her. I thought I'd play it cool, sit back and give her a nice 'How have you been, Red.' Instead, I was instantly tongue-tied.

"I—I—Uh, hi." *Nice, Cait, real smooth.*

"Uh, yeah," she said, a frown crossing her face that pulled on a long scar that ran down the side from forehead to cheek. She ran a hand through her short hair in what looked like frustration.

I stood, and we stared at each other for a few moments. Then I threw my arms around Morgan's neck and hugged her as pressure built in my eyes. I sniffed. "I missed you."

She didn't hug me back at first, seeming not to know how to respond, but then she patted my back gingerly. The whole encounter started to feel weird. Though I'd dreamed of this moment for years, I hadn't thought it would be some romantic movie. Still, I'd thought it would be better than this. This was awkward, and the unease continued until my heart thumped in my chest, and a flush crept up Morgan's neck as she looked everywhere but at me.

I turned to Freyer and finally broke the shitty silence. "We served two tours in Iraq, side by side."

"She saved my life—twice," Morgan elaborated with a tepid smile.

"Oh, well, that explains the chilly reception," Freyer commented sardonically.

"Yeah," I mumbled, and there was another moment of weird quiet.

Freyer shook his head in confusion and then meandered away, leaving us standing there, unable to meet each other's gaze. I couldn't figure out what to do with my hands. I rubbed them together, then pushed my arms to my sides.

"Y—you want that coffee?"

"Sure," Morgan replied noncommittally. "But I hear the coffee here is fucking awful."

I barked a nervous laugh. "Yes, it is, but Carlos has a secret stash." *Fuck, why is this so hard?*

We walked to the breakroom in syrupy, uncomfortable silence, and I started a pot of the good stuff. I watched the coffee brew, trying to think what to say, but Morgan didn't wait as her temper flared, and she laid into me.

"What the fuck, Cait? I called you and called you. I wrote you. And you ghosted me. I know I—"

I slapped my hands on the countertop, rattling the glasses in the sink. "Hey! You dumped me, remember?" I spun around, jabbing a finger at her. "I was an absolute wreck after—wait for it—saving your fucking life, and you just took off. The next thing I knew, the woman I loved was getting married. Worse yet, to a guy." My voice dropped, choked. "I loved you, and you abandoned me."

Morgan blinked and sat down hard in one of the chairs. "Shit. I didn't realize—"

"Cait? You okay?" Carlos called from the hallway.

"Yeah," I called back, trying but failing to steady my voice. I pulled the handkerchief from my pocket and wiped my nose.

Morgan sat there, abashed, a dumb look on her face.

I sniffed and thumbed the tears off my cheeks. "Damnit, Morgan, say something."

"What would you like me to say? I fucked up? I told you that in my letter, but you never answered. Why didn't you just call me if you felt the same way?"

I looked away, embarrassed, still furiously wiping at my tears. "I didn't read it—at least not until a couple of weeks ago."

Her eyebrows shot up. "Wait, what? Jesus, Cait, are you fucking neurotic or what? Let me get this straight. I sent you a letter pouring out my heart, and you didn't read it. Instead, you carried it around for ten God damn years, suddenly deciding to open it? Wow! Just—wow." She sat back hard in the chair with a look of disbelief and irritation.

"I wasn't the one who opened it," I admitted quietly. "My friend, Liz, did. Honestly, it probably would have sat there forever if she hadn't. I was always afraid to."

"What the fuck for? I left you three messages just like it, throwing my heart out there."

"I didn't listen to those either."

"What? And you have the gall to bitch me out?" I couldn't decide if Morgan looked enraged or just incredulous.

"I was a fucked up kid drowning in PTSD. You just up and left one day while I sat terrified that my arm would never work again. Then I got the wedding invitation. It was like a slap in the face. I—" I gave up trying to explain. I was just making it worse. "Fuck. Look, Morgan, I'm sorry."

She stared at me, her jaw working as if deciding what to say. In the end, she didn't say anything. She stood, walked over, and pulled me into a firm hug. We stayed like that for long minutes. I didn't want to let go, and I guess she didn't either. Then Carlos' Texas drawl called from the doorway, and we separated, both a little teary-eyed.

"This her?"

I sniffed and wiped my nose again. "Yeah. Detective Morgan Kennedy, this is our lead, Carlos Ramirez."

Morgan shook his hand as I poured each of us a cup, then she stared at my arm as I held out her mug. "Holy shit, Cait. What happened to your arm? That's some first-class plastic surgery."

"What?" I looked down. The last time Morgan had seen it, my arm had been covered in a web of scar tissue. "Oh, that? It's not the same arm."

Morgan blinked. Then she spoke very slowly, "I'm sorry, what?"

"Okay, so—" I pressed my lips together to gather my courage, then pressed on. "I was trapped in this medieval cuff and tore it off rather than drain the blood from a sixteen-year-old girl. But then this asshole vampire named Schmidt tore her throat open, and I had to turn her anyway. So, so much for that idea. My arm grew back, but then I went into some kind of vampire remission that almost killed me, and Marcella, my vampire girlfriend, dumped me."

She looked at Carlos, who just shrugged.

I held out my arm. "Here, have a feel. Good as new."

Morgan felt my arm, astonishment playing on her features. "I thought Freyer was pulling my leg."

I took a sip of my coffee and shook my head.

"So vampires are real?"

Carlos chimed in. "Yup."

"And you were one?" Morgan asked, her eyes slowly getting wider and wider.

"Yup," I said, then nodded as I took another sip of coffee, hiding a slight smirk behind my mug.

For a moment, Morgan gawped like a fish, looking for words. Then, she sat back in the chair and took a long, hot gulp of her coffee. Again, she opened her mouth to say something, but she didn't get very far as Freyer strode into the breakroom, tripping over her outstretched legs.

"Damnit, Kennedy! Carlos, Cait, Bill wants to see you in his office asap."

I pursed my lips like I'd eaten a lemon. I loved Bill Larson. Then I found out that he and Mike, the man I used to call my father, were both on the take back in the day, among other sundry horrible things. Unfortunately, I was forbidden by Nastasia from disclosing that tidbit to anyone. So, as we left Morgan and walked into Larson's office, I carefully schooled my face into impassivity.

Larson stood as we entered and gestured to two empty chairs. Carol was already in the room, along with a young

Asian detective with a triangular face and a little nose. I recognized her immediately, though I'd only met her once before. "Hi, Maki. How's your father?"

Maki turned to me. "Detective Reagan. Dad's fine. He misses working with your mom."

Larson interrupted. "Have a seat."

I sat quietly, saying nothing and waiting to hear what Bill had to say so I could make a quick exit, but Bill had to ask.

"Cait? You okay?"

I tried to keep the emotion out of my voice. "Yeah, I'm fine. Just got a lot going on, personally."

Bill looked skeptical but sat back down and proceeded anyway. "I just had a long conversation with the Commissioner. With the recent revelations about what's been living just below our feet, she wants your unit to head up a new special squad." Bill referred to over a thousand preternatural creatures living as refugees in nine different underground camps around the city.

Most recently, Channel 7 ran a very sympathetic two-hour special on the camps and the pitiful plight of the various creatures in them. My ex had orchestrated it before she'd left town. The real stroke of genius was using the mermaids, Gretchen and Kaja, as spokespersons. It gave a sympathetic face to the entire ordeal. What parent wants to tell their child that they didn't care about Princess Ariel? Vampires and Werewolves were not part of that 'exposé,' however. We—or rather they—had decided to remain quietly in the background, lest they become a hindrance to efforts to improve the situation.

Bill continued, snapping me out of my musings. "Second Squad Homicide is now officially the Preternatural Investigations Unit. In addition to a very light load of human-on-human homicides, your team will be responsible for handling anything with a supernatural bent. That means human-on-preternatural violent crimes and vice versa. Except for the two vamp murders you have right now, all your current cases will be handed off. In addition, the Caldwell and Rodriguez cases are considered officially cold and will be shelved—indefinitely." He opened his drawer and pulled out four detective shields. They were the same as the ones we carried, but rather than the typical gold, they were plated in shining red.

I raised an eyebrow. Carol's mouth dropped open. Carlos just waited, patient as always.

"I know there aren't many cases, but the Mayor and the Commissioner want to get ahead of what they believe is coming. To help you and fill out the team, I've assigned Detective Imai to the squad." He gestured to Maki. "She's got more than a passing familiarity with all things supernatural, so I expect you to welcome her with open arms."

"Yes, sir," Carlos said. "Anything else?"

Bill gestured to the others. "For you three, no." He turned to me. "Cait, stick around for a moment."

Fuck. I tried not to look too sour. "Yes, sir."

After we'd exchanged our badges and the others had left, Larson started in on me. "Okay, Cait, I've known you your entire life. What the hell is going on?"

I stood up, turning one foot toward the door as if to leave. "Nothing you want me to talk about."

"Huh-uh. Sit your ass back down, young lady, and tell me why it is you've suddenly decided that I'm the devil himself."

I wasn't going to get out of this without giving him an answer. "Fine, you want to know why? It's because of you, Mike, Erik Schmidt, and the Patriarca Crime Family, that's why." Larson had been right in the middle of the insanity that had gotten my father killed, my sister essentially kidnapped, and my memories erased.

"That wasn't my fault, Cait. Your dad—"

"He wasn't my father," I shot back hotly, standing and advancing on Larson. "And how can you say that? You were on the take, too."

Larson flushed in anger, and he didn't back down. Instead, he got in my face, and I could feel his hot breath as he dressed me down. "I was never on the take, Cait. That was Mike. And, of course, he was your father. He raised you. Donny Moylan certainly didn't have a hand in that."

My mouth fell open. "You knew that Uncle Donny was my da? And you never told me?"

"Why would I? You weren't supposed to know, and your mother forbade it. I'm sorry that your family had secrets, but they weren't mine to tell. But, I did my best to protect you kids and your mother."

"How long have you been working for Marcella?" It was a legitimate question. After all, he'd assigned me to the Caldwell case at her request, the same case that had twisted my life into the pear shape it was now.

"Hey! I don't work for Marcella; I owe her my life. I'm sure you can appreciate that. Your dad died instantly from the first shot. Marcella kept me alive until the ambulance arrived." His voice rose precipitously. "So, yeah, I do small favors for her sometimes, but I don't take a dime, and I don't do anything illegal. I'm a good fucking cop. You get me, Cait Reagan?" Larson was crimson-faced and as angry as I'd ever seen him.

I flopped back into my chair, stunned, then sighed, rubbing my forehead and taking it all in. God, I was an asshole. "I'm sorry," I said softly.

Bill took a deep breath and calmed. "Are we okay, then?"

"Yeah, I'm sorry, Bill."

"You said that, Cait. Apology accepted. It's done." His voice turned kind, and he smiled, bunching up the star-shaped scar on his cheek. "I'm going to go visit your mom in rehab tomorrow. I wanted you to know. Have you taken her out to see that snake lady friend of Marcella's?"

"Bian?" I blinked. Shit, why hadn't I thought of that? "No, but I might do that this week." Bian had more than just modern medicine to work with. I was betting she had powerful magic at her disposal now that the gate was open.

"See that you do," Bill said firmly. "Get out of my office."

I stopped at the door, turning back before opening it. "Bill?"

"What now, Reagan?" He snapped, probably louder than he'd intended.

"What will we do when one of the vamps or werewolves goes rogue? They're a shit ton stronger and faster now."

"I don't know, Cait. But just because we're outmatched

doesn't mean we don't try. So keep a blade and a stake handy."

"Yes, sir."

"I wish I still had a vampire on my team," Larson said as I left his office.

I sighed heavily as I closed his door.

CHAPTER FIVE

Leaning against the wall next to Larson's office door for a few minutes, I watched Morgan. She sat in my chair, leisurely sipping her coffee and looking out the window at the parking lot across the street, the one used by just about everyone. Given her physique, there was no question why Freyer had taken her for the Fugitive Apprehension Squad. She was confident and professional. It probably didn't hurt that she dwarfed most of the guys and could put them down with one arm behind her back.

Morgan looked up, caught me staring, and raised her mug in salute. I flushed a little at getting caught but didn't move or turn away. Instead, I crossed my arms and continued watching her. She smiled, then flushed a little, too. Then she looked behind her as if I might be looking at something out the window, and I grinned at her discomfort. She looked back at me, a little frantically, I thought, and, seeing I was still staring at her, she gave a nervous laugh and made a 'what are you staring at' gesture, finally giving me the finger. I chuckled.

She was the same woman I remembered from Iraq, maybe a little older, more seasoned, but the same woman. Her big green eyes still looked at me from under her shock of red hair, cropped short now. Each of those eyes sat over a light punch of freckles on high, elegant cheekbones that framed a middling nose. Her plump, pink lips were just as inviting as I remember. The scar down the right side of her face didn't mar her beauty; it seemed to enhance it, giving her a rakish cast that suggested she was not a woman to fuck with. After a few more moments of study, I finally uncrossed my arms and walked over to her.

Morgan cracked the crooked grin she always gave me when I did something silly, and my heart skipped a beat. It tugged her scar into a crescent curve across her right cheek, and I decided that was okay. I'd always thought scars were cool as a kid, anyway.

She said, "You know, there's a fine line between a coy glance and the piercing stare of a serial killer. I think you crossed it."

My grin widened further until I couldn't help but laugh, the humor banishing my earlier awkwardness and replacing it with a warm, familiar feeling. I gave a quick glance out the window, trying to suss out what caught her attention, but there was nothing, just rows of cars, mostly small imports. They were covered in the cracked, gray dust that douses everything this time of year, a mix of salt, exhaust, and de-icing chemicals that poisoned the streets, our lungs, and, ultimately, after a few rain showers, the harbor.

"So, Red, whatcha lookin' at?" I asked, bumping the chair.

She turned and looked back out to the lot, her emerald eyes flicking back and forth from lamp post to lamp post. "The far lot's camera coverage. It's abysmal."

"Still looking for insurgents?"

When we'd walked guard duty together in Iraq, we often played this game, spot the shitty security. We'd look for entries too easy to open, rusted portions of the fence, or broken bits of wall. We always bitched about the motor pool. It usually had one poor guard, sweating like a pig, walking back and forth among the humvees.

We regularly joked about stealing one of the vehicles and disappearing into the desert for a girl's night out. Each time, we'd take the fantasy a step further. Morgan would say, 'We ought to steal one.' Then, a few nights later, I'd add, 'And throw a beer keg in the back.' Then it was, 'Grab a sleeping bag.' The next night I'd say, 'only one?' with an expression of mock hurt. And on our last night, Morgan would tack on, 'We'd share it for warmth. It gets cold out there.' I'd laugh nervously, and the next duty cycle, we'd start at the beginning again, sometimes with a slightly different twist, sometimes not. Christ, we were a mess. Fucking don't ask, don't tell. *I'd almost had it,* I thought. *But then again, probably not.*

"Old habits die hard, I guess," Morgan said, then she turned and smiled at me again. Genuine and rosy-cheeked, it lit her eyes and turned her face incandescent.

My heart fluttered like it had when I'd first seen her at OSUT. I'd been this skinny little shit from Boston, scared of her own shadow. Morgan's easy grace and fit body had drawn me to her almost immediately. Well, that was a bit of a lie. We'd all been fresh recruits, sitting voicelessly on our first trip to the mess. She'd dropped down across from me, reached out, grabbed a bit of my chopped eggs, and popped it in her mouth, saying with a grin, "You know, if you eat too much of this stuff, it'll make your tits shrink. I wanted to let you know now because it's too late for Drill Sergeant Smith." I had let out a peel of laughter, drawing scowls from the Drill Sergeants. And with one joke and a little easy charm, she pulled me right into her world. I'd forgotten all about that moment. But now, it made me grin wildly at the pleasant thought, and I said, "I missed you, Red."

Morgan stood and stepped right into me, wrapping both arms around my shoulders and pulling me to her, which had the attractive benefit of mashing my cheeks into her breasts. I didn't say anything. And despite the thoroughly embarrassing display of cop-on-cop affection, I leaned my head harder into her chest, as I'd done a thousand times years ago, and hugged her back. And I held on to her like she might turn to vapor if I let go even a little bit.

"I missed you too, Kitty Cait," she whispered, and I caught Carlos' muffled snort of laughter from another cube across the floor. *Great,* I thought, *I am going to be Kitty Cait with the unit forever. Fucking werewolf ears.*

Someone cleared their throat behind us. "Ahem." Morgan and I broke the embrace and turned. "Oh, Maki. Sorry, this is my long-time friend from the Army, Detective Kennedy. She's on Freyer's squad. Morgan, this is Detective Imai. She just joined the—"

"Zombie Squad," Morgan finished rudely.

I blinked, taken aback. "I'm sorry?"

Morgan smirked, crossing her arms and leaning against the cube wall. "That's what everyone's calling it."

I frowned. "We're not the fucking Zombie Squad; we're the Preternatural Investigations Unit."

"Pleasure to meet you, Morgan." Maki shook Morgan's hand, then looked at me. "Cait, if you're not careful, they'll take PIU and turn it into the Pee-ew Squad or maybe the Pew-pew squad. We should take the wins where we can get them."

Morgan guffawed at that, and I looked at Maki sidelong. "You're not helping."

Carlos snorted again from somewhere else on the floor.

Morgan eyeballed Maki. "Oh, I like her. Can I keep her?"

Maki responded before I could. "You couldn't handle me, Kennedy. I breathe fire."

"Wow, Maki, you're going to fit right in," I stated, then chuckled and shook my head in disbelief. I thought I might have to look out for her with her quiet demeanor and soft voice, but it seemed not so much. She was pretty bold for someone so small. My tongue flicked out unconsciously, catching a whiff of something strange. It was a familiar scent, and it brought back memories of Tourmakeady and Mameó's farm, but I couldn't get a grip on it.

"What the fuck was that?" Morgan exclaimed, eyes growing wide.

I giggled. "What, this?" I flicked it again, this time exaggerating the snake-like wiggle.

Morgan blinked in surprise. "Yeah, that."

I smirked and stuck it out again, letting her have a good long look. "It happens sometimes. I can't help it."

Morgan furrowed her brow, thoughtfully tilted her head for a moment, and then asked, "Why is it blue?"

"Why is it blue? That's what you want to know?" I rolled my eyes and gave a semi-silent snort. "Okay, well, in short, I was infected by this parasite that messed up my genome, mixing it with a snake goddess. It took some getting used to, but it's actually kind of handy."

Morgan raised a suggestive eyebrow, and I could see her wheels turning at the more obscene implications. "Handy, how, exactly?"

I laughed loudly, then said, "Not like that—well, maybe. But, for example, I can smell Tom Ford Oud Wood cologne and bad coffee wafting toward us. That'd be Freyer." I counted down silently with my fingers. Three. Two. One.

Freyer's voice snapped over the cubes. "Morgan! We're out of here. Quit grab-assing your ex and get your gear. Work to do, you know?"

I winked. "See, handy."

"Yeah, I wonder what else you can do with it. Dinner Next week?" Morgan asked as she turned to go.

I blushed. "Uh, sure," I stammered, and she was gone.

Carol strode over and leaned against my cube, waggling her eyebrows. "Your ex, huh? I thought Marcella was your first," she said, loud as ever.

"Jesus, Carol, can you blab my shit around any louder?"

Carol pressed her lips together and had the grace to look somewhat abashed, even if a naughty smile ruined the look slightly.

Maki looked up from her desk, eyebrows raised in interest.

"Yes, Marcella was. And no, Morgan is not my ex. We were close once, but we were never really involved, at least not like that."

"Like what?" Carol said with a laugh. "Use your words, Cait."

"Ha ha, Carol, you know what I mean. We were never together as a couple. After we left Iraq, while I was recuperating, we stayed at my mother's for a couple of months, mostly in separate rooms."

"Mostly?" Carol raised an eyebrow.

I sighed. "No, Carol, we never had sex. Christ, you're nosy."

Carol's response was classic Carol. "West Indian, Cait. When I was born, I was issued a mouth with no filter, a

Trinidad and Tobago flag, and a busybody nature."

I leaned back in my chair, making slow circles on my legal pad with a pen, and my mind ventured back to memories that still sat vivid in my thoughts from time to time. "I was in pretty rough shape. Some nights, I'd wake up from nightmares, and she'd come to hold me until I fell back to sleep."

"Speaking of, how have your therapy visits been?"

I rolled my eyes again. It was no use, and I began to wonder whether Carol did it on purpose or if she simply had brain damage when it came to letting other people in on my personal issues.

"They're going surprisingly well. Jennifer is a great therapist. Some days are better, but she's given me good tools to heal my trauma. The nightmares have all but stopped. She's taught me that journaling is vital to processing emotion, so that's what I do." In all honesty, the nightmares about Iraq had quit, but I had new ones these days that were almost certainly related to my time as a guest of the Vampire Council. I kept that to myself. I was confident that they'd subside eventually.

"Hey, Carlos!" I called across the cubes.

"Yes, Ma'am!" He answered from his new desk, formerly occupied by Vic. It had been sad moving Carlos there, but we had to make room for Maki, and I'd heard we had a transfer coming in to take Mill's desk, which was also a tough change. Also, the department had funded a new crime analysis group for Homicide, which had taken three other desks. The unit was getting crowded.

"We need to huddle on the vamp murders."

A familiar face popped up over the cube wall where Mills used to sit. "Let's do it!"

"Jess? What are you doing down here?" I asked, seeing Doyle's cherubic face smiling down at me.

"They've gone vertical for the Zombie Squad, so I'm assigned as the Lead Forensicator!" The unabashed glee on her face was, as always, very disturbing. She liked the gooey stuff.

I gave her a tart grin. "Forensicator isn't a word."

"Yes, it is. Now, lighten up. I've been assigned to provide

forensic expertise to the team and to study the scientific aspects of Preternatural Crime. It's going to be so cool working together, too!" She waggled her eyebrows.

"All the more reason I can't date you, Doyle," I said with a laugh.

She made a kissy face and threw me the finger before disappearing behind the cube wall. She wasn't back there long, though, crowding into mine and Maki's little corner for the case update. Doyle squeezed in closer than seemed necessary, making it a point to lean over my shoulder. Her heartbeat thrummed in my ears, making me wonder what her blood would taste like. *Fuck*, I thought, *would this ever go away?* I shook my head to ditch the feeling. It didn't work, but I pressed on anyway, licking my lips unconsciously.

"Alright," I said. "So we have two dead vampires. Both were restrained to tables. Both were decapitated. Interestingly, only one was staked. For the uninitiated, staking does not kill us— uh—them. It paralyzes them. They can hear, see, smell, and taste but cannot move. Don't ask how that works; I'm not a witch. It's part of their curse." I looked back to see Doyle writing furious notes on her tablet. I turned to Maki, catching her just sitting there, looking bored. "Maki, are you following?"

"Sorry, Reagan, I'm familiar with vampires. Keep going, please." She took a slightly more attentive stance and seemed interested in the case, but the education on vampires might as well have been a treatise on bullet grains.

Irritated, I said, "Maki, these aren't vampires from books. They exist and are extremely dangerous. Much of what we learn from movies and books is wrong. For example, you all know they don't go poof in the daylight. That's a fallacy from the 1936 film Nosferatu with Max Schreck. Side note—"

"I'm aware that they don't sparkle, Cait," she said somewhat snidely, taking us all aback. "Please, continue."

I stared at Maki in annoyance, my lips pressed into a thin line. She was starting to get on my nerves, and I saw her less as wunderkind and more snot-nosed, know-it-all junior detective. "I was going to mention that the sunlight myth started because the director, Murnau, lost the last few pages of the script and had to improvise."

"Now that is interesting," Maki said. "Not that they don't go poof, I knew that. But that the myth came about because of lost script pages. I need to note that. I always wondered why people thought that."

I raised an eyebrow. "Are you writing your doctoral thesis or something?"

"Not exactly, no. But I'd like to be an expert in this area, and every tidbit helps."

At least something about this briefing interests her, I thought. "The two victims are Cynthia Ann Wilson and Dwight Merano. Wilson was found in the cellar of an abandoned home on Norfolk Street in Roxbury. The first victim, Merano, a local, was also found in a cellar just three blocks away on Cedar. Both Merano and Wilson disappeared roughly a week before they were found murdered. I re-evaluated the time of death estimates from the medical examiner. I adjusted them based on a vampire's baseline body temperature of eighty-six degrees, for which I deserve a commendation, given my math skills."

Everyone laughed, even Maki, which was good. It might take a minute, but she'd gel with the team eventually.

"Both were found less than twenty-four hours after they died. I have no clue why they were held for a week before being murdered. Any theories?"

"Probably interrogation," Maki said. "Or experimentation. According to your notes, they were kidnapped during the day. No one leaves a vampire chained up in a basement for a week; there's too much risk they'd escape. And neither vampire was desiccated enough to suggest they'd been drained or starved. These guys held them somewhere else before moving to the final locations where they were murdered."

Not bad, I thought. "Sounds plausible. But why take them to the new location to kill them? Why not just kill them in whatever location they were holding them?"

"Disposal, maybe?" Carol said. "Wherever they're holding them might have some foot traffic that might not be predictable."

"It's a good theory. Let's see if we can validate it." I looked up to Carlos for further suggestions, but he nodded in approval. He was having me do more of these since I'd expressed an interest in promotion.

"Okay, the case notes are in the system, along with the witness statements. Right now, we have no leads and one clue. In Cynthia's pocket was a calling card of sorts, shown here. I pulled up the image of the card."

Doyle jumped in, interrupting me. "I'll see if I can find any reference to that crest. I think I've seen it before, somewhere."

"Great, Doyle, thanks. That's all we have." I closed out the case file on my computer. "Any questions?"

Everyone shook their heads, and we split up. I had a mountain of paperwork to do before I could finish transferring my cases, so I got to work on that. I looked at Maki. She was reading the case files and scribbling notes furiously.

"Something on your mind, Detective?" Maki said without looking up.

I didn't answer immediately, my eyes tracing the outline of her face, from her beautiful, deep-brown irises that seemed to swallow her pupils, down the contour of her wide, flat nose, to her full lips, pursed in concentration—or perhaps, annoyance. Her face was like a work of art with a mix of Japanese and Chinese features blended into something that seemed almost carved of flesh and bone. Maki's constantly shifting gaze launched back and forth from paper to screen as she scribbled notes at a frightening speed, betraying the same sharp intellect I'd seen in her father.

Finally, Maki, an eyebrow raised and lips pressed firmly in annoyance, placed her pen deliberately on her legal pad and turned a questioning gaze in my direction. "What is it?"

"I know that Larson assigned you to our team because of your expertise, but—"

Maki interrupted. Her tone suggested that she'd been questioned on this subject many times. "You'd like to know how someone my age, whose only experience seems to be law enforcement, can have much expertise at all. In the preternatural, that is."

I nodded. "Well, yeah. I know your father, and his

experience with the supernatural seems to be limited to the tablets we used to open the black gate."

"As strange as it might seem, I learned everything I know of the preternatural from his mother and grandmother. I am also much older than I appear.

"Of course, I've done my own studies as well. You might be surprised that preternatural creatures are relatively common in Japan, at least the ones native to our country." There was something about her tone that intrigued me. She looked no more than twenty-five or twenty-six, and her overall demeanor was quiet and reserved, but she spoke with absolute confidence and authority. And, again, her eyes seemed to gaze at me as if I were a child despite my more advanced years. It reminded me a bit of how Schmidt had looked at me while explaining his evil plan. I quailed briefly at the unbidden memory.

I grunted in acknowledgment. "What do you know about vampire hunters?"

Maki responded like a professor giving a lecture or a computer delivering data from some science fiction film. "There are forty-three known hunter families. Of those, the hunting line within thirty-eight has either ended or the entire family was extinguished. Such endings were typically violent. That leaves five families. Only two of those are known by name, the De Medici—yes, those De Medici—and the Rognvaldr. As for the other three, who knows?"

I raised an eyebrow. "De Medici? I thought they died out."

"It would seem that Cardinal Leopoldo had some indiscretions of his own in the 1650s."

I whistled. Either Maki was exceptionally well informed, or she was putting me on. Knowing her father and the kind of daughter he'd raise, I believed the former. "How do you know all this?"

Maki smirked. "Family secret. I'll tell you about it one day. Now, regarding my thoughts on the murders, the killers are almost certainly professional vampire hunters."

I crossed my arms and waited for her to explain her reasoning, genuinely interested in her take.

"The techniques and, more importantly, the calling card, suggest a hunter family. In the 19th century, such tokens were common among them. And, while the sloppiness of Ms. Wilson's kill, specifically the broken restraint, suggests the opposite, I think, given that both vampires were identified, kidnapped, and held for a week prior to their murder, we can chalk that up to lack of practice."

I sighed in irritation. "Which also means they'll refine their techniques, just like any serial killer."

She nodded. "These guys knew right when to grab both victims to avoid both detection and having to fight with a vampire at night."

I nodded back my agreement. I remembered how Haimon Blackman had killed two Detectives and torn through six other highly experienced officers with nothing but a sword. I'd even plugged him with four shots from an M4, which had barely slowed him down. On the other hand, I'd easily been snatched off the street right in front of the house during the day. Vampires weren't a tremendous threat in the daylight hours. Though they still had some defenses. They could heal incredibly quickly, and their glamour was still very much a concern.

Maki continued, mirroring my thoughts. "I find it interesting that neither Wilson nor Merano could control their attackers. That type of resistance is often inherited."

I jotted that tidbit down in my notebook. "Anything else you can tell me?"

"Not that I can think of at the moment." Maki tapped her finger against her lips thoughtfully. "But I do have a question we all want to think about. How did they know who they were looking for? Even for a trained eye, vampires look generally human. They're hard to spot in a city of six hundred thousand."

"I considered that. And it's a good question. I'm going to ask the currently available council members to come by and sit down for a chat so we can get their thoughts."

"Wait, you what?" Maki asked, her eyebrows shooting up. "Is that wise, bringing Liz and Nastasia here?"

I raised an eyebrow. Maki seemed to know a lot. "Bringing Nastasia here, probably not. Liz is actually pretty nice. In any event, we need more to go on, and given that they are keeping all the baby vamps in line right now, they might know some of the comings and goings of our two victims."

Maki barked a laugh. "Baby vamps? Is that what they call new progeny these days?"

"Nope, just me. Anyway, thanks for your insights. It gives me some ideas. In the meantime, I have a ton of notes and reports to write before I hand off my other two cases."

Maki nodded and went back to working on the vamp case. I began typing up the various and voluminous notes from my other cases that I hadn't yet put into the system. It was going to be a long day.

CHAPTER SIX

I looked at my clock about six times between two and three. I'd sucked down a cheeseburger and a Gatorade to alleviate the last of my hangover, and thankfully it was gone, even if I was still irritable and tired. A sliver of worry was stuck firmly down my chest, straight under my sternum, and into my gut. I was meeting with the Finchers at four, and I couldn't fuck this up. I tried to suppress the feelings by burying myself in work, but that only worsened the anxiety as I watched the clock making sure I didn't miss the appointment I'd set with them. Finally, the clock ticked over to three-thirty, and I packed up.

"Maki, I have to go. I'll be back in a couple of hours. I have to meet Katie's parents." Maki looked up at me and nodded. Then she went back to documenting something to do with vampire hunting tactics and habits, some of it was spot on, and some of it was dead wrong. I frowned, wondering if I should fix it or let it be, but I didn't have time to think about it. Instead, I hightailed it downstairs and hopped into my Jeep.

After a twenty-minute drive, I arrived at a dilapidated triple-decker on Spaulding Street. Taking a deep breath before leaving the car, I thought about what I might say to them.

'Hello, Mr. and Mrs. Fincher. Your daughter is now a vampire and can't come home. Would you please sign these adoption papers? Also, you're awful parents for leaving your kid on the street and never filing a missing person report. And it's clear from the DCF reports that you've abused the fuck out of both of your children for years.' My jaw clenched, and I gripped the steering wheel in anger. This wasn't helping, so I shook my head to clear the building rage, hoping I'd figure it out. I steeled myself and walked to the door.

The doorbell didn't work, so I banged a few times in typical cop fashion until an angry-looking bald man in his mid-forties with a long, unkempt beard answered the door in his boxers and wife-beater. "Yeah?" He sounded like a three-pack-a-day smoker with a thick Southie accent.

I flashed my badge. "Hi, Mr. Fincher. I'm Detective Reagan. We spoke on the phone. I'm here to talk about Katie."

He stood there for a minute, looking at my badge with a sour expression. "Yeah, come on in. I'm Jim."

Well, at least he wanted to be on a first-name basis. "Cait," I said, and he grunted in acknowledgment, which seemed positive.

We trod up the stairs and into the apartment in silence. A young girl, maybe ten or twelve years old, with long black hair in a messy bun, watched some anime show on a small television.

"Leah! Get the fuck outta here! Now!" Jim barked, causing the little girl to jump in terror and dart quickly from the room. As she left, she peeked at me sidelong with soft, questing, grey eyes. As if just remembering something, she yanked the scrunchy out of her hair and tried to hide a fat bruise encompassing the left side of her face, but I had seen it. It looked about the size of Jim Fincher's fist, and my own hands clenched and unclenched with helpless fury. I took in a deep breath to calm down. A small evil voice in my head said, *Let them have Katie. It'll only last a night or two.* One corner of my mouth crooked up at the malicious thought, but I pressed back on the feeling. *Where did that come from?*

After Leah had gone, Jim hollered for his wife, Anne, who walked into the room from somewhere in the back. "Jim, what the fuck—" she started, then saw me with my badge in my hand and snapped her jaws shut, but with all the screaming, my right hand twitched toward my sidearm reflexively. Ten years out of Iraq and I was still wired to expect danger with every loud noise.

I'd checked on the Finchers before I'd set up the meeting. They were real fucking peaches, pillars of the community. Their file with the Department of Children and Families was as thick as a dictionary, and every other page seemed to be a complaint about child negligence or abuse. I couldn't begin to guess why the kids hadn't been pulled out long ago. Of course, if you pull children from a home, you have to have someplace to send them. I noticed Leah watching us surreptitiously from her bedroom door. *One thing at a time, Cait.* "I'm here about Katie, Mrs. Fincher."

"What has that girl done now?" Anne asked as she sat down on the couch. Jim gestured to a worn easy chair with a broken arm, and I sat down as well.

"She hasn't done anything wrong, Ms. Fincher. She was involved in an incident and was—" I paused, looking for the right word. "She's had some significant trauma." You'd have thought I was talking about a total stranger by their blank, uncaring stares, and I couldn't help pressing my lips together in frustration. "You may have heard about the incident at Elliot Norton Park?"

Jim scratched his beer gut. "There was an explosion, or something wasn't there? Something toxic? What about it?"

"Well, through no fault of her own, Katie was caught right in the middle of it. Physically, she's very healthy, but mentally, she's suffering from a kind of amnesia and bouts of aggressive behavior."

"Well, that figures," Anne sneered. "She creates a bunch of trouble and then can't remember a thing."

I glared at her. "I'm sorry?"

"What my wife is saying, Detective, is that Katie's been a handful ever since she was little. She's run away from home more times than we can count. Finally, this past summer, she took off, and we just stopped looking for her. We thought she might come home, but she didn't. We've given up."

I chewed at my cheek to keep from letting my jaw drop or

losing my temper. Katie had been a scared kid, and these neglectful shits had just left their own daughter on the street like some unwanted pet. She was only sixteen.

I plastered on a smile and said, "Well, Mr. and Mrs. Fincher, I've been taking care of her since the incident, and frankly, I've become quite fond of her. I'm here because I'd like to adopt her."

A thick silence, almost palpable, filled the room. The Finchers stared at me for a moment, eyes wide, mouths open like two kids waiting for a dose of medicine they couldn't stand but had to take anyway. Then Jim's jaw worked so hard for a minute I half expected to see bits of fine, white enamel-dust spit out of his mouth when he spoke next. "You what? You can't do that."

"I'm sorry, Mr. Fincher, but you just said she was more than you wanted to deal with, and I'd like to take care of her. Her needs are considerable, and I think it would be in her best interests—"

"Oh, you do, do you?" Jim interrupted, now so red-faced I thought he might have a stroke on the spot, which I thought would be super convenient about then. "That's my daughter." In three seconds, he'd gone from neglectful parent to possessive.

I ran a hand through my hair and sighed. I'd been here five minutes, and I hated these people. This wasn't going to work the way I'd hoped. "Mr. and Mrs. Fincher. You just admitted to neglecting your daughter's welfare to a police officer. Do you have any idea how much trouble you are in already? I would be perfectly within the law to arrest the both of you right here, right now." I paused to let that sink in before I continued quietly. "But all that would come of it would be putting you in prison and your daughters being placed in the foster care system, and that's not what I want."

"No, you want to steal one of our kids for yourself. Do you get paid more if you have a kid or something?" Jim asked.

Shit, I thought. *Of course. Now his attitude made total sense.* "No, sir," I replied, eyes squinting. "But you do, don't you?"

Jim Fincher shut his mouth, and rightly so. This was about

money, not Katie's welfare. The Fincher's DCF file had noted that they were on public assistance. If I adopted Katie, they'd lose a significant amount of income from the government. From the looks of the apartment, they probably needed every dollar they could get.

If they had been good parents and weren't abusing their kids, I'd probably try to work something out for her to just stay with us, get her into school, and keep it off book. I certainly didn't need the money right now. But I had a pretty good bead on them. Anything I did to keep Katie with me would be seen as a threat to the money. Besides, who knows what else was going on in this place? They probably wouldn't want their daughter talking to a cop.

Fuck. I should never have tracked these people down. I should have taken Nastasia's advice and had Nastasia arrange a new identity for Katie. God, I thought. *I used to be such a straight-arrow cop. I* could almost hear Nastasia's voice in my head, saying, *my, my Cait, how you've changed.*

I bit my bottom lip in frustration. I had a not-very well-controlled urge to beat the ever-loving shit out of Jim and Anne Fincher and snatch Leah away to my house forever. But the department didn't take kindly to officers randomly assaulting citizens and kidnapping their children. I closed my eyes and steadied myself for what came next.

"Mr. Fincher, why don't you come and see Katie? I think it would be good for her. My—" I paused, considering what to call Liz. "My roommate, I'm sure, would love to see you both. You can bring Leah, too, if you like. I think it's important that you see her, understand how she's changed, and let us explain the—repercussions if she cannot stay with us."

"Is that a threat, detective?" Jim asked, face screwing up in indignation.

I sighed and ran a hand through my hair again. "No, Mr. Fincher, it's nothing of the sort. I want you to understand Katie's health issues, that's all."

Jim leaned back on the couch and spread out, legs splayed, arms behind his head, a dominance display called spreading or hooding. It always irritated the fuck out of me. In response,

I leaned forward a bit, sliding the chair closer to the couch and intruding on his space. I even pushed my feet out until one was almost in contact with his. He moved back and crossed his arms and legs, his confidence broken. It was a petty thing to do, but I wasn't getting anywhere with these people anyway.

I was about to say something else, but my phone rang. "Homicide, Reagan."

It was Carlos. "Sorry to bother you on a personal matter, Cait."

"No, it's fine."

"We've got a break in the vamp case, and we need you back here. How much longer will you be?"

I looked at the Finchers. Jim watched me as I spoke, his face a mixture of anger and grim satisfaction. I was sure he could tell from my expression that I wasn't happy, and he took absolute glee in it. I had a sudden urge to call Liz and just turn her loose on him, but I quashed it. I really wanted to do this the right way. I wasn't Nastasia.

"I'm pretty much done. Be there soon." I hung up.

I wrote our address and my burner number on a sheet of notepaper and gave it to Mr. Fincher. "Please call me, and we can get together. I want to work this out. I'm sorry, but something's come up, and I have to leave. It was a pleasure meeting the both of you."

I saw Leah peek her head from her room as I left, and a lump settled in my throat. I was worried that my antagonism might get her punished just out of Jim's misplaced rage. Shit like this just wrecked my world, and there wasn't a damn thing I could do about it. I thought somewhere in the back of my head that I wished that Jim and Ann Fincher would die. Even deeper than that, I wondered what I might do if I'd still been a vampire.

"So, Mr. Fincher, can we expect you to come by?"

Jim Fincher stood, arm gesturing toward the door. "Oh, you can expect a visit from us, for sure, Detective."

Fincher wasn't done flexing yet. He was going to make this as unpleasant as possible. *Bring it, asshole,* I thought as I opened the door and left.

Outside in my car, I breathed heavily, trying desperately to quell the fiery rage that burned in my chest. I wanted to commit violence, and I didn't know why. I'd dealt with abusive parents before, and I'd always kept my cool. It was beyond distressing the way I was feeling now. It took a long time for me to simmer down enough to drive back to HQ, and I still did it in hard jerking motions, taking corners too quickly and popping my siren more than a few times to get slow motherfuckers out of my way. I was in no mood.

I had been a fool to think Anne and Jim Fincher would be reasonable. Some naive part of me had really believed that they would just hand over their child, given that they didn't seem to care about her. But that had been stupid. Nastasia had been right. *Why didn't I listen?*

"Fuck," I swore, my mind running through the maze of shitty actions the Finchers might take.

"Rough visit?" Maki asked, interrupting my self-flagellation as she set a mug of coffee in front of me. I hadn't asked for it, but I could probably use it. I felt like shit: exhausted, bleary-eyed, and miserable. The coffee would at least keep me going.

I held up the mug in thanks and took a sip—and almost spit it out. "Oh, God, you made the open case? Ugh."

"The what?" Maki said, giving a puzzled look.

"The open case. The orange shit. As in the unsolved case of homicide by poisoning."

What erupted from Maki isn't something I'd call a laugh. It was more like a series of sound bubbles that floated from her throat as she grinned, each popping with a high-pitched squeal-like sound. It was probably one of the weirdest things I'd ever heard. The closest thing I could remember hearing was a screaming fox on Mameó's farm back in Ireland, which gave me chills. Of course, I was about eight at the time.

"To answer your question," I leaned in and lowered my voice. "I turned a sixteen-year-old kid to save her life a month ago, and now I'm trying to raise her. I met with her birth parents today, and it didn't go well."

"What do you mean you turned her?"

"I'm a vampire, Maki, or at least I used to be," I said, and then I explained what happened, keeping the details a little vague.

She raised an incredulous eyebrow. "Really, now? I thought there was no cure for vampirism."

I shrugged. "I guess I found the only one, but it was a one-shot, not likely to happen ever again."

"Okay, assuming I buy that, I thought vampires were forbidden from turning anyone, especially that young, because of revenants or something."

"Jesus, you're well informed," I said, and Maki's face lit up like a shower of fiery lights, all dimpled and red and proud.

"I told you I know a lot about vampires," she held up a hand. "I can't tell you how, at least, not yet. But I will at some point, I promise."

I nodded. "Anyway, extenuating circumstances were in play." Then I smirked and added, "I can't tell you what they were, but I will someday. I promise."

She looked at me as if to say, 'Touché detective, and fuck you very much.'

I moved on, though, telling her about Katie's parents, and Maki frowned at that, saying, "They sound like sick fucks to me."

I blinked in astonishment, an amused grin spreading across my face. Maki had surprised me again, dashing my view of her as this prim and proper young woman.

Maki glared at me, reading right into my expression. "Yes, I look young and Japanese, but that doesn't make me some anime schoolgirl. I'm a grown-ass woman who can kick the shit out of just about anyone she meets."

I was unsure how to react, stunned as I was at her response.

"I'm not a child," she said flatly. "I'm a fucking professional, a Detective, just like you. By the way, since we're on the subject, you offended the hell out of me earlier. Your whole demeanor was condescending. You assumed I was inexperienced and stupid because I look young. You thought I didn't know my shit about vampires, too. I don't like being infantilized."

I frowned. She was right. I deserved the chewing out she'd just given me. "Sorry, Maki. I'll try to check my unconscious bias better." I rubbed my temples, then scooped a couple of Tylenol out of my desk and knocked them back to forestall a budding headache.

"Sorry, it's not you." I didn't know why I was apologizing for taking Tylenol, but I suddenly felt like I should. "It's been a rough morning. I'm afraid the Finchers are going to do something stupid like try to come to take Katie."

Maki looked at me intensely until the stare became uncomfortable, and I finally cleared my throat. Then she said, "They'll probably try something, but I have a feeling it will all work out for her, so don't worry."

"What makes you say that?"

"Just a feeling." Maki turned back to her work. "It'll be okay." She sounded almost dismissive, but there was something in her confidence that made me feel a little better.

I shrugged and focused on wrapping up the minutiae of my casework, transcribing case notes, and typing up scene reports that had been waiting. After I'd made a dent in the paperwork, I sidled around to Doyle to ask her what she'd found on the vamp case.

She looked up at me with wide eyes. She was probably surprised I didn't go off on Maki like I had Carol. But Carol had gone in on my—what?—family? Maki was giving me what for, and she'd been right to do so.

I shook my head, warning her off from saying anything. "Whatcha got, kid?"

Doyle pulled up a couple of videos. "Check this out."

In one video, a late-model, black GMC suburban with Florida plates and heavily tinted windows drove past the corner of Morton and Cedar, right near where Merano was murdered and shortly after the estimated time of death.

"Okay, does it show up somewhere else?"

"Yup." Doyle hit play, and I watched what looked like the same SUV, this time with Georgia plates, drive past the corner of Norfolk and Morton, near where Cynthia Wilson had been killed, again about when we believed she died.

Of course, it could be a coincidence, but my gut said otherwise. If it was the same vehicle, someone was taking pains not to be identified by using stolen plates from out of state, meaning it likely belonged to one of the perps. Criminals didn't typically change the plates on a stolen car. They would steal another one if they were at all intelligent. From what we'd seen so far, I couldn't say our perps were pros, but they were competent, having pulled people from their homes in broad daylight without a single witness.

"What do you think?" Doyle asked.

"I think we put out a BOLO for a black GMC Suburban with stolen plates. That's what I think. Then we have someone go canvas Cynthia's apartment building."

"BOLO's already out. Anything else?"

"Not yet. Check the rest of the video and see if you find more. Great work."

I went back to my desk to make a dreaded phone call. We still needed more information, so as much as I hated it, I picked up the phone. This was going to suck.

"Hello?" Nastasia answered Liz's phone.

"Where's Liz?" I asked impatiently. "I need to talk to her."

There was a very long pause. "Cait, we've talked about respect, darling." Her voice was low and chilling. She sounded like a psychopathic school teacher by the way she was talking down to me. "I don't want to teach you how this works the hard way. Now, give me a proper greeting."

I sighed. "Hello, Nastasia. Can you put Liz on the phone, please?" Maki jerked her head up and turned slowly, mouthing Nastasia's name. I nodded.

"That's better. No, I cannot. She is on another call. Is there something I can help you with?"

Fuck, fine. I thought. *Let's get this over with.* "Actually, yes." I swallowed, my throat suddenly very dry. "Um, can the two of you come down to HQ? We need to ask you some questions about our dead vampires and their habits."

"Oh," Nastasia said, sounding almost crestfallen. "That's all.

I was hoping you'd be coming to stay with me for a bit. Learn how a proper vampire lives. How sad. Well, we can make time this evening after we feed Katie. We'll see you at midnight. Now, say goodbye, Cait."

I growled in frustration and said, "Goodbye, Cait." Then I hung up. "Fucking bitch," I muttered. Wait, had she said she was taking Katie with her to feed? *Fuck.* I didn't want Nastasia within a hundred yards of Katie if at all possible.

"When are they coming in?" Maki asked after I'd finished fuming.

"After midnight."

"You mind if I take the interview with you? You shouldn't do it alone."

"That would be grand," I replied. "Thanks." I hadn't wanted to meet them alone, anyway, but Carlos had an event tonight with Marcus, and I didn't dare bring Carol. She'd get us both killed.

I snatched up a still of the Suburban that Doyle dropped on my desk and looked at it. The photo reminded me momentarily of the night I met Marcella. Carlos and I had sat on a park bench near the house. A black SUV had dropped off someone we thought was Marcella. It turned out to be Liz, but we didn't find that out until much later.

For a moment, I let myself remember how fabulous Marcella had looked that night and how completely twatted I'd been over her. God, she had seemed so stunning. I remembered wondering how she looked so good after a six-hour flight.

A six-hour flight, I thought, and the cold finger of panic ran down my spine like water. I snatched up my phone to dial the TSA duty officer at Logan.

The guy who answered had so much gravel in his voice that he sounded like he spat rocks when he spoke. "Officer Myles."

"Officer Myles, this is Detective Reagan at Boston Homicide," I said in a rush so fast that it probably sounded more like one long run-on word. I took a breath and slowed down. "I was wondering if you could do me a small favor. It's regarding a current case. Can you get access to a flight manifest from two months ago? I need to find out if someone boarded a plane."

There was a long pause, and I held my breath, waiting for him to give me the run-around. "You got a warrant?"

"No." Another pause. I waited for him to tell me to piss up a rope or hang up.

Instead, he said, "If I get it for you, will you get one?"

"I suppose that depends on what's in it."

Then he barked a laugh like granite on flint. "Yeah, I hate paperwork, too. Alright, it'll take some time. How soon do you need it?"

"The sooner, the better. I'm working the murder of two individuals who had something in common with the passenger, and I want to make sure she made it out of the country safely." I mentally kicked myself for not doing this after the first murder turned up. Marcella had been out of contact for way too long. I hadn't expected her to call me, but Marcella should have checked in on Liz and the company at some point. I'd been so wrapped up in the idea that she'd abandoned me that it hadn't even occurred to me that something might have happened. *Fuck.*

"BA flight 212, the 4th of November. Her name is Marcella Carson." I spelled it out.

I heard him mumbling as he wrote it down. "Carson, right. Okay. I'll check. Usual homicide number?"

"No, call me on my cell the minute you have something, please." I gave him my number, and he ended the call. I returned to my paperwork with a stone placed rather unkindly in the pit of my stomach. *Please be on that flight, Marcella.*

CHAPTER SEVEN

Hours later, I squinted at my computer screen, not out of fatigue; I was simply bored. I watched the image blur and twist, passing the time like a child holding a pencil in front of them and alternately opening and closing each eye, watching the image move left, right, left, right. Then I doodled around, even at one point drawing goofy images on my pad. It was a weird hobby I'd picked up lately for which I'd found I had some minor talent. I drew a quick sketch of Liz, finding some resemblance in the finished product, but not much. The eyes were too even, the nose too wide, but her smile was right.

I looked at the clock, whose hands seemed ridiculously sluggish. I still had an hour before they arrived. So I drew a caricature of Nastasia, her nose too long, eyes squinty and mean, her mouth split far wider than possible. The top of her head was tilted cartoonishly back like a PEZ dispenser, a giant hand dangling me, kicking and screaming, over her mouth. A long demonic tongue snaked out as she prepared to swallow me up. I chuckled when it was done. It didn't look like her or me, but it was still funny and eased my fear. I labeled each character in the sketch with a name and an arrow.

To my left, Maki had her head down on her desk, snoozing away. The cutest little bit of drool had pooled by her mouth, and a small, deliciously evil, extremely childish part of me wanted to lick my finger and stick it in her ear. I stifled a laugh so as not to wake her. I didn't know her that well, and I wasn't five, not physically, anyway.

I looked at the clock again. It was four minutes after midnight. They were late, and the anticipation of confronting Nastasia weighed on me again as I picked up my mug, and the coffee slopped a bit over the side. My hands were shaking. I didn't need to put much effort into dissecting my emotions, but I shoved the thoughts violently aside in a fit of anger. *No, I* thought. *This is what she wants. She wants me to feel just like this. She wants me to both be afraid of her and attracted to her.* Nastasia was the kind of woman that made you say, 'This person will completely fuck up my life. God, wouldn't that be grand.' I needed to focus.

My phone rang. "Homicide, Reagan."

It was a woman's voice I didn't recognize, giving me a moment of relief from my anxiety. It wasn't the front desk. They weren't here yet. "This is Officer Dietrich at Logan TSA. Myles wanted me to tell you that Carson never made her plane. Her bags were checked, but she didn't board. Someone down here said that federal agents picked her up." My whole body seemed to fold in on itself, and my head spun. Shakily, I thanked Dietrich and bid her goodbye.

Every organ in my body seemed to sink all at once, as if gravity had a particularly heavy pull on my insides, dragging them down along with any energy I had. I rested my head in my hands and cried, terrified I'd never see her again.

"Fuck," I swore softly. And I had thought I was over her. Clearly, I wasn't, even after everything she'd done. "Fuuuck," I said louder, then remembered Maki was asleep one desk over. I turned as my phone rang again and wiped my eyes. Maki was awake, watching me. Her fox-like facial features twitched, and she said, "She's not dead. You'll find her."

I wondered how she knew, but I didn't have time to ponder that as my phone rang for the third time.

"Reagan, Homicide." I couldn't help the shaking in my voice.

"Hey, Cait, it's Kathy down here at the desk. There are two

ladies here to see you." Kathy was an older patrol officer who'd semi-retired but then come back to work the front desk out of sheer boredom.

I pulled myself together. "Let me guess. A pretty blond and a brunette that seems like she ought to be working an S&M gig, both pale as fresh snow?"

Kathy grunted a laugh. "Yes, ma'am. That's them."

"I'll be right down."

When the elevator opened, both women were standing directly in front of the doors. Nastasia was dressed to kill, almost literally. She wore a black dress with a tight leather-corseted bodice, black seamed stockings, and patent leather heels strapped at the ankle. A leather, biker-style jacket adorned her shoulders. Her long dark hair was done up in a tight bun, and she even had a pair of reader glasses on. I'd been joking, but she looked like the naughty librarian headed to her after-hours S&M gig. Hell, maybe she was. Nastasia was the walking epitome of sensual sin, and despite my anxiety, my heart thumped hard with something else entirely. "Ladies, come along."

Both women were obscenely quiet until the doors closed, then Nastasia spoke up.

"So, Cait, how have you been? You and Liz have been getting along. She's been able to speak of nothing else."

I fidgeted with my pen nervously, hands rigidly at my sides. "I—" My voice cracked nervously, and I cleared my throat. "Liz and I are doing fine, thank you."

Nastasia turned toward me. "And how about Katie? She's quite the little monster."

I frowned. I opened my mouth for a nasty retort when the elevator bell dinged.

"Ah, saved by the proverbial bell," Nastasia said, and she strode from the elevator as the doors parted, turning right.

I grabbed Nastasia by the arm, and she jerked loose, turning on me and making me quail. "Do not handle me, child." My stomach dropped at the menace in her voice.

"Then don't turn your back on me when we're talking," I shot back with more bravado than I felt. "You demand manners. Well, so do I. There's no reason to be rude. Besides, you're going the wrong way. Homicide is this way." I gestured toward our desks.

Nastasia didn't move. Instead, her eyes flashed, and she spoke in a low, frightful tone, showing her fangs. I froze. "Let's get something straight, little girl. I have had it with your disrespect. Marcella was much too loose with you and every other newborn. I demand the courtesy of my age and expect to get it. I have been roaming this planet for eight hundred years, and you can't imagine how patient and cruel I've learned to be. I hear your mother is ill, and what about your sister?"

I blanched at the implied threat and backed down immediately. "Yes, Nastasia. I'm sorry."

"Nas, really?" Liz said. "Try not to be a total twat, will you? You keep saying Cait is one of us, but you keep treating her like chattel. If we're all beneath you, why don't you treat me that way?"

"Because you haven't tried to kill me twice, Liz. And this one needs to remember who and what she is. She won't figure that out with your mollycoddling." Nastasia tilted my head up with a finger, searching my eyes with her own, and I found myself unable to move. My eyes flicked over her face. There was something in her expression I didn't understand, almost pensive. Very slowly, her face crooked up into a wicked grin. "I can't wait," she said with a mysterious and altogether terrifying air that made my stomach drop, then turned away.

Liz frowned deeply and shot Nastasia's back a hateful gaze, but she said nothing else. I looked to her for support, but she was staring straight ahead, her usually bright expression spoiled with helplessness. She couldn't protect me. I was alone against Nastasia in this contest of wills.

I am going to have to play things smarter, I thought. *What would Nastasia do?* I snorted in mild amusement. *Probably something evil.* But I'd have to start thinking like her if I wanted to survive.

Arriving at the interview room, I escorted them in and retrieved Maki. Once we were all seated and as comfortable as we could be with an eight-hundred-year-old murderous vampire in our midst, we started.

"Detective Imai, this is Elizabeth Tyler and Nastasia Volkova. Ladies, Detective Imai."

They shook hands, and Maki paused momentarily as she took Nastasia's and looked into her eyes. Then she said, "Ms. Volkova, that won't work on me, so don't waste your time."

Nastasia sat, a slight frown on her face. I was envious. I'd give almost anything to be immune to glamour like that. Of course, I had been once. This sucked.

Maki and I sat, and I started the interview. "So, Nastasia, you were closest to Cynthia. Do you have any idea who might have wanted to kill her?" My hands were steady, but my leg was trembling under the table.

"From what I understand, she was found beheaded, like Mr. Merano, though not staked, which is odd. One of the remaining five hunting families would likely be to blame. Though, I find that very disturbing." Before I could ask, Nastasia elaborated. "We've heard neither hide nor hair of the families since the fire in Oulu."

Liz grimaced.

"I'm sorry, the fire in Oulu?" I glanced at Liz, but she gave nothing else away.

"My, my, Cait. Marcella was remiss in your education. You and I will need to talk later." I paled but recovered, and Nastasia continued. "We all met for a conclave every ten years or so. Mostly they were debauched parties, but on this occasion, the council, which, at that time, was five of us, demanded attendance from everyone to talk about depleting the number of revenants. It had become clear that we were unable to turn anyone reliably. I'm sure Marcella explained at least that."

"Yes, she made it clear that was the reason why you opened the gate. Magic is needed to fuel the transfer of the curse reliably."

"Well, you and your mother opened the gate. I was just a bystander, really. Thank you for volunteering to participate in that endeavor," Nastasia said past her malicious smile.

You fucking bitch. "I'll give Schmidt your regards." I finally felt a little more myself, so I sat back, picking up my pen. Nastasia, for her part, gave a short, glittering laugh at the retort, a surprisingly lilting, warm sound that slid deliciously over my skin. I wondered if it was just me or if she had somehow added glamour to it. Either way, it creeped me out.

Nastasia continued, and a deep frown marred her features. "Our ability to turn people began to fade almost four hundred years ago. By the late 1800's it had reached a crisis point. Too many vampires were trying to make companions, servants, and such. As a result, hundreds of revenants scuttled about Europe, attracting too much attention. Believing that no one would go against the council, we decided to, how do you say, 'put the kibosh on it?' So, in 1882, we held a conclave in Oulu, Finland, on the second of November. Based on the census taken during the initial stages of the conclave, we are certain that all but two known vampires attended. As we opened the conclave, someone set fire to the next-door pharmacy."

Nastasia turned toward Maki, reached out, and placed a delicate white hand on her pad. The movement was smooth, almost wraithlike in its grace and gentility. "Please stop taking notes. The rest of what I say is not on the record, is that understood? If I find out this has been spread around your department or anywhere else, I will have no choice but to eliminate anyone who knows. I hope that is clear enough for you." Nastasia's tone wasn't loud or menacing, yet it was clear that she expected compliance.

Maki placed her pen carefully on the table and waited. Maki's face didn't so much as twitch, but her posture shifted immediately, closing up with her arms across her chest.

"Of the roughly four-hundred vampires in attendance," Nastasia continued gravely, "only twelve of us survived."

My eyes turned into dinner plates as I did a quick mental count. "Twelve? Plus two not in attendance, that's fourteen. With the ones that Schmidt turned plus Katie, that means only twenty-seven vampires survive after the last two murders."

"Twenty-eight, Cait," Nastasia countered. "Don't forget yourself."

"I'm not a vampire anymore. Why do I keep having to say

that?"

Nastasia turned her gaze on me, and I shrank back in my chair. A strange feeling sank into me, almost pleasant, as I gently folded my hands in my lap and closed up. I looked at my hands, my knees, then the carpet, my eyes searching aimlessly as I tried to understand the emotions running through me. My breath turned heavy, and my cheeks burned. I was terrified of her, yes, but closing up and giving Nastasia what she wanted was making me aroused. I crossed my legs. *God, what the hell?* I thought. *I'm wet.* I squirmed uncomfortably.

Liz placed a hand on Nastasia's arm and said. "Nas, stop. It's distracting, and this is important."

The fear fled, and the arousal lessened, but it was still there. I shook out my hands and sat back up. *Fuck,* I swore inwardly. *She's glamouring me. Right here in front of Liz and Maki, she's glamouring me.* I did my best to shake it off and tried to pay attention. But it was too late. I couldn't take my eyes off of her skin and the way the bodice of her dress cupped her breasts, creating an enticing line of cleavage that—

"Just a second," I said and bolted to the ladies' room to splash cold water on my face trying to jolt away the intense thrill, but it only intensified as the door opened behind me. I closed my eyes. "Oh, shit." I breathed.

The soft clack of heels tapped up behind me. I didn't look up into the mirror at first, not wanting to see her with her soft, kissable lips and flawless skin. A hand brushed my hip, and I stood straight, stiffening. I felt the touch of each finger at my waist as Nastasia pressed to my back and inhaled. I spun about, almost losing my balance in a sudden headrush.

There was no one there. I looked in the stalls, even under the countertop. The room was empty.

"What the fuck?" I whispered and splashed another handful of water on my face. It took a few minutes, but I finally managed to stop my heart from racing. *Now I was seeing things? I didn't think she could do that to me, not this far away.* I shook my head and stalked from the ladies' room. *Enough of this shit.*

Nastasia was still speaking to Maki as if nothing had

happened, but she paused as I entered, saying, "Cait, darling, you look positively flustered. Are you alright?"

I squinted at her. "Knock it off, Nastasia. We're supposed to be working here."

"What do you mean?" She asked. She looked perfectly innocent sitting there if you didn't count the emo dominatrix outfit and the way she had her legs crossed, so her skirt was perched precipitously high on her legs, uncovering the tops of her stockings and lace garter straps.

"You know what I'm talking about," I shot back hotly. "In the bathroom—"

Liz interrupted us. "Cait, Nastasia has been sitting here talking to Maki the whole time you've been gone. She didn't do anything. Are you okay?"

I looked at Liz skeptically, and she raised her eyebrows waiting for me to explain. I gave up arguing and sat back down. The fear was gone, and so was the heat I'd felt. Now I was just tired, and I rubbed my eyes. "I'm sorry. Keep going."

Nastasia continued. "As I was saying, it's not something we advertise. Now that the gate is open, we will turn others, but Liz and I are working on some rules. Just turning any idiot we fancy won't be tolerated. Being a vampire means inheriting extreme power, and with that is expected a certain level of decorum, shall we say." I understood completely. With only twenty-nine—well, twenty-eight—vampires, the numbers were gravely lopsided in favor of humans if it came to violence.

"So, what does the fire have to do with the 'five families?'" I asked, picking up my pad and pen and making a quick mental note to talk to Liz about my 'education.'

Liz finally spoke, picking up the narrative in a more fact-oriented manner. "On November 2nd, 1882, we gathered in Oulu, Finland. During the fire, it became clear that someone in our midst had coordinated with at least one of the families, as any of the vampires who escaped the fire were quickly cut down by a group of hunters surrounding the building. Those of us who did escape only managed to do so across the rooftops. The presence of the hunters made it clear that we were the target; the fire was not an accident. Ultimately it burned down half the town, but I digress.

"After the fire, we all agreed to remain quiet and not draw attention to ourselves. We also agreed that we would make no more progeny until a way could be found to make the process more reliable. Of course, some of us failed to abide by that decree." Liz paused. She meant Marcella, of course. "In any event, we heard nothing from the hunters after the fire and had surmised that they believed us all dead."

"Until now." I finished for her.

"Until now," Liz confirmed. "That's not shocking, though, Cait. After your chase with Haimon in West Roxbury, we expected some attention. But, we're not an obvious group in a city of six hundred thousand people. Pale as we might be, nothing we've done gives us away, and we've been meeting secretly. So, the real question is, how did hunters track down and murder two brand new vampires in a week without leaving a single shred of evidence other than the method of execution?"

Maki looked up from her pad. "Well, I wouldn't exactly say none." She pulled out her phone and brought up an image of the card we'd found on Cynthia's body, sliding it across the table. "Do you recognize this? It seems to be a calling card of some sort."

Both vampires looked at it and shook their heads. Liz slid the phone back across the table. "No. It's neither De Medici nor Rognvaldr. It could be from one of the other families."

I tilted my head in curiosity. "So, dumb question, if you don't know all of the families, how do you know how many remain? I mean, there were forty to begin with, right?"

Nastasia's eyes snapped to me with rapt attention. "And how do you know how many families there were, Cait?"

Shit, me and my big mouth. I struggled to find a satisfactory answer without bringing Maki into it.

"I told her. It's from my own research," Maki said before I could stop her.

Nastasia raised an eyebrow, and Liz looked at her suspiciously. "What research?"

Maki didn't flinch. "Hideyoshi Ito is one of my ancestors." Now, that was interesting. She was descended from one of the elders in some way; it explained a lot. The explanation seemed to mollify Nastasia, though Liz still eyed Maki.

"Okay, so we have one clue," Liz said. "I think Marcella may have some materials tucked away somewhere on the families, and I know Schmidt was keeping up with them for some time as well, though with him dead, I'm not sure where we might find any research he had. We'll go through Marcella's information when you come home."

I nodded, then swallowed, afraid to be the bearer of bad news. "One more thing." I was surprised that my voice didn't shake as I spoke. "Marcella is missing. Has been for two months now. She never made her flight."

You could have heard a pin drop, then Nastasia said in a low and threatening tone, "And why are we just now learning about this?"

"I just found out myself," I said and pressed my lips together. Nastasia didn't say anything else, but there was something in her eyes, a touch of worry perhaps. If they could get at Marcella, they could get at her. On the other hand, Liz looked stricken, but she kept her thoughts to herself.

We spoke no more of Marcella for the rest of the interview, instead going over Cynthia's and Mr. Merano's victimology, gathering as much detail as possible and focusing on their movements.

In general, there was nothing weird or unusual if you took into account that they were vampires, of course.

Cynthia had been working as a night dispatcher for a local ambulance company. Dwight worked for a software company as a customer advisor of some sort. Based on the evident struggle at Mr. Merano's apartment, he'd been grabbed at home during the day; his apartment had been trashed during the fight. I expected Carol and Carlos to find the same at Cynthia's.

Cynthia spent most of her time feeding at local bars in Back Bay, and Merano was living over in Quincy, hitting bars around there. We knew of no overlap, and they didn't feed together. Honestly, other than being vampires, they had nothing in common. The lack of indications of how they were stalked was frustrating.

"There should be a database," I mused after we'd finished.

"What's that, Cait?" Liz asked. "What do you mean?"

"I mean, we should keep track of who feeds on whom. It'll eliminate the possibility that we—sorry, you—feed on the same person as someone else."

"Perhaps we need an app for that," Nastasia joked. "Available from the Apple Store and Google Play for all your vampire needs."

I laughed, despite myself, at her uncharacteristic show of humor.

Nastasia turned abruptly sober. "Yes, it's funny, but I'm serious. It's not a bad idea. At some point, we're going to have to go public. This might be a good way to hook in a younger crowd."

"I'm sorry? A younger crowd?" That sounded icky.

"The twenty-somethings. Looking at us, you'll notice that Liz and I look about twenty-five. Between twenty and thirty is the usual age for turning someone. You were kind of old, to be honest."

I blinked. Was I the old lady of the bunch? I hadn't considered it, but she was right. Of all the vampires I'd met, only Schmidt had appeared older. Even Marcella had been in her mid-twenties when she'd been turned. *Fuck. I am the old lady!*

Nastasia laughed almost charmingly. "Oh, Cait, I'm only teasing you. You're, by far, not the oldest who has ever been turned. Schmidt was just over fifty. But, if you think about it, it should be clear why. Any of us could easily pass for twenty-five to forty-five-ish. Twenty years in a single identity is considered a good run."

I realized that Nastasia was a wealth of knowledge. Maybe spending more time with her wouldn't be so bad, as long as she didn't murder me in a fit of pique. *What was I thinking? I didn't want to spend more time with her than—*

"Okay," Nastasia said as she stood, pulling me from my

thoughts. "I think we're done here. Liz, can I count on you to work with Cait to ferret out who is hunting us?"

Liz frowned. "Yes, Nastasia, but I'm not a detective. This isn't my forte."

"Perhaps not, but it's not like we don't have one on hand that has more than enough experience for the both of you." Nastasia winked at me. If the gesture was supposed to set me at ease, it had the opposite effect. I didn't particularly appreciate having her attention like this, and I got the feeling she was planning something—something I wasn't going to like at all.

But I wasn't quite finished. "Nastasia, I need to put surveillance on the other vampires. They're in danger."

She seemed to think about that for a moment, tapping her lips. "Okay, but please keep it to Freyer's team or yours."

I nodded, then quickly added, "Yes, ma'am."

Liz rose, and they both left the interview room. Maki and I followed them out, making sure they entered the elevator.

As they were leaving, Nastasia stopped the door with one hand. "Be seeing you soon, Cait," she said with a smile that chilled my blood, then she let the doors slide closed, leaving me standing there shaking.

Maki watched me with intense curiosity, bordering on creepy. "Are you feeling okay?" She gestured to my trembling hands.

"No, I'm not." Tears of frustration and terror stung my eyes, and I tried fiercely to blink them back, finally failing and taking one of the random seats near the elevator.

"Jesus, Cait, What did she do to you? Everyone around here says you're a tough-as-nails, hard-ass bitch."

"I used to be. I am." I sniffed and wiped my nose with my handkerchief. "But Nastasia is a pro when it comes to vampire glamour. She could make me her willing slave at her whim, and there'd be nothing I could do about it. And we had an altercation, where—" I wiped my nose and eyes on my handkerchief again and fought to pull myself back together.

Maki sat down in the chair next to me. "Cait, you have every right to be afraid, but—"

"You're not listening. Her glamour is flawless. It took a while for me to figure it out. She feeds my fear when I upset her, feeds my pleasure when I submit, and she won't let me go. Now she makes veiled threats whenever I see her, comments about Katie, and comments about my mother. She enjoys keeping me on edge, terrified that if I make any mistake, she'll end my world as I know it and keep me alive. She broke me!" My voice turned shrill. "Nastasia broke me! Do you get it?" I stood and paced for a minute, wringing my hands.

I let out a nervous, maniacal bark of laughter and tried to compose myself, wiping my eyes once more. "Maybe I'm just tired of dealing with—" I paused. I had been about to say life, or maybe vampires, but there was Katie—and Liz.

"Why do you live with them? Liz can take care of Katie by herself."

"Because Liz is my friend, and Katie is my responsibility. I turned her. And I love them both. I can't leave them with her." I jerked my head toward the elevators, indicating Nastasia.

Maki sighed and put a hand on my shoulder. "Well, you'll figure it out. I know you will."

Will I? I wondered. But it wasn't Liz I was thinking about just then. It was Nastasia, and it caused a well of longing to sink into the pit of my stomach to lie next to the twisted mass of fear she engendered, and a thrill shot through me at the thought of being with her, seeing her naked, just touching her. It was maddening.

"In any event, that was mostly useless," Maki said, interrupting my thoughts. "They hardly told us anything. I already knew all that business about the fire in Oulu."

I blew out a breath. "No, we did learn one thing of use. Somewhere in Marcella's or Schmidt's files is the answer we're looking for. We just need to find it before another vampire dies. And we need to put surveillance on the others, now."

CHAPTER EIGHT

Saturday, December 18th

Three weeks until my murder. . .

I contacted two of the remaining vamps and put daytime surveillance on them the following morning. We were less concerned about the nights, so their homes would be watched between an hour before dawn and an hour after sundown. As for the third of Schmidt's progeny, Andrea Saint-Fleur, there was no trace. Carlos and I had tried her home, cell, and her work. All to no avail. After almost three days, we finally put out a BOLO, even contacting the press for help.

Back at Marcella's, Nastasia had a shit fit about bringing in the press.

I reminded her that one of our vampires was missing, that I was the expert in this area, and that a good leader didn't browbeat their teams over what they couldn't control. It had gone over like a turd in a punchbowl, with her doing plenty of grousing about my 'so-called' expertise, but at least she didn't get violent. She just huffed and went home, demanding I call if anything turned up. Score one small, minuscule point for me in the respect category—sort of.

After that, all we could do was wait. But I didn't expect to wait long. She'd been missing almost a week, which was no bueno. Both Merano and Cynthia had been found about five days after they'd gone missing, so if Andrea didn't turn up soon, we could expect her dead.

Finally, long before sunrise on the sixth morning, the call came in. I had been gazing numbly at another forty-minute video of people buying gas and snacks, looking for any more footage of our elusive SUV. I was about to go home and pass out when Carlos walked over, grim-faced, to tell me that they'd found Andrea Saint-Fleur.

I barely heard him and rubbed my red eyes. I'd tried to focus on the vampire murders, but for days Leah's gray eyes had been haunting me, bruised and pleading. I'd seen the look a thousand times. Her eyes screamed for help, begging for a million things. Don't take away mommy and daddy. Please make sure I eat enough. But most of all, they begged me to make them stop hurting her. I'd worked a few abuse cases that had turned into murder cases. In one case, a woman's daughter wouldn't stop flicking the light switch, so the boyfriend beat her to death. In another, a mom smothered her own child so the baby wouldn't cry when she went to get a fix from her dealer. It was horrendous. Even after I'd been cured, I'd ceased thinking of myself as part of a species that could do that. I stuck out my tongue, taking a moment to examine it in a small mirror I kept at my desk. What had once been an annoyance and a little scary had become a part of me, a little piece of Bian that made me something other than these evil fuckers who murdered each other and beat or neglected their kids.

"Hey, Reagan, we've got a case," Carlos repeated, looking at me expectantly and pulling me from my dark thoughts.

"I heard you." I sighed and ran a hand through my hair. Then I gathered my gear, but my motions were slow and depressed. This was going to be a long callout as the anxiety and worry over Katie gnawed at my gut. I was about to walk out the door when I heard a snippet from the TV in the conference room. A couple of guys were watching the news.

The anchorman spoke with that Midwestern non-accent all newscasters shared, "That's the fourth ship lost in the Strait of

Messina. Italian authorities have been unable to identify the creatures we now know to be responsible. This footage may be unsettling for some viewers."

The last thing I heard as I hit the stairwell was the sound of screaming Italian men and the rushing of water. I hadn't seen any of the visuals, but the noises told me all I needed. The Strait of Messina was infamous. Several decisive naval battles were fought there in Ancient times. But it was its rather singular ignominy in Greek myth that I thought of as the door to the stairwell closed, silencing the sounds of carnage issuing from the television. It was the home of Scylla and Charybdis, two gigantic monsters that sank and destroyed ships, consuming the men aboard.

I tried to summon any care for the men who had been dying in the video, but all I felt was that somehow, in all this, we'd given humanity precisely what it deserved. Humans destroyed everything in their path, constantly pushing the edge of their own destruction. Well, now, there were things to push back, and I simply didn't care. No, I was glad about it. And with that thought, I struggled to understand what was wrong with me. *I hadn't been this way before the gate, before I was turned, had I?* I took a deep breath and accepted the callous feeling. Fuck it. I had a job to do. I rushed down the stairs and out to Carlos' waiting cruiser.

As soon as I buckled my seatbelt, Carlos roughly threw the cruiser into gear, and we left. Carlos' jaw worked as he drove. He was aggravated about something.

"What is it?" I asked after a prolonged silence.

"Just tell me why?" He said, eyes glued to the road and hands wrapped tightly on the wheel.

I sighed in exasperation, immediately feeling defensive. "Why what, Carlos?"

"After all the shit we went through and what happened to your mother. After all you learned about them. Why Elizabeth Tyler?"

I bristled and lost my temper. "Not you, too. Carol just asked me the same question on the way back from Cynthia's murder scene. I've had enough of everyone passing judgment on my personal choices. It's my life, and I'll be damned if I explain it to you or anyone else." Tears of rage and frustration burned in my eyes.

Carlos pulled into a small parking lot in front of a convenience store and turned off the car.

"What are you doing, Carlos? We have a crime scene to get to."

"They'll still be dead when we get there." Carlos threw the car in park and squinted at me. "Cait, I'd like to consider you a friend, but shacking up with a vampire again?"

"Come on, Carlos. Can we not do this?" I pulled my handkerchief and dabbed at my eyes.

"Cait, I'm worried. Hell, we're all worried, and with the gate open—"

"Fine!" I barked. "I'm one of them, Carlos, still. Every so often, I can feel it burning under my skin." I squinted with impotent rage. "And you know what else? I liked being a vampire. I liked being able to push people around when I wanted to. I loved the bite. It was like sex in a can. I could do what I wanted when I wanted, and no one could stop me. I was strong and fast—" My steam ran down as I struggled through the last few words of what would likely have been a great speech. "And no one could hurt me. No one could—" I paused for a long moment, stifling a hiccuping sob. "God, I'm so fucked up." I stared at the car's ceiling and let out a growl of frustration.

"Darlin', I'm sorry. I know part of this is wrapped up in Katie and that you feel responsible for her, but—"

I cut Carlos off. "No," I snapped. "I'm not shirking my responsibility to Katie. I turned her. I erased her life. Me, no one else. And she's been through enough, whether she remembers it or not. I can't just abandon her and pretend I don't care. I wouldn't be able to live with myself."

The tears were free-flowing now as I thought about Katie and what I'd done. But she'd been so innocent and desperate, and I couldn't let her die.

I sniffed and blinked. "I know my involvement put you at risk last time, and I'm sorry, but you don't have to protect me.

I'm managing okay."

Carlos put the car in gear and backed out of our parking spot. "That's my risk to take. Besides, we did good last time."

I grinned at that, wiping away my tears. "I know. You tore the shit out of an eight-hundred-year-old vampire."

Carlos grinned. "I won't lie; that did feel pretty good knocking Nastasia's dick in the dirt. I don't get the chance to cut loose like that often. Now, just tell me you haven't slept with Liz."

My face flushed crimson, and I floundered for words, stuttering slightly. "N-no, I haven't slept with either of them. It's a bit of a dilemma." I suppressed a smile. I was teasing him a bit.

He laughed at first, but then his eyes went wide as he caught on. "Either of them? You don't mean? Good God, darlin', you like to live dangerously."

I gave him a sidelong glance and smirked. "Come on, Carlos. You can't tell me that you haven't noticed that Nastasia's sexy as hell."

"I'm gay, Cait, not dead. I've noticed. But she's beyond mean. She's fuckin' evil. She'll probably sleep with you, sure, then pull your fuckin' heart out, probably literally. Besides, I figured you'd be into Liz. I hear the way you two talk on the phone."

I quirked my lips. He wasn't wrong. Liz and I talked about when I was coming home from work and how Katie was doing. Sometimes, we just chatted for a few minutes about nothing. A warm feeling crept into my chest when I thought about it. *Crap.* I didn't say anything for long minutes, letting the conversation stall out. Carlos finally broke the silence.

"What are you gonna do when Marcella comes back?"

"If she comes back," I muttered. "She's missing. She never made her plane. But after what she did, she'll be lucky if I don't stake her ass for a few years."

"What! When did you find this out?"

"Last week," I replied and flinched.

"Well, that's something I'd have liked to know. This is serious, Cait. If they can get at Marcella, they can—"

"I know!" I snapped. "I'm sorry. It's just vampire business, you know?"

Carlos squinted at me.

I frowned at him, irritated. "Now what?"

"It's police business, too," Carlos muttered but didn't say anything else as we turned into a neighborhood street in Hyde Park, arriving at the scene moments later, squelching any further conversation. Before exiting, I looked in the mirror. Shit, my eyes were puffy. I looked like I'd been crying. *Fuck.*

The whole team was at the scene except Maki, who had the night off for a personal matter. Doyle walked up as soon as we exited the vehicle.

"Things just got a lot worse," she said, her face ashen gray. "We've got a dead cop; it's Soledad."

My eyes went wide. "What? What was he doing here?"

"It's easier if you just come and see." Doyle stalked off toward the house, and we followed. Unlike the other two crime scenes, this house wasn't abandoned. It was a tiny two-story A-frame with gray Hardiplank siding, a cute little red door, and a 'For Sale' sign out front. Two officers were posted outside, chatting, a pissed-off look on both of their faces. Carlos and I nodded to the two officers as we donned our gloves and entered the home, following Doyle downstairs into the cellar.

The cellar was empty except for a blood-covered table, the heating appliances, and two bodies in one corner.

One was Soledad, formerly one of Freyer's guys. He didn't like me very much, mainly because I was a vampire. It freaked him out badly, and he'd transferred out of Fugitive Apprehension right after their run-in with Haimon Blackman, where two good Detectives had died. Soledad's throat was torn out, though there was almost no blood around him. A discarded axe lay next to him.

The other was Andrea Saint-Fleur, a young African-American vampire of mixed Puerto Rican and Haitian descent. She wasn't moving, but her head was still attached. A thick wooden stake protruded from her chest. Finally, we had a fucking witness.

Carlos let out an ear-splitting whistle. "Everyone out! Except for you, Reagan, you stay with me."

I waited for Carol, Doyle, and another patrolman I didn't recognize to leave, then joined Carlos down next to Andrea. "Alright. She'll likely be freaked and maybe even blood-starved when she comes to, so you'll need to hold her down."

Carlos nodded and straddled her waist, placing both hands on her shoulders. It gave me just enough room to remove the stake.

"On three," I said, and Carlos nodded again in acknowledgment.

I took a deep breath, counted to three, and pulled the stake from Andrea's chest with a grunt, the back end of it whacking Carlos in the gut. Surprisingly, she didn't freak out or even say anything at first. It took a minute, but Andrea's eyes fluttered open, wide with terror. Then she looked at me, and some of the fear dissipated from her expression. Carlos and I looked at each other, and then he lifted off of her.

"Cait?" Andrea uttered through trembling lips. "Is that you?"

I sat her up, breathing a sigh of relief when I noted her chest was healing quickly, a sign that she'd fed recently. "Yeah, it's me. Are you okay?"

"Fuck no," Andrea spat as she pulled her legs up to her chest. "I'm not okay."

I looked at Carlos. "We have to send patrol home. They can't be here when she walks out, or the cat's out of the bag. Nastasia will go apeshit."

Carlos frowned and looked at me like I'd lost my mind. "We can't charge a guy with attempted murder if there's no evidence of attempted murder. And we can't very well put someone behind bars without a victim. Otherwise, what are we doing this for?"

He was right, but Nastasia would have a shit fit, and I knew it. She'd probably blame me. She hated me anyway. I sighed and nodded. "Okay, but can you have Doyle come down with a smock and evidence bag?"

Carlos started for the stairs.

"And Carlos?"

He paused mid-stride, turning to look at me.

"Remember that this will come around to the Vestry, too, eventually."

"I know," Carlos replied and headed back up the stairs.

Andrea was shaking badly when I turned back to her. I wanted to hug her, but I couldn't. I didn't want to contaminate her clothing further. "It's okay, Andrea. You're okay. When did you last feed?"

Andrea looked back toward Soledad. "I got a little bit out of him before they staked me, so I'm okay for the moment, but it's rising. I didn't kill him, though. I don't understand what's happened here. He was alive when I last saw him, Cait, I promise." She started rubbing her arms, and fat tears began to fall over her lashes.

Doyle came down the stairs with a paper smock and a large evidence bag, followed by Carol and Carlos. Doyle was gentle, shushing her as she opened up the cellophane pack containing the smock. "Okay, take it easy. Let's get those clothes off you, and then we can get you out of here."

While Doyle worked to get Andrea situated, I called Liz. She didn't answer. She and Katie must be out. Katie had to feed frequently. I sighed and pulled up Nastasia's number. My finger hovered over the entry for several seconds before I finally pushed it, sucking a breath to steel myself.

"Hello, my pretty. Is this a pleasure call?" Nastasia answered.

I steadied my voice before answering, but it still sounded shaky to me. "No, Nastasia, it's business. We've had another hit. Andrea Saint-Fleur."

Nastasia swore loudly, and Carlos looked up at me, an eyebrow raised. I waved him off.

"She's alive. She was just staked. But I need someone to come and take her to the station and give her some blood." Carol's brow furrowed, and she frowned heavily. I waved her off, too. "Can you help her? I can't have patrol take her. I don't think it's safe. I could take her, but—"

"No. You do your job," Nastasia said flatly. "I'll come to get her. Where is she?"

I gave Nastasia the address before she continued.

"She'll have to stay at your place, though. I have no room in my apartment. But at some point, I want to talk to you about all this. I have questions. Like how is it that your team is always the call-out for these cases? And what will happen when we find these bastards?"

"Won't that be lovely?" I hung up. "Fuck."

Doyle took Andrea outside while Carlos, Carol, and I walked the scene. Nothing in the scene made much sense, though. From what we could see, Soledad's body was largely unharmed, though his left wrist had a bruise on it where, I assumed, Andrea had grabbed ahold of it. That jibed with Andrea's statement that she'd fed on Soledad. But, on closer inspection, the wound on Soledad's neck suggested it had been clawed open. If Andrea had done this, her hands would have been covered in blood, but they weren't. They'd been clean.

I moved away from Soledad's body, which stank heavily of decay, and tasted the air. Like in the Wilson case, I smelled stale cigarette smoke and cheap men's cologne, definitely Old Spice. I also smelled something new, a little like a wet dog. Before I could say something about it, though, Carlos chimed in.

"Do you smell it, Cait?"

"Yes. What is that?"

"Werewolf. Like humans, we all have a unique scent, but it always has a bit of the wolf in it, too. It's how we know each other. It's too subtle for most humans to pick up, but—"

"I'm not all human," I finished for him.

"I was going to say that you're special, but yeah. At least two others were here. I'm willing to bet the werewolf did that to Soledad. I don't recognize the scent, so it's a wolf I've never met."

I walked around, scenting the air with Carlos.

"It's strongest over here," Carlos said finally from the stairs.

Doyle came bouncing down the stairs with her kit. "What's strongest?" She asked, eyes bright and sparkling. I shook my head. The woman loved a good murder scene.

"Smelly werewolf," Carlos replied.

"Huh. I don't smell anything," Doyle said as she trotted back over to Soledad's body. "Is it that tongue thing you do again?"

"Yes," I replied, watching intently as Carol and Carlos examined the stake we'd pulled out of Andrea. It reminded me of the one I'd seen Blackman carrying at Marcella's a couple of months ago. It looked like the same wood and was the same style, if a bit shorter.

"Hey, look at this," Doyle called from Soledad's body, holding up a pair of business cards identical to the ones we'd found at the previous scene.

"Where were these?" I asked as she handed them to me.

"Sticking out of his jacket pocket."

I examined the cards. They were definitely the same as the other crime scene. I frowned and looked back at Soledad. *Two cards? Why two?* Then it hit me—one for each vampire, Andrea and me. My eyes flew open.

"Stop!" I shouted as Doyle was about to start swabbing a spot on the table. Doyle froze, and I leaned down, looking underneath. My heart turned to ice.

Attached to the table by some sort of adhesive was an explosive device, an antenna sticking out of it. Fixed dead center of the mechanism was a mercury switch. Good god, the slightest movement of the table could set it off. It was a miracle we hadn't blown ourselves to bits already. Suddenly, a red light began to blink on the thing.

"Fuck! Everybody out, now! And don't touch the table!"

I didn't have to ask twice. Everyone bailed like roaches with the lights coming on. Doyle and I brought up the rear. The exterior door was just within reach when the bomb exploded, and the house came down on the two of us.

CHAPTER NINE

I coughed and gagged on dust and pulverized drywall. I pulled out my flashlight and glanced, brushing the larger chunks of debris from my face. I'd landed in a small void, hemmed in on all sides by debris. I slid my foot out from under a splintered board. Somehow, I'd curled small enough when I'd fallen to avoid my limbs being crushed by the falling house, but I could barely move. Doyle hadn't been so lucky. Pinned next to me, she groaned loudly and tried to drag herself forward. Her agonized scream nearly blew out my eardrums as the massive beam pressing into her back shifted slightly.

I put a gentle hand on her shoulder, barely touching her. "Jess, don't move."

"Cait! Jess! Can you hear us?" It was Carlos.

"Yeah, we hear you," I called back. "I'm in a void, but Doyle's hurt badly and pinned under one of the upstairs joists. We need to get her out of here." I sniffed and then flicked my tongue. Mixed in among the smells of broken wallboard, mine and Doyle's body odor, and a thousand other things was the distinct smell of something like burning plastic and propane gas. *Shit.* "Carlos, something is on fire!"

"Okay, hold on. We're going to get you out of there. We've got people on the way. You sound close, so it shouldn't take too long."

"Hurry, Carlos."

"Cait?" Doyle mumbled.

I turned my flashlight on her and stifled a gasp. Her back was out of alignment. The support on her back had severed her spinal column. Blood flowed freely from underneath the beam, down her hips, to the floor. I shined my light on her face and spied a burgeoning bruise that covered most of the left side. Her nose was broken as well. "I'm here. Hold on, honey. They're coming. They'll get us out."

Doyle's voice was small, scared, and agony filled. "Cait, the house is burning. I can smell smoke. I don't think we have much time." She grunted as the rubble shifted again.

"I know. I smell it, too." I shined the light in her eyes. Her pupils were sluggish but responsive. She probably had a concussion. "Can you feel your legs?"

"No. I think my back is broken. I'm in a bad way, Cait. I'm going into shock." I could see tears welling in her eyes. Thankfully, my phone was still in my pocket, so I dug it out and dialed Nastasia.

"Relax, Cait, I'm on my—"

"Nastasia, there was a bomb," I blurted out quickly. "Jessica and I are trapped under the house. We need help. Her back's broken, and I don't know how long this void will last."

"Son of a bitch," she swore. "Okay, I'm on the way." I heard the whine of her car engine as she stepped on the gas, and then the call dropped.

I whispered to Doyle, "Stay with me, baby. We'll get out of this." After some struggle, I wriggled out of my coat and put it loosely over her, careful to keep her head clear. The warmer I kept her, the longer she'd survive.

She chuckled weakly. "Heh, you called me baby."

I snorted in disbelief. "Good grief, you have a one-track mind."

"Just trying to stay," she grunted once more, "conscious."

Outside, more emergency equipment arrived, fire engines this time. "See, the Fire Department is here. They'll get us out."

"Yeah, but Cait, I'm going to be paralyzed from the waist

down for life. I wish you were still a vampire."

Yeah, I thought, *me too.* "Why would you want me to be a vampire? It wouldn't help right now."

"So you could bite me. I wanted to know what it's like, before—"

I interrupted her morbid musings. "Trust me. You'll get your chance here shortly. Now stop talking like you're dead."

The building shifted again, and Doyle screwed up her face in pain, grunting and heaving to breathe. "I feel—like the whole house—is on me."

I tried to keep it quiet, but I couldn't stifle my tears of frustration. Doyle was being crushed, and there wasn't a bloody thing I could do about it. It was agonizing. Shouts sounded outside, men and women calling to each other. I couldn't make out any words, just sounds. Water sprayed noisily; the Fire Department was putting out the fire wherever under this heap it burned. Every so often, trickles of water filtered down from above, landing on Doyle and me. It was ice cold. *Fuck!* That would send Doyle into shock faster.

"Hey, you still with me?" I asked and stroked Doyle's hair.

"Yeah, it doesn't hurt as much as it did."

I closed my eyes for a moment in silent prayer. She didn't have any time left.

"What are your thoughts on the case?" I asked, deciding it was best to keep her talking as long as possible.

She sucked in a painful breath. "Really?"

"I need you to stay conscious, so answer the question."

Doyle seemed to think for a moment. "This would be easier without a house on me, but okay. So, this is quite the escalation in their MO. Odd for a serial killer."

"They're not traditional psycho-sexual killers," I responded. "So, with these new behaviors, what did we learn?

"To be second to last escaping from the bomb," she snorted caustically through a pained chuckle.

"I'm serious, Doyle. This is stuff you need to know. Now, what did we learn?" She was quiet for a moment, so I poked her arm. "Hey, you still with me?"

"Jesus, Cait, give me a second to think. I'm crushed under a lot of weight here." She paused for a few minutes, presumably collecting her thoughts. "This fits the mission-oriented profile. They're motivated by a code of belief that says they need to eliminate a particular group rather than getting off on the killing itself."

"Gold star," I replied as brightly as I could. "What else?"

She grunted in pain again but continued. "Assuming this is the same bunch, Soledad clinches the fact that there is law enforcement involvement, which is not good. That means you were the target this time. Soledad knew you used to be a vampire and would have known you were assigned to the PIU and that we would have been called in for this."

I nodded. "So far, so good. What else?"

"They still see you as a vampire."

"Yes, keep going."

"Someone in the group or working with them has bomb-making expertise, former or current bomb squad, maybe, or EOD. That was a sophisticated bomb. You told me not to touch the table, so it must have had a motion trigger. But it went off anyway, which means a radio receiver, too. To set it off when we were all scrambling to get out, they had to have eyes on the house. That means they're probably out there right now. Some of the parts should be easy to trace once we get ahold of them."

"Good, you're doing great."

Doyle thought for a moment. "I don't know. I can't think very well. I keep thinking about this guy who got caught between a subway train and the platform. When they lifted the train—"

"Stop. We're not going there. We're getting you out in one piece. Now, what else about the case?"

"How did they know the victims were vampires in the first place? Yeah, vamps are pale, but picking a vampire out of all the people in Boston is like selecting a slightly whiter needle in a haystack of mostly white needles. Someone is giving them information on who the vampires are and where they live."

I'd already figured out that part, but I let her run with it. Maybe she'd come up with something I couldn't. "Let's assume it's not another vampire. Who else could it be?"

Doyle was quiet again for a moment. "Um, someone in the department, the mayor's office, or Nastasia. From what you describe, Liz doesn't—" She grunted again and was quiet for a moment. Then she said, "I'm sorry, Cait, I can't think about this anymore." Slowly, her breathing steadied, her inhalations turning soft and shallow, another sign of shock. She was dying right in front of me.

I leaned down and kissed her cheek. Helpless tears fell from my eyes. "That's okay," I whispered. "After this adventure, we'll have a lot to analyze. We can do it later."

"You can," Doyle whispered so softly that I almost couldn't hear her. "I'm, uh, I'm not going to be there." Her lids drooped heavily over her eyes.

"Don't say that, Jess. You will be there. Look, I'll make you a deal. You get out of this, and I'll make sure we get you back to tip-top shape. Then we'll go on a date, okay?" My weeping was steady now. I couldn't lose anyone else, especially not Doyle. I tried to blink back the tears, but I couldn't. *God damnit.* "So, see," I said, sniffing. "We have something to look forward to. You have to stay conscious and with me, okay?"

"That sounds nice," she said. Then she blinked slowly.

"Hey!" I shouted, voice cracking. "Where are we with that rescue, guys? Come on!"

"We're coming, Cait," Carlos shouted from the other side.

I coughed amid all the particulate crap that was floating about. I couldn't think of anything else to say to Doyle. Fortunately, just moments later, the whirring of a drill sounded against the crumbled drywall next to me, and a 4-inch hole appeared, letting in cold air from the outside. *Thank God.*

"Detectives, can you hear me?" A voice called.

I looked at Doyle, who wasn't moving. "Yeah, but we have to get Doyle out of here, like now. Please hurry."

"Okay, we're sending in a snake camera to see what we can do to get you out." The voice disappeared, and a small snake camera with a blinding light slid through the hole. It panned around a few times and then slid out.

I looked back at Doyle. "Jess, honey, you still there? We're almost out." She mumbled something unintelligible, and a voice I recognized filtered through the hole, drowning out Doyle. Nastasia was here.

"I can do it faster. Just put the fucking jacks under the joist, and I'll do the rest."

We heard a chainsaw cutting outside during the next five or so interminable minutes. Then, someone pulled out a piece of drywall next to me. The hole wasn't big enough to climb through, but I could now see the outside world and what had us hemmed in. A steel-reinforced beam sat slightly torqued underneath the pile of exterior lumber that had fallen between me and what used to be the doorway. The beam was slightly canted, and Nastasia felt under it for a handhold. *Holy shit,* I thought. *She's going to lift the whole damn house.*

Several fire engines, ambulances, and patrol cars surrounded the building. Bright lights were shining toward the house, and a crowd had gathered in the distance, including the press. Nastasia was standing next to the hole in slacks and stockinged feet, a pair of heels lying in the grass behind her.

"Nastasia?" I called through the hole.

"Yes, Cait? I'm kind of busy here."

"What's the plan?"

"The plan is that we're going to push some jacks in there to lift the joist off Detective Doyle, and then I'm going to lift this steel beam, and they'll pull you two out. In the process, I will look stellar for the news vans while doing so." She flipped her hair mockingly like a high-fashion model. "So, not to worry. I had planned for us to stay out of the news for a good long while, but it can't be helped."

"I have a favor to ask. Doyle's back is broken. She's dying. Can you—"

Nastasia bent down to the hole and looked inside with a small pen light, speaking quietly. "I'll try. That's all I can promise. But, you owe me for this."

I frowned, wondering why Nastasia couldn't ever, for one moment, be a little more human. I turned back to Jessica. "You hear that, Doyle? You're going to get that vampire bite we were talking about."

She didn't say anything but gave me a weak thumbs up.

It took only a few minutes to set everything up, but it seemed like hours. They slid two small hydraulic jacks through the hole, attached to long hoses. As the firefighter directed me, I pushed them under the beam on either side of Jess. Once they were in place, a compressor motor fired up, rumbling with a deep base that shook the dust and reverberated in my chest.

"Okay, Detective, get ready," a firefighter said. "On three." Then several people counted down.

Three. Two. One. Nastasia flexed and screamed as she lifted the steel beam. The compressor squealed loudly, powering the jacks and lifting the joist on Doyle's spine. Big hands grabbed me and dragged me, half scrambling, out of the void and into the frigid night. Then they grabbed Doyle, pulling her out just in time as Nastasia lost her grip on the edge of the wall, and the entire front of the house fell inward.

Nastasia didn't wait. As soon as she dropped the beam, she knocked everyone aside and knelt, cradling Doyle's upper body. Doyle cried out but abruptly silenced as Nastasia, whispering gently, gazed into her eyes, stealing Doyle's pain with her glamour.

It looked like she was hugging the auburn-haired woman from almost any angle, but I knew better. Doyle moaned softly, her right arm curling around the small of Nastasia's back, stroking. I shivered momentarily with the lubricious noises of Nastasia's feeding, remembering the strange sensation of having my heart stutter as blood flooded to my neck and out in deep, long pulls, and dark, malicious envy overwhelmed me. Nastasia drew life from Doyle like a lover beneath the cover of her hair, and I finally had to turn away, biting my lip as another quiver of icy-cold want ran down my spine.

I turned back as Nastasia laid her down on the concrete and hovered over her, delivering changed blood in a long, passionate kiss. Doyle coughed a few times, then her back arched, and she screamed in pain as the blood began to heal her wounds. Most importantly, though, within seconds, Doyle curled her legs up to her chest as she cried out in agony.

Two EMTs standing near rushed to get situated with a c-spine and backboard as they hauled her off to the hospital. Doyle moaned loudly, but in pleasure or pain, I wasn't sure. Her eyes were heavy-lidded, looking spellbound, glassy-eyed, and dreamy. I pulled my handkerchief from my pocket and gave it to Nastasia, who still had her head bowed, hiding her blood-covered face beneath her hair. When she finally stood, most of the blood was off, though a bit still lingered at the corner of her mouth.

I stepped between her and the spectators, wiping it off with my thumb. The scent of it shot through me, and I wiped it off quickly with a shudder.

"See, darling? Not cured." Nastasia said as she reached down, snatching her pumps from the ground.

Without thought, I pulled her to me and wrapped my arms around her in a long grateful hug. "Thank you," I whispered. To my surprise, she returned the hug and patted me on the back before releasing me. She stared at me for the briefest moment before pulling her heels on. Then, shoes adequately squared away, she stood and smiled cryptically, but she didn't say anything. Instead, she handed me the keys to her little Honda and took Andrea to a waiting patrol car, where they both got in. As the car pulled away, I saw the two talking over something through the window. I wasn't usually insecure, but I wondered if they were talking about me for some reason. Were they? Andrea looked up at me with a strange expression that looked a lot like pity. Then they were gone.

It took several hours to continue the investigation. I was completely unharmed. There wasn't a scratch on me for all that had happened. It would take days to retrieve the bomb components and sift through them, so we left that to the experts and headed back to Schroeder.

I called Liz as soon as I got into Nastasia's car. She and Katie had indeed been out and hadn't seen the news. They'd been blissfully unaware that I'd almost been blown to hell and crushed under a building. I also told Liz about Doyle's bite fetish and what Nastasia had done.

"That's interesting." There was something strange, almost

strained, in her voice. "Tell me more about Doyle."

Doyle? Why Doyle? Okay. "She's twenty-four and cute, with reddish-brown hair like mine and a genius IQ—"

Liz interrupted me. "Just Nastasia's type, young, red-headed, and dreamy-eyed. You'll want to keep an eye on that. If I know Nastasia, she'll be courting Doyle hard, trying to get her to agree to be turned. You said she was interested in what a bite would be like?"

"Yeah, she was all about it. And honestly, I'm pretty sure it was all she could have imagined. When they took Doyle away, she looked totally star-struck, like I did when I met Marcella for the first time. It's not good."

"Why?" Liz asked.

I thought about that. *Why was it bad?* Doyle was a big girl. She could make her own decisions. I wouldn't choose Nastasia, but that was me. "Well, Nastasia can be pretty abusive," I said, reaching for a reason.

Liz paused for a moment as if thinking about it. "Cait, she bullies you. I don't know why, but that's not typical. With most women, she's protective. She's not sweet, but she's not a sadist, either. She's powerful and knows it, but most of her strutting around is just bluster. In all the years I've known her, she's never treated her paramours poorly. She hasn't treated them well, either, mind you. She doesn't let them live with her and emotionally keeps them at arm's length. But she's not mean to them or abusive."

I grunted. It hadn't occurred to me that Nastasia had another side to her. All I'd ever seen was the raging bitch. But, then again, I hadn't considered what kind of patience, cunning, and overall mental fortitude it took to be alive for eight hundred years. I'd have to give that some thought. "Okay, well, I'll at least let Doyle know what she's getting into."

"That's wise. This needs to be an informed choice, and it looks like we're going public with or without Marcella, so—" She trailed off for a moment, then her voice softened. "I'm just glad you're okay. Please be careful out there. I'm not sure what I'd do if something happened to you."

I blinked. "I'll try to be careful, but the job is what it is, Liz. You know that. But I'm glad I'm coming home to you guys, too."

"Okay. See you soon, love." She hung up. That warm feeling started creeping into my chest again, but I wrestled it away. I wasn't going to fall for another fucking vampire. I wasn't.

Nastasia and Andrea were waiting at HQ when I arrived. Nastasia didn't say much. She just greeted me, took her keys, and left. Andrea sat in the interview room, still wearing the plain white disposable smock she'd been given. They were so undignified. Like a hospital gown, but somehow worse.

Carol sat with me for the interview. Andrea looked better, far calmer, and more relaxed than at the scene. Honestly, she looked bored.

"Andrea, this is Detective Washington. Do you need anything?" It was a dumb but habitual question.

"No, thank you. I'm fine. I want to get this over with so I can get cleaned up and eventually get to bed. I'm emotionally exhausted and frankly scared."

Carol stepped in. "Please explain, from the beginning, how you ended up in that house."

"I work on the overnight shift for a cybersecurity operations team at Chandeva Cyber. I'd just pulled five overnight shifts in a row and was starving, so I headed to the bar scene up in Lowell to find a donor."

"A donor? Is that what you call it?" Carol asked snidely.

I snapped my head toward Carol, frowning at her unprofessionalism, then broke in. "I'm sorry, Andrea. Please continue. Why Lowell?"

Andrea made a disdainful face at Carol but moved on. "I go to Lowell because it's far away from my home and keeps me from treading in the same places as the others. Anyway, this guy starts coming on to me at the bar, the dude you found in the basement. He said his name was Juan and suggested we go back to his place. I agreed, and we left. We ended up at a small apartment in the Highlands. We talked for quite a while. He seemed nice. He asked me about my family. I asked him about his family and so on. I thought I had all night. But it started getting close to sunrise, so I thought I'd glamour him and get on with it, but it didn't work. His mind was all static and weird.

"Since that was no good, I started to dress to leave. Then he started getting a little rough with me, insistent that I stay. He even blocked the door. I could have plowed through him, but I didn't want to hurt the guy and wasn't afraid of him. Then the sun came up while we were still arguing, and he grabbed me. At that point, I didn't fuck around. I bit into his neck and started draining him, but his buddies burst in and tackled me. One of his buddies was strong, really strong, like vampire strong, but in the daylight. He held me in place and threatened to kill me if I didn't fix the first guy's neck. They all had machetes, so I gave him a little changed blood. As soon as I was done, they dragged me downstairs and threw me into the back of a black SUV. We didn't get far before they got sick of my struggling, and the big asshole, the strong one with brown hair and creepy eyes, staked me. That's all I remember until you pulled the stake."

I finished noting all that she had said. "Could you find the apartment again? If needed?"

She made a derisive sound. "Of course. I know right where it is. I made a mental note of the address when we got there; it's an old habit, something I used to do—" She paused, suddenly uncomfortable. "Anyway, yeah, I know where it is." She gave us the address near the corner of Robins and Pine in Lowell.

"Hang tight," I said, and Carol and I left.

As soon as we got outside, I pulled Carol away from the door. "What the fuck," I hissed at her. "I'm getting sick of your prejudice. She's just trying to survive. Look at her. She's brand new and recently turned. She's trying to do things the right way."

"Cait, all we have is a staked vampire and a dead cop. Soledad was a clean guy. He wouldn't do what she's saying."

I pursed my lips. "You don't know that. Soledad flipped the fuck out and quit the unit after he learned I was a vampire. He went over to work for Stanley in Drug Control. People do weird shit all the time when something pushes them over the edge. Look at all those idiots who thought vaccines had fucking nanites in them. Ignorance has no friends."

"You're perspective is skewed because you know her. You should bow out of the case."

My eyes went wide. Carol had lost her grip. "What? Because I've met the woman a couple of times? It's not like we're pals or something. I barely know her. Hell, I barely knew Soledad. Maybe it's you that has a perspective problem. Like you, I'm inclined to believe that cops are on the level, but that doesn't always make it so. Please don't go there, or I'll have to go to Carlos. Besides, what do you think happened? She killed Soledad in Lowell, planted a bomb, then staked herself in an abandoned home in Hyde Park. What for? More likely, they were going to kill her, and Soledad freaked out, so his werewolf buddy killed him for it. Regardless, we can check out her story easily enough. They'll have footage at the bar."

Carol put her hands on her hips. "Fine, but if her story doesn't check out, we haul her ass back in here and find out what really happened. This smells like bullshit to me."

I shook my head. "Fine. But, Carol, something you should know."

"What?" She snapped, turning toward me.

"This is the world now. And with the dreams you're having, you're part of it whether you fucking like it or not, so you better woman up and get used to it because it's not going away."

"Whatever," she said as she turned away with a dismissive wave.

We walked back into the interview room and collected the details on the bar they went to and the route they took to get to the apartment. I told Andrea to wait at my desk after that. I'd take her home. Carol left as soon as we were done without so much as a word.

Fuck her, I thought. *She'll have to get over it.*

I called the hospital to check on Doyle.

"This is Detective Reagan," I said when I finally reached the charge nurse in the ER. "I wanted to check on Detective Jessica

Doyle. EMTs brought her in after the bomb blast in Hyde Park."

The nurse put me on hold for only a second, then returned. "She left AMA Detective. She certainly didn't look like she'd been in a bombing."

I breathed a sigh of relief and offered my thanks. Then I said goodbye and hung up.

I tried Doyle's cell, but it went straight to voicemail, and I wondered how she'd gotten home, but I let it be. She had friends who could pick her up, I was sure.

I gave Carlos the lowdown on Andrea's whereabouts before he sent me home and told me to take a few days off, per department policy. I didn't bother him about Carol's attitude during the interview. He'd look at the video in due course.

Fuck this, I thought. *I could use a day off. I'd rather hang out with Liz, anyway.*

CHAPTER TEN

The shock of the day's events wore off as I stepped through the front door, taking the last vestiges of my energy with it. Andrea followed me in, and I closed the door. My hands were shaking again as every loud noise, explosion, gunshot, and horror of Iraq tumbled back into my head. I slid down the door and sat on the floor.

God damnit, I am so tired of this. I had worked so hard on my trauma from the war, and now this happens. *Fuck!* After a few long minutes and several deep breaths, I pulled myself off the floor despite wanting to curl up into the fetal position and lay there.

"You okay?" Andrea asked.

"No, I'm not okay. This case is fucking up my team and fucking up my head. Besides, I should be asking you that."

Andrea walked to the stairs and dropped onto the second step. "Of course, I'm not," she said quietly. "But I can take it. All I want to do right now is shower and sleep."

I looked at her for a moment and realized she had a haunted look on her face. "Abusive boyfriend?" I asked.

"Three different boyfriends. I have shitty taste in men." Slowly she stood, looking for all the world like a scared little girl.

"How old are you?" I asked.

"Twenty-three, why?"

"Just wondering. Why did you become a vampire?"

"I was in a pretty bad place when Schmidt found me, you know? Ready to pack it in. He gave me a second chance, though I don't think he liked what he got."

"Why's that?" I asked, now genuinely interested.

"I didn't adore him like the others. I didn't even like him. Look, I'd love to chat about this, but I need to get ready. The sun will be up any minute, and I can't always keep myself awake. Sometimes, I collapse where I am."

I pointed toward the staircase. "Third floor, last door at the end of the hall. It was my mother's room, but she's in a rehab facility and won't be using it for some time. Hopefully, we'll get you back to normal life."

She gave a sarcastic laugh and said, "Let me know when you figure out what that is, will you?" Then she headed up the stairs, the paper smock making her sound like a walking newspaper.

After Andrea disappeared into the stairwell, I looked around. The house was deathly still, the silence punctuated only by the whoosh of the central heat. Katie was probably dreaming of blood-filled tootsie-pops or something equally gruesome, which brought a grin to my face as I imagined her licking her way to the center. *One, two, three. Squish. It takes three licks to get to the center of a bloody-pop.*

I ambled into the kitchen, bone tired. Liz sat perfectly still at the table with her head in her hands. A dozen pink tissues sprawled around, the box still in front of her.

I stopped in the doorway. "Liz? You okay?"

Liz looked up, a stricken expression on her face. Her eyes glistened in the overcast morning light. She'd been crying. No, she'd been bawling. She sniffed. "Some badass vampire I turned out to be," she said with a mirthless laugh. "I've been sitting here for hours, just waiting for you to come home. After you told me what happened, I tried to play it cool on the phone, but all I could think of was, 'what if?' What if you'd been crushed under the building? What if you hadn't seen the bomb? What if you'd died?" Fat, pink tears flowed down her face once more.

My heart sank and a lump formed in my throat. For a moment, I couldn't speak. I'd scared her. I sighed in frustration. This was why I'd lived alone for all those years. My job is hard and sometimes dangerous. And at that particular moment, I just wasn't equipped to take care of someone else's feelings. I was sick of living in a morass of guilt for just living. I stood and stalked to the back stairs.

"Cait?" Liz called after me. "Wait."

I ignored her, stomping up the stairs in frustration. I couldn't deal with this right now.

"Cait, stop, please," Liz called, hurrying up behind me. I sped up, but she caught me in the third-floor hallway outside my room and grabbed my arm. "Would you please wait a minute and tell me what's wrong? What did I say?"

"Nothing," I muttered and stalked into my room, but Liz stuck her arm in the door when I tried to close it. "Damn it, Liz. I'm tired. I was just in a fucking explosion that almost killed one of my best friends. I can't deal with your emotions right now."

Liz put her hands on her hips and glared at me. "What? You asked me if I was okay. You fucking asked! Don't get mad at me because you can't handle your own feelings."

"What?" I asked incredulously.

Liz exploded. "You think, after three hundred years, I don't know when someone thinks they have to take care of everyone else and feels shitty because they can't? You may think I'm just some girl from the streets of London, but I have centuries of experience. I have lifetimes on you, and I can read you like a fucking book. You feel bad because I was worried about you. But that's because you think it's your job to keep me happy. It's not. And, an important life lesson here, you can't make people happy anyway. My happiness is my own responsibility, not yours. I know you care, and I appreciate that, but you can't take responsibility for my feelings. You don't control them! So don't put your shit on me!"

I blinked. Liz had never yelled at me before.

Liz continued, lowering her tone and turning far more

gentle. "Now, tell me."

I stood there staring at her for long moments, my hands clenching and unclenching, even as they trembled. Then I broke down. I hadn't wanted to. I was tired of crying and bawling and dumping my shit on people. But I couldn't hold it in. "I'm sorry, I—" I couldn't get the words out.

"I know. I was just worried. You'd think, after three hundred years and countless paramours, I'd be less—I don't know—invested. But, no, my blackened vampiric heart, it turns out, is made of mush."

"Mama? Auntie Liz? Is everything okay?" Katie asked from the door.

"Yes, Katie. Mama just had a rough day. It's okay." She went to the door and spoke to Katie, sending her back to whatever she'd been doing. She should have been in bed. I sat down.

"Tell me," Liz said softly.

I waited until Liz had closed the door and sat down beside me, then said, "Liz, I was so fucking scared." My whole body trembled now. "I was crammed into a little tiny space, and Doyle was crushed under a support beam. And the house was on fire. They started putting it out, but water started trickling in, and I know how much those hoses pump out. I thought that was it. We'd either be crushed, burned, or drowned. But I couldn't let Doyle know. I put it aside like I always do, focusing on the problem at hand. But, Liz, I don't know how much more I can take."

Liz pulled me into a hug. "You should stay home today. You don't need to go to work. Enough is enough, Cait. You need a real break. You've been going non-stop since you went back, working six or seven nights a week."

I snorted at her timing. "Funny you should mention that. I'm on three days' leave. It's probably a good time to get scarce anyway, what with Nastasia being on the news."

Liz's eyes grew wide. "She what? You said there were people there, but not that the news caught it on camera."

I blew out a breath and dried my eyes. "Yeah, she lifted tons of material off us right in front of a half dozen news crews."

Liz scowled and pulled me off the bed. "Come on. This I

have to see."

I followed her to the media room where Katie was watching *Alien*.

"Hey, Mama, do you think a vampire could take an alien?"

"No, honey," I replied automatically. "They have acid for blood. Now, what are you still doing up? You should be in bed."

Katie scrunched up her face in irritation. "I'm finishing the movie, duh."

I scowled at her. "Don't talk to me that—"

"Hush!" Liz hissed, snatching up the remote and putting it on CNN, much to Katie's disappointment. The timing was impeccable, though. The video of Nastasia lifting the edge of the house played in crystal clear detail. You could almost see the specs of dirt on my face as they yanked me out. When it got to the part where Nastasia was saving Doyle, the commentary turned comical.

"So what is it that you see here, Doctor?" The anchor guy said in a split frame.

"I have no idea. It looks like she's giving mouth-to-mouth. But I can tell you. When someone's adrenaline pumps like that, they don't realize the damage they do to their bodies. That woman will be feeling that tomorrow, that's for sure. She probably gave herself a serious hernia lifting that much and probably broke a few bones as well."

Liz busted out in peels of scorn-filled laughter. "That's amazing. When confronted with the most awesome spectacle of vampire strength, they chalk it up to adrenaline. Then she practically drained that poor girl and gave her changed blood, and they called it mouth-to-mouth. You could see the blood running down her cheek. Unbelievable." She clicked it back over to Alien as she ran a hand across her face in disbelief. "Just unreal." She turned to Katie. "Don't ever let yourself get caught doing something like that."

"I know Auntie Liz. I'm not stupid." Her tone was both disrespectful and incredulous, as if what Liz said was the most obvious thing in the world. She was becoming a true teenager. *God help us.*

I shook my head in mild amusement and followed Liz back into my room, leaving Katie to finish watching the greatest sci-fi horror movie in history. Melancholy stole over my thoughts as we left the media room. Not only was I tired, angry, and guilt-ridden, I was depressed.

"Do you feel any better?" Liz asked when we reached the door.

"Some. Now, I'm just down," I whispered as I turned to enter my room.

She kissed me on the cheek and turned away, heading toward the stairs.

I put a hand on the doorway. "Liz?"

Liz stopped mid-stride after just two steps. She turned her head slightly, not quite toward me. "No, Cait. You're tired and lonely, I know. But I don't think it's a good idea for you to stay with me tonight. Please have a good night." Then she continued on, disappearing into the stairwell.

Crestfallen, I stepped into my room and closed the door. I sat in the emotional space where friendship begins to develop into something more, and I felt unsure of what to do. I readied for bed silently, moving about in strange, almost wistful unhappiness. And yet I could find no culprit, no reason to be so dejected. Perhaps it was the day's events or maybe the fact I'd been rebuffed by Liz, but nothing in my life seemed without some pain, even Katie. I decided that thinking was more effort than I could stand, so I cleaned up and went to bed.

Sleep was a long time in coming, and I lay there, watching the moon outside. Liz had been right to refuse. I thought of Marcella and her fabulous frost-blue eyes for the thousandth time and about the first time she and I had spent an evening together. Or part of one, anyway.

I had been so broken, laying in the very same bed, drugged into a zombie-like slumber, with her curled up around me. God, I missed her.

I laughed mirthlessly to myself as I considered how I'd thought I'd had it all worked out when I moved in here. Liz and I would live together and care for Katie until—until what?

I had no idea. What did I think I would do, find another human woman to live with? That'd be rich. I'd come home one night and find her lying on the floor, my daughter having accidentally used her as a drink box. Hell, what woman would want to live with a sixteen-year-old vampire, anyway? *Besides me. Or Liz. Or*—I paused, weighing whether Marcella would be good for Katie. *Probably not.*

Eventually, things might change, but for now, Liz and I were stuck together. Whether a victim of the hunters or off on her own, Marcella probably wouldn't be coming back anytime soon. My mood began to sink further at the thought of never having the romantic life she promised me.

I needed to go to sleep. I was overtired, and my nerves were shot. But, as I drifted off, finally, one pleasant thought did stick with me. I had a home. I had a good friend who cared about me. And I had a child that loved me. This honestly wasn't so bad.

CHAPTER ELEVEN

My first day off went exactly according to plan, mostly. I went shopping for groceries and sat around watching TV. I even took a short nap. Then, later, as Liz worked on business for Carson Logistics, I took Katie out to Leslie's so she could feed.

I felt horrendous as I watched her walk right past the bouncer, not even showing her fake ID, and I had half a mind to bust his chops right there, but then again, it wasn't like she'd be drinking alcohol, and I had to remember why we were here. I glanced around, thinking I might find Pauline, but her pixie haircut was nowhere to be seen. Instead, the traffic was pretty light—only a few folks at the bar and on the dance floor. Maybe three of the ten or so tables were occupied. The usual crowd was probably being kept in by the cold.

It was only a few minutes before Katie was chatting up some young girl who looked about Katie's age, but it was hard to tell with her makeup and the dim light. For a kid who was awkward as hell in every other social situation, Katie had no problem enticing a victim. I assumed there would be a bit of the whammy in play, but if there was, it wasn't obvious. The girl didn't look glamoured in the slightest, which I found even more disturbing than the alternative.

I watched the girl step outside as Katie hit the bathroom, then Katie left moments later. *Good girl*, I thought. *Never let them see you leave with your victim.* I hoped Katie wouldn't have one of her episodes, but those seemed to be happening less frequently, and Liz had told me she should be fine.

'Should be' being the operative words.

I fidgeted at the bar, nursing a glass of scotch for almost an hour before Katie finally texted.

Katie: Ummm. . . I have a problem.
   Me: What kind of problem?
   Katie: She wants me to do it again.

I paused, feeling suddenly very uncomfortable. I just knew I would regret my next question.

Me: Wants you to do what, exactly?
   Katie: U know. She's in the bathroom right now. The whammy didn't work. :wide eyes emoji:
   Me: Oh, Jesus.
   Katie: I'm freaking out. What if she dies?

I'm pretty sure that a part of me had just died already. On the other hand, the entire situation was so ridiculous. It was really fucking funny.

Me: You should probably just leave.
   Katie: But I like this girl.
   Me: :facepalm emoji: Katie, darling, you need to leave.

There was an extended period of time before she texted back, and I started to get nervous. What if the girl died? What if Katie had an episode? Why was she taking so long?

Me: ???
   Katie: Busy right now.
   Me: Everything okay?
   Katie: Yes. Get me in an hour. We're just talking. I told her I was full.

I did a spit take into my scotch, and the bartender looked at me funny, so I just held up my phone. "Teenage daughter," I explained, and the bartender chuckled, going back to whatever drink she was making.

Me: :facepalm emoji: Okay.

She texted me the address, and I left Leslie's in a hurry, alternating between absolute amusement and total panic the entire way home. Liz was in the sitting room in front of the fireplace when I returned.

"Forget something?" Liz asked as I walked in.

I shook my head and handed her my phone so she could read the exchange. At first, Liz snorted, then as she scrolled, she started laughing uncontrollably.

"That's the best one I've ever heard," she said as she went into hysterics. "I'm full. Honestly."

"Having fun?" I stared at her in disbelief and barely suppressed glee, my hands on my hips.

"Oh, this is lovely. Our little Katie has a girlfriend," Liz tittered and tossed me my phone. "I was beginning to wonder if she wasn't some sociopath the way she was always so perfunctory with her victims. Where did you take her?"

"We went to Leslie's. Where else?"

Liz tilted her head. "Leslie's? No wonder. I never take her there. I figured Katie was straight. No wonder she went after the guys with about as much aplomb as a starved leopard. And she never said a word."

"I know, right? I went there because I would be comfortable. I figured one victim's as good as another to her, you know?"

Liz just continued to laugh. Then she asked me to sit down on the couch next to her. "Cait, we need to talk for a minute."

I studied her face, looking for a hint of her mood, but she was still smiling. "Nothing good ever starts with 'we need to talk.' Can I get a glass of wine?"

Liz was still clearly amused at the situation with Katie. "Sure." She chuckled again as I left the room. "I'm full. That's brilliant."

My anxiety rose as I poured myself a hefty glass of wine in the kitchen and then sat on the sofa. I had to grip my wine glass with both hands because they were fucking trembling again. "Okay, so what did I do?"

Liz fixed me with a smile and waited for me to take a few sips of my wine before she spoke, leaving me in absolute terror over what she was about to say. I tried to keep calm, but my heart was racing. Was I developing an anxiety disorder?

"Cait, are you okay?" Liz asked.

"Yeah, fine. Just go ahead. I'll be okay." I was definitely not okay, nor would I be. But Liz had something to say, and she deserved a chance to say it, whatever it was.

"I like you very much." She paused.

"But?"

"But we can't get physical. You know I want to. And I know you do, too. But if I did, if we did, it wouldn't be fair to me." She held up a hand to forestall any protest. "We're good friends, and nothing will change that, but I don't want to play second fiddle. Until you have closure on your feelings for Marcella, I can't trust that any relationship we strike up won't end if she returns."

I sighed, mostly in relief. "I know, you're right, of course."

"Cait," Liz said, taking my hand. "It's okay. I'm not upset with you. As a matter of fact, I'm flattered. But we've become such good friends in the last two months, and I want to keep it that way. Please don't be angry with me."

I jerked in surprise as if she'd slapped me. "Angry with you? Why would I be angry with you? I feel bad because I was just thinking of myself last night. You haven't done anything wrong."

"Then why are you shaking?" The worry on her face was achingly sweet, but I promised myself I was not going to come apart.

"I'm having an anxiety attack," I said through trembling lips. I took a gulp of my wine, trying desperately to settle my nerves. The burn of the alcohol helped, but not much.

Liz stood and took the wine glass from my hands. "Cait, come with me." I took an offered hand, and she led me to the elevator. Once inside, she hit four on the panel.

"But—"

Liz shushed me. "We're not going to have sex, and you're not staying up here all night. But what I need is in my room. Tomorrow, you need to call Jennifer and see about getting a prescription for an anti-anxiety med."

"But what about Katie?" I asked.

"I'll get Katie," she said as the elevator dinged and the door opened. "You go strip, get a shower, and lay down. I'll be back shortly. Katie needs to come home anyway. She's supposed to be feeding, not getting off with some girl she met in a bar."

Despite my shitty mood, I couldn't help but laugh. "You know that means something a little different in the States."

"Yes, I know. She shouldn't be doing that either," she said as the doors closed.

As soon as Liz was gone, the anxiety returned. I'd had anxiety attacks before, especially after the war, but never like this. My chest was tight, my hands tingled and shook, and I felt at any moment like I was going to fall to pieces. It was awful.

Jennifer had warned me of this in therapy. The mind can only take so much trauma, which brought me back to the same thing as always. Vampires don't have this problem, except maybe when they're starving. Vampires can have anxiety, sure, but not anxiety attacks. And they can squelch their feelings pretty damn efficiently when needed. Being a vampire meant most emotion was muted, softer, all of them except rage, lust, and love. Those emotions were heightened. I thought about asking Liz to turn me again. It was really fucking tempting.

Regardless, it was no wonder I was breaking down, though. I had been on edge for weeks, unable to find five minutes to myself. I was helping Liz manage household chores and the budget. I'd even been taking calls with her for Carson Logistics, helping her re-organize the company after it became clear that Marcella had left the finances in a shitty state.

Marcella had had the best intentions, but the camps had drained too much from the company and her personal accounts. Adding on top of that three weeks of taking care of my mother in her declining condition, Nastasia and her bullshit, and figuring out how to best work my life around Katie's needs, I hadn't had a second to breathe. Then there were the murders and the bombing.

Liz finally showed up almost an hour later, and I was still wired, unable to sleep, my mind racing with every possible catastrophic outcome if I didn't manage everything. I was still aghast at how horrible the anxiety attack was. I wondered briefly if this was what had driven my friend Specialist Rutherford to suicide after she'd left Iraq. I could see how it could happen.

"Katie okay?" I asked as Liz walked around, getting herself situated for bed.

"Oh, she's over the moon," Liz replied irritably. "She thinks she's in fucking love. The girl is almost five years older than her."

"Oh, good lord. Really? Does the girl know that?" I asked around a yawn.

"Of course not. I thought about telling her not to talk to her anymore, but you know how that'll go. She'll start sneaking out behind our backs."

"She wouldn't do that."

Liz looked at me skeptically. "Cait," she said as if I were standing firmly on the primrose path, and she had to pull me back.

I stuck to my guns, though. Katie was a good kid. "I mean, that's what I'd do. It might even be what you'd do. But Katie—"

"—is a sixteen-year-old girl who thinks she's in love. I told her she had to come clean about her age, or I would. "

"Ouch," I said and winced. That would likely end it. And Liz wasn't wrong about that. The girl was too old for Katie. And, if telling this twenty-year-old, whoever she was, that Katie was sixteen didn't end it, then 'Detective Reagan' would be paying her a visit, and nobody wanted that, least of all me.

"You get some rest there for a minute while I see to a couple of things. I'll be right back." Liz walked out before I could protest. I had thought she was going to give me a back rub.

She probably still would if I could stay awake long enough.

That sneaky bitch, I thought as I woke up to find Liz in the bed next to me. *She waited for me to fall asleep.* I rolled over and looked at her. I'd never seen her play the innocent before, and it was kind of cute the way she batted her eyes in that 'Who? Me?' kind of way.

"You did this on purpose."

"I did not," Liz said, but a cheeky smile tugged at her lips. "You were asleep last night, and I didn't want to wake you. But since you're awake and seem to be feeling better, you can go back to your own room."

"But I'm warm," I whined.

She gave me a sly smirk. "Whinging is unbecoming for a hard-nosed detective. Now go."

"Oh, fine," I grumped as I got out of bed, swearing like Yosemite Sam as I walked to the elevator.

"Take your clothes," Liz said with a laugh.

I turned back, grabbed my clothes off the floor with a curse, and headed to the elevator. "Oh, Liz. I'll remember this." I headed back to my room.

"No doubt you will," she called after me.

Back in my own room, I pulled on some pajamas and curled up in my bed. It was fucking cold, but Jabba immediately hopped up on the bed and curled up in my knee pit. I stroked his head.

"At least you'll keep me warm," I said as he rolled over, demanding belly scritches. "You stupid Hutt."

I tossed and turned for about an hour before I finally got up to make myself some breakfast. As I was cooking, the front door opened. "Fuck," I swore under my breath. Other than Katie, Liz, and me, only one person had a key. I peeked around the corner and locked eyes with Nastasia. *Shit.*

I dashed to the stove and turned it off. As I turned to flee the kitchen, I nearly jumped out of my pajamas, finding Nastasia standing inches from me. I hadn't even heard her move. *Fuck.*

"Alone at last," Nastasia said seductively, reaching up to stroke my cheek with a finger. I jerked my head back and stepped away from her.

"Please, not now," I said as I turned to walk the long way around the island.

Nastasia intercepted me. "Now, now, no running off, дорогая."

"Хуй тебе," I replied.

"Oh, Cait, what a potty mouth you have." Nastasia donned a wicked smile, looking me in the eyes. Surprisingly, nothing changed. There was no glamour, no sudden urge to strip and throw myself at her—well, at least no urge that wasn't already there. She reached up again, stroking my cheek with the back of one hand, and I flinched.

"Oh, Cait, I'm not here to hurt you. I just want to ask some questions. If you recall, I said we needed to discuss the sudden changes in the department."

"Nastasia," I said and swallowed hard. "You know I can't really talk about—"

"Sit!" Nastasia ordered, pointing at a chair at the table. I obediently walked over and sat.

"Much better," Nastasia said. "Now stay put." She trotted into the foyer and returned carrying a plain brown leather satchel-style briefcase which she placed at her side as she returned to her seat.

"You fucking bitch," I snarled, my hands clawing into the wood. But I could do nothing. I was helpless, and in moments, my impotent rage turned to tears. "Please, Nastasia, don't do this."

"Well, if you cooperate, I'll leave you be." She placed a hand on mine. "I'm not doing this to hurt you, Cait. I need answers, and you have them. I am protecting our kind. Something you should appreciate, don't you think?"

"I'm not a vamp—"

"You keep saying that, but you and I both know the truth, and, soon, I'll prove it," she said, her tone ominous and dark.

"How?" I whispered, quailing at the implications.

"That's for me to know, as they say. But, to other matters."

Nastasia reached down and pulled a tablet and digital pencil from her satchel. Oddly, she also retrieved a pair of half-moon reading glasses with platinum temples which she placed on the bridge of her nose. Finally, she pulled out a red scrunchy which she used to bun up her hair. The entire effect was comical, giving her more the look of a naughty librarian again than a cold-blooded killer. It didn't do anything to assuage my fear, but I still screwed up my face in absolute amusement at the sudden transformation.

"Why is your team the only one investigating the murder of our kin?" She asked, pad in her right hand, pencil in the left.

I sighed and closed my eyes. I really should have known it would go this way, and I could have saved myself more humiliation if I'd just told her. I was just being obstinate. "Release me, please, and I'll tell you whatever you want to know."

Immediately whatever hold she had over me lifted, and I could move again. I blew out a relieved breath and leaned back in the chair. I studied her face, taking a moment to really look at her. There wasn't a line on it. No scars, no wrinkles, nothing. In many ways, other than being that of a beautiful twenty-something, it was like the face of a baby.

I set that aside for a moment to answer her questions. "My team has been re-assigned to the newly formed Preternatural Investigations Unit. Carlos, Carol, Detective Maki Imai, and I are the core of the unit. In addition, Detective Doyle, whom I'm sure you remember, is also a member."

At the mention of Doyle's name, Nastasia ceased scribbling on the tablet and looked up. "Yes, Jessica is quite the woman. She is sharp, not squeamish, and, I might add, quite taken with both of us."

I pressed my lips into a thin line in frustration. So that's where Doyle had gotten off to when she left the hospital, right into Nastasia's arms. I grunted. "Yes, well, she has a thing for vampires, I think."

Nastasia only nodded before moving on. "And who assigned you to this unit? Was it Bill or someone else?"

"No, it was Bill, but he did so at the orders of the

commissioner and, I think, ultimately, the mayor."

Nastasia continued to write, asking questions as she grilled me. The interview was short. She asked a few questions about Carlos, but I couldn't tell her anything she didn't already know. She asked a few questions about Maki, but I didn't know Maki very well, so I was stumped at most of them, other than who her father was. I told her about Carol's visions, but she seemed almost uninterested in that, noting it but asking nothing further. In fact, most of what she asked, she already knew. I realized some of the questions were simply to determine if I was being honest and forthcoming. When she was finished, she closed the cover on the tablet and put it and the pen away.

"So, do you have any questions for me?" She asked, drawing a blank stare from me. I hadn't expected that, but I recovered quickly.

"What happened to your face?" I reached a hand up to touch it.

She examined me for a moment, deciding whether to answer. In the end, she said, "You have an expert eye. I was captured a few years after I was turned by a small band of Mongols, the same people who destroyed my village and tried to kill me.

"Anyway, they wasted no time in flaying most of the skin from my body. Imagine their surprise when, within a few minutes, it grew back. Then they tried to burn me alive. When that failed, I used the opportunity to escape. Then I killed them to a man later that same night."

"Oh, God," I whispered softly. I couldn't imagine the pain that she must have endured.

"It's true that I prefer women, but I did have a husband and a family once. And though my husband was a cruel man with a foul temper, I didn't develop my hatred for the male sex until the Mongols raided my village in the steps of Russia. I will tell you now. I have had my fill of killing. I don't enjoy it, but I am not above executing enemies of our kind."

She held up a hand to forestall my planned retort about being human. "Please, let's not debate that. I hate men, Cait, and I know that, as a general rule, you do, too. I can see it in your eyes. I know a bit of your background, but there's something deeper, something angrier. You're brilliant and recognize the injustice that men visit upon women all over the world to satisfy their own fragile egotistical aims. We're far more alike than you realize. I am not a monster, at least not when I don't have to be. We really should be friends."

I balked at that. "I will never be your friend Nastasia. If for no other reason than what you did to Katie and what you do to me on a regular basis."

Her eyes flashed dangerously. "Do not say that again. I never laid a hand on Katie. That was all you and Schmidt, but you can believe what you want."

"I believe that even if you didn't commit the act yourself, you went along with it. You even taunted me. What was it you said? 'Enjoy your snack?'"

She pulled up the corner of her mouth in a wicked, knowing smirk. "And what was it Liz said? 'We'll take her out of there as soon as you tell us what we want to know.' That seems like a double standard."

Shit. She wasn't wrong.

Nastasia's expression turned incongruously sweet, as if she were gazing at a cherished lover rather than a victim. "Cait, darling, aren't you tired of this? Being pushed about by everyone? Gabe used you as arm candy. Marcella used your sister as a bait and switch. Liz uses you to assuage her guilt. I am trying to make a better life for us. I could use your help rather than having you fighting with me all the time."

"Nastasia, darling," I spat. "Kiss my lily white ass."

She ignored me, instead saying, "I already see it inside you, the sliver of me that burrows in and winds about your heart. I will show you how to live as a queen, strong and capable and fearing nothing, not even me." She paused and stood.

"Now, I have things to do. You sit there like a good girl until I leave, understand?"

The compulsion returned, gluing me to my seat. Nastasia bent down and tilted my head up. Then she did the most unexpected thing. She kissed my lips gently as she ran her hand smoothly through my hair. And despite all of my protesting to the contrary, I didn't find it unwelcome. The hair stood on my arms, and a thrill raced through me. I surrendered to her, closing my eyes and tilting my head in obeisance to her tugging fingers. She slowly deepened the kiss, drawing overwrought breath from my chest as I reveled in the glossy, slick wetness of her lips.

"I'll see you again soon," she whispered as she drew away.

I opened my eyes and watched her pack her things and stalk out of the house, satchel in hand, taking the compulsion with her.

After she was gone, I inhaled deeply, catching her scent on my tongue, and pressed my thighs together. The kiss still burned on my lips, and I touched them absently. My entire body trembled in a dreamy mixture of terror and desperate want. Much to my surprise, I wasn't as frightened as I had been. I felt something else entirely, something that I scarcely expected. Admiration.

I blew out a breath and dropped my head to the table. "Fuuuuck!"

CHAPTER TWELVE

I jerked awake, shaking and exhausted from a deep slumber. My head rested on my arms at the table, and Liz gently shook my shoulder. An annoying buzzing filled the air periodically, and Liz thrust my cell phone in my face. "You have a call."

"Hello?" I answered in a sleep-clouded voice, wiping a bit of humiliating sleep drool from my chin.

"Ms. Reagan? This is Janeane from Freeman. Doctor Rodriguez wanted to find out if you could come to see him about Róisín."

I blinked confusedly, trying to clear the fog from my brain. "Has something happened?"

She paused for a moment. "I think you need to speak to Dr. Rodriguez."

Panic welled in my chest, but I tamped it down and used my job as an excuse to get some answers. "Well, put him on the phone. I'm a homicide cop and can't just drop everything like this unless I know why."

"Let me see if he's available." She put me on hold.

"Let's just take her to see Bian," Liz suggested in a tired voice, echoing Larson's recommendation days ago. "She's probably not getting any better. Tell him we'll have her transported somewhere else."

"Hey, Cait," Dr. Rodriguez greeted in his deep baritone. "I

didn't want to upset you. Róisín is doing fine physically. But she is still deteriorating mentally. We've been unable to stimulate her further, and the decline is starting to become significant. I think we need to start talking about hospice."

I closed my eyes and sniffed. "Okay. I have another option I want to try, so I'll arrange transport. I appreciate your efforts, Doctor."

"Transport to where?" Dr. Rodriguez asked. His tenor had changed, and it irritated me. He'd just said he couldn't help her, so I didn't understand why he cared.

"To a specialist who might be able to help her."

Liz made motions for me to end the call, so I hit the mute button. "What?"

Liz sat up. "It doesn't matter. You have power of attorney, and you're next of kin. You have the right to take her to Timbuktu if you wish, so don't engage in this conversation. He doesn't need to know. Just tell him we'll be there with Medical transport today."

I unmuted the phone. "Dr. Rodriguez, we'll be there shortly with medical transport. I promise we'll take good care. Thank you for all you've done. See you soon."

"But—" Dr. Rodriguez started, and I hung up.

Liz chuckled. "Okay, that wasn't quite what I was saying, but it'll do. Hey, you okay?" Liz used a thumb to wipe away the tears as they fell over my lashes and idled down my face.

"Fuck, Liz. I can't do this anymore. I got blown up by a fucking bomb, one of my worst nightmares, by the way—quite literally. I just know the Finchers are going to create problems and probably try to take Katie from us, getting themselves fucking killed in the process. Nastasia is constantly screwing with me. She was here today, by the way. My team is the primary callout for anything that even smacks of a paranormal event, which, based on what I've seen on the news, will mean no more days off. Not that we really have the expertise to handle anything but vampires and werewolves. And now, I have to face the fact that my mother is dying. I just can't."

My tears turned to shaking sobs. *Dear God, what will I do without her?* She'd made plenty of mistakes, but she'd shielded me from the worst of what she'd faced for almost all of my life. *And where the fuck was Aoife?* I picked up my phone and dialed her.

"Cait, who are you calling?"

I held up a hand as Aoife answered on the first ring. "Hello?" Even though I had my memories back, the sound of her voice, so similar to mine and yet with a thick Irish brogue, seemed oddly surreal, like listening to myself captured in a recording I don't remember ever being made.

"It's Cait. Mom's in a bad way. This may be it. I think you should come here."

There was a long pause. "Cáitlín, I can't."

My temper spiked. "What? This is our mother we're talking about, Aoife. She's dying, and you can't be bothered to make the trip. If it's money, I'll—"

"It's not money, sis. I can't explain right now, and it breaks my heart that I can't come, but I just," her voice cracked, and she paused, then she hiccuped in my ear and sniffed. Another pause. Finally, she came back on the line, and I heard aching pain in her voice. "Feck, Cáitlín, I just can't." She burst into tears, and then she hung up on me.

"Fuck!" I yelled, staring at the phone in absolute confusion and disgust, and came apart. Every weird emotion about Aoife and my mother swirled in my head, clawing its way to the surface in a morass of guilt, anguish, fear, and rage. I threw my phone across the kitchen, hearing it tumble away into the foyer and strike the wall.

Liz pulled me to her and let me bawl on her shoulder as I clawed at her shirt.

"Why, Liz? Just—why?" I felt even worse for keeping her awake in the middle of the day, which only sent my thoughts more profoundly into the dark places of my heart. "What the fuck good am I if I can't keep things together? It's like the reverse Midas touch; everything turns to shit. Do it, Liz. Do it now. Turn me. Right fucking now." My breathing came in jerking, sobbing puffs that wracked my entire frame.

"Shh. Slow down. This isn't over yet," Liz cooed. "Try to take a deep breath."

I tried to get air. I hyperventilated like that for some time until I finally stopped the gasps with long, drawn-out breaths.

"That's it. Easy. I don't know what's going on with your sister, but something is wrong. She sounds sincere when she says she's heartbroken that she can't make it. In the meantime, we will go through this together, you and I. You hear me?"

I nodded, furiously wiping my nose on my shirt.

She looked at her watch. "It's only eleven thirty, so get some more rest. I'll make a couple of phone calls and arrange everything. It won't take long. I'll be right back."

"Liz, I can't afford to move her. That's a twenty-thousand dollar ambulance ride."

"Cait, Carson is a logistics company. They have resources we can tap into for this. I can call in some favors. So, please, relax. We'll get this done."

"But—"

"Stop." Her voice was a gentle whisper, but the power she put into it snapped my mouth closed. "I'm sorry, but you need to stop, Cait. You're spiraling. Now, look at me."

I turned my face to hers. As I met her gaze, her mind washed over mine, slow and gentle, bringing tremendous calm and an overwhelming urge to sleep. My face drew slack, and my eyelids grew heavy. My thoughts fogged up.

"That's it, love," Liz said. "Don't fight it. Just let me help you." Liz lifted me up and carried me to her room, where she lay me on the bed, squelching my will once more, and I fell into a deep, dreamless sleep.

Liz woke me several hours later with loving gentleness. "It's time, love. Get dressed. We'll meet the ambulance at Freeman in ninety minutes. I've arranged everything, so not to worry. Bian thinks she can help."

Still depressed but well-rested, I dressed and headed downstairs. Liz was waiting for me in the kitchen when I stepped from the elevator.

"Ready?" Liz asked, her face a mask of concern.

I stepped over to Liz and pulled her into a tight hug. "I don't deserve you," I whispered and looked up into her emerald gaze. "Thank you for everything."

She smiled kindly, then said, "It's my pleasure, love," and kissed me on the forehead, and we left to collect my mother.

The Freeman Rehab facility sat in Natick, Massachusetts, just off the turnpike. Its ancient brick exterior dated back to the mid-1800s, lending the building an austere appearance that looked more like a prison than a hospital. In the early 1900s, one ward had even been dedicated to the criminally insane. But now, it stood as a beacon of hope for the neurologically devastated.

The interior was neither posh nor beautiful. Every surface spoke of years of efficient function and solid care, from the battered linoleum floors to the box-like rooms provided to the patients. Welcoming and warm, it was not. However, its reputation was stellar, and it had come highly recommended by several neurologists whom we'd spoken to about my mother's case. The doctors were all accredited and qualified in their field, and employees were required to pass technical and psychological evaluations before employment. It was a solid facility.

We were taking my mother to Camp Three, where Bian had relocated part of her now bustling practice rather than living year-round in her cottage in the middle of the Hockamock Swamp. The recent disclosure of the hidden world around and under Boston had enabled her to be at least a little more open about whom she was and what she did. My mother was likely her first human patient, other than myself, but there would be others, mainly those in desperate need, for whom modern human medicine had failed. And while I had only modest hopes that Bian could help my ma, even the shadow of hope was better than no hope at all.

When we arrived at Freeman, we were greeted by John Faison, my mother's care coordinator. Dr. Rodriguez wasn't available. I didn't fault Faison for being skeptical, but at that particular moment, he was pissing me off with a million irrelevant questions.

"So, where are you taking her?" Faison demanded, arms crossed. He was standing just in front of my mother's sparse room.

I looked at the man, my eyes hard and lips pressed in a thin line of irritation. "Mr. Faison, I get that you are my mother's care coordinator, but Dr. Rodriguez already acknowledged there's nothing more you can do. She's deteriorating rapidly. I am meeting with a specialist downtown to see if anything more can be done. And, honestly, you know this is best for her." I tried my best not to be confrontational, but all I wanted was for him to get the hell out of my way so we could take her to Bian. And do what? I had no idea.

Mr. Faison finally uncrossed his arms and sighed. "Okay, I suppose it couldn't hurt anything."

"Mr. Faison," Liz said, walking up with the transport crew. "You are aware of the population that has been living underneath Boston? The ones in the news?"

Mr. Faison raised an eyebrow and frowned. "Yes. What about them?"

"We're taking her to see one of them. They have—" Liz paused, searching for a word, "options that you do not. We promise she'll either be right as rain or we'll be taking her to hospice care." Liz put a hand on Faison's shoulder. "Either way, we will keep you in the loop."

I couldn't keep my composure any longer and I had to blink furiously to keep from crying. The idea that I'd be here, considering hospice care, was still a shock. When I lost my father, I still had Ma. If I lost her, I'd be alone, except for Aoife, which, right now, seemed more like I had no one.

"Fine," Faison said, pulling me from my thoughts and stepping aside.

An orderly was adjusting my mother's bed, lowering her head so we could move her onto the stretcher. My mother's gaze seemed far away as she stared out the window. Gone was the woman who had raised me, replaced by a hollow shell of pale, thin flesh wrapped in sallow skin that neither heard nor saw anything around it.

"Ma?" My voice cracked. "It's me, Cait."

She didn't turn or move or acknowledge my presence. A feeding tube snaked up her nose, held in place by medical tape. She hadn't been like this when she came to live with us two months ago. She'd been aware if a bit lost. She still spoke then, though she had often confused me with my sister, Aoife, or with my aunt, Mary. I found myself wondering, now, if she was still in there at all. Her formerly bright eyes were dull, lifeless, and empty.

A tall, handsome young man with a dark beard and pretty blue eyes appeared in the doorway with a clipboard. "We're ready for you now. Are you sure this is where you want us to take her?"

Liz dealt with him while I walked over and took my mother's hand. "Ma, we're going to go on a little trip now. I'm going to introduce you to one of my dear friends. She saved my life once, and I hope she can make you better."

There was no response, so I kissed her on the forehead as the EMTs loaded her onto the stretcher.

Liz walked over and tried to pull me away by the shoulders, but I waved her off. I needed to do this. I needed to be here from start to finish. Rage and guilt knocked about in my head as I thought about how she'd gotten this way. Schmidt had done something to her to make her pliant and suggestible, but he wouldn't have known where to find her if I hadn't told Liz.

An irrational part of me still burned at Liz's involvement, but she hadn't known me then, and it hadn't been her fault. They'd found my mother and the tablets in the imaging lab at Boston University, just like I'd told them. And, at first, it all seemed fine. Schmidt did nothing but bring them to the gate facility. But when they'd arrived, Schmidt glamoured her to believe she was saving Aoife and me by helping him and that he was her dear friend. That was all it had taken to break her mind. Glamour was a dangerous thing. If a vampire forced someone to see things that were too far outside a person's sense of reality, it could end with a psychotic break.

In the end, though, Schmidt's glamour hadn't been what had done most of the damage. My mother had suffered a liver laceration. Blood loss caused her heart to stop during transport to the hospital, and she was down for too long, resulting in brain damage. Truthfully, my hopes were modest. I believed the situation was hopeless, but she was my ma; I'd do whatever I could. But this was probably my last resort. If Bian couldn't help her, I wasn't going to prolong her suffering. Her soul deserved peace.

I continued to sob as they wheeled her down the hallway, and Liz practically had to pour me into the car when we left. We followed the ambulance, escorted by Carlos in a cruiser, lights flashing.

The drive only took about a half hour, but it seemed far longer, stuck as I was in the passenger side, rubbing my forearm with worry and fear, watching the familiar landscape of the pike pass us by. It finally ended on a small dock in the seaport district.

The EMTs unloaded my mother, and Liz carried her down the dock to a waiting boat, an old battered blue and white Smartliner water taxi that had seen better days. Once the three of us, Liz, my mother, and myself, were loaded, I thanked Carlos and waved goodbye as we cast off, and Liz drove us out into the harbor and toward the mouth of the Charles River. It was a circuitous route. There were several places we could have put into the water. However, the entrances to some of the camps were still carefully guarded secrets, and we wanted to identify any taggers-on, specifically from the press, before we got anywhere near the camp. Shandra was trusted, others not so much.

I was struck by the serenity of the Charles as we rode. The sky was clear, and the waxing gibbous moon showed high above, spilling bright silvery light across the still surface. I probably would have thought the river scene beautiful if it hadn't been for the somber mood. Instead, it felt eerie, motoring up the glass-like Charles River without another boat in sight, only the lights of the city to keep us company. It was almost as if the river had stalled, waiting for us to pass in solemn solidarity for my mother's plight.

We passed MIT and the Harvard Bridge, their lights casting a faint glow as flowing mist rose, throwing everything into a murky haze. The mist became thicker and thicker, and soft tendrils of a magic I'd never felt before wafted over my skin. I'd learned from Liz in one of our late-night chats that sensing magic wasn't a vampiric trait, and yet, as soon as the gate had opened, I'd become aware of it. No one could explain it. Usually, being able to sense magic meant you had witch blood, but my family had never demonstrated any such capacity before. Even before the gate opened, true witches still had some magic to draw on, remnants from days long gone, I assumed. Just another mystery of my fucked up genome, I guessed.

Liz drove us beyond the Boston University Bridge before she doused the running lights and turned toward the northern shore. I'd never been to Camp Three. It was populated exclusively by lamiae and was off-limits to all humans, and any other creatures for that matter, except for Marcella, Liz, and Bian. Even the location was a carefully guarded secret.

I would be the first human to see it and likely the first human to see a lamia in a hundred years or more. I did know there were two entrances to the camp. I'd overheard Liz discussing problems with one of them that was in Cambridge somewhere further upriver. The other, though, I assumed, was the gated tunnel of brick and concrete dead ahead of us. It sat like the great black maw of some serpentine beast that lay beneath Magazine Beach and Memorial Drive.

As we entered the dark tunnel and I lost visibility, I felt a vague sense of anticipation. I truly hoped that Bian could help my mother, if for no other reason than this would be something she'd want to see and experience.

My mother had been on archeological digs and visited ancient sites around the world throughout her career as a linguist, but this was history in situ. Many of the lamiae were ancient, according to Liz, and the eldest, the one they called 'Mother Lamia,' had been around since before Christ was born. My mother would love to get a first-hand account of the world they'd seen change and develop over that time.

We were deep within the tunnel when torchlight appeared in the distance. Two small sconces cast a dim light over a small dock, barely large enough to birth our small boat. I gasped as we approached and one of the lamiae came into view. She was beautiful. From the waist up, she had the body of a fabulous black-skinned woman of African birth that blended at her midsection with the dark scales and tail of a snake. Similar in many ways to Bian, but smaller. Her torso was dressed in a t-shirt and a bright blue Canada Goose jacket. She smiled at us, and white teeth shone in the wan firelight. Soft brown eyes crinkled in genuine pleasure as she greeted us.

"Elizabeth Tyler and Cait Reagan," she said as Liz cut the engine of the boat. "I am Alitash, and I welcome you to our home. Please disembark and follow me. I apologize, but we are unable to bring a litter for your mother this far out of the camp. One will meet us when we cross the water door."

Liz helped me out of the boat, then scooped up my mother, carrying her onto the dock. "Alitash, it is very good to see you. May the eyes of Lilith look upon you, and may her presence bless you."

Alitash bowed her head and took a torch from a small drum. Then she lit it from one of the wall sconces with an almost ceremonial flourish. "To light the way," she said before we followed her away into the darkness beyond.

The sound of Alitash's passing in the narrow brick-lined passage was fascinating, all slithery, like silk over sand, and the gentle weaving of the torchlight as she moved forward was almost hypnotic. For the first time since we'd placed my mother at Freeman, I began to feel a strange and irrational hope; there was magic here. I could feel it coursing through me like the anticipation before Christmas morning.

"We are all excited. Mother Lamia foretold of your coming," Alitash said as we closed on a watertight bulkhead door at the end of the short passage. "Normally, we do not permit others to enter the sanctuary, but your mother is special, as are you." She addressed that last to me directly. Liz turned and looked at me, raising an eyebrow. I just shrugged.

Alitash spun the wheel and opened the door. Beyond was a stone staircase leading downward, lit on each side by soft ambient electric lights. The walls were of carefully crafted stones laid so close together that you couldn't fit a sheet of paper between them. Though the stone was grey granite, it reminded me most of the pictures I'd seen of the interiors of the pyramids and other structures in Egypt. None of the stone blocks was exactly the same, and yet they were all cut precisely. The perfectly smooth surface told of their newness, and yet the style was ancient and so genuine as to be awe-inspiring.

We followed Alitash down the steps, and Liz finally spoke, breaking my reverie. "So, what do you think?"

"It's amazing. How long has this been here?" I asked, figuring it must have been built in the 19th century by Freemasons or something.

"Forty years," Alitash said flatly. "We started building it in 1979."

"How did you accomplish something like this in forty years? That seems impossible. And under the noses of all of Boston."

Alitash smiled mysteriously. "That's our secret, little one. If you think this hallway is impressive, the next chamber will blow your mind. Come along."

The steps ended in a short hallway, and Alitash took my hand, asking me to watch out for her tail as we walked or slithered or whatever. At the end of the hallway stood two truly massive stone doors, each easily ten feet tall, above which sat the ouroboros carved in the Egyptian style, representing both life and death, the beginning and the end. Alitash placed my hand on the edge of one of the doors.

"Give it a light push."

I gave the massive door a very gentle shove, and it spun open easily, perfectly balanced. Beyond stood four lamiae next to a beautifully crafted wooden litter carved with vines, reeds, and what looked like Egyptian feluccas sailing on the Nile. The interior of the litter was laid with mats of braided reeds. The doors were shaded with the same. I had no idea where they found reeds like that in Boston and didn't ask.

The floor sloped gently down for a distance of about thirty feet beyond where the litter sat and opened up into a massive stone passage. My mouth hung open. The ceiling was supported by carved black and grey marble columns. Each of the columns was wrapped by a carved marble snake that twisted and turned. The detailing was exquisite.

Alitash moved next to the litter and gestured. "Place Róisín inside. My sisters will carry her to the ceremonial chamber where Bian and Mother Lamia are waiting." She grasped my shoulders and kissed each of my cheeks. "Do not fear. We will bring your mother back to you. Though—" Her face clouded for a moment as if hesitant to say more.

"Though what?" I furrowed my brow.

"I will let Mother Lamia explain. I can do no justice to her—designs." The other lamiae picked up the litter. To their credit, though she could not feel it, my mother's ride was perfectly settled and smooth, with only the slightest hint of rocking. The sense of anticipation and magic I'd felt earlier only heightened as we traveled the torchlit corridor. Twelve alcoves lined the walls, six on each side. Within stood sculptures depicting lamia in various mundane tasks: gathering water, swimming, and preparing food.

"The sculptures remind us all of where we come from. All of the lamiae you see were once women as you are today. And, to a one, we were transformed into the creatures you see. It is our only desire to better the world, bring balance to nature, and return to the surface to live under the sun once more." There was a wistfulness to her tone that spoke of heavy regrets, a tone I knew well.

"I believe I understand," I said softly.

"I know that you do, Cait Reagan. We have watched you for many years through many eyes."

"Watched me?"

Alitash merely smiled sadly and continued forward. At the other end of the great corridor were two more large doors that Alitash pushed open. The procession then moved into a large chamber even more grand than the preceding hallway. The walls were decorated with a mixture of hieroglyphs and cuneiform writing, as well as frescos. Four massive columns supported the ceiling, one in each corner. Unlike the previous room, these columns were made of stacked roughly hewn hexagonal stones, implying a culture more ancient and wise than the previous rooms by far. Roots hung through holes in the ceiling. It was humid and warm here, and I began to sweat, even after removing my winter coat.

The entire chamber was lit by some sort of ambient silvery light cast from above. It took me a moment to realize that it was moonlight from the surface, somehow magically translated down into this place, giving everything an unreal, almost ethereal appearance.

As I entered, I gasped slightly as a rush of something powerful and beautiful passed across my soul. In this dark place, deep beneath Cambridge, there was true magic and power. Unlike the gate tablets I'd held once, this magic was wholesome and pure, full of beauty and light, bringing tears to the edges of my eyes. It felt like untempered joy.

Bian and a much older lamia, ancient by the look of her, rested on their coils on a dais at the far end of the chamber.

The old lamia spoke loudly with a voice that rasped like sandpaper. "Welcome, Cait Reagan, and welcome to your mother. Long have we watched you, and I have shared in your life's grief and joy. Elizabeth has shared your plight and that of your mother with us. Bian and I will do what we can. Though, I suspect you will have a difficult choice ahead of you. My daughters, please place Ms. Ó Néill on the altar so that Bian may examine her."

Bian slid gracefully from her coils, moving quickly and precisely, so differently from the cramped quarters of her cottage. She slid up to me and grasped me in a gentle hug.

"Cait, I am truly happy to see you again, even under such sad circumstances. I will do what I can. I believe, though, we can bring your mother back to you. Her examination will take some time, so please, why don't you rest? There is a room through that hallway." She gestured to an opening in the back of the chamber. "You'll find food and water as you may need, child. You may trust Mother Lamia and her children. They mean none of you any harm, I promise."

I looked into Bian's glittering snake-like eyes and broke

down once more, clutching Bian in desperation. "Please help her. She's all the family I truly have left."

Her clawed hand brushed tenderly across my head. "Hush now, my child. I will tend to her. I know that you are afraid, but I promise that we will do all we can, and we have far more at our disposal thanks to you and your mother. There is hope for her yet."

Liz joined us and pulled me close. "Come, love, let's get you some rest." I took a last glance at my mother, now lying on the stone slab of the altar. Her dead eyes seemed to fall on me as I left through the side corridor, guilt and fear following behind, both in good measure.

The room they provided was small and sparse, lit by a small candle. A pile of soft cushioned mats in one corner provided bed space, and a low table held a plate of fruit and a carafe of water with a single glass. The most inviting part of the room, though, was the silence. Liz blew out the candle and led me to the cushions where we lay down. I rested my head on her chest for some time and listened to her breathe. The sound was soothing even though she only did it for my benefit.

"Do you think they'll be able to bring her back?" I whispered into the darkness.

Liz stroked my hair with her delicate fingers. "I don't know, love, but I believe so. Mother Lamia is old and powerful. She knows a great deal of magic that is long forgotten and, in many cases, known only to her. If there is a way, I believe they will find it. What I don't understand is why."

"Huh? Why what?"

"Why she has chosen to try. The lamiae are secretive and highly protective of each other. They have developed ways of passing unseen by others. It is almost unheard of for them to mingle with mortals. For that matter, I have never been this far into the cavern, and Alitash has been my only contact among them. Almost everything I know is second-hand knowledge, but, for some reason, Mother Lamia chose your mother for some higher purpose."

Before I could question it further, my mother's voice sounded from down the hall, a pained and desolate scream, not someone in physical pain but the voice of deep emotional agony. It was a mixture of rage and desperation I'd never heard from her. Liz and I jerked out of our reverie, and Liz flew out of the bed, pulling the door wide so I could see. We heard her again, and I took off at a run, Liz hard on my heels.

CHAPTER THIRTEEN

Back in the massive throne room, two lamia guards I didn't recognize, one of South Asian descent and the other Caucasian with salt and pepper hair, blocked our way with crossed spears. My mother lay writhing on the altar as Bian held her down with a clawed hand. She hadn't so much as moved in so many weeks that I'd lost hope. And while she seemed to be in distress, she was, at least, responding to stimuli.

"Cait! Please help me!"

She's still in there! I thought and charged forward, my heart twisted by the torrent of emotions that spun through it. The two lamiae grabbed me by the arms. "Let me go," I snarled, jerking hard against them.

"Let her through," Bian called with labored breath. The two guards released me, and my momentum took me to the floor, but I bounded up and rushed to my mother's side.

"Ma! Ma! What is it? What can I do?"

"She's locked in, Cait," Bian said softly, placing her hand on my shoulder.

I looked up, horror-stricken. "Has she been this way the entire time? Locked in her head? Oh, God." I'd been locked in my own body once, able to feel but unable to respond. It had only been a few minutes, but it had been horrifying.

"No," Bian said. "She was completely unaware until I

started my examination. When she screamed, I had just begun to unravel her mental state. I still have much to do to understand what we can do to help her."

Bian's voice was serious, but then she smiled beatifically at me. "But Cait," Bian paused, placing a hand on my shoulder and one under my jaw, keeping my attention. "She's alive. She's in there. Now, let me work. Despite what you hear, I'm not hurting her; just sifting through her memories. Her body is simply retelling the story. She is not reliving them. But, it is difficult and laborious work for both of us. On top of that, she fears me and fights me, making this harder. Perhaps, if you speak to her, let her know about me—"

"Ma, I'm here. I'm here." I sputtered quickly, unable to get the words out fast enough. "It's Cáitlín. I'm right here with you. My friend Bian is the woman in your—" I struggled for a word.

"The visitor," Bian whispered. "Tell her I am her visitor, and she can trust me."

I took a breath and slowed down. "Okay. Bian is the visitor. She's the woman I told you about. She can help you come back to me—me and Aoife. You can trust her."

My mother's lips moved, blowing the faintest breath of air. I leaned down, trying desperately to discern what she said, but I couldn't make it out. I looked up at Liz.

Liz's eyes glistened with tears. "My babies," she said softly.

My hand flew to my mouth, and I collapsed into Liz's arms, a sobbing mess. "She's in there, Liz. It's really her."

"Yes." Liz held me for a moment before a soft, warm hand with long nails tugged at my shoulder.

"Come with me, child." The raspy voice belonged to Mother Lamia. "There is certainly nothing you can do right now, anyway. So, let me distract you from your anguish while Bian works. Elizabeth, if you'll excuse us."

I looked up at Mother Lamia, stricken and conflicted. I longed to be next to my mother. But after a confirming glance from both Bian and Liz, I realized I would only be underfoot, so I gave my mother one last squeeze and kissed her forehead before finally stepping away.

Mother Lamia led me down a long corridor behind the dais. Warmed air blew from open vents along the way, and I wondered how far under Cambridge we walked. We passed many rooms as we traveled the massive complex, arriving ultimately at a small chamber barred by a door ornately carved with more snake iconography.

Inside, the walls were painted with finely detailed murals showing a series of historically significant scenes. Some I did not recognize, but others contained features instantly identifiable, the pyramids of Egypt, the hanging gardens of Babylon, and the city of Apollonia. Centered in the chamber were two enormous bowl-like stone chairs covered in soft cushions and blankets. Mother Lamia hoisted herself into one and coiled her lower half, resting her upper torso strangely, almost reclining on her own tail, then she gestured for me to sit in the other.

I kicked off my shoes and climbed awkwardly onto the pillows, sitting cross-legged.

At first, Mother Lamia said nothing, staring at me. Before long, the soft rhythm of my breathing, the warm air, and the gentle movement of Lamia's eyes lulled me into a hypnotic state. Every hair on my body stood as a whisper of gentle magic stole over my skin. Then she spoke, and her voice became all-encompassing, drawing me into a vision of the world she described.

"My name is Lamia. I sat as the queen of all Libya over two thousand years ago. My subjects adored me. In all things, I endeavored to be diligent and just."

My mind seemed to both wander and focus. I gazed across a vast city on the shores of the Mediterranean, Cyrenaica, maybe. From the heights of a tall palace, I looked down on a bright and vibrant port where jetties and berths splayed like fingers jutting from the shore into phthalo blue waters. Vessels of every stripe and color made landfall below, bringing fresh foods and goods from afar, and carrying away the produce native to the region.

"You may find what I am about to tell you somewhat—offensive. Contrary to popular belief, the gods of old were not myths. They were real beings who came to our world from others, not from space as some humans conjecture, but via gates similar to the one you recently opened."

I sighed in mild exasperation. "Please don't tell me those ancient astronaut idiots were right."

Mother Lamia smirked. "Not exactly, no. To call them aliens suggests something far too simple and rather mundane. And it does take a bit of the mystery out of godhood, don't you think? But they were beings of great magical power from another world, so, in a sense—" She stopped as a fit of coughing wracked her ancient frame. Another lamia, beautiful with brown and orange colored scales, entered bearing two glasses of ice water. Her coloring blended gently into the body of a gorgeous young olive-skinned woman appearing, perhaps, Doyle's age.

Mother Lamia and I each took a glass of water, and the younger lamia nodded and then exited the room in the light rushing of scales on stone. Mother Lamia drank, then continued.

"Humans at this time were thriving, primarily as hunter-gatherer societies. As cultures began to spring up, these so-called gods guided their early development and were known by many names. Which god was which and to which culture was sometimes a nebulous thing. But the one known as dyeuspater was the most powerful of them and always the leader, their king."

The vision began anew, and my eyes lost focus. When it returned, a powerfully built man appeared, dark and handsome, tall and swarthy. A word from my mother's teachings slipped from my lips. "Sky-Father."

Mother Lamia simply continued in her rhythmic, hypnotic cadence. "As for the old gods' interests here, that is at best unclear. And though I can see many things in my visions, the past, the present, and, sometimes, the future, I cannot see minds or motivations. Much is still hidden from my sight." She paused, taking another sip of water.

"About three thousand years later, a second group of these beings arrived, led by an entity of unfathomable power called

Danu, the Mother of Waters."

"The Tuatha Dé Danann." I could see them, all of them, a hundred of them, stepping forward from a shining golden gate beneath a great mountain. People of many races, it seemed. They stood proud and tall, and the one who led them carried with him a spear that shone in both sunlight and darkness. It was Lugh, and next to him stood the goddess Danu, carrying an immense golden bowl.

"Yes, the Tuatha dé Danann, the Children of Danu, issued an ultimatum to the group we'll call 'the Gods.' Cease meddling with humans and return home or face war. Of course, war immediately ensued, lasting several human generations. As the Danu seemed on the verge of victory, all holy hell broke loose, quite literally. The original Regos gate to the realm you might call Tartarus or Hell opened not far from the coast of Ireland, and the forces of Mother Darkness spilled forth, rising from the waters."

"The Fomori," I whispered, an ancient name for creatures from the sea battled by the old Irish Gods.

"Yes. The Tuatha dé Danann abandoned their efforts to oust the invading gods and took to defending humanity from the monsters gaining a foothold on the eastern shores of Europe and what are now the British Isles."

"While the Tuatha dé Danann or Sidhe, as you call them now, fought the Fomori, the Gods thrived. Great civilizations sprung up wherever they placed their efforts: Mesopotamia, Greece, Egypt, Rome, India, China, and so on.

"During this time, Dyeuspater, now known as Zeus Pater by my people, was a sometime participant. Most of the time, it seemed, he was intent on fathering as many children as he could among humans. An interesting side note, Dyeuspater was later called Dispater by humans, a demon and enemy to Christianity in the Ars Goetia. This is the epitome of irony for reasons that will become clear. Humans love to demonize things." She waved her hands about, clearly indicating herself and the other lamiae.

She wasn't wrong. Humans demonized everything we didn't understand or didn't believe in. We still do. Even my people degraded the Tuatha dé Danann to demons, reducing the Morrigan to a screaming harbinger of death and mighty Lugh to a little fat man with a pot of gold at the end of a rainbow.

"I knew Zeus," Mother Lamia continued. "He came to me many times. At first, his visits were kind and courting. Then, they became seductive and insistent. Before long, we lay together, and he blessed me with three beautiful children over as many years. Of course, I knew he was married and that Éria, his wife, known to my people as Hera, was a jealous creature. But he was well known to father many children, and in most cases, Hera ignored them. Besides, I was a queen; what did I care for such things? I was righteous and gave homage to all gods, including Hera. I expected she would overlook my transgressions with her husband. I was wrong.

"The Queen of Lillies, as we sometimes called her, visited me late one night, murdering my children and cursing me, transforming me into the form I still wear today."

I felt the tears welling in my eyes as the vision turned tragic. Two young boys and a daughter before me, none older than eight years, lay on the stone floor of a great palace, faces contorted in agonized death throws. They became my children as the vision took a stronger hold, and my heart shattered, drawing a pitiful wail from my throat. My daughter struggled in my arms as she hemorrhaged internally, wracked by horrible wounds and screaming. I gasped as, for a moment, I gazed into the pained and twisted face of Katie instead of the dark-skinned babe. I shook my head. The vision cleared and then returned to the three slaughtered children. I dashed from the palace but didn't get far as Hera struck me down. I felt my legs collapse, boneless as they drew together and scales painfully sprouted across them. Claw-like nails sprung from my fingers, spewing blood as they pushed through the bloating skin. My teeth fell to the stone steps as fangs grew to replace them. Unable to walk and unused to my new body, I dragged myself through the streets of my beloved city. My people, who had once thrown vast revels in my name, now recoiled in horror as I passed.

The vision faded and yet still burned in my mind's eye, and I once again heard Lamia's words. "When I prayed for Zeus to help me, he came, but only to blame me, the victim in all this. He then cursed me with a long and fruitless life. At least he didn't remove my eyelids, as the legends state. Perhaps I should be thankful for small blessings." The hate in her voice was unmistakable.

"Regardless, some curses have a way of becoming twisted and strange. They can have unintended effects. Poseidon was my father. And cursing a child of another god is— unpredictable. In a sense, even a curse gives some power to the creature that is cursed. And demigods contain the blood to wield such power. Even normal humans can learn to twist their curses to better their condition. At least sometimes.

"But I digress. Eventually, the war against Mother Darkness' forces ended, and the Sidhe turned back eastward, driving the Gods back to the Dwarka gate. In a desperate gambit to fend off the onslaught by the Sidhe and their human allies, the Gods drowned the great city, killing all within. Many Sidhe and humans died. Of course, the creature we once called the Sky-Father was nowhere to be found during the battle. But, he had not been idle." Mother Lamia gave me a crooked smile.

"While the other Gods had spent their time exploiting various cultures and squabbling over the resources of this planet, the Sky-Father was busy cultivating monotheistic beliefs among Semitic tribes around the Jordan. He whispered in the ears of prophets and created 'miracles' to prove his might."

It took a moment for all of this to sink in, and Mother Lamia paused, freeing me from the visions and giving me time to comprehend her implications.

"Are you saying that the creature that you called Zeus, that the earliest people called the Sky-Father, is the same being that modern humans call God? Like, the Judeo-Christian God?"

She smiled, almost wickedly, like she was spilling a deep dark secret. And, I supposed she was. "Yes. The existence of other gods is written in the Bible rather clearly. The book of Isaiah states, in chapter 46, verse 4, that 'I am your god.' Why would 'God' need to say he was 'your God' unless there were others? Even earlier, in the book of the Exodus in the Torah, 'Who is like You, Yahweh, among the gods.' The Bible acknowledges the existence of other gods, even if men no longer do. And they didn't vanish from all creation just because men say so.

"The rest is history. All else that followed in Judeo-Christian belief is really just confirmation bias. Men cemented their belief in him as the one, true God, demonizing all others and demonizing women as well, even demonizing his original 'nom de voyage.'"

My mind reeled as I followed her logic to its most prominent and disturbing conclusion. "That would make Jesus Christ a demigod child of the Sky-Father? The very 'false god' that the New Testament warns of." She was right. The entire concept was beyond ironic. I wasn't sure I believed any of this, but given all that I had seen, all that I knew now that I hadn't before, it wasn't impossible. It was even far more plausible in many respects than the alternatives.

"As Zeus furthered his hold around the world, ensuring that he was seen as the unquestioned ruler of all humanity regardless of whether polytheism or monotheism won out, he fathered one more child among humans. Hera was gone, so he needn't worry himself that this child might be murdered. He imbued the boy with the power to perform what you might call miracles. Of course, the irony is that his son was still murdered, just by his followers. And you would certainly be forgiven for perhaps wondering why he allowed this to happen." Mother Lamia smiled a hateful, spiteful smile full of vengeful satisfaction. "Where is his offspring? Where is the great return he supposedly promised? Why didn't he save his boy from the cross?"

As a kid, dragged to church on every holy day of obligation, I'd asked that very question of my mother. Ma had never had a satisfactory answer, usually answering 'scripture' or 'God's plan.' At least, at first. Later it became, 'who the fuck knows what men think?'

Mother Lamia continued, almost gleefully. "The reason is

simple. He was indisposed. Though the Sidhe were either murdered or driven back through their own gate by humans, under the auspices of burgeoning Christianity, three Sidhe sisters, Badb, Macha, and the Morrigan, remained. Known as the Morrígna or the Erinyes to the Greeks, the daughters of Ernmas born here on Earth closed all the gates, then confronted Zeus himself. For he had been so busy futzing about in the Middle-East, that he wasn't prepared when faced with their fury and power. But, having no way to return him to his plane of existence, they locked him away. And he sits, buried somewhere, encased in a crystallized gray-stone cell until someone frees him, for he cannot die."

I sat stunned, unable to respond for long moments. "All religion is a lie?" I whispered finally.

"No. It is simply not as people believe it to be. Humans are desperate to believe that something watches over them. The creature they call God has gone from a jealous God to a caring God who, somehow, abandoned his own child to a miserable death and then to the creator of all things. And all those who came with him have been relegated to demon, myth, legend, or outright lie."

"I can't accept this," I said finally, shaking off the strange feeling and getting my wits about me. "Besides, even if it were true, why are you telling me all this?"

"You should know your history."

Something sickening began to settle in my belly. I was getting tired of being pushed around at the whims of fate. "My history? I'm a kid from Dorchester. I'm a cop. I'm not even a vampire anymore, but I've been fucked over by them plenty. That's my history."

"Is it? Is that all that you believe yourself to be?"

"Of course. I'm certainly not special. I'm pushed around by everyone around me."

"Cait, take a moment and think. Didn't you activate the tablets? Was there nothing special you could do while cursed with vampirism that Marcella and Elizabeth could not? I just told you that the daughters of Ernmas closed all the gates. They couldn't leave. And, as I said, curses could have unexpected effects on the offspring of gods."

"No! No way!" I struggled from the weird chair and backed toward the door.

"Cait, the black gate is open, the forces of Mother Darkness will return, and, more importantly, with magic now loose in the world again, Zeus will be maneuvering to escape. Imprisoned as he is, he cannot exercise his power to a great degree, but he can still influence people. Do you really want a malignant narcissist god running all over, well, creation?"

"I don't understand. Mother Darkness and Zeus are not exactly entities I can contend with. I don't have the kind of power to fight that."

Mother Lamia didn't argue. She simply looked at me as if I were a petulant child and rose from her seat. "Bian is likely finished now. Let us see what she has uncovered, shall we? After all, it's the real reason you came."

I followed Mother Lamia out of the room of murals and back to the throne room or temple or whatever it was, all the way trying diligently to forget all she had said and failing spectacularly.

CHAPTER FOURTEEN

My mother was still unmoving when we returned. Bian was sitting, if she could ever be truly said to sit, on her coils and writing on a tablet, a new iPad by the look of it. Liz was nowhere to be seen. Lamia said nothing, opting to return to her spot on the dais, so I approached Bian.

"Well? How is she?"

Bian looked up from her writing. "Mentally? All of her is in there, somewhere. Her mind is disconnected. Her consciousness can't access her body properly, and her memories are beginning to deteriorate. You brought her to me just in time." Bian turned to Mother Lamia. "You were right, by the way."

"I'm always right, dear," Mother Lamia said. She didn't make it sound like a joke. More like she really believed that. Christ, she was arrogant. I still wasn't convinced about her whole 'Zeus is the Christian God' bit, but whatever. It didn't matter.

"Right about what?" I asked.

"The problem isn't her mind. We can pull that back together easily enough, but her body is another story, specifically her brain. It's significantly damaged."

"Can you help her or not, Bian? Just cut to the chase. I get the feeling I'm not going to like the answer." I was tired and irritated and struggling not to crumble to the floor as it was. It had been a long day, and my nerves were shot.

"Yes. Mother Lamia and I can help her, but I need to know if she can handle it. There are roughly twenty lamiae here. They were all once human, and—"

I stared at her, wide-eyed. *She couldn't be suggesting—* "No. No way. It's not that she can't handle it. She's too practical not to, but I can't make that kind of decision for her. Is there no other way?"

"Well, I could place one of the parasites in her, which might reform her body. Those parasites evolved to replace the host brain, absorbing the memories of the host as they do so. But based on your experience and my research, they hold the life and memories of several lifetimes, a complete person. She would be someone else who had your mother's memories, but it wouldn't be her. It wouldn't be your mother anymore. If the lamiae transformed her, she would still be her, just in a different, more sturdy, capable body. She'd also be physically younger."

"You said Mother Lamia was right. You suspected this was the situation all along."

"No," Bian said softly. "I did not. Mother Lamia foresaw you coming here. She also knew of your mother's condition. She's a powerful oracle. She knows many things that seem unknowable. She believed this would be the case."

"Why didn't you tell me?" I sounded like a whining child. I was stalling, trying to get up the nerve to say yes. It's not like there was a choice. I could take her to hospice and watch the woman who raised me die slowly. Or I could have her back, albeit changed. I wondered what she would want. I thought about Katie. If it were me, I'd want as much time with her as possible. I loved her, and just as she wouldn't want to lose me, I wouldn't want to lose her.

I sighed and rubbed my tired eyes. "Alright, what do you need me to do?"

"Nothing," Bian said, placing a comforting hand on my shoulder. "Nothing at all. Just be here for her. She'll be disoriented when she wakes up and need someone to anchor her. We will all be quite foreign, except Liz, of course, and I don't think she likes her very much."

"Will it hurt?" I looked to Mother Lamia for support.

She looked at me with sympathy. "No child, she won't feel a thing until it's all over. It won't be like my own transformation. You may stay with her throughout."

Bian turned, astonishment clear on her face. "You will let her watch?"

Mother Lamia smiled, warm and genuine, in a way that was strangely comforting. "Yes, she may stay. She needs this, I think."

Bian's reaction told me all I needed to know about how rare this was, probably unheard of.

"Thank you, Mother Lamia," I said, inclining my head in reverence. "I accept this for the honor that it is." *Why are the 'monsters' always so much more humane than humans?* I wondered for probably the thousandth time.

"Hey, how are you holding up?"

"We're about to turn my mother into a creature of legend. How the fuck do you think I'm holding up?" I snapped and instantly regretted it, covering my mouth in shame.

Liz jerked as if she'd been slapped. "I am just the help, love." Liz shot back nastily. "I'm only here for you, as always."

I covered my mouth and stood, wrapping her in a tight embrace. "Oh, Liz, I'm sorry—I'm just—I—" Tears welled in my eyes. "Please, just hold me."

Liz returned my hug, squeezing me gently, and for that short time, it felt like being wrapped in love. She'd made her point. Liz had just been making sure I knew she was there for me.

"Shit, I'm sorry. I shouldn't be crying all over your nice blouse."

"They're just tears, Cait. They'll dry."

I gave up and leaned into her, closing my eyes and letting the tears come until I felt a touch on my shoulder, and Shari from Cincinnati said my name. "Cait, We're ready. Why don't you and Ms. Tyler join us."

Liz corrected her gently. "It's Medlyn among us, dear."

"Sorry. Ms. Medlyn, please follow me." Shari led us over to a large square mat of thickly woven reeds on the floor, maybe a few feet from the head of the altar, where Mother Lamia slithered over and spoke to us.

"Caitlin, this is a powerful ritual, and you may find it disturbing, but I promise you, your mother will be in no pain."

I nodded, and she continued.

"However, you and Ms. Medlyn will not be unaffected by this. It will likely feel strange, even a little transcendent. The incense we use induces a powerful psychic state and is often overwhelming for humans. Proximity also breeds a certain shared experience, so Ms. Medlyn, you may feel much or all of what Cait experiences. Either of you may leave now if you wish."

"No, I'm staying," I stated flatly. "I'm going to be here."

Liz crossed her arms and looked at me. "Well, don't expect me to leave. Where you go, I go."

I turned back to Mother Lamia. "I guess we're both staying."

"Very well," Mother Lamia said and slid back onto the dais. She waved her hand, and Shari moved to a lever and pulled it down. The sound of immense gearwork rumbled through the chapel, lowering the altar slowly until it was flush with the floor, followed by a massive thunk. A series of small boxes had been placed in a circle around my mother. Each was opened, and what must have been a hundred snakes slithered from the boxes, crawling over and around my mother's body. I was about to rise, but Mother Lamia placed a hand on my shoulder.

"Relax. They will not harm any of you. Your mother doesn't have enough mass for the transformation. These snakes are sacrificial. Their essence will become a part of your mother, giving her the power to heal her wounds, recover, and transform."

I felt a sudden reluctance as I realized what was about to

happen. Part of me wanted to scream at them to stop, but I couldn't. She was going to die without this. Maybe I might have found another way to save her, perhaps one that wouldn't involve all this, but even this had been a long shot. We were committed.

"When we begin to chant, the magic will draw energy from all of us, you included. You may feel faint or lightheaded. The incense we use causes mild hallucinations and may make you feel—strange, almost euphoric. That is normal. Do you understand?"

"Yes," Liz and I said together.

"This is not without risk to both of you if something goes wrong. It is small but very real. Do you accept the risk?" Mother Lamia asked, her tone now very serious. "Do not take this lightly. None of us will be in a state to help you during your mother's transformation or for some time after."

Liz and I both nodded.

"Very well. We will begin." She paused for a second and turned back to Liz. "No feeding, it will disrupt the ceremony, and you may not know on whom you feed."

Liz nodded, and Mother Lamia turned away, directing two lamiae to bring baskets and simple robes of red-dyed linen. We were asked to remove our clothes and put on the robes, and we obeyed. I felt a little weird getting naked in front of so many eyes, but I pushed it aside.

The baskets were placed away in one corner of the room; then, we knelt in the center of the mat. Dim sconces were lit, providing the only light in the room, leaving it much darkened since the moon had set. Several lamiae placed small braziers about the temple and lit the contents. A sweet-smelling smoke filled the chamber as the lamiae surrounded my mother. Mother Lamia resumed her position on the dais as Shari, who appeared to be leading the ritual, began to sing.

I coughed a few times as the smoke entered my lungs, but in moments, the discomfort passed. I felt a little silly and uncomfortable, kneeling in nothing but a robe on the reed mat. I looked up at Liz, who just shrugged. Then the room swirled for a second, and a pleasant buzz set itself in my head. Slowly, the singing took on a three-dimensional quality, echoing in my mind, the sound seeming to flow across my skin like water. Then ripples shook the air in time with the singing, almost as if I could see the sound waves, and the colossal stone columns seemed to breathe. *Holy shit,* I thought with a snort of laughter and not a little surprise, *I'm high. I hope they don't make me take a piss test at work.*

"Let's hope not. But if you get fired, you can stay with me as long as you want." Liz said, but her voice seemed far away, as if echoing down a long tunnel and yet right next to me.

I tried to shake my head, but it moved slowly, and I couldn't take my eyes off Shari's back. It was as if I could see every glistening drop of sweat sliding down. Then I jerked, absorbing Liz's words. "Wait, what did you just say? Did you just hear my thoughts?"

Her reply was lost in a rush of magic that blew through me like a cyclone, causing me to gasp and shudder, filling my mouth and nose with the taste of loam, forest, and flowers. It was like having love and the power of life flowing in and around my very soul.

I bent forward, my arms crossed, and my fists clenched as my body spasmed uncontrollably. When I'd recovered, I drew myself up, finding my hair floating around my head, weightless. And I tasted other strange flavors and scents in the air, too, mingling with the smoldering masala and dragon's blood aromas of Liz and me. New feelings flashed through me, intense desire, followed by love and affection for Liz, low and needful. I couldn't separate my feelings from the emotions of the others in the room, which cascaded through my thoughts in a cacophony of euphoria. This wasn't like the power vampires have over the mind. It was soft and serene, a beckoning rather than an intrusion.

Several lamiae began beating drums, and one played something like a didgeridoo. Another began finger-playing a hang drum whose tones seemed to beat against my chest. I tried to turn toward Liz, but my neck refused to comply. I found I wasn't frightened at all, though. Instead, I laughed, and it came out in a strange hissing sound that siphoned through my ears with the same peculiar echo as Liz's voice.

My breathing deepened, and something odd seemed to be happening to me. I felt as if I were being held up by some unseen force, just on the verge of floating into the air. The snakes crawling on my mother expanded. When they became bloated beyond recognition, they merged, forming a dried husk around my mother, a chrysalis.

An old crack in the floor caught my attention, and my eyes followed it as it ran across one of the stone pavers.

"What was I thinking?" I asked Liz, but when I turned to her, she looked strange, naked, with her body undergoing some kind of transformation. Her robe pooled and moved about her feet appearing to flow away from her. Her tongue flicked, long and forked, and her irises morphed before me, becoming vertically slit and snake-like with a sparkling emerald quality. Splendid mother-of-pearl-colored scales sprouted and flowed across her body. She hissed at me playfully, and I reached up, stroking her head. "You look—" I lost the thought as I gazed into her eyes, and everything became confused. I felt her mind and emotions flow into mine as the room twisted around us.

"Your eyes are glowing, Cait," Liz said absently.

We both jerked abruptly as wave after wave of magical, electric euphoria moved through us. With each wave, the chrysalis moved and spasmed as well. The transformation had begun, but the ritual seemed not to be over as the lamiae started moving away and pairing off.

"What is going on?" I tried to say, but it came out indistinct and garbled. Something rough brushed against my skin, feeling like sandpaper. It took me a moment to realize it was the linen robe. I shrugged it off and looked at my legs. Deep black scales flowed across my lower body. My vision shifted, everything turning a blue-green color as if the color red had been drained from the world.

"How do you feel?" Shari asked, a playful grin on her face. "I would give anything to feel what you're feeling right now. Our magic has strange effects on humans, though I've never heard of anything like this."

The rapturous effects of the magic and the hallucinogenic smoke slurred my reply, turning it into a breathy, hissing sigh. "I feel s-s-so good."

Shari brushed the back of her hand against my cheek and ran her hand across my abdomen, where scales met skin. "This is a good look for you. You should see your eyes. They're alight with green fire. I've never seen anything like that before." She touched my face, running a calloused thumb across my cheekbone. "I don't think this is our magic."

I knew I should be alarmed, but I only felt peace. I wondered if this would be permanent. It might be neat to be a lamia. I giggled as I thought of myself slithering after bad guys through the streets of Boston.

Shari surprised me with a deep, delicious kiss, then slid past me to kiss Liz as well. A pang of jealousy mixed with the hot current of arousal in my stomach, but Liz and Shari parted quickly, and Liz swept a hand down my front, pulling an ecstatic noise from my throat, part human, part hiss. "Oh, that feels—" I started, but the words just drifted away as I closed my eyes, and a universe of sparks, stars, and swirling galaxies spun across my vision.

Something wet and soft stroked across my mouth. Instinctually, I opened my lips, and a forked tongue swept through, then the soft lips and tongue withdrew. Time seemed to be moving in fits and starts, so I didn't know how long I sat there, touching my lips, mourning the lost kiss before I spoke again. "Oh, God, Liz. Where are you? I need you," I moaned with a feeling of longing that physically hurt in my chest and gut.

Laughter hissed and crackled in my ears like the tinkle of crystal on marble as I watched a distant star go nova behind my eyelids.

"Please, Liz, love me," I whispered, desperate for her touch, and a wet tongue licked across my left breast. I moaned with the sensation. The reeds of the mat crinkled and crunched satisfyingly underneath me. *Am I lying down?*

"Oh, Mother Lilith, grant us the wonder of this night," a dozen voices said in unison. "Give us the gift of your happiness and contentment in the beauty of your children. Bring us together on this night of love and tenderness that we may truly feel the love you impart." Magic again rushed through the chamber, and the smoke became thicker. I felt my consciousness was extending beyond my body, my awareness all-encompassing. I could perceive the weight of many bodies around us, entwined and moving rhythmically. Dark whispers and quiet lustful noises filled the air. A forceful presence I could only describe as feminine power coursed through and over me, sending a divine flutter through my body that traveled along my spine and down through every inch of me.

"I love you. I'll love you forever." Liz whispered, and I opened my eyes dreamily. Liz had entirely changed. She lay lazily with her tail draped across mine on the floor. She stroked gently, caressing my chest and my face. I felt the pass of each finger individually, and heavenly tingles bloomed in their wake. Her skin felt like a mixture of velvet and leather as my fingers drifted over her.

"Liz? Is that you?"

"Yes, my love. Who else?" Her voice was clear and ringing but reverberated with a strange metallic echo.

"But, what happened to you? Are you okay?"

Liz looked at me oddly, her brow furrowed. "I'm fine, love. God, everything feels so wonderful."

"But, you're a vampire," I said slowly, lolling my boneless neck to one side. "You can't get high."

She leaned down, kissing me. "I don't think it's my high that I'm feeling," she whispered in long, lazy words. "Besides, I'm not a vampire right now, am I?" Her pupils were blown with drugged-out bliss. She kissed me again, her breath warm and inviting, filling my lungs with life-giving air as if she were giving me part of her soul, bright and hot. Liz ran a hand up my body, and someone stroked my tail in a way that drew a gentle hiss of pleasure from my throat.

My eyelids drooped once more as a leisurely wave of ecstasy began building within me, like an orgasm but slow and with no specific center. I made soft, indelicate sounds as I ran my hands down my own body. Liz pressed her lips to mine, far more passionately now, and the feeling of her mouth was lovely and sweet. I sucked at her tongue.

A dim embarrassment at this semi-public sexual display tried to worm its way out, but another random sensation stole away the emotion as arms, hands, and scales brushed against me from all directions. Wet kisses and soft wet tongues lapped across one part of us or another as Liz and I coupled in the rapidly dimming light of the temple. I had no self-control, but this wasn't wild abandon; it was sensual lovemaking, soft and sweet, filled with light and hope. Gentle moans could be heard all about us. Someone cupped one of my breasts, a thumb playing at my nipple.

In moments, the rising tide of ecstasy crested deep within me, and I arched my back, hissing and gasping softly in the long, warm orgasmic feeling that followed. Liz's sensual sounds told me she felt the same. I swished my tail about leisurely, basking in the utter splendor of it all. I grasped her hand and squeezed it as I gazed into her crystalline green eyes, letting the delicious sensations flow over me. She smiled a wide, loving smile, and we both laughed, and it was a sound so bizarre it made us giggle uncontrollably.

This is so—I couldn't finish the thought as another cascade of sensual pleasure, more potent than the last, stormed through my senses, leaving me heaving, tail thrashing. And I wasn't alone; we were all feeling it, twisting and shifting with ecstasy. As the pleasure drifted away, I closed my eyes, completely relaxed and lost in the afterglow.

It took many long moments before I returned to my thoughts, feeling confused and with a deep sense of loss and longing. Liz and I were most definitely naked and lying on the floor, legs and bodies entwined. We were ourselves again, almost as if the transformation had never happened. And as we lay like that, my breathing and that of a dozen lamiae about us drew deeper and more rhythmic. Sweat ran across my body, soaking my hair. Even Liz was wet with perspiration. There were no other sounds save the occasional shush of a shifting body. I sighed contentedly and closed my eyes, relaxing for long minutes on my back before opening them again and staring at the vaulted ceiling, shifting and twisting with the brazier-lit shadows.

I jerked up as the sound of stretching skin and tearing flesh came from the chrysalis. A pale hand with deep red claw-like nails pushed out. Beside it, another hand appeared, tearing slowly through the surrounding fleshy material. There was no blood or gore, as I'd expected. Instead, the chrysalis desiccated, turning to dried paper-like bits, then flaking away to powder.

My mother's head appeared, looking so young, almost teenage. She shifted and moved, shaking off the powdery flakes of the destroyed chrysalis and revealing a beautiful creature with my mother's upper body, albeit much younger, and the lower half of a snake with gorgeous green scales dotted with yellow patches in a not-quite regular pattern. Her hair lay long, reaching the bottom of her back and restored from its former patina of gray to dark green, contrasting with her very human-looking skin.

Then, without a word, my mother sat up and licked her lips with a delicate pink forked tongue, not unlike my own. She opened her eyelids, revealing exotic, blue-green, snake-slitted eyes that glittered, wet, and alive. Then she fell backward in exhaustion.

Suddenly sober, I looked for my robe. Unable to find it, I gave up and hurried to her side, taking her hand. "Ma," I whispered. "Ma, it's me. Can you hear me?"

She glanced about for a moment, blinked, and smiled at me. "Oh, Cáitlín, I had the strangest, most wonderful dream."

I pulled her to me, dousing her shoulder in tears as sobs of joy shook my entire frame.

"Cáitlín, dear, why are you naked?"

My sobs turned to heartfelt laughter.

"Cáitlín, dear?"

"Yes, Ma?"

"Why do I have a tail?"

I laughed through tears of joy and hugged her even harder.

CHAPTER FIFTEEN

Liz and I sat in the temple, now cleaned and bereft of all others. A single brazier burned near the dais casting deep shadows across the chamber. Soft wraith-like shapes flickered and moved in the firelight, changing the formerly welcoming environs to that of something tomblike and eerie. If I were some kid who didn't know what was waiting out there to eat me, I might have thought it adventurous. But I did know and wondered what more could be waiting out there that I'd never seen or imagined. Was some monstrous form set to detach itself from the flickering shadows, intent on snatching me away to some horrid place? It was all more than enough to set the imagination on fire.

The lamiae had taken my mother off to another room to bathe her. They were concerned about potential skin parasites, which had never occurred to me. But many snakes carry parasites, and my mother had been reborn through sacrificed snake carcasses. So I hadn't seen her since about five minutes after she'd acknowledged my presence. Bian had, though, pronounced Ma mentally healthy and, officially, a pain in the ass patient.

Ma seemed to be handling the transformation incredibly well, far better than I was. I still had a knot of guilt in my stomach. I tried not to think about it. My mother was alive, and I wasn't going to self-sabotage. Maybe there would have been a different way, but she had a long life ahead of her, and she'd be like a pig in shit talking to Mother Lamia after she adjusted to her new life. And I got to keep my mother.

I was a little pissed that Aoife wasn't here, and I promised to pick up the phone and call her again. She needed a piece of my mind, assuming she answered. I got that she was jealous or angry or something, but it didn't excuse her not flying here to see her own mother. I tried to put that out of my mind as well. *God,* I thought, *my ability to look at the dark side of things could fuck up a wet dream.*

"Did you declare your undying love to me?" I asked, playfully smirking at Liz and trying to lighten the mood.

Liz scoffed. "I'm not responsible for that. I was drugged and high."

"Vampires can't get high. Besides, in inebrietate veritas," I said, twisting the Latin phrase.

"Apparently, we can when the person we're b—" Liz snapped her mouth shut, halting her statement.

"When we're what?" I asked, raising an eyebrow, genuinely curious what she was about to say.

"When the person we are with gets high in the middle of a weird lamia ritual that causes us to share the experience. That's what I was going to say."

"Uh-huh. Sure."

Liz turned her back on me, and a bit of pink showed on her neck, so I ceased my ribbing.

"Mother Lamia says I'm not human," I said, changing the subject.

That clearly piqued her interest because she turned back to me with an intense and questioning stare. "I'm sorry?"

"She says I am a demigod. She thinks I'm the daughter of the Morrigan or one of her sisters. Do you believe that?"

Liz seemed to think about that, and I'd have preferred she'd just told me it was ridiculous, but instead, she said, "You know, I have wondered where your green eyes come from. I mean, who else in your family has green eyes?"

"No one, just Aoife and I," I answered, seeing where she

was going. "I mean, Mike did, but he wasn't a blood relative. Ma has blue eyes, and Uncle Donny has brown eyes."

"Don't you think that's odd?"

I looked up at her. "What? Not really. I mean, yeah, but look around you, Liz. Everything about my family is odd these days. It's probably just a recessive gene."

"Brown eyes are always dominant, Cait. Always."

I rolled my eyes and rubbed at a rough spot on the stone next to me. "I get what you're saying, but it's impossible, Liz. I think my mother would have known if she hadn't given birth to us. Besides, Aoife and I look just like her, except for the eyes and nose."

"Yes, but I've met your Uncle Donny. Neither of you looks anything like him. And, for that matter, where did you two get that thin nose? I think you might want to ask your mother if she had any other liaisons while she was separated from your father. When she recovers, that is."

"Girls don't get girls pregnant, Liz," I said flatly and shook my head. What the hell was she thinking? These people were all nuts.

"And Zeus screwed Europa as a bull. Of course, I'll never understand the attraction there."

I barked a laugh.

"I will say this, though. Right after Mother Lamia tells you that, you transformed us into lamiae by instinct. If that's not demigod power, I don't know what is. Just remember us little people when you're rich and famous."

I scoffed at that. "Yeah, that'll be the day. I like being a cop. I'm not interested in some two-thousand-year-old war or any godlike power. I just wanna catch bad guys and come home to you and Katie." Now that I'd said it, I realized that was the truth. That was what I wanted, and it sounded very nice and, in a weird way, normal.

Liz spun around and squinted at me. "What about your true love? Morgan? What about Marcella? I don't want to be the rebound fuck."

I frowned and stood. "Why would you say something like that? That was low." Hurt, I stalked out of the room toward the back, Liz calling after me. *What the hell is taking so long?*

In the back, Bian lay deep inside her coils. Her glittering eyes peeked out in the lamplight as she rested in a shallow bath, not all that different from the one in her cabin, though deeper and, from the looks of the steam, much warmer. "Where's my mother? I want to see her," I said with a miserable sniff.

"She's deeper in the complex with the others. Give them time. I promise you'll see her soon. In the meantime, come and tell me what is wrong. I would expect you to be joyful, not miserable."

I walked over to the large basin and stripped. The water was definitely warm, much warmer than I was used to, and it took a few minutes of gingerly lowering myself in to get comfortable. Then I swam over to Bian and rested my head on her coils, looking through them into her pretty yellow eyes.

"I don't know, Bian," I said miserably. "I'm thrilled that mom is better. Of course, I'm afraid she'll hate what we did to her. She loved her work, and now that's gone. I have no idea how I'd feel if it happened to me."

"Why? She can still work. It'll take a bit of cajoling, but I think we'll be able to get her back into class."

"It's Boston College, Bian. The board of trustees is more conservative than you'd think for a university around here. They may not budge."

"Oh, I doubt that. Your mother seems to be pretty assertive, and she's got tenure. As long as she's capable of teaching, she can take the fight to court if necessary. What's really going on? I know that's not what has you down so suddenly." A hand reached out and patted me on the head like a kid. I snorted in bleak amusement. I always felt about five years old next to Bian.

I sighed heavily. "It's my personal life in general. I'm trying to take care of Katie. Liz is helping, but our relationship is getting a little weird."

"It's turned serious, and you're not sure you're ready for it?"

"You'd make a good shrink. You know that?" I pushed my

hand through the water, feeling it flow over my skin as flakes of the desiccated chrysalis floated off me. "Yes, that's probably not far off. I like Liz. I think I love her, but I'm not sure if I'm ready to jump back in the water with a vampire. It gets pretty deep. And I have other interests at the moment. I don't think I'm ready to be monogamous, and Liz deserves better consideration than that."

"Then I'd recommend you take your time. Liz isn't going anywhere. I see the way she looks at you. She values your friendship. And I've known Liz for many years. She's not Marcella. She's patient and kind, not prone to play head games. She'd certainly make a better queen than Marcella or Nastasia."

"Well, better than Nastasia, for sure. Wait, queen? I thought the council led the vampires."

"They do, and you can see how well that's worked. They're all but extinct. Most older vampires are too conniving and manipulative for their own good. Around five hundred years ago, Marcella was the undisputed queen of vampires, a title she took by tooth and nail. Everyone hated her for it. But then, several vampires joined together and tried to depose her.

"Rather than risk all-out war among rival factions, she offered a compromise. She would lead a council." Bian lifted her head and rested her arms on top of her coils. "I think that was a mistake. Vampires are an unruly lot. You need someone who is both ruthless and kind. Someone who can make the hard decisions. Most importantly, you want someone doing that job who doesn't want it. And—let's be honest—it's a shitty job sometimes. You have to punish people who get out of line pretty harshly."

I blinked. It had never occurred to me that there may have been another power structure before. "Well, at least Nastasia isn't the queen."

"No, not in name, but she's the oldest vampire around right now, and there's no one to challenge her. Except maybe you."

I scoffed. "Yeah, whatever. She'd snap my neck."

"Don't underestimate yourself, Cait. You have power you haven't even begun to uncover. Besides, I get the feeling that

Nastasia likes you." Bian smiled almost wickedly, like it was some kind of fantastic joke on Nastasia.

"Hardly. All she does is terrorize me and screw with me. She almost killed me the other night. The only thing keeping me alive is that she's afraid Marcella will come back." Now that I'd said it, it sounded like bullshit, even to me.

"No, Cait. Liz told me what's been going on. If Nastasia wanted you dead, she'd have had no qualms about doing it, and you'd be dead already. Nastasia isn't afraid of Marcella. Look at the facts. She hasn't killed you. She hasn't fed on you. All she's done is intimidate you and bully you a little. She'd probably kill you if you did something insane, but she's pretty savvy. I've known her for a hundred years, Cait. You're not dead or totally in thrall to her. Trust me. She likes you."

I was skeptical, but I didn't argue. Bian was older than all of us put together. If anyone knew the makeup of the people among our little group of monsters, it was her.

"So you think my mother won't hate me for this?" I asked earnestly, changing the subject.

"No, dear, I won't." I turned back to find my mother leaning in the doorway. She dropped down, half pulled, and half wiggled along the floor. "Sorry, I'm still getting the hang of this."

After a few moments, she slid into the water and moved around quickly, swimming naturally. She dunked her head and came back up, wiping the water from her face and pushing her long hair down her back. "I could never hate you, Cáitlín. And I'm thankful for you every day."

I hugged her, and it felt a little weird. First off, we were both naked, and I looked to be the older of us. Then she cupped my face and kissed my forehead, and I relaxed as she cruised over to the basin's edge and sat on a submerged ledge. "You did good, mo chroi."

"Thanks, Ma. I'm just glad to have you back." I sniffed and blinked away a few loose tears. "What are you going to do about work?"

"Work? I haven't even thought about that. Sweetheart, I died in an ambulance, and now I'm whole and new, and while it's all a little strange, I want to experience this. I'll call Gregory on the board and take a leave of absence. Then, when I'm ready, I'll go back and see if they still want me. I might even try to find some young guy to date." She winked at me, and I laughed uncomfortably.

"Ma, I do not need to know that."

She smiled. "Honey, this is by far not the hardest thing I've gone through. At my age, I just roll with the punches. So, Elizabeth Tyler, huh?" She waggled her eyebrows at me.

"She goes by Medlyn now, and it's not like that. Well, it kind of is, but it's complicated. Also, Morgan's back in town."

My mother raised an eyebrow. "Well, that would be complicated. I know you've always carried a torch for her."

"Yeah, and I still do. It's just a little awkward since we haven't talked in so long. We're supposed to go to dinner this week, and I'm a little worried about what she'll say and how Liz will feel about it, and then there's Nastasia."

My mother's face turned hard. "That evil bitch, what about her? Wait, Cáitlín. Oh, don't tell me you've got a crush on her? God, you like the bad ones."

I blushed furiously. Leave it to my mother to call me out on something like that. "It's not a crush, but I do find her attractive." *Liar,* a voice in my head said. "But I also know she'd just fuck up my life. I'll stay away from her. I promise. Besides, she hates me."

Bian cleared her throat.

"Well, Bian thinks she likes me just fine, but I think she hates me. And then there's Katie."

My mother's eyebrows shot up. "Another one? Good God, Cáitlín, you really have them beating down your feckin' door."

I chuckled at my mother's confusion. "No, Katie is my daughter, Ma. My vampire daughter. Remember that sixteen-year-old kid who walked into the gate room with me? The one with the black hair?"

"Vaguely. That part is all still very hazy. Anyway, go on."

"I turned her—long story. Now I'm stuck with her. Not in a bad way. I love her, and she loves me. It's just I never expected to be a parent, and that complicates things further. Even if I could have a relationship with another human, that'd make things almost impossible."

"Darling, you will figure this out. You always do. I have faith in you."

"That makes one of us. On a completely unrelated note, since we're just here chatting as if you weren't neurologically devastated for the last two months and weren't just turned into a lamia of myth and legend, is Donny really my da?"

My mother tilted her head, confused. "I would assume so. Who else could it be?"

"You assume so? That's not encouraging. What are you not telling me?" Meanwhile, Bian slid back down into her coils, apparently thinking better of getting involved.

"Honey, at that point in my life, I'd only slept with two men, Donny and Mike. That's all that matters." She crossed her arms, and something in her demeanor told me there was still something she was hiding. Then it hit me.

"The only men? Is that an important distinction, Ma? Have you ever slept with a woman?"

My mother flushed crimson from her head to her waist, and she looked away, suddenly bashful. My eyes shot wide.

"You did! You slept with a woman! Oh, Ma!" I was in total shock.

My mother's mouth pursed in mild irritation at my outburst, and she squinted at me. "So, Donny and I were hot and heavy for weeks. But we had a fight, and I didn't want to be around any men. So Mary took me to a bar in Galway, a little hole of a place."

"Your sister Mary? Aunt Mary? Gay Mary? Lesbian Mary?" I was dumbfounded. But then again, I'd only recently figured out my Aunt Mary was gay. I'm not sure why in my whole life I'd never put two and two together before. She'd lived with the same woman for thirty years in an itty, bitty house.

"Yes, I was very uncomfortable when I got there, so I started drinking shots. I was pissed in no time. A beautiful woman about my age at the time approached me. She had gorgeous black hair and pretty eyes. I was bollocksed, and she was pretty persuasive." My mother's flush deepened to a lovely dark crimson, and I suddenly felt a pang of sorrow. She'd obviously liked the woman and found her attractive. It had never occurred to me that my mother might be bi or gay or anything but straight. And maybe it was just this one time, but still.

I tried to go easy and not sound accusing. "Why didn't you tell me? Even when I came out?"

"Because my sex life is none of your business, and honestly, I still felt guilty. I was raised Catholic. But regardless, she was a woman, so Donny has to be your da."

I rolled my eyes. "Ma, who was this one-night stand? Did you get a name?"

My mother flushed. "I can't remember. Honestly, I barely remember the event itself. I was so drunk, and we ended up screwing in the back of Mameó's car. It was sloppy and weird, and I had the worst hangover the next morning." She barked a laugh. "I pretended to be sick for two days so your mameó wouldn't catch on. God, I haven't thought about this in thirty years. I was so angry at Donny that I didn't talk to him for over a month after that. You should have seen him in the drizzle outside the garden gate, drooping wildflowers in his hand."

"Oh, you are in so much trouble!" I exclaimed, poking her and giggling like a schoolgirl. "If Mameó were still here to see you, you'd be so busted. And after all the shit you gave me over dating too young. Oh, mom, you suck."

My mother turned an even deeper red. But what was she going to say? 'I'm still your mother, and you'll talk to me with respect.'

She pouted. "I'm still your mother, and you'll show me respect, girl."

Close enough. I laughed even harder. "It's okay, Ma. I forgive you. I'm sorry."

She moved to the corner of the basin. Then she stuck out her tongue and gave me a pitiful raspberry. I returned it, doing far better. She tried to look angry, but a smile was tugging at the corners of her mouth.

I swam over and pulled her into a long, squeezing hug. "I

love you, Ma. I would have been lost without you."

"I hate to break this up, but Donny Moylan is not your father, Cait," Bian said, rising from within her coils. "Did you carry the twins to full term, Róisín?"

My mother frowned. "No, they came early, thirty-two weeks. But they were fine. Healthy and fully grown, both over seven pounds. The doctor said I must have been eating like a horse."

"The doctor," Bian pronounced rather pointedly, "was an idiot."

I sat on the ledge and blinked. "But, Ma just said—"

"That she had a liaison with a stranger at a bar in Limerick a month before she saw Mr. Moylan and that you and your sister were very premature." Bian finished for me and continued. "While early delivery isn't unusual for twins, two months early is. In addition, you were both of good weight and length by your mother's admission. I'm sorry, Róisín, but no amount of heavy eating makes a baby grow that fast. The twins, on average, should have been born at around three to four pounds. On top of that, I heard you tell Liz that you share no facial features with Mr. Moylan. Goddesses and gods are known to be extremely facile at impregnating women under rather odd circumstances. Finally, their offspring are often excellent at things like transformations, given enough available magic, such as you might find during a major ritual."

"Europa and the bull," I said as I absorbed the facts.

"Europa and the bull," Bian repeated firmly. "I'm sorry to tell you this, Ms. Ó Néill, but your children are demigods."

I shook my head. "Fuck me."

CHAPTER SIXTEEN

The whiplash between my state when I arrived, my joy that my mother was okay and didn't hate me, and the shock of finding out that Donny probably wasn't my father any more than Mike was had left me mentally numb. I was actually thrilled to leave at five in the morning. I was exhausted. Besides being up all night, I was in emotional shock.

My mother stayed, for now, to learn what she'd become and get used to her new body, and something like envy crept up on me. It was peaceful there, and I understood why they allowed few visitors. It was a space where people considered monsters could be safe from the judgment and bigotry of humanity, just like all the camps. Marcella had done something exceptional in setting them up. After making the camps public knowledge, I hoped they didn't lose that privacy. Though, as I recalled, Camp Three and the lamiae weren't public knowledge either, for which I was imminently thankful.

The comments on social media, of late, had turned less than encouraging, ranging between skepticism and outright hate. There were some bright spots, though, people who defended them and thought it incredible that there might be a little magic left in the world. Little did they know.

We left by a different route, taking the surface exit and catching a ride share home. Liz was icily quiet for the entire ride, exiting the car and stalking inside the house without a word when we arrived. She was running hot and cold. If I hadn't been so preoccupied, it might have pissed me off. As it was, I was glad she'd chosen to keep to herself. I also felt like absolute shit. My chest felt tight, and my throat was scratchy. I was coming down with something.

When I rounded the corner into the kitchen, I found Katie standing stock still, a bag of blood in her hand. I stopped cold, fear sinking hard into my stomach as a shiver ran through me.

"Katie? Honey? You okay?"

Katie's head swiveled slowly toward me, eyes devoid of recognition. Her fangs showed in a grotesque mockery of a smile, predatory and malign.

"Oh, shit." Katie was having a regression, and Liz wasn't here. "Katie, honey? I know you're in there."

I screamed for help, and Katie shot forward, grabbing me by the shoulders.

"Katie, stop!" I shouted as forcefully as possible, hoping my voice might trigger something in her consciousness. But only Liz or Marcella could control her in this state.

Katie licked her lips, locking eyes with me, and I felt myself falling into her gaze. I fought against the glamour, my mind rebelling against the intrusion. I hadn't known that revenants could use glamour, but then again, Katie was no typical revenant, and her power was overwhelming. Black tentacles of her curse reached through my thoughts. This wasn't like Marcella or Nastasia. There was no seduction, and it wasn't gentle. She just snuffed out my resistance like a candle.

I continued to stare into the eyes of my beautiful child glowing with an unearthly red light. Within that animalistic stare was the little girl I'd created, the one I'd turned. She had been so frightened in the cell, and I'd tried so hard to find any way to spare her this, but I'd failed. It was only fitting that she should have my blood to sustain her. I relaxed, bending my head backward and exposing my throat. Yes, this was the way it should be, my life for hers, fitting penance for turning a child.

As she ran her tongue across my neck, finding my pulse, I

thought about the first time she'd called me mama.

"Mama," I whispered, now floating in a sea of contentment. "You called me mama."

"Mama?" Katie breathed, her voice confused and tiny. I looked down. Her chin quivered in budding horror. She released her painful grip on my arms, and I looked back into her eyes. Gone was the beastly hunger that had claimed her, replaced by the little girl I'd been raising and nursing back to sanity for the last two months. "Oh, mama," she whispered. "Oh, no."

Before she could bolt, I locked both arms around her, pulling her to me in a firm hug, whispering encouragement in her ear. "I've got you. It's okay, baby. You didn't do it. You didn't hurt me."

My heart tore as she clutched her mouth and sobbed on my shoulder. Tears rose in my eyes, but I blinked them back.

Finally, Liz flew down the stairs. "Cait! Cait! Where are you?"

"I'm here," I called from the kitchen doorway. "It's alright. We're okay. We're both okay. Right, honey?" I pulled back and looked into Katie's face. Tears still streaked down her cheeks, but she nodded. I picked up the blood bag she'd dropped at my feet and handed it to her. "Here, drink."

"What happened?" Liz said at my back, a mild panic still evident in her tone.

"Just a bad moment, but she recovered. We're okay." Well, Katie was okay, and Liz was okay. I was definitely not okay. My hands were shaking again with mind-numbing terror. "Can you sit with her while I go to the loo?"

"Of course, baby," Liz said. I looked at her for a moment, befuddled at how she called me baby. Then I went to the foyer restroom.

Once inside, I broke down, trying very hard to cry silently. I knew they'd hear me, despite my best efforts, but I tried anyway. I hadn't been scared for myself at that first moment when Katie grabbed me. I'd been afraid for her. I ran my hands over my face and through my hair. And after a few moments, I wiped my eyes and washed up.

In the kitchen, Katie was still crying, now wrapped in Liz's arms.

"I'm so sorry, mama." She sounded like the child she was. Despite the moments when she seemed almost a grown woman, emotionally, she was a twisted mess, both sixteen and about five years old.

"Hey," I said, pulling over a chair and sitting up against them. "You don't have to apologize. It's not your fault."

Katie looked up, shaking off Liz's arms. "No! It's your fault." She screamed at me, jumping out of her seat. Her voice rose with each word. "It's your fault I'm this monster. It's your fault I can never go outside, go on a date, or live a normal life. It's your fault I'm like this. You did this to me!" She stood and stormed out of the room.

I sat there, stunned, unable to say anything, the cold weight of shame and culpability pressing down on me. Finally, I closed my eyes and sighed, laying my head on the table. *Fuck.* I started to rise, but Liz grabbed my hand.

"Hey, this is the first time she's had an episode without me. It just scared her, that's all. She doesn't mean any of that. Now I want you to go upstairs and get some rest. You've had a long day, and your in no condition to deal with a bitchy teenager."

"She's not wrong," I whispered, failing under the weight of the rage that had been in Katie's eyes.

"Yes, she is. It wasn't your fault. Schmidt knew exactly how to twist you to get what he wanted. He was good at that. And he got precisely what he deserved: beheaded at your command without pomp, circumstance, or funeral. Now go upstairs and get cleaned up. I'll be up shortly." Liz kissed me on the cheek and left the room.

Later, showered and in pajamas, I lay in my bed. The house was warm, but I was viciously cold, shivering, in fact. My whole body had begun to ache. Outside, fresh snow had begun to fall in fat flakes that drifted in the heavy wind across the picture window, lit by the street lights below, and low clouds reflected the yellow-orange glow of Boston. The night had turned maudlin and dark, much like my mood.

My mind raced with everything that had happened. I felt

dirty. I'd participated in an orgy of sorts, and that made my stomach do flip-flops. But it was what happened with Katie that was troubling me more. Liz was right, of course. Despite what Katie had said, I had saved her. She would have a very long life full of opportunities to learn and grow as a woman. But I still felt tightly bound skeins of remorse and pain tugging at my heart over the opportunities she wouldn't have. Most of all, Katie loved me, and I was going to grow old and die in front of her eyes while she remained, physically at least, sixteen forever. After almost losing my mother and the cold, wretched helplessness I'd felt, I realized Katie would have to endure that, too, at some point. It was all so unfair. So I lay there, shaking in the dark as tears fell onto my pillow. And maybe I was feeling sorry for myself, but I didn't care. It wasn't a crime.

Liz entered the room a bit later. I didn't see her. I only heard the swish of her clothes as she moved to sit on the bed. I barked a loud cough, and all I wanted was for her to hold me. I thought about getting up and maybe cranking up the heat, but I felt too shitty even for that, and this was nice despite feeling miserable and sick.

Liz moved entirely onto the bed and said, "I'm sorry for what I said at the camp. We're friends; if that's all we ever are, I'm okay with that. I shouldn't have gotten so possessive. You know what vampire love is like."

I did, indeed. But finding nothing to say that would matter, I didn't respond. Instead, I turned over and pressed my face into her chest, letting her curl her arms around my shivering body. Liz reached a hand up to my forehead.

"Oh, goodness, darling. You're on fire. Why didn't you say something?"

My teeth were chattering now, and Liz went into the closet, digging out a heating blanket, which she plugged in and lay over me.

"What are your symptoms?" She asked, sitting on my side of the bed, feeling my neck to find very swollen glands.

"I feel cold and achy. I think I've got the flu." I scoffed and laughed weakly. "Some demigod I turned out to be."

"Is that it? Any other symptoms? Headache?"

"A bit of a cough, and yes, I feel a headache coming on."

Liz sighed and disappeared, only to return and stuff a thermometer into my mouth. A few minutes later, it beeped, and she read it. "Jesus. You're one oh four. That's it. You're staying in bed until you get better."

Liz shook her head and picked up my phone from the nightstand, keying in Carlos' number on the cracked screen.

"Well, hey there, darlin'. Everything alright? You know you're on leave." God, he was loud.

"Carlos, it's Liz. Cait is sick—"

Carlos interrupted her. "She alright? Anything serious?"

"No, Carlos. She's fine. It's likely just the flu, but she won't be in for a few more days. That's all I called to tell you."

"Put her on the phone," Carlos demanded. He didn't sound upset, just concerned.

"Nope. She's resting. She can call you when she wakes up."

"Carlos," I croaked, my throat suddenly dry. "She's putting me on house arrest. Tell her to quit."

Liz shook her head and handed me the phone. "Fine, here."

"Tell her to quit what?" Carlos asked. I almost giggled at how he said what, like it had an h in front of it. His Texas accent always tickled me at the weirdest times.

"Tell her to let me go. She's got me trapped." My voice was tired and scratchy, and my throat hurt.

"No can do, darlin'. We'll just have to scuffle along without you. You get some rest. No argument. Put Liz back on the phone."

I handed Liz the phone. "Here, he wants to talk to you."

She took the phone and walked away from the bed. "Uh-huh. Uh-huh. Yeah, of course I will. No, I'm not doing that. She's got the flu, Carlos, not ebola."

Carlos said something else I couldn't make out.

"Okay, I'll tell her. By the way, her mother's all better. Bian took care of her. Let Larson know, would you? Okay, thanks." There was a pause as Carlos said something else. "Yes, I know that maybe one day she will. Thanks, Carlos, I appreciate it." Liz hung up and put my phone on her nightstand, out of reach.

"Tell me what?" I asked as she headed for the door.

"Some Bureau Agent named Schaeffer is looking for you. She's conducting more interviews about Elliot Norton Park."

I rolled my eyes and coughed. "Oh. Whatever. I've already told them everything I'm going to. She can piss up a rope."

Liz chuckled and left the room, returning with hot chicken broth in a mug, a glass of orange juice with some immune booster, and two NyQuil.

I sat up and made the sign of the cross at her. "Bless you, my child."

She recoiled in mock horror, hissing like a movie vampire. "I'm melting. I'm melting," she cried, sinking beneath the sheets.

I started laughing, but it turned into a loud cough. "Ow, that hurt. Don't make me laugh." I couldn't help the grin on my face, though. I downed the pills and food she'd given me and curled back up in the bed, still chilled, but not as much. It wasn't long before the NyQuil kicked in, and I passed out.

CHAPTER SEVENTEEN

Two days of misery. Two days of coughing, puking, headache, and—other things sick people do.

It was horrible. At first, Liz had been sweet, but that had been a front for an evil bitch woman who took Liz's place on day two. She mutated into Nurse Ratched, waking me up every few hours day and night to feed me medications, make sure I was hydrated, and monitor my vitals. I began to suspect she learned her bedside manner as a prison guard—in the seventeen hundreds. Even Jabba refused to hang around in the bedroom whenever she showed up, the perfidious feline.

Then again, I couldn't complain about the results. By the third day, I was feeling a little better, and I hoped that she'd back off because I was in no mood to get out of bed. I had this glorious plan to snooze away the day and then sneak into the media room with ice cream and watch scary movies with Katie half the night. But, no. Around nine in the morning, Liz came in. Apparently, she was done.

"Up, we have work to do."

"But I'm still sick," I said, my voice sounding like cotton in my ears because of my stuffy nose. It might have been a little whiney, too. Okay, a lot whiney. "And it's Christmas Eve."

"Not sick enough. We have things to get done. You are such a baby when you're sick."

"Kill!" I said to Jabba. "Attack!" He just lifted a leg, licked himself, and laid back on the bed next to me. "Some friend you are," I muttered to the orange pest.

"Cait, Nastasia has been on my ass to find out what's going on with these hunters. Now up!" She jerked the comforter off the bed, Jabba charged out the door in a huff, and from somewhere back in my throat, I hissed. Not a snake hiss, either, like a vampire's hiss, like a 'give me my blood before I rip your tits off' hiss, like the hiss I'd thrown at Marcella in Bian's cabin right after I'd been turned. Liz immediately drew away, hissing back and baring her fangs. I covered my mouth as Liz glared at me, her expression somewhere between feral defensiveness and stunned disbelief. Then she grinned and laughed and said. "What the fuck, Cait? Where did that come from?"

"Oh, God, I don't know." I gave a wide-eyed, nervous titter, suddenly feeling very weird.

Liz relaxed slightly, then made a half-hearted joke, trying and failing to lighten the mood. "Well, wherever it came from, don't hiss at me, missy. I'm ten times your age and will turn you over my knee."

I thought about saying something naughty but deferred and got out of bed. The weird feeling lingered as I put on some sweats and sneakers, at Liz's direction, and followed her to the elevator. She pressed the call button, and I leaned against the wall, feeling the thrum of the lift motor buzzing through my head. The soft hiss of the pneumatic lift and the subtle whine of its electric pump was perfectly clear, and I found myself trying to pick apart individual ticks of the mechanism lifting the car. Then that perfect clarity stopped, and the subtle noises vanished.

"I wanted to strike while the iron was hot on whatever information Marcella had about 'the families,' but then there was the bomb and Róisín, and then you got sick. So we need to do it today before you have to go back to work." The elevator dinged. "Come along, darling. Much to do."

Liz fished a key out of the pocket of her skirt and unlocked the infamous 'B2' button.

All fatigue vanished as I realized where we were going. "We're going downstairs? Holy crap. It's been killing me for months, wondering what's down there. I bet it's like the bat cave, all dark and brooding." I rocked on my toes, positively giddy with excitement.

Liz snorted in amusement and pressed the button. My anticipation was palpable as the elevator descended, taking much longer than I expected.

"How far down is the sub-basement?" I asked, waiting for the elevator's usual ding, indicating we'd reached the bottom floor.

Liz smiled knowingly. After a minute or so, maybe seventy to a hundred feet down, the lift stopped, and the doors opened.

"This tunnel," she said as we stepped out, "almost connects to the corridor between the Faeries and the Mermaids. Unfortunately, there's unstable ground there, and the tunnel was never finished, so it's blocked off."

Immediately to my left, at this end of a long corridor, was a door, which I assumed was a staircase. It sat right next to the elevator. The other way, the hall ran about fifty feet to a steel hatch, as you might have on a submarine.

"What's back there?" I asked, craning around her to get a better look at the big steel door.

"That's the armory."

I raised an eyebrow. "The armory? Marcella has an armory? Is it like a medieval armory or modern gear?"

"It's modern gear. I mean, there are swords, of course. But most of it is guns, bullet-resistant vests, and other knickknacks we might need to hold out against a large number of assailants for a short period of time. There's also a secondary exit to the street. It's blocked off so that only a vampire could open it—or a bulldozer, maybe."

I shook my head. "I never pegged Marcella for the survivalist type." Liz glanced at me but ignored the dumb quip.

We walked down the hall. About halfway down, on the right-hand wall, sat a more typical wooden door painted in a gorgeous dark red. In its center sat a brightly polished brass knob. There was no locking mechanism that I could see. As we approached the door, I noticed a rune circle inscribed on it, also in brass. It was the same emblem that decorated the floor of the foyer.

Liz opened the door with her free hand, and I gasped as Liz threw a switch, lighting a series of electric sconces and illuminating the room beyond.

We stood on a metal staircase that descended about ten feet to something like a cross between a wizard's study and a museum built from the imagination of Jules Verne. A series of bookshelves filled with various ancient texts lined two of the walls. Some of them I recognized as nineteenth or twentieth-century literature. All of them looked like first editions.

One bookshelf contained row after row of leather-bound volumes whose spines were unmarked. Across the floor were display cases full of artifacts of every shape and kind. Everything in the room centered around an ornate gilded wooden and glass case that held a shining orrery. Just next to it sat a breathtakingly beautiful brass telescope that, while polished to a perfect shine, looked to be several hundred years old. The room was a treasure trove of history beyond reckoning.

I put my hands on my hips and turned toward Liz. "Dear God! She collected all of this over the years?"

Liz didn't respond except to smile and draw away, pulling my hand as she descended the stairs. I followed, letting her lead me through the cases.

The room must have been fifty feet across and about as deep. As we walked among the cases, we passed a display with several swords, all in the gladius style. A display case next to those contained several stone tablets in cuneiform, similar and yet very different from the tablets we'd used to open the gates. Passing rows of smaller items, we came to an ornately carved mahogany desk that sat against the wall opposite the door. Upon the desk sat a desk lamp, a pencil box containing various types of pens, and a leather-bound journal, still open to a half-written page.

November 2nd

I have decided to free Cait. Today, it was clear that I've done far more harm than good. I failed to stop Schmidt. Cait's mother will likely never recover. Moreover, Cait has returned to being human. And though I fear the change is not permanent, she deserves the chance to find love, be happy, grow old, and pass away. Would that I had that choice now. While it's certain that I love her, it is also certain that my presence in her life is damaging. So, I return to Stockholm to settle some affairs. I will reach out to her when I return in a month. Maybe I will have changed my mind. Perhaps I'll feel differently, for I am undoubtedly heartbroken.

I ran a hand through my hair and felt tears pushing at the backs of my eyes, but I refused to let them fall. I flipped through the journal, stopping at another entry.

October 19th

I saw Cait for the first time in fifteen years today. As I'd asked, she's been assigned to Jessvin's case. Goddess, she has grown into a beautiful woman. I knew she would, but it caught me off guard. I feel drawn to her in a way I haven't felt since Elizabeth so very long ago. Her green eyes sparkled with the color of life, and her auburn hair made—

The words turned blurry when the tears I'd been fighting flowed over my lashes. My breath came shallow, and my chest squeezed with grief as Elizabeth reached over and closed the journal.

"You don't need to be reading that," she said softly, brushing a gentle hand over my head. "No good can come of it."

I wiped my tears away, sniffed, and looked up at Liz. In her eyes, I saw kindness, but underneath I saw something else— desire, maybe?

Up to that moment, I'd accepted Liz's hospitality without question, mostly because I had assumed that she felt guilty. Now I wasn't so sure. "Can I ask you something?"

"Of course, Cait. Anything." Liz picked up a glass of blood she'd apparently left sitting there when she came to collect me and sipped from it.

"Why are you my friend? I mean, why did you decide to befriend me?"

Liz tilted her head as if confused. "Why wouldn't I? When we first met, all we had in common was that Marcella had used us. But I knew immediately that you were honorable and forthright. You tore your arm off to avoid feeding on Katie. It wasn't terribly smart, but it was courageous and compassionate. You never run from danger. Quite the contrary, you run towards it. In many ways, I admire you."

I sat back for a second and considered what she said, feeling the sting of tears in my eyes. It was probably one of the nicest things anyone had ever said to me—like ever, and I was momentarily speechless.

I said, "I just realized that I've been horribly unfair in my estimation of you. I find myself always looking for the ulterior motive in what you do, but I seldom find it."

"I'm not Marcella, Cait. I'm more a lover than a fighter or a politician. I do what I have to to survive, but I don't have the knack for gamesmanship that she does. I prefer to be direct. Marcella likes to talk about herself as if she were human, but she doesn't understand the concept, not really. On the surface, she seems wonderful and compassionate, but underneath, she's a manipulator, ruthless in her own right, though not as brazen or unfeeling as Nastasia or Schmidt.

"I know what I am. But unlike the others, I still appreciate good friendship and love. I think it's just my nature. I believe it girds me against the predations of the hunger. And perhaps it's a conceit or a self-delusion, as Nastasia believes, but I don't think so." She patted my shoulder in a motherly gesture. "Now, let's get to work." She pointed to a bunch of file boxes stacked in a corner near the bookcases.

Before we started, Liz moved behind me and started rubbing my shoulders, working out a kink in my neck I hadn't realized I had.

"Oh, that feels so good," I moaned. "But you need to stop,

or we won't get any work done." I patted her hands and stood, hauling up the first box onto the desk. She pulled over an old wooden chair stuffed in the corner, and we got to work.

Most of the files were in English, though some were in German and some in Swedish. We set aside the Swedish ones. Liz read through the German files while I read and made notes of the English ones. Each file contained a story of a sort made up of letters, writings, and essays on a hunter family. The papers were written by both members of the families in question as well as the vampires who had studied them.

We found references to the names of about twenty-five or so families. From there, we were able to cross-reference the crests of all of the family names. None of them even remotely resembled the card Carol had found. It was all a dead end. In several places, there was mention of a set of files kept by Schmidt, but there were no details on where they might be found. That was until Liz found a handwritten note lying loose in the bottom of one of the boxes. The note wasn't special in any way. There wasn't even a name on it, just an address, one I recognized instantly.

I remembered the insane run I'd made down a darkened tunnel at that address. The tunnel where a gray worm-like creature infected me with a bunch of parasites, almost ending my life. "Fuck me," I whispered, shuddering slightly at the memory.

"I mean, if you insist, darling, but I must warn you. You may never want another."

"Wait, what?" I glanced up at Liz, and she wore a cheeky smile.

"Oh. Ha, bloody, ha, very funny." I knew it was a joke, but I blushed all the same. Liz was just my type. Over six feet tall, Liz had beautiful blond hair, though cut shorter, and she stood on a pair of column-like legs, just like Marcella.

When I'd been Schmidt's prisoner, she'd been downright friendly. I'd thought, at the time, she was just using me to get back at Marcella, but that wasn't it. She'd just wanted me to know how manipulative Marcella really was. But I'd been so smitten with Marcella that little Liz said would have made much of a dent in my worship of the woman, so she'd shown me. She had been trying to help me right from the start. Liz was a good person, and, while private, she didn't mince words when she decided to speak her mind, with no secrets or half-truths.

I decided I liked her, maybe even trusted her.

CHAPTER EIGHTEEN

After we were done, I returned to bed and passed out, only to be awakened a few hours later by an inquisitive "Mama?" from my bedroom door.

Wracked by a fit of coughing and then blowing my nose, I peeled open an eye and looked. Katie and Liz stood with the door open just enough to peek their heads in. Katie was practically beaming.

As shitty as I felt, I couldn't help but crack a wide grin and croak out, "Merry Christmas, sweetie." Then I sneezed loudly and sniffed. "I'm so sorry that I'm sick." I even sounded like shit, with my voice hoarse and my throat miserably sore.

"Merry Christmas, Cait." Liz gave me a sympathetic look and then a dopey smile.

"Go on down to the sitting room," I said through a long, drawn-out yawn. "I'll be right down."

Katie nodded vigorously. "Come on, Auntie Liz! It's time to open our presents." They disappeared down the stairs, Katie practically bouncing away.

I heard Liz say, "Not without mama, you don't," as the stairwell door closed, and I chuckled to myself.

Once they were gone, I dug into the back of my closet and pulled a pair of smartly wrapped presents decorated in goofy Halloween-style wrapping paper from under two shoe boxes.

Living with Liz and with her helping considerably with Ma's treatment, I'd had a little bit of expendable cash, so a few weeks before, I'd picked up Katie's present. Buying for Liz had been much harder, but I'd found a small painting of her from the early 1800s in a drawer in Marcella's office a few days after I'd moved in that gave me the perfect idea. I'd gone a little crazy, but I didn't care. I loved giving gifts. I snatched up the two small presents and headed downstairs.

I hadn't had a Christmas morning with someone I truly cared for in years. Gabe and I had spent one Christmas Eve together while we were dating, but he left the following morning for Christmas with his parents, an event I refused to join, afraid of a repeat of the one disastrous meal we'd had with his mother and father. Ma was always overseas at Christmas with Aoife, though I hadn't known that at the time, and it still hurt, even though I understood now why she'd left.

Liz and Katie sat in the sitting room, and Liz had even started a low fire in the fireplace. I paused in the doorway, suddenly flooded with an overwhelming sense of hominess and love. I couldn't help myself as tears of joy overflowed my lashes and spilled out.

Katie sat in her PJs, and Liz was in a nightgown and robe. Both of them sat quietly and, in Katie's case, not so patiently. They'd be going to bed soon, but this was going to be the best Christmas ever.

Liz stood and pulled me to the couch. She didn't ask about my tears. She understood implicitly that I wasn't upset. Katie was confused, though.

"Mama, why are you crying?"

"Because I'm happy, honey. It's what people do when they have everything they want, you know? Or if they feel really loved—or both." I glanced at Liz when I said that last bit, and she crooked up the corner of her mouth.

I handed my gifts to Liz and Katie. Liz gave a wry laugh at the wrapping paper covered with cutely drawn little vampire bats and pumpkins and said, "Nice wrapping paper, you nutter." I grinned until my face hurt. Katie looked about to open her gift, but Liz stopped her, saying, "No, Katie. Mama has to open hers first."

I gave her a knowing smirk and scooted on my butt to the tree. I pulled out the three gifts. There were two small parcels, both from Liz and the atrociously wrapped thing next to them from Katie. I looked expectantly at Liz, and she waved a hand, prodding me to open them.

"Go on, Reagan. Get to it."

I shook my head and opened the first gift and had to laugh. It was a coffee mug stamped with a chibi-style vampire with blond hair that read 'I Only Date Vampire Lesbians.'

"Nice," I said sardonically and set the mug on the floor next to me.

The second gift from Liz was much more serious. Inside the wrapping paper was a small wooden box ornately carved with thorny rose vines and our names. I looked up, blushing a little at the intimacy of it. Inside lay a small teal bag from Tiffany & Co. I gasped.

"Jesus, Liz, you shouldn't have done this. It's way too much."

I opened the bag to find two gold bracelets inside. I pulled one out, and Liz came to sit next to me on the floor.

Liz pulled out the other bracelet and turned it over. "They're friendship bracelets. One for each of us."

The bracelets were simple cuffs, each engraved with both of our names and the words, 'best of friends.' She snapped one of them on me and then held out her wrist, where I placed the other one.

"Well, I don't feel quite so bad for splurging, then," I said. "Open your gifts."

Katie opened hers and freaked and gave an old-fashioned fist pump. "This is the one I wanted. Yes!" It was just a new iPhone, but she was thrilled like I knew she would be. She'd been begging for a new phone for weeks after dealing with the cracked screen on the hand-me-down I'd given her.

Liz picked up her gift and gently, methodically began unwrapping it.

"Really, Liz? Just open the damn thing."

She grinned evilly and continued to open it slowly. When

she finally saw the plain brown box inside, she said tartly, "A box! Just what I've always wanted."

My lips pulled into a ridiculous, if a bit villainous, smile. "Well, lucky for you, it came with bonus material inside."

In the painting I'd found, Liz had been wearing a pair of gold earrings. Fortunately, the painting had been marked with the date on the frame, so I called a friend of my mother's, and he pointed me to an antique dealer who helped me find a pair that looked just like them.

Liz opened the box, gasped, and nearly dropped it. Then she made a terrible face like she was reliving a horrible memory. *Oh God,* I thought. *Did I just fuck up? Did they belong to someone she hated or remind her of some dreadful event?*

"Thank you." Her voice was quiet and tremulous as she took out the gold drop earrings adorned with three different colors of citrines—and began to bawl.

"Oh, God! I'm sorry, Liz. Are they from an old lover who died or something? Did I fuck up?"

She shook her head vigorously, still staring at the earrings, and then threw her arms around me and cried more.

Fuck, I thought. *Nice job, Cait. One of the hazards of buying something for someone who's been around for nearly half a fucking millennia.* "I got them from an antique dealer in London a little over a week ago. I thought—I'm sorry. If they bring back bad memories, I'm sure I can—"

"No!" She said quickly, wiping her nose on the sleeve of her robe. "I love them. I just—I never thought I'd see them again. Good God, Cait, how much did it cost to get them?"

I blinked. "Well, it's kind of gauche to ask, don't you think?"

"Cait, you don't understand. These were my mother's earrings. I was forced to sell them over a hundred years ago. They're one of a kind."

My eyes went wide. "What? Marcella has this little portrait of you upstairs. You were wearing those? Those actual earrings? I had just thought a little throwback jewelry would be nice. I mean, you've done so much for me—"

She went on as if I hadn't spoken. "My mother gave these to me when I got married. In eighteen sixty-five, I sold them so that I could get out of London in a hurry. It killed me to do it. I loved my mother. You have no idea."

It took a moment to sink in. Then a broad smile stretched across my face as it suddenly occurred to me that I had given a vampire, who'd probably been given every other gift in the world at some point, a present that had made her cry tears of fucking joy. *Yes! I win!* Of course, then I started bawling, too, because it was just too sweet of a moment not to.

She laughed and grabbed my face, and kissed me. "Thank you. Thank you so much. And I thought I'd overdone it with the bracelets. Do you like them?"

"I do," I said softly, feeling unexpectedly very shy. "They're wonderful. Thank you."

We sat there for several awkward minutes, just looking at each other before Katie cleared her throat. "Um, what about the one I bought for you?"

I cleared my throat and tore my gaze from Liz's eyes.

"Oh, I saved the best for last," I said with a grin and pulled the present from under the tree. The gaudy paper was wrapped haphazardly and practically strung with tape from every corner. It took me a moment to get it out, but rolled up inside the silly wrapping job was a t-shirt that said, 'Some Moms Run a Tight Ship. I Run a Pirate Ship. There's Drinking and Swearing.'

I broke out in peels of laughter and held up the shirt just before descending into another coughing fit that left me wheezing for breath.

"Now, back to bed with you, Cait. I'll bring you some OJ."

"But—"

"No buts. I said go."

"I love it, Katie," I said as I grabbed my presents and sniffed back more tears. Katie joined us on the floor and hugged us, again, way too tight. But it didn't matter. I could die right here, and all would still be right with my world.

Eventually, though, Nurse Ratched got her way, and I grumped my way back to my room. Liz returned later with a bit of orange juice, tucked me in with some NyQuil, and bid me goodnight with a kiss.

"Best Christmas Ever," I whispered as she kissed me on the forehead and left, closing the door behind her with a smile.

CHAPTER NINETEEN

Wednesday, December 29th
Two weeks before my murder. . .

I lay in bed, sick for three more days, and, honestly, they were three wonderful days of quiet, no more Nurse Ratched, no plaintive requests from Katie. Katie did turn up at one point with a get-well card, which was adorable. She also showed me some of the educational work we'd been doing. She was advancing phenomenally, and her math skills were already better than mine. It made me proud. She had two loving parents now, and we would ensure she had all she needed the best we could. Her regression last Wednesday was long forgotten.

I finally decided that I'd definitely hit the mark with the earrings when Liz woke me gently and carried me bodily to the big tub in her bathroom to give me a lovely bubble bath. She pointed out that I did not live a typical life in any way, shape, or form, reminding me that the average girl on the street did not have a tireless vampire to take care of them when they were sick.

Liz even checked on my mother, who was doing well but having adjustment issues. I wanted to go to her, but Liz begged me off, telling me, "A few more days or weeks of letting her recover in her new world won't kill either of you, Cait. We saved her. That part's done, and that's what matters."

With all the coddling and pampering, warm feelings for Liz started bubbling around in my skull and my stomach. I tried to stomp on them, but they wouldn't go, and I found myself touching her needlessly, holding her hand a bit longer than necessary when she gave me things. I even snuck into her room and stole her pillow, taking it to my bed and stuffing my face in it when I slept so I could smell her scent. While she cared for me, I watched her, admiring how she moved around so gracefully. By that Tuesday, I found myself counting how many times she said 'love' or 'dear' to me. For all this, I willfully refused to acknowledge that I was really done in over her, but I still smiled every time she came into the room. *God, I am so fucked*, I thought.

The royal spa treatment ended on Wednesday as Liz finally ordered me to return to work. I whinged and grumped a bit, even going so far as to make fake coughing noises, but eventually, she just pointed at me and then to the elevator and told me to get out of the house. I frowned like a spoiled kid and stuck my tongue out at her.

Later at work, the team welcomed me back as soon as I walked in. Carol looked at me strangely and pulled me aside, marching me to the break room where she gave two Detectives a stern look, and they cleared out.

"That Bureau Agent, Schaeffer? She's coming in tonight. She's expecting you to be here. Also, Mayor Kim is coming in this afternoon, and she wants to meet all of us. She'll be here in an hour."

"Fuck me! Really?" I shook my head. Well, so much for four days living in the lap of luxury home care. Maybe I could get Liz to give me a massage when I got home. *No, no, no, I* chastised myself. *That wouldn't be fair to her or you. Stay in your own room, Cait.*

We didn't have any more leads on the black SUV, and no more vampire murders had been discovered. The surveillance we'd put on the remaining vampires had turned up bupkis.

"Thanks for the heads up, Carol. You doing okay?" Now

that I was looking at her, I could see the bags under her eyes. She looked exhausted.

"Not really. I'm having new dreams now that won't quit—every night. A few nights ago, I dreamed that your mother was talking to you again, but it wasn't your mother. It was one of those snake women, like from Ancient Greece. It looked like your mother, from the waist up, anyway. She—"

My eyes went wide with shock. We hadn't told anyone about ma's new condition other than she was okay. "Wait. You dreamed about my mother, talking to me, and she was a lamia."

"Yeah, that's the word I was looking for. Anyway, it was bizarre. You two were in this big bath, like a Roman bath, with steam all around, and you were talking to each other. I couldn't hear everything, but I think you were talking about your father. Your birth father, I mean. Not Mike."

I dropped heavily into one of the chairs, and the leg broke, spilling me onto the floor. "Fuck, that hurt." I grabbed my lower back.

"Oh, Cait, are you okay?" Carol jumped forward to help me up.

"Thanks. Yeah, other than the nasty bruise I'll have on my ass and my lost dignity, I'll be fine. I'm—" I stopped to figure out how to discuss this. "What night did you have that dream?"

"Um, Sunday, I think. I'm not having the same dream anymore. Lately, they've been weird, most of them more mundane. But some of them are fucked up. I even had a dream where you shot some guy who was chained up."

I grabbed Carol by the shoulders. "Carol, you need to keep track of every dream you have. I mean every dream. That dream you had Sunday wasn't a dream. It was a vision, a vision of the future. That happened."

I told her about what we'd done to help Ma on Monday night, and it was Carol's turn to look stunned.

"Ma always said that some of the women in my family had the sight, you know? One of those old family legends. My grandmother could supposedly tell when women were pregnant just by looking at them, like before they were showing. I figured that if it were true, she was keying in on changes in body language. I guess not." Carol sat down in an unbroken chair. "I don't need this, Cait. What is going on? Vampires, werewolves, mermaids? Now I'm seeing the future? I haven't had a solid night of sleep in a month."

I grabbed another chair, checking it first before I sat down. "We talked about the black gate? Well, now that it's open, magic is back in the world. I think that's why this latent ability you have is amped up to eleven. It's the only thing that makes any sense. You told me the dreams started right after we opened the gate, right?"

She turned sarcastic. "Yes. Fuck. Cait, thanks for that."

"Hey!" I protested.

"Well? What do you expect me to say?" Carol ran a hand across her face. "Anyone you know that'll have any thoughts on how to control this?"

"I do," I said, laying a gentle hand on Carol's shoulder. "Look, I get it. You're stressed, not sleeping, and freaking out. I understand how it feels when things are happening to you, and you have literally no control over your own body. But you're not alone. We will get through this."

Carol sat quietly for a moment, then turned a horror-stricken expression toward me. "In one of my dreams, Janelle died. Is she going to die, Cait?"

"Carol, sometimes dreams are just dreams. I know someone, Mother Lamia, that has the same gift. I'm sure she'll have some advice."

"Great, how do I get in touch with her?" Carol asked, suddenly sounding a little more like herself.

"You can't, but I'll arrange for you to see her this week. But, Carol," I said, my tone earnest and pointed. "You have to promise not to breathe a word of anything you see or hear."

"Sure, anything. I just need to get my life back."

Carol was shaking, so I took her hands. "Listen to me. You're not going to want to hear this, but this is your life now. You can run from it if you want, but you can't run from yourself. So, let that go. You and Janelle will be fine. You'll be able to handle this, I promise. Let's put this aside for the moment and get back to work."

"Okay, okay. I got this." Carol said, reassuring herself. She stood up.

"Let's go see what the mayor wants, shall we?" I stood and put an arm around her shoulders. "Will you be okay until this evening?"

"Yes. Thank you so much." Carol said, then she added, "Something else I wanted to say."

"Yes?"

"Andrea's story checked out. The bar footage showed Soledad chatting her up and taking her away in his car."

"I figured." I didn't rub her face in her own bigotry; it wouldn't help her or our friendship now. She was freaked out enough as it was. Instead, I asked about the apartment Andrea had mentioned.

"Yeah, Cahill from CID checked it out. She said it was empty, unrented, and completely scrubbed, no evidence, no furniture, no nothing."

I frowned but wasn't surprised. These guys had been one step ahead the whole time.

"Also—" She stopped, looking uncomfortable.

"Also?" I prodded.

"Vampires scare me, Cait. It took me a minute to realize that's why I didn't like them and why I was so hard on you. I should have taken your word about Liz. I'm—I'm sorry."

I hugged her. "It's alright, Carol. You're my friend, and nothing is going to change that. And I have your back."

"I know."

Carol and I left the break room together and returned to the cubes. I pushed yet another knot of guilt into some internal box and kept going. I didn't need to blame myself for this, too. These were unintended consequences. I knew there'd be more, a lot more.

I handed my more mundane case files to Dooley, the admin sergeant. After that, I called Liz.

"Hello?" She croaked, sounding exhausted.

"Hey babe, sorry to wake you. Can you arrange for Carol to

see Mother Lamia? She's developed some kind of precognition since the gate opened, and it's driving her mad. I'm hoping Mother Lamia can give her some advice. "

"I'll try. Mother Lamia is secretive, and she may not want Carol there. But she seems to have a soft spot for you, so it may not matter."

I snorted. "She's not the only one. Go back to bed, sweetie." I said, then inwardly cringed.

"Of course, honeypie." She said with a chuckle and hung up.

The mayor rolled in an hour and a half after I did. Mayor Kim was an interesting bird. I'd met her father once, a super nice guy from Seoul who'd moved to the states with his wife to learn cooking. They'd opened a restaurant in Boston's unofficial 'Korea Town' along Harvard Avenue. I'd seen her in the restaurant a few times but never spoke to her.

She arrived with her protection detail, including Sesi Williams, who'd pushed me to shoot for Detective. We'd been almost friends at the time, but we'd drifted apart as our jobs and family life, well, her family life, took over.

Sesi wore a well-cut black business suit and a white button-down that contrasted nicely with her dark skin and sensible but nice shoes. She spotted me immediately as they swept into our part of cube town, giving me a subtle wink as the mayor strode in behind her. I gave her a crooked smile. It was nice to know she still remembered me.

The Buddhist prayer beads on her right hand revealed what a complex person Sesi was. She had an interesting background. Born in the US to a South African father and a mother from Chicago, she was a polyglot who spoke six of the eleven official South African languages, something she said was expected there. The conversion to Buddhism had come with Sam, her husband. At first, I'd thought she was humoring him, but she really got into it. Now she volunteered at the local temple.

We all filed into the conference room. Freyer's team was already there, and I sat beside Morgan.

Morgan leaned over and whispered in my ear. "Wow, here five minutes, and I get to meet the mayor. That's nifty."

"Don't be so impressed. She's kind of anti-cop," I responded with a slight frown. "She's cut the department budget by twenty percent and ran on a defund platform. Not thrilling. Even after the reform act, she's still gutting things."

Morgan frowned, and her brow furrowed. "Well, that's a bummer."

Carlos dropped into the seat next to Morgan. "This ought to be interesting," he said. "Mayor Kim's like a horse apple in midsummer, so I'm just thrilled to hear what she has to say."

Morgan laughed, and I looked at them, puzzled.

Seeing my confusion, Morgan explained. "A horse apple is horseshit, Cait. You have to grow up on a farm to know that."

I raised an eyebrow and replied in a sharp hiss, dropping into an Irish accent. "We just call it shite, and I did grow up on a farm, Mameó's farm, you feckin' dosshouse wagon."

Carlos looked at me like I'd lost my mind.

Morgan erupted into laughter. "I don't know what that means, but it doesn't sound nice."

"So, Morgan, how's the family?" I asked absently as we waited for the Mayor to finish chatting with her press secretary.

Morgan made a sour face. "Mom and Dad are at least talking to me, but it's rough."

"Is your sister okay with it, at least?"

Her eyes turned tight at the mention of her sister, Caileigh. "Oh, yeah, she's alright, I guess, but she's off at college." She paused and rubbed her forearm nervously. Obviously, there was something going on between them. "Look, let's talk about this later."

"Alright, settle down over there," Larson called, interrupting us, and we straightened up.

The mayor took the small podium in the room. It was then that I noticed that several photographers and reporters had entered behind her. She was flanked by Sesi and another of her security detail.

"Hello, everyone. Thank you for meeting me on short notice," Mayor Kim said as she scanned the room. "First, I want to thank the second squad night's group for taking on the responsibility of dealing with preternatural crimes. You'll notice they are all wearing the new red badges for the preternatural team."

Morgan looked down at my hip as if noticing that my badge was different from hers for the first time. I reached down and twisted it slightly, showing it off. Morgan rolled her eyes.

"Secondly, I have underestimated this department's value in the last two years. Growing up in an immigrant community, police are not seen as friends but as a necessary evil at best and enemies of our community at worst. And I apologize to the people in this room if I have created a somewhat adversarial relationship between my office and the department.

"To rectify that, I am announcing a new initiative at a dinner a week from Saturday. The teams assembled here, PIU and Fugitive Apprehension, will be my guests of honor. Each of you involved will receive a commendation for your work in protecting the public from Haiman Blackman and for your defense of the city during the events of Elliot Norton Park. I will also ask the city council to re-establish seventy-five percent of the last year's budget cuts to provide new equipment and training."

Everyone clapped, but Larson looked upset, and I eyeballed him. He gave me a surreptitious hand wave, begging me off.

The Mayor continued. "In addition, we will be announcing the retirement of our very own Lieutenant Larson. We will thank him for his service to the department, and he will be awarded the key to the city."

There were gasps and whispers all around the room. We were all stunned.

"What the hell?" I whispered to Carlos, who just shrugged.

The mayor stepped aside, and Lieutenant Larson stepped to the podium. "Settle down, please, everyone. I know this is a surprise, but the Mayor and I have decided we need new leadership for the Homicide Unit. I was offered a promotion but have chosen not to take it. After more than thirty years as a cop, it's time for me to take time for my family while I still have time left. If anyone has any questions, feel free to drop by my office. You'll meet your new Lieutenant next week as we begin the transition of responsibilities. I want to thank the Mayor for coming down here personally to announce this and for her recognition of your efforts. You're dismissed."

Larson stepped away from the podium and left the conference room without looking back. The Mayor followed without answering questions. I was out of my seat in a flash and charging out the door.

"Madam Mayor! Can you please tell me why?"

"Detective Reagan," she said, gesturing toward the interview room door. "Please step in here, and I'll explain. You probably, of all people, deserve it."

I followed her and Sesi into the interview room, and they shut the door. I looked up; the camera light was off.

"Detective, I know your family has been friends with Bill for a long time, but the FBI has been snooping all around the department, and Bill is on their radar. This was the easiest way to get him out of the line of fire. On top of that, as you know, he has exercised the prerogatives of his job with some questionable judgment. Namely, he placed you in charge of the Caldwell investigation at the request of Ms. Carson."

My jaw dropped. No one was supposed to know that. I couldn't imagine how she'd found out. Then my brain finally caught up with all that had happened in the last few days: the new unit, the new badges, and now a new Lieutenant. And the conclusion I came to was beyond ugly.

My mother, being a linguist, was also quite the historian. So, in addition to subjecting me to endless hours of droning about reconstructed dead languages like Proto-Indo-European and Proto-Celtic, of which I remembered only a little, she also rode herd on my history grades. I hated history, finding it boring, but I learned a great deal, especially about the formation of the first police departments.

In the north, their primary function was to protect the shipment of goods, but in the south, it was a whole different matter. The policing organizations of the southern states were formed to capture runaway slaves; to this day, black communities were overpoliced like hell in the south. If you were a politician and wanted to score points, tell people you're tough on crime. Translation, you're gonna keep those black and brown folks in line. That lesson burbled its way out of Mr. Nolachuk's history lectures and into my head.

This whole realignment ensured that the PD had a firm grip on the preternatural creatures in the area. Whomever the Mayor assigned as the new Lieutenant would be her hand-picked spy, feeding her information on any cases we took. Why else create a particular unit to patrol two thousand people in a population of six hundred thousand? And why else issue us the ominous red badges? When something happened, which it invariably would, when a preternatural creature killed someone, she would use us to score political points. She might even start rounding them up. They were already conveniently contained in camps around Boston. Fuck, our unit might as well be the fucking Gestapo. And worse than that, there wasn't a damn thing I could do about it.

"If there's nothing else, I think we're done here."

I looked at Sesi, but her face was impassive. If she had any opinion one way or the other, she was keeping it close to her chest.

"Madam Mayor, I live in Ms. Carson's home. I'm sure you know that."

"Yes, Detective. I assume that won't be a problem for you. If you feel you have a conflict of interest, I can ask the commissioner to have you reassigned."

"No, Ma'am," I replied, eyes slightly wide. "No conflict."

"Good." Then her voice softened. "Please understand. I did offer Larson a promotion to another unit, but he declined. I didn't want him to leave the department."

I nodded. *I understand, alright,* I thought. *You fucking fascist.*

Sesi opened the door, and she and the mayor left, leaving me standing in the interview room, shocked and trembling with rage.

Later, I knocked on Larson's door to find out what was

happening, but Bill sent me away. He told me he'd tell me the details after his replacement came in.

It was a few long minutes before I walked out. Carol was standing outside the door. "This is fucked up," she said, watching the last of the Mayor's entourage walk around the corner toward the elevators.

"Yeah. Yeah, it is."

"Well, something's wrong with her."

"Yeah, there is. She's using us to play politics. But that's what Mayors do."

Carol shook her head. "No, there's something off about her. Like it's the mayor, and it's not. I don't know how to explain it. It's just a feeling. While she was talking, I had this impression that she was a puppet or something, just reading a script. It wasn't the way she spoke either. Like I said, just a feeling."

"Huh," I grunted. "You make it sound like she's possessed."

"Yeah, that would be how it felt." Carol gave an exaggerated shiver. "It gave me the willies."

I decided to put aside my immediate worries about the unit and the department. I couldn't fix any of it, so I focused on paperwork.

Carlos had me doing various bits of administrivia for the team. I bitched about busy work, but he made it seem important in typical Carlos fashion, pointing out that if I wanted to lead my own squad one day, I needed to get used to it.

It was a good point, so even though it was shit like checking time sheets and paperwork reviews, I plowed through it quickly and with attention to detail. It also put me in a better mood than I'd been in all week, being back to work and having shit to do. As much as I had felt like I might not be cut out for police work anymore, this reminded me how much I needed this job. It helped my sanity as much as it challenged it.

Of course, my good mood went to shit when Schaeffer arrived with the promise of several hours of Bureau interviews. What's worse, she was accompanied by Special Agent Carter Reese, Matt Reynold's old partner and, from what I'd heard, Reynold's replacement as Special Agent in Charge.

I schooled my face carefully and played with my pen, flipping and clicking it in rapid succession. It wasn't an actual habit. I was doing it to be annoying. Besides, they didn't need to know I'd developed a semi-permanent shake in my hands that didn't seem to want to go away.

"Special Agent Schaeffer, hello," I said, appraising the woman when she approached. She wore a plain but tastefully gray suit with a white top and sensible black shoes. Her brown hair was in a tight bun. She looked like a typical tight-ass fed, but I noticed little details that belied that view. Her breast pocket held a pair of aviator sunglasses, and her shirt was a simple, no-frills button-down, open one button too many. Also, a lump showed under her pant leg at the ankle. She had a holdout weapon down there. This was a badass chick. I made a mental note to get to know her better.

"Detective Reagan," Schaeffer greeted. "I believe you already know Agent Reese."

I looked at Reese, and despite his best efforts to keep his expression neutral, I could see the disgust in his eyes. *He knows*, I thought. *He fucking knows! He knows what I am, what I did to him. Fuck.* I pretended not to notice his discomfort, keeping my expression carefully pleasant. "Reese, good to see you again. Still wearing that Old Spice? Wear it all you want. You'll never be Matt." Schaeffer's facade of pleasantness slipped into a rather pointed frown. Reese's expression slid from carefully covered disgust to absolute hatred. "Speaking of, where is Matt these days?"

Reese continued to stare daggers at me and didn't answer, so I stuck out my tongue. Schaeffer did a double-take but recovered quickly. "Uh-huh," she muttered. "Okay, are we ready to do this?"

I snorted. "Do I have a choice?"

"No," Reese said flatly, and Schaeffer frowned at him. I wondered what their relationship must be like. Knowing how laid back Reynolds was, maybe working for a young asshole like Reese didn't sit well with her.

We retired to the interview room. This was several hours of my life that I'd never get back.

CHAPTER TWENTY

"So, let's go over this again, Detective. Tell us exactly what happened, in your own words."

I'd been in the interview room at HQ with Special Agents Schaeffer and Reese for four hours, repeating the same shit over and over. I was really beginning not to like Schaeffer.

I leaned back in the chair and sighed in exasperation, twirling my pen. "Special Agent Schaeffer, this has to be the fiftieth time I've told the story. It's my sixth interview with federal agents of one kind or another. Do you need to go over this—again? What exactly is it that you want to know?"

Schaeffer set down her legal pad and pen, glaring at me. "Detective, what is not clear is how a hole in space and time, chock full of nightmares, just popped into existence underneath Boston. The federal government is looking for answers, and I aim to give them some. So, please tell me what you know about how the gate opened. We know you were there. We need the details to do something about it. We have a whole team of scientists, soldiers, and bureaucrats milling about under Elliot Norton Park and examining—what did you call it?—" she glanced at the file in front of her, "the Gate Chamber?"

"Ms. Schaeffer, like I said. I'd love to tell you more, but I just can't."

Schaeffer leaned forward. "Can't? Or won't? Detective, need I remind you that I'm a federal agent? I can have you arrested for obstruction."

I barked a laugh. "Obstruction? Of what? Justice? I haven't committed any crime, and no one can point to one statute that has been broken regarding this other than some local trespassing laws, for which I have qualified immunity anyway. You can try to intimidate me with that bullshit, but you and I both know that won't stick. And don't give me that national security nonsense again. I've heard it a dozen times, and so far, it's been an empty threat. I'm going to step outside and make a phone call and see what I can do because, despite your bitchy attitude, I know you're just trying to do your job." I stood up and walked out the door leaving the agents to their thoughts.

I called Liz, and she answered on the first ring. "Well, hello there, beautiful."

I blinked. *Beautiful?* "Um, okay. Hey. What's got you in such a good mood?"

Liz laughed on the other end. "Nothing in particular. Just feeling good. What do you need?"

"I am getting grilled for the sixth time by federal agents. I need to tell them something. I can't stonewall forever. The department can only cover for me for so long before it gets political and I end up suspended."

"Nastasia is here. Let me see what we can come up with. Just a second." The line went quiet as she put me on mute. I leaned against the wall, placing the phone on speaker so I didn't have to hold the damn thing to my ear. I didn't want Nastasia involved with this, but that wasn't up to me, as usual.

"Cait? You still there?" Liz said a few minutes later.

"Yeah, what did she say?" I was getting a little anxious.

"She said you should go back in and wait for her to get there. She'll deal with it. I think Nastasia has had enough pussyfooting around."

"She's not going to do something crazy, is she?" I asked, now more worried instead of less. I had just wanted to be able to throw Schaeffer a bone, not put her on the radar of the second most dangerous creature on the planet.

Liz's demeanor became serious. "No, love, I don't think so. She just said she's let this go on for too long."

"Are you coming down too?" I asked, hoping she would. The thought of being anywhere near Nastasia gave me severe anxiety.

"No, I'm staying with Katie. But don't worry, I made Nastasia promise to be good." There was something weird in her voice, though. She sounded—I don't know—protective.

"Everything okay?" I asked nervously.

"It's all fine. She'll be there in twenty or so minutes." Liz hung up, and I frowned at my phone.

"I'll go get her when she comes up," Carlos said as he walked up.

"I take it you heard?"

Carlos nodded. "Yup. Things are about to get crazier than a dog at a hubcap factory."

I snorted a laugh. "Okay, whatever that means. I'll go back in and wait. Nothing else I can do."

I returned to the interview room, giving Carlos a wan smile as I closed the door.

My breathing was a little short, and my palms were sweaty as I sat back down across from Reese and Schaeffer. The truth was I was scared. I had no idea what was about to happen. I expected Nastasia to come in and whammy Schaeffer out of her gourd as I'd done to Agent Reynolds a few weeks ago. At least, I hoped that's what she was going to do. The other possibilities were too unpleasant to think about.

"Are we ready to begin again, Detective?" Agent Schaeffer picked up her pen and got ready to write.

"Not just yet," I said as calmly as possible. "Nastasia Volkova, who was there, is coming to join us. She can answer all your questions. She should be here in about twenty minutes."

Schaeffer raised an eyebrow. "Who is she?"

I answered cryptically, not at all sure how to represent Nastasia. "I'll introduce you when she arrives. Please, humor me, Special Agent."

Schaeffer sighed in frustration and dropped her pen back on

her pad, crossing her arms. She and I stared at each other for almost twenty minutes, neither of us saying a word. I smirked slightly as I realized she was probably watching me the way I watched her, looking for any indicators of behavior that might be useful. Reese excused himself to hit the restroom and left us alone for a few minutes.

"So, what happened to Reynolds?" I asked. "I liked him. Reese seems, um, challenging."

Schaeffer snorted, and the beginnings of a smile pulled at the corners of her mouth. "Agent Reynolds left the bureau. He had some issues going on. I want to say Reese is an interesting man to work with, but he's just angry."

"Yeah, I got that about him."

"What's between you two anyway?"

"Oh, well—" I was about to make something up when Carlos opened the interview room, admitting Nastasia.

"Cait, get out," Nastasia demanded as she walked in. "I need to have a word with Special Agent, ah—"

"Schaeffer," I answered helpfully and stood quickly, snatching my notepad off the table. "Special Agent Schaeffer, this is Nastasia Volkova. I think she'll address your concerns. But my desk is straight out the door, and I'll be here if you need anything after talking to her." She was probably going to need a change of pants.

Schaeffer about jumped out of her seat. "Wait a minute. We're not done here. No one said you could leave, Reagan."

Before I could answer, Nastasia stepped into Schaeffer's space, giving her an imperious glare. "I did. She's dismissed. Now sit." Schaeffer sat obediently back in her chair, hands folded. Then Nastasia turned back toward me, giving me a sly smile and a wink. "I said leave, Cait. Not to worry." I suppose I should have been relieved by the statement, but I wasn't. God only knew what she was about to do to Schaeffer. I visibly cringed as I closed the door.

Carlos and I went to the surveillance room to watch, only remembering the feed was off when presented with a blank screen. "Shit," I swore and went back to my desk to wait.

It was a very long half-hour before the interview door

opened again. I watched as Nastasia exited briskly, throwing me a wink and heading for the elevators. Moments later, a very scared, disheveled, and pale-looking Special Agent Schaeffer followed. Her hair was mussed, and another button was undone on her shirt. *Oh, Nastasia, why do you always have to go there?* I thought.

Schaeffer looked at me as if unsure if she should talk to me further or leave, turning a complete circle before finally walking over. Her hands were trembling violently. Schaeffer was beyond shaken; she was terrified.

I stood and offered her my chair. "You look like you need to sit down."

"Th—thanks," she stuttered as she plopped into the chair. I realized that she hadn't even brought out her briefcase or legal pad, so I went to retrieve them.

"Here," I said as I handed Schaeffer her things when I'd returned. "You okay?"

"No, Detective. Just a couple of months ago, we all learned that mermaids and faeries were real. Now, it's vampires."

Carlos walked over with a cup of water, handing it to Agent Schaeffer.

She thanked him and downed it. "Is she as ruthless as she says?"

I smiled and nodded, happy that, for once, I wasn't Nastasia's target. "Yes, Special Agent Schaeffer, she is."

"Call me Angela," Schaeffer said as she accepted another cup of water from Carlos.

"Angela, that woman is the second most dangerous thing on this planet. She can get to anyone at almost any time. Now, I think you understand why I wasn't exactly forthcoming about what happened. Also, you can call me Cait." I held out my hand, and Angela took it. "So, what did she tell you?"

The flush had returned to Angela's cheeks. "She detailed what happened in the tunnels under Elliot Norton Park, then explained that she would kill my daughter if I didn't leave you alone. She also said there'd be serious repercussions if I took this to my superiors. How did she even know I have a daughter?"

"She probably made one phone call on the way over here. She's well connected." I leaned back against my desk. "You need to understand something. Nastasia plays the long game, the long, long game. If you try to have her arrested, she'll ghost, and you won't see her for years, but when she surfaces, she'll be the last thing you see, ever. If she promised to kill your daughter, then be assured that she will, even after you die. She doesn't live by human rules. Even when I was a vampire, she terrified me."

"You were a vampire? Reese tried to tell me that, but I thought he'd lost his shit, like Reynolds."

"Yes. I'm not anymore, so please keep that to yourself for my protection. There are people out there that would happily kill me if they knew."

She nodded. "What did she do to me? She made me see things. I thought I was going mad." Angela fumbled to put her notepad in her satchel, dropping it on the floor. "Shit."

I knelt and picked up the pad, placing it in the satchel and setting the bag against the wall. "Alright, I know you're spooked. Trust me, I know. You need to take a deep breath. You look like death warmed over." And she did, pale and starting to hyperventilate slightly, her exhalation coming out in short breaths. "What else did Nastasia say?"

"Only that she might need my services one day and not to stray too far from town. Fuck, how did I get into this?"

"Same way I did," I said and pulled two glasses and a bottle of scotch from Freyer's desk drawer. I poured one for me and one for Schaeffer. She didn't even give me that 'I'm on duty shit,' instead upending the glass. "I got assigned to a case, and next thing I knew, wham, I'm through the looking glass."

"Thanks for that," she said, setting the glass down.

"Another?" I asked, the bottle still in my hand.

She nodded. "Keep it coming."

I poured her a double and sat down, placing the bad scotch between us. "Welcome to the fold, Angela." I held up my glass in a toast. She looked at me for a moment, probably wondering if it was something worthy of celebrating, then finally clinked glasses with me anyway.

"Will I see her again? I mean, do you think she was serious about needing favors?"

I laughed at her naïveté. "Nastasia does not fuck about. She's a game player, but she always gets what she wants, and everything she does, so I'm told, is for a reason, everything."

Angela glanced around, realizing the floor was almost empty. "Where the fuck did my asshole boss go?"

"I suspect he left the building," I said casually. "I'm sure you noticed he had to visit the little boys' room as soon as I mentioned Nastasia's name. He knew who she was." I thought about that. He knew who she was. And he smelled of cheap cologne. "Motherfucker!" I swore.

Schaeffer had her head down, elbows resting on her knees as she swirled her drink. She looked up at me. "What is it?"

"What kind of car does he drive?" I asked, pulling up the video Doyle had pulled the other night.

"Who? Reese?"

"Yeah." I turned my laptop toward her. "Does that look like it?"

Schaeffer examined the grainy picture. "Could be. He does drive a black Suburban. They're pretty obvious. But a lot of us drive home in our Bureau vehicles from time to time, and it's one of the most popular SUV brands on the road."

"Could he have access to license plates from other states? Maybe stolen ones?"

"What are you driving at, Detective?" Schaeffer asked. Her eyes turned hawkish, and her expression suspicious. "What is this all about?"

I closed my laptop and studied Schaeffer's face. She seemed like a good sort, who generally followed the rules but knew not everything was black and white. She wasn't some kid. She was a seasoned agent. "Can I trust you to keep something to yourself?"

"Depends on what it is, you know that."

I screwed up my face in a moment of indecision, then pressed on. "Okay, so the fact that vampires exist is a closely guarded secret. Only a dozen or so of us at the department know about them, plus the chief, the commissioner, and the mayor. That being said, there are such things as vampire hunters."

Now I had Schaeffer's complete attention. She set down her glass, only half empty. "Okay."

"They follow family lines. We've been having a problem with some here. So far, we've been able to keep it quiet, but eventually, something will happen that people will believe and that will be it. It's only a matter of time."

"I'm not following." Schaeffer leaned back in her chair, waiting for me to continue.

"Two of our youngest vampires were murdered. They were young and stupid, but it doesn't matter. They were people with jobs and families. They weren't monsters."

"And you think Reese is tied up in that somehow?" She asked skeptically. "I'd be shocked. He's a Mormon kid, Cait. You know they always stick to family and do what they think is right. They're better known for a unique brand of Christianity, interesting underwear, and leading relatively healthy lifestyles that typically don't include murder."

"I know, and it's just a theory, and I have few facts to support it, but can you at least check on a few things for me?"

She shrugged. "I suppose. But I don't expect to find anything."

"Thank you," I said and explained what I needed.

"I wish Reynolds was here. He wouldn't have left me hanging like this. He disappeared almost a month ago, and no one has seen or heard from him. The Bureau is looking for him, but we all pretty much think he's dead. You know he murdered his wife."

"Oh, God, I didn't know that. I'm so sorry. I liked Reynolds."

Carlos glared at me accusingly around the cube wall. *Shit.* All I'd wanted was to get Special Agents Reynolds and Reese to leave me alone, not send one of them round the twist.

"So, what are you going to do?" I asked. "Please tell me you aren't going to send this up the chain."

"Me? Fuck no. I'm going back home to drink myself into a stupor and calling in tomorrow. I might even re-evaluate my career path. Ms. Volkova told me that a guy named Schmidt opened that whatever it is downtown, and now he's dead. That's good enough for me. Just one question, though." Angela looked pointedly at me, "Do you work for her?"

I snorted. "Hell no, but I know better than to piss her off. I have family, too. She almost killed me once, and I'm in no mood to give her reason to try again."

Angela stood and grabbed her things, looking a little calmer. "Well, that's it then. I'm going to file my report. Reese can kiss my ass."

As she started walking toward the elevators, I called out. "Angela. For what it's worth, I'm sorry you got mixed up in this."

She just waved and kept walking. "Thanks for the scotch."

"Well, that's not good," Carlos said as he watched Schaeffer depart.

No, it is not, I thought and decided it was time to knock off for the day. "I'm going home."

CHAPTER TWENTY-ONE

I repeatedly pressed the button on the garage door opener, but nothing happened. The light came on, but the door stubbornly refused to open. *Damnit.* "I'm fucking tired. I do not need this," I muttered, finally opting for parking on the frozen streets. I'd had enough of this day. Despite my calm demeanor for most of it, Agent Schaeffer, and especially Reese, had rattled me. I finally found an empty spot on the square, just across the park from the house, so I would only spend a few minutes freezing my ass off.

A cruel wind blew across the city, rocking the trees and driving spiraling drifts of snow about through the air. I was one foot on the steps of Monument Park as the massive spotlights illuminating the monument died with a loud bang from somewhere very close. My free hand was almost on my weapon as I realized what I was doing. *Relax, Cait, it's just a transformer.*

I took a deep breath. The park was now pitch black and creepy. City lights reflected from the low cloud cover, casting the entire park in a soft gray light that deepened shadows and twisted the trees into strange shapes. The branches cracked and shook in the wind, making strange noises, almost like scrabbling legs. Underneath, I thought I could hear a strange chittering noise.

Okay, fuck this, I thought and hustled to the house as fast as I could without falling on my ass. I found the front door unlocked, and every hair on my body stood on end.

"Liz? Katie?" I called as I stepped in. "The garage door opener is broken." No answer.

My eyes quickly adjusted to the single dim wall sconce lighting the entryway. I hoped that Liz had decided on some mood lighting because my sense that something was wrong wouldn't quit.

I dropped my backpack and drew my service weapon, working my way through the house, floor by floor, clearing each room and closing doors behind me. It was slow going, but by the time I'd reached the fourth floor, it was clear that the house was empty. Returning to the first floor, I collected my discarded backpack and locked the front door. On the side table, I found a note that Katie and Liz had gone out—to feed, I assumed. I still felt something was off, but finding nothing, I decided a workout was in order. There was a beautiful full moon out, but I closed the curtains to my window as I changed; no need to flash the world.

I lifted weights for about an hour, then went at the heavy bag. I pounded it in frustration.

Right hook, elbow, knee, duck-left, left jab.

Everything in my life had gone pear-shaped. I loved Katie, Marcella, and Liz. But, damnit, my life was completely fucked up over vampires.

Roundhouse, snap-kick, quick side-kick.

And the fucking Finchers, I just wanted to shoot those two.

Jab, jab, jab, cross.

And even though she'd gotten me out of the jam with the FBI, I was sick of Nastasia and her shit. I hated being afraid of her. I hated her threats. I hated her perfectly pert breasts, gorgeous hips, and spectacular legs.

Right jab, left, right, left.

Most of all, though, I hated that she haunted my dreams at night, almost every night, a beautiful poison flower of my darkest, most prurient, twisted fantasies, enchanting and perfect and powerful.

Quick jabs, hook, hook, roundhouse, snap-kick, knee.

Of course, if I were a vampire again —

I let that thought go. That way, as I liked to say, lay madness and foolish choices. But, God, I was sick of being a cop sometimes.

By the time I was done, sweat clung to my body, and my arms and legs ached from the exertion, but my thoughts still hadn't drifted away from Nastasia. "Fuuuck," I screamed and made the long climb up the stairs to my room for a long, cold shower.

I stripped off my workout clothes and looked out the open window admiring the moon once more as the cold air brushed a chill over my flesh. Then my heart stopped. *The moon? I didn't leave the window open.* I lunged for my gun in a panic, but it wasn't on the nightstand.

Nastasia stepped silently from the shadows into the dim light of the table lamp, my holster dangling nonchalantly from one hand. "Looking for this?"

Oh, shit.

I wanted to run, but my brain seized, and my legs wouldn't move. My heart thudded in my chest, and I began to hyperventilate. I tried to speak, but my throat was suddenly dry, and I couldn't swallow. Terror had me in an icy grasp, stealing the heat from my body even as a flush of excitement poured through my blood. I couldn't take my eyes off her.

Nastasia glided across the hardwoods in bare feet, making not so much as a whisper on the creaky floor. She wore a shift of sheer, black chiffon that clung to soft round breasts and shapely hips as she swayed mesmerizingly with each languorous step. She placed my weapon on my wardrobe and closed the distance between us until she was within an inch of my face.

I bit my lip to keep it from quivering as my legs finally responded, almost of their own volition, backing toward the lamp as if the light would protect me from the predatory gleam that lit Nastasia's eyes. It only made it easier to see. Some terrors are best left in the dark.

Nastasia moved toward me again, forcing me back. My calf

hit the bed, and my hip bumped the nightstand. She drew a manicured fingernail across my jawline, the hard nail tugging delicately at my skin. I still couldn't speak a word of protest.

She uttered something, just a whisper. "Are you afraid of me, little girl?"

The question didn't register in my fear-clouded mind, and I cleared my throat, finally finding my voice, small and stricken. "Please." It was a plea, but for her to leave or to touch me, I wasn't sure.

Her hand caressed my cheek again, just her fingertips this time, feeling like soft, cold velvet. "You're exquisite." Her fingers lit across my collarbone and over one shoulder. "Sculpted, like one of Corridini's veiled figures."

I swallowed hard and, unable to control myself, slipped my hand to her waist, my fingers brushing her thigh, my lips half pursed in anticipation of her burning kiss.

Nastasia continued whispering as if I hadn't moved, leaning in cheek to cheek, her soft, velvet, bloody lips narrowly missing my own and making me tilt my head slightly to better feel her smooth face on mine.

"Did you know that every vampire has a unique scent?" She asked, her voice low and inviting. "Marcella smells of sandalwood, Elizabeth of burning dragon's blood. Yours—" Her heavy intake of breath caressed my ear, sending a shiver down my spine and gooseflesh across my semi-naked body. "You smell of a mix of cinnamon and burnt embers, perhaps reminiscent of a smoldering masala spice. The same scent I noted the first time I met you. It's how I know."

I breathed in, unconsciously inhaling her scent of pine needles and crisp winter mornings where distant clouds threatened deep snows. My hand came reflexively to my neck as she placed gentle, cold fingers on my throat, and another violent shiver rattled my teeth. But rather than pull at her fingers, I caressed them before my hand fell to her hip once more.

Nastasia reached behind my head and withdrew my hair from its ponytail, pausing to push aside an errant lock from in front of my eyes. She curled it behind my ear, gently grazing the skin as she did so. "You think you fear me." She leaned closer, her breasts to mine. Her voice was a gentle cold breeze, smelling of mint and copper, promising pleasures to my mouth, filling my lungs. A cascade of chaotic sensations flooded my head: ice-cold fear, burning lust, and an almost giddy abandon that defied any reason. I wanted to be something dark and malign, something powerful. I wanted to be like her, unfettered by conscience as I saw fit. That desire, above all else, was both most powerful and yet most distant, floating on the edge of my consciousness.

Her lips were a hair's breadth from me, and she spoke again, her voice sultry and low—intimate, like a lover's, her words a creeping echo of my own thoughts. "Have you considered that perhaps it's not me you fear? Yes, I am amoral and passionate, taking what I desire, which frightens you as much as it tempts you. In truth, though, it frightens you because it tempts you. You want to be like me. I know this because I used to be like you. Fighting to follow human rules in a world where the most powerful ignore them altogether.

"Cait, do you know what a black mirror is? Witches, true witches, use them to see beyond or within. Unlike reflective mirrors, black mirrors are a window to the soul.

"I am your black mirror Cait, the villain that lives within the hero you struggle to be. I am the truth within the lie you tell yourself. Look into my eyes and see what you are." I looked up; I couldn't help it, and she gazed into the deepest part of my soul. This time, she wasn't gentle as she intruded upon my thoughts. She was rough and probing. The black tentacles of her power ripped aside my happiest moments to dig at the memories that pained me most, even as she shared horror after horror from her own life.

A memory of Mike screaming at my mother over something inane. That mixed with Nastasia's memories of a small village in Russia as it was overrun by Mongol horsemen. She dug through every horrid moment of my rape at the hands of Sgt. Holley, and it twisted with her own by a man who stank of horses, foul sweat, and rotted teeth.

A million other indignities, large and small, bestowed by

men swirled together until it made no matter whose memory was whose. And I saw a darkly brilliant goddess standing above me, offering me the choice to become the night as I clawed my way, broken and dying from a shallow covering of dirt, filth, and leaves. The mild misandry I'd felt for years blossomed into our shared burning rage against all men. I became her, tearing my way through the horsemen who'd left her for dead. We were vengeance, now given form. She became me tearing the head off of a vampire guard deep within my cell next to the gate chamber, then crying desperately to save Katie, begging for help that would never come. Opening my throat to turn her, praying it worked.

Tears streamed down my face as she clawed away all of my defenses, the walls and deep holes I used to protect my psyche from the things I'd seen in my job and my life—dead children, murdered women, senseless crimes of both passion and premeditation, ending with the pivotal moment of my life that had burned away so much of my sanity, an explosion that ended the life of a child when I pulled a trigger, leaving a blood-soaked marketplace in a desert so very far away.

A choked sob slipped from both of our lips. For the briefest of moments, we were one. Nastasia had seen the darkness within me, a seed ripe with potential for both malignant joy and devastating power. She nurtured that seed as it bloomed into the monster I wanted most to be. A sense of power, confidence, and righteousness that I'd never known grew with it. We were dark angels able to do as we bid without restraint. And I reveled in it. I wanted more. I wanted her.

The depths of her dark eyes burned with the fire of her unbridled passion and ruthlessness. "I know you find me attractive. Don't bother to deny it. And, after all, am I not attractive?" She shrugged from the black shift and lazily hit the switch dousing the table lamp.

In the moonlight, with her flawless skin, like magnificent marble, perfect breasts, and voluptuous figure, she was a succubus of old, both beautiful and enticing, full of sinful promise. Like some errant, corrupt goddess of the moon, cast merely of shadow and light, given the breath of life by the darkness itself, she stood there watching me as my eyes flicked over her body, and I wet my lips in anticipation. Desire flared in my breast as I reached a trembling hand to her face, feeling the cold softness of her cheek, my thumb caressing the line of her bottom lip.

"Yes, my dear. This is what you truly are—a predator, unbound and uncaged. This is what it means." Nastasia's eyes flared as she spoke. "You will always be one of us, Cait. It is your destiny to do what you wish, when you wish, without apology and without remorse."

The fear clutching my chest mixed with an uncontrollable need to close the distance and press her full, red lips to mine, to be as she was. I was so sick of following the rules and getting nothing. What was being human to me, anyway? A rigged system that victimized me over and over. The only justice I'd ever find would be that which I made for myself.

"Fuck it," I whispered with finality. "Let it all burn." And then I slid my hand to the back of Nastasia's neck, pulling her forcefully into a desperate and passionate kiss. Her fangs grazed my lips in a brief, triumphant smile as she crushed her body to mine. She had me, and we both knew it. And I didn't care. I moaned, opening my mouth to admit her tongue, her sin, her power.

She shoved me onto my back, and I moved up the bed, beckoning her with a finger. She followed, pushing me into the mattress, nibbling at my ear, my chin, and my throat. My sweat-soaked hair lay cold against my back as my head sank into the soft, down pillow. An intense thrill of excitement filled me as Nastasia lifted her face from mine and smiled, fangs clear and shining white in the moonlight, eyes alight with lust.

The thought of tasting the ecstasy of her bite erupted into an uncontrollable lust for her. Then Nastasia flooded my thoughts with fear, fear of her, and a desire to let her have me, body and soul. My pulse raced as the delicious taste of terror and dread coursed into me, raising an unstoppable urge to surrender my throat to her. I'd give her anything, do anything. I relaxed, pressing myself into her, letting Nastasia take whatever she wished.

Nastasia's dark demand cut through it all. "That's it, dear. Let it all go."

The fear evaporated, banished by my surrender, but within my deepest soul, I had wanted the fear. I had liked it. I wanted to be afraid of her. I wanted her to own me. "More," I whimpered, begging for the fear to return and heighten my desire like a drug.

"There is no more," she whispered as she bit into my lip with her fangs, drawing droplets of blood that coursed into my throat, salty and warm and full of the succulent copper taste I'd missed so much. I was a vampire to my very core. Deliciously evil thoughts, controlling and manipulative, sang in my head; whether they were mine or born of her glamour, I neither knew nor cared.

I sat up, pressing my face to her milky white skin and luscious breasts. I licked and bit them, tasting the succulent flesh under my teeth and tongue. The torrent of emotions coursing through me was primal and beautiful and genuinely wicked, sinfully vulgar and harsh. I jerked Nastasia violently onto her back and bit her throat, my blunt teeth tearing uselessly at the flesh. She drew her fingernail hard across her carotid, tearing it open in a burst of her blood, which I lapped as the wound closed. The blood was thick and cold, but the salt-copper taste was everything that I remembered, and the hunger rifled down my body like a wave of crawling insects, causing me to arch backward, moaning in an alien swirl of pleasurable discomfort. *God, I missed that.*

"You feel it, don't you?" Nastasia asked with a wicked smile as she placed a hand on my chest, guiding me gently onto my back once more.

I returned her depraved smile with one of my own. "Yes," I whispered with an almost maniacal titter.

Without further foreplay or preamble, Nastasia violently pushed my arms to the bed and laughed. Then she smiled like the demon she was. Her skin was liquid silk as her body caressed mine, sliding lower and tearing away my panties.

She took me in her mouth, licking and nibbling at my labia, then my clit, and pushing her fingers inside me, making me gasp in brutal ecstasy. Never in my life had I taken such pleasure in sex, and its intensity frightened me, causing me to tremble, even as sparks of pleasure rushed through me.

Clawing at Nastasia's hair, fingers digging into her scalp, I moaned, and my body shook, closing so swiftly toward an unbelievable climax. She slowed her pace, drawing out my pleasure, then stopped, causing me to whimper in weak protest.

"Not yet," she breathed as she licked a long line up my body to my throat.

"Yes, I want it," I growled. "Give it to me! Take it all; end it. Make me whole again." I pressed the back of her head, feeling her lips meet the skin of my throat.

Her fangs sunk into me, tearing a heaving gasp from my lungs as pain mixed with unearthly pleasure, and my mind seized with an earth-shattering orgasm that ripped my thoughts asunder, setting a wash of warmth across my entire body and raising every hair. I arched my back, mouth agape in a silent scream, as I clawed desperately at Nastasia's back, drawing long bloody rents in her flesh. Each forceful pull of her consuming draws caused my pulse to stutter as it pounded in my throat. Strangled cries and choking gasps of ecstasy labored their way past my lips as she swallowed all I was, stealing my soul on a river of blood.

My head buzzed as blackness and stars swarmed the edge of my vision. My breathing became overwrought and shallow as my heart slowed, pumping what little blood remained with furious, desperate contractions. Nothing hurt as my hand fell lifeless from her back. The drunkenness of death whispered on my breath.

Nastasia's lips mashed into mine, pushing the warm magic of my transmuted blood into my mouth, forcing it down my throat in the blackest communion. I swallowed and swallowed until I choked and coughed, spewing blood between our pressed lips to slide hot and slick across my chin and cheeks. Still, there was more. I drowned in my own blood as the light and heat of it flooded my every sense bringing a thundering calm.

Nastasia withdrew from my mind, and a gentle quiet took residence in my head as my flesh knitted and the demon fled. The insectile shimmer of the hunger flitted under my skin as bone numbingly cold and peaceful blackness drew me away to enfolding darkness.

I woke an hour or so later to find Nastasia lying beside me, watching me. The lamp was still out. The curtains were still pulled back, admitting the glowing light of the full moon. Every muscle in my body ached as I dragged myself to a sitting position.

"Ë-моё! That was fun," she said as she pulled a glass of orange juice from the nightstand and handed it to me.

"Now, who has the potty mouth," I responded with a bit of a smirk and a touch of snark.

Nastasia giggled, and it came out both cute and seductive, deep and resonant, warm and soft, something I felt almost physically. It caught me off guard and made me laugh as well. Then she asked, "How do you feel?"

I took a long sip before answering, feeling the cold juice travel down my parched throat. "I—I don't know, Nastasia. There was something—" I trailed off for a moment, lost in the maelstrom of emotions, desire, guilt, fear, and something much more intimate and soul-bearing for which I had no name. I jerked myself from the mental spiral.

Nastasia smiled a sweet smile, lacking the cruelty she often displayed. "Call me Anya." She reached over with a languid hand and plucked the orange juice from mine. "Drink it slowly, or it will taint the changed blood."

I didn't argue. I rolled onto my side to face her, resting my head back on the pillow. Damn, vampires were so stunning, especially by the cold white light of the full winter moon. I was in awe of her, drawn to her in a way I'd never been with anyone else. Of course, everything about her was wrong for me. If I fell for her, she'd break my heart or use me until I had nothing left to give, but I was the proverbial moth, blithely flitting nearer and nearer to its inevitable incineration.

As I lay on the blood-soaked sheets, trying to ignore the feeling of it sticking to my body, a thought occurred to me. "Was that true? Were those real memories?"

Nastasia turned away and gazed far away out into the frigid night. "Of course. And I won't lie and say I've never shared them with anyone else, but I knew you would understand."

I'd forgotten the window was open, and I realized I was freezing, but I understood, alright. We'd both been raped. And, whereas she'd been left for dead and I hadn't, the end was the same. We both felt the same rage over what had happened. It occurred to me that if I ever got my hands on Holley, I'd kill him. And it wouldn't be so he couldn't do it again. It would be to avenge myself upon him, just as Nastasia had avenged herself upon the horsemen who'd assaulted her. That feeling had created a bond between us that was beyond the trauma itself. It was a kinship of sorts, an understanding. I wondered, though, if when she'd slaughtered those Mongol horsemen, she had given a moment's thought to the rest of her family that they'd killed, or had it been only to avenge her own brutalization? I realized that I was gaining insight into her mind, and I was intrigued. I also decided that the purity of her motives didn't matter.

"And the creature who came to you, who turned you? What of her?"

Nastasia still stared out the window, refusing to look at me. And I began to believe that maybe she hadn't meant to share so much with me.

"I don't know who she is, honestly. Marcella and I were both made the same way. Neither of us was turned the way we turn others, the way you were turned."

"The dark goddess," I whispered.

"Yes. It seems that Liz, at least, is teaching you something."

My teeth began to chatter, but I was too weak to do much more than pull the covers up.

"Oh, Cait, my apologies. I forgot." Nastasia stood and slowly closed the window and then returned to the bed, pulling me close and sharing my stolen heat with me.

"What are you planning?" I asked lazily as a strange feeling of freedom and self-acceptance sifted through me. It was palpable and pleasurable, raising gooseflesh along my arms.

"Planning?"

"Yes. There are so few of us left, and we're dropping like flies. I also know Liz is on the council to give it an air of legitimacy, but without Marcella, you're the one in charge."

"Well, it's good to see that you've accepted what you are. But I'm only planning what's best for us. With such an existential threat to the council, the protocol is to scatter. But I believe we must stand firm this time and end this threat."

I sighed. "That's not quite what I meant, but please, go on."

Nastasia smirked. "I know what you meant. I have no real plan for you, Cait. Honestly, I'm just enjoying your company."

I looked at her, astonished, my voice rising. "Enjoying my company? You've done nothing but terrorize me for two months now."

She smiled wickedly. "Cait, I was proving a point, one you haven't grasped yet." She took another sip of her blood, swirling the glass about, allowing the thick redness to coat the inside. I licked my lips unconsciously, then shook my head.

"What do you mean? What point?" I pressed my lips together in a thin line, whether to ward off the sudden desire for the blood or in anger over her prevarication; I wasn't sure.

"Cait, darling, every time I saw you, I was doing my dead-level best to make you as afraid of me as possible."

My eyes went wide, and I shot out of the bed, yelling at her. "What? Well, it fucking worked because—"

Nastasia just cocked her head and raised an eyebrow. "No, Cait, it didn't."

"Of course it did. I've been terrified—"

She held up a hand, stopping me again. "No, Cait, it didn't. I am the best of all of us at glamour. No one holds a candle to my abilities. I've had captains of industry, battle-hardened soldiers, and even kings at my feet begging for my forgiveness with just a taste of what I did to you."

"So you're saying what, exactly? I'm immune or something?"

"No, Cait, you're not immune, obviously. You're the most resilient creature I have ever encountered in eight hundred years. Despite all that I did to terrify you, make you afraid, you simply soaked it up and took more. What I told you, just a bit ago, that there was no more. That wasn't a metaphor or mercy. I literally had no more. Fear just isn't an emotion that stops you."

"Well, you certainly stopped me on the floor when we fought. I wanted to kill you, and I was so scared I couldn't pull the trigger."

"No, Cait, that wasn't fear. I literally grabbed ahold of your ability to move, just like I did at the kitchen table a few days later. It was all I could do. I was fucking terrified that you'd actually kill me."

"But it broke me, Anya! It fucking broke me." I sat down on the bed and ultimately moved back under the covers, shivering again. I wasn't going to cry again. I wasn't. Not this time. I furiously blinked back my tears. "My hands shake all the time now. I was scared to be around you." I looked at the ceiling and sniffed, blinking back the threatening tears. "I'm so sick of this. I'm sick of the head games. I just want to have some semblance of normalcy in my life."

Nastasia lowered her voice. "Cait, darling, you are, right now, quite full of shit."

I turned and glared at her. "What?"

"You hate normal. When I came out of the shadows of your room, why didn't you run? Why didn't you protest? Why didn't you say no? You grabbed me and kissed me. Why?"

Any denials died on my lips. "Because I didn't want to say no," I whispered. "Because, despite how fucking evil you are, I wanted you. I wanted this."

"And is that so wrong? Having what you want?"

"But you're—"

She scoffed. "What? Evil? Bad? A vicious meany?" She laughed. "What is evil, Cait? A hundred years ago, a woman who had sex with men as she saw fit was considered evil. Lesbianism was considered absolute witchery. Women were burned at the stake for less.

"I don't kill indiscriminately. I use every resource to protect my own and don't show a lot of mercy when doing it. Is that evil? When men do it to protect nations, they're called heroes and great statesmen. Evil is a four-letter word that only means what society says it does."

"No, that's not true. There are things that are objectively evil."

"Like murdering babies," she said flatly, sounding almost like she agreed.

"Yes, like murdering babies."

"Really? Let's look at your example of objective evil, then, shall we? In my village, a boy was born with two poorly formed arms. After examination by one of the village elders who declared him crippled, his father suffocated him."

I looked up at her, horrified. "Not helping your case," I said with a scowl.

"Really? Consider this. How would that child survive? He couldn't hunt, he couldn't farm, he couldn't wield a weapon. He couldn't contribute at all. Keeping such children alive meant someone would go hungry in the family. Most likely the crippled child. Harsh as it may seem, it was considered mercy, not murder."

"That's horrible." *How could anyone do that to their own child,* I thought. But then I stopped for a moment to consider the reality she described. There were no hospitals, no medical treatments, not even so much as a wheelchair.

"What would be more horrible? Watching him die slowly of starvation? We lived hand to mouth. It was eight hundred years ago. We had no way to help a crippled child. Every mouth had to have strong arms and legs attached to it."

I opened my mouth to say something, but I couldn't think of anything.

Nastasia said, "Maybe if the child had been healthy, I would agree with you. Let me ask you this? Do you blame me for killing the men who destroyed my village?"

Now it was my turn to scoff. "Of course not."

"Only because you think it was justified. Mongols were conquerors, that was their culture, and they considered a raid like that to be a good use of resources. My rape was par for the course. Awful as it may seem, they were probably congratulated after they murdered everyone and raped the women. It wasn't evil to them. But to the victims, like me, they were monsters."

"Are you trying to tell me that it was okay that they raped you?"

"Of course not. But they thought it was just fine. Objective evil is hard to find, Cait. I hate to break this to you, but you have a child's view of morality, and you need to learn that. I can see that you still love as we do, with compassion only for those you truly care for, none for any others."

I thought about the newscast from the Strait of Messina. That was it—the thing I'd been denying all along. I wasn't human anymore, not in the way that counted. I didn't care a lick for strangers.

"Do not worry, Cait. You'll be back in the fold soon enough, just as you were, all fangs and clammy skin. I'm here to make you ready to make the hard decisions. A war is coming between us and pretty much everyone else. How friendly do you think the world will be to Katie when they find out what she is?"

It was one of my worst fears. I was afraid I wouldn't be able to get Katie ready for life on her own soon enough, constantly hoping she would gain enough control and self-possession to gird her against her revenant-like moments.

"But, not to worry, Cait. We will come out on top."

I looked at her askance. "It sounds like you have a plan."

"I do. I plan to consolidate us in more open-minded cities, London, Dublin, Boston, Seattle, Vancouver, Munich, and Capetown. We will then go public, campaigning for 'human rights.' Conservative countries will fear us. Liberal countries will want to protect us. It's an old story. We will play on the appeal of social justice and set humans against each other for our benefit.

"More authoritarian countries will rail against us, but they want us for what we can do and what we know. Such countries are easy to control from the shadows. If Schmidt had been anything but a bean counter, Germany of the late thirties would have been his to command. In the end, we win, no matter who is in charge. It's as simple as that."

"Holy shit," I whispered.

"In the meantime, I'll be moving around a bit." She stopped and gulped down the rest of her blood. I licked my lips as a tremor ran down my spine. She had a drop of blood still perched precariously on the edge of her bottom lip. I leaned in without thought and licked it off, then pulled back, slightly horrified at my own action.

She smiled a smile that seemed to say, 'I told you so.' Then she continued. "I've selected a half dozen candidates around the United States that I need to evaluate and see if they are worthy of turning. We need desperately to increase our numbers. Schmidt also believed this, but he was haphazard and stupid about it. He selected people he felt he could control, people who would be so grateful to be turned to escape bad relationships or dire personal circumstances that they would worship him. He wanted lackeys, not true vampires. And, unfortunately, I wouldn't call any of them 'stable geniuses.'

"I suppose I'll have to clean up his mess. Then I'll be looking for a more select group to start. And no more men. Men should be locked in cages and let out when someone needs a pickle jar opened."

I laughed at that. She didn't, raising an eyebrow instead.

"Men," she said, "are self-indulgent children who do not deserve our power. They start wars, rape, intimidate, and manipulate. They lie without concern for whom they hurt. Let the werewolves have them if they want. I will, as you say, take a hard pass. In the meantime, Detective Reagan, you need to get some sleep. You are worthless as it is. We don't need you unable to function."

I laughed at the light-hearted insult and rolled over, closing my eyes. Nastasia, or Anya rather, spooned up behind me, placing a warm arm across my midsection. She stroked my hair in an almost motherly gesture.

I woke in the dark sometime later, rolling over, feeling the vacant space in the soft sheets. Nastasia was gone. It had been a one-night stand, after all.

I felt strange about it, the empty place in the bed. A violent twisting of unmanageable emotion swirled in the reminiscence of last night's masochistic delight. Between the forced sharing of our respective trauma, the pounding fear and hopelessness I'd felt, and my imploring Nastasia to make it worse, I was lost. In the end, I'd felt so small and helpless, waiting for her to have her way with me, and not once had I asked her to stop. Instead, I'd begged her to push me further into abject terror and kill me. In a deep, very dark, very secret part of me, the part that I was terrified to explore, I wanted to be like her. I shuddered slightly at the thought, but there it was. She had been right all along.

Her sheer nightgown had revealed her voluptuous body and, it seemed, her solicitous purpose in coming to my room. But she'd had another less fathomable reason beyond sex and blood. And while it occurred to me that Nastasia's hatred of Marcella had fueled some petty desire to take what Marcella had possessed, my gut told me that wasn't why. Whatever her reasons, our coupling had made it clear that I was part of a group of apex predators, far more capable and powerful than any human. The vampire I had been still lived within me, and it wanted out.

'You're becoming like them,' Carlos had said when I'd glamoured Special Agents Reese and Reynolds. I hadn't felt a shred of guilt about overpowering them or how easy it had been. I still didn't. Instead, I felt an intense satisfaction. My intent had been thoroughly corrupt by human standards, making them forget that vampires existed and interfering with a federal investigation. By my accounting, though, I wasn't so sure. What were they to me, two men who thought their jobs made them superior? What made them more righteous than us, other than the dictates of human law? The more I thought about it, the more enraged I felt about how they'd cornered me, thinking themselves capable of strong-arming me. *Fuck them and the men they worked for,* I thought. *If they wanted me to be a villain, I could be one.*

I was certainly no worse than the men that Anya hated so much, leaders who sacrificed countless lives in service to ridiculous religious causes, their own malignant narcissism, or both. Being a vampire was so much more straightforward, purer somehow. Anya's sentiment about doing as we pleased without remorse and without restraint turned over in my mind. *I am far more like Anya than Marcella,* I thought. And that thought frightened me, yet again, not because I felt any kind of regret but because it gave me a strange, intense sense of giddy, malicious delight. A deep-rooted part of me wanted to be the monster, the thing they feared in the night.

CHAPTER TWENTY-TWO

My skin burns, and the bees buzz beneath it as I curl into the corner. The cell looks familiar, like the one under Elliot Norton Park, yet it is not. A thin blade of light slides under the metal door. My senses are beyond heightened, and the light burns my eyes. There is a guard outside; I can taste his sweat and fear drifting in the air. It is beyond disgusting. Underneath that stench, though, I catch the scent of his blood, like a mixture of copper and salt, bustling its way lightly through the reeking mildew of this concrete box. My arm is once again scarred and trapped inside the horrid cuff. I pull experimentally. There should be a stabbing pain, but there is nothing but a vague tugging sensation in my skin.

The hunger returns, keening through my head like a gale, as I stand on wobbly, tired legs and bang the dented steel door with bare knuckles, breaking my gaunt, brittle fingers. I feel nothing but desperate need. My animal screams echo through the cell, heard, certainly, but unanswered. I no longer know how long I have been here. A week? A month? A year?

My hair is no longer beautiful; it is dry, white and strawlike, and sickeningly thin. Only a few waxy threads dangle from my scalp.

My thoughts venture through the door, trying to glamour the guard outside, but his mind is a slippery thing, all self-indulgence and narcissism, oily and disgusting. Without contact, I cannot drive to his core and influence his thoughts. Yet his surface thoughts of sex and food and sports waft to me. Disgusting.

I bang the door again and growl in frustration, finally returning to the corner where I've been sitting for what seems like an eternity. My arms wrap weakly around my chest in desperation and hopelessness. If only I hadn't sought to save her from herself. If only I hadn't rejected her. If only I hadn't tried to control everything. If only.

Regret was something I long thought myself beyond. It doesn't matter, though. I have no more tears to offer. Would, though, that I had a river of them, then perhaps I might give proper homage to the vastness of my sorrow.

I stifle a wail of misery as a shudder runs through me, and the hunger crawls up my flesh once more.

The door opens. I expect to see Katie, but they toss in a man, old and decrepit and gaunt. By his smell and his clothing, he's a transient. His tanned skin is cracked and dried. He kicks away from me to the other side of the cell on torn feet with caked yellow toenails.

I try to resist, but I know this game. They'll feed me to sate the hunger and then try to break me with starvation. It'll do them no good. I am too old for petty torments like this. The worst tortures are in your mind. This is nothing by comparison. I've been through worse. So much worse.

I latch onto the man's will, calming his fear. At least he will not die in terror. He will feel peace before the end, that much I promise myself. I draw him to me, stripping away all of his emotions. I have no choice. I recognize the man, though. His name is Daryl, Daryl Cummins. Shit. Those bastards. How did they know? It makes no difference. I may be lost, but I will give them nothing.

"Marcella!" I cried into the darkened room. For a moment, the hunger prickled through me, and my vision swam, but then it subsided. My breath heaved through my aching ribs and all of my limbs hurt. And I was starving. A low cloud cover had closed over the city, shrouding the tallest buildings in a thick orange acetylene-lit fog. A soft, miserable drizzle fell from the sky as bare mournful trees swayed in the wind and a middling breeze swept past my window. After my terrifying revelation about myself and Anya, I found the weather depressing, and it pulled me back to everything I didn't want to think about like an impossible weight.

"Mama?"

I turned to find Katie standing in the doorway, holding Vlad, her little stuffed vampire bat. Jabba walked around her legs, rubbing up against them. I wiped the sweat from my brow and pulled back a smear of blood on my hand.

"Yes, darling. I'm sorry. Mama just had a nightmare. What can I do for you?"

"Can I sleep in your bed today?" Katie asked sweetly. "Also, Auntie Liz is in the kitchen. She wants to talk to you." She sniffed the air. "That's your blood." It wasn't a question.

"Yes, dear, it is," I replied as I got up and stripped the bed. I washed the blood off of me with a wet rag and put down fresh sheets, stuffing last night's linens in the laundry hamper.

Katie's expression turned horrifying, full of unbridled rage. Her fangs extended, and her eyes grew brutal and cruel. "Did Nastasia hurt you?"

"No, baby, it was my choice." I coughed, and my chest muscles spasmed in pain.

"Oh, well, that's okay then." Katie's expression shifted back to her cherubic smile like flipping a switch, which was probably even more terrifying to anyone who didn't know her.

"Let me go see what Auntie Liz wants."

Katie giggled. "Um, mama, you're still naked."

I looked down at myself and immediately tried to cover up, totally embarrassed. "Turn around, baby, while I put some clothes on."

"Mama, I've seen you naked before. Remember, you had to wash up when Schmidt had us. Besides, I'm sixteen; I know what a naked woman looks like."

I sighed and got dressed. She was right, of course. She was almost a woman. I tended to forget that she wasn't a little girl; she never would be. That thought stuck in my craw. She deserved a normal childhood, not one full of abuse and misery. Guilt gnawed at me, but I brushed it aside. Right now, she was better off.

"Okay, get comfortable," I said as I stood in the doorway. "I'll be back before sunrise. I'll even tell you the story of Queen Medb if you're still up."

"And Cú Chulainn?"

I smiled at that. "You remembered. Good girl."

"Don't worry, mama. I'll wait. I've been practicing. If I want to go to school, I'll need to learn to stay up and manage myself."

School? I hadn't even thought that far ahead. I just wanted to keep her safe for now. But, I supposed, given her needs for socialization, we'd have to figure that out at some point. As I left and headed to the Kitchen, I thought I understood how most parents felt about their children. I'd die for Katie, simple as that, not because she was beautiful, or intelligent, or even sweet. She was all of those things, most of the time, anyway. It was because she was mine. Something had happened in the last two months. I'd started as Katie's caretaker, and I had truly become her mother. I loved her more than life itself.

As I stepped out of the elevator, a sickening sense of dread rose in my stomach. Somehow, I just knew Liz would say something about my night with Nastasia. I found Liz sitting at the table, working on her laptop.

"Fun night last night?" She asked, stopping her work and looking up as I padded in on bare feet.

I rolled my eyes, deciding honesty was best and taking a moment to gather my thoughts. "It was—confusing. How was the hunt?"

"Oh, it went swimmingly. Quite the little predator we've raised. She doesn't fool about, you know? As adults, we tend to target people looking to get laid. It makes things easiest. But Katie, she goes after whoever suits her fancy and drains them damn near to death before giving them changed blood. More efficient, she says. She doesn't even give them a moment to recover before glamouring it all away." Liz sounded both impressed and proud. And, to be honest, I understood. Liz and I had both been turned intact, complete with memories and regrets, and guilt. Katie had no memory except that of being a vampire. For her, it was just dinner time. People were people, and Katie saw them that way, but she was a true innocent. She had no morals and, like all vampires, only carried empathy for those she loved. At the moment, it didn't bother her that someone might die during feeding any more than I felt remorse for a delicious cannoli.

"She said you wanted to talk. What about? Not last night, I hope."

Liz frowned. "Not really, but since you bring it up. Do you know what you're doing?"

I sighed, grabbing more orange juice and dropping into a chair next to her. "No, Liz, I don't. It wasn't like that. Anya showed up in my room and was very persuasive." I didn't want to get into the details; somehow, I didn't feel Liz would appreciate it.

"Anya?" Liz raised her eyebrows. "My, my, she must like you. She doesn't even let me call her that."

I ignored the comment. "I'm sorry."

"Sorry? Whatever for? We're not attached. You don't need to apologize to me for anything, Cait. I just want to make sure you understand what you're getting into." She talked a good game, but her eyes were tight. She was upset.

"Getting into? It was a one-night stand. But it was—" I was at a loss for words. "She shared things with me. She showed me things. And I—" For a moment, I was overwhelmed.

"Cait, you need to be careful. Nastasia never does anything without reason. She's calculating in the extreme. I've told you that. Everything she did or said last night was designed for a purpose."

I swirled the remainder of the juice in my glass, watching the bubbles spin around the edge as despondency set in. "I'm becoming like her, Liz. I can feel it. There's this darkness in me, and she brought it to the surface in a way I didn't think possible."

Liz turned away from her spreadsheets, took my face in her hands, and spoke gently. "No, love, you're not becoming like Nastasia. Yes, there is darkness in you. I have seen it, that deep rage you carry with you. But you also have love for others and people who love you. Nastasia has none of that, and there's a good reason. She snuffed out her own light a long time ago."

I sighed heavily and ran a hand through my hair. "Can I ask you something?"

"You just did, dear," Liz said with a pert grin.

"Do you think I make a better vampire than a human?"

Liz paused, carefully sizing me up before she answered. I could almost see the wheels turning in her head as she judged my mental state. "Cait, how shall I put this? You are a phenomenal vampire, strong and sometimes ruthless yet compassionate beyond the norm. You have a genius intellect. That is clear. You're courageous, sometimes to the point of recklessness, but it always seems to work out.

"Most importantly, though, despite your protestations, you like being a vampire, and you know it. Your fear of being turned again comes from your lack of trust in yourself, not in any of the human trappings you complain about, the food, the sweaty workouts, and all that rubbish. From what Marcella told me, you took to feeding like the proverbial duck to water. Was she wrong?"

I shook my head as gooseflesh rose on my arms, and I flushed slightly. "Hardly, that had been easy, and I'd enjoyed it."

"And, yes, you're a shitty human. You hate being a human. I know you do." She raised a hand to forestall my burgeoning objections. "You wouldn't have asked otherwise. Now, are you asking because Nastasia made you think you weren't?"

"God, no. Just the opposite, and I've been considering—"

"Ah." Liz smiled wickedly then. "Well, when you decide you want to be turned again, you be sure to let me know first."

I snorted in amusement. "Oh, no doubt. I certainly wouldn't let Nastasia do it, and one of the baby vamps might kill me."

"Enough philosophy, though. So," Liz's eyebrows waggled suggestively, "How was it?"

I flushed furiously. No matter how much I tried to square in my mind that Liz was three hundred years old and had very likely, no, definitely, heard it all, I was still embarrassed. Besides, I still didn't know how I felt about it. "As I said, it was confusing. I really don't want to get into it. Nastasia got inside my head pretty hard."

"Well, I'm sorry, then. Sex should be something you enjoy, not something full of head games." She looked me in the eye rather pointedly then. "Perhaps she's just not the right partner for you."

I twisted my mouth into a wry smile. "You know, I had this worry that you might be jealous."

Liz's demeanor shifted abruptly, a brief frown forming at the corners of her mouth. "I won't say I'm not surprised. I thought I was more your type, and I am probably a tad jealous, but we've made no promises to each other, so who you sleep with is your business, and no one should judge you for that." Then she smiled playfully. "Except me, of course. I'm judging you quite harshly." She turned to the laptop, pretending to be aloof, striking a haughty tone. "Nastasia, indeed. So sad." Then she clucked her tongue.

I laughed as she gave me a sidelong glance and smiled, thankful she'd broken the tension. "So, what was it you wanted to talk about? I want to get back to Katie before the sun comes up."

Liz looked back up at me. "Just that we'll be going through Schmidt's files tonight, so try not to be overworked when you get home. It'll likely be a long night."

"As if there's any other kind living with vampires." On a sudden whim, I walked over, leaned in close and kissed Liz on the cheek, and cupped her face. "You're a good friend, Liz. I don't know what I'd do without you." I held that pose for a moment longer than I intended, looking into her fabulous green eyes. I wanted to kiss her lips, but I relented and turned for the elevator. At the door, I paused, turning back. "Liz?"

"Hmmm?" She was back to her spreadsheets.

"Can I ask? If Marcella is so powerful, how did Schmidt capture her?"

"She let herself get captured so that she could rescue you. But, Cait, we're not invincible. You know that. In the daylight hours, we're not helpless, but—" The comment trailed off, and Liz looked up from her computer. "Why do you ask?"

"Just working on a theory for my case." It was a lie, but only a small one.

I trudged back upstairs, almost falling from the elevator as it opened. I was exhausted. Nastasia had taken far too much blood. Then she had given so much of it back, so much so that I'd woken to her drinking the bagged stuff. It made no sense.

As I entered my room, I blew out an exasperated breath, emotionally confused and dog-tired. Katie lay in my bed, curled up around Vlad, eyes closed. I lay down beside her, and she moved to put her head on my shoulder. She was surprisingly warm, the previous night's feeding still running through her body. Part of me felt sorry for her, being stuck at sixteen for the rest of her life.

On the other hand, I'd noticed that I wasn't recovering from my workouts as quickly as I used to, and having those sixteen years back didn't seem so bad. At least vampires, even adolescents, didn't have to deal with puberty. God, an eternity of hormones running through you like that would suck.

"What did Auntie Liz want?" Katie asked as I closed my eyes.

"To pry into my business, what else."

Katie giggled. "She heard you two up here when we walked in. She was so pissed, mama. You should have seen her pacing around downstairs."

I turned over to face her. "Who was she pissed at?"

Katie yawned a very vampire-like yawn, fangs and all. "I don't know. She kept mumbling about stupid Cait and that bitch, Nastasia. That's all I heard before I went to go watch TV."

I snorted a laugh. "Really? Huh. That's not like her."

"Says you." Katie sat up and looked at me. "Mama, for being such a good Detective, you really don't have a clue."

I wondered what she meant by that but decided to let it go. "I've been told that before. Now lay back down. The sun will be up in a moment."

Katie did as I asked and lay her head in the crook of my arm. Moments later, a sliver of harsh winter sunlight slid through a gap between the curtains, and Katie was dead to the world. I took a moment to adjust the curtains, then returned to bed to get some more rest. It took a while, but I finally fell back to sleep.

CHAPTER TWENTY-THREE

Work sucked. I was exhausted most of the day. Every muscle in my body still hurt, and I couldn't stop thinking about Nastasia. The war of emotions was almost palpable. One minute I was stuck in the memory of her bite, and the next, I was drowning in the terror she pushed into my mind. The horrible memories and trauma we'd shared blended within it all, shading it in a terrible dark stain. And God, the desire I felt to be a proper vampire again, powerful and ruthless, horrific and fearsome, it was almost more than I could handle and still get anything done. It wasn't until early evening before I could pull myself back together and put it out of my mind.

"Hey there, Kitty Cait."

I looked up at Morgan. She was leaning against my cube wall and eating an apple. "Will you stop calling me that at work, please?"

She grinned. "Sure, as soon as we have dinner. Remember?"

I hadn't forgotten. I'd just been so fucking busy I hadn't had time to think about it. "Yeah. Fine. Wait, aren't you supposed to be watching what's his name?"

"He's asleep, and Freyer took this shift. He gave me half the day off. I thought I might convince you to do the same. You should know the BOLO on your suburban hasn't turned up much. So far, we've only pulled over three limo drivers.

Except, and I take great joy in this, I personally had the pleasure of pulling over Agent Schaeffer. You should have seen her face, all red and angry. It was cute. She badged me, and I let her go, but I fucked with her a bit first."

I laughed, then looked at my desk. I wasn't getting anything done anyway. I looked at my watch. It had just turned six. "Fuck it." I stood and put my arm in Morgan's. "Let's grab dinner. Meet me at my place around eight."

Morgan smirked. "Our reservation is for nine, so that'll be perfect."

I shook my head and laughed. "See you in an hour and a half." Something awful, though, roiled in the pit of my stomach. Guilt.

I shooed Jabba off the bed. "No, no. Get away from there. No fur on my dress." The little furball was just about to plop down on my evening gown. It was a cute little thing, a calf-length, spaghetti-strapped midi of black charmeuse that hugged every curve, not that I had a lot of them, but that was the trade-off for building up so much muscle mass. Next to it sat a pair of Louboutin medieval torture devices disguised as patent leather heels. Next to those sat two flesh-colored bandaids for my feet, because they weren't broken in. My feet were going to be miserable, but that was the price of fashion. I was trying to decide if I should go with a pair of lower heels when Liz walked in.

"What's all this?"

I looked over at Liz. "I'm going on a date tonight. I think it'll take my mind off of things. I'm thinking of wearing this."

"A date." Liz looked skeptical. "With whom? Anyone I know? Please tell me it's not the bouncy one."

"No, I'm not going on a date with Doyle. She's too young for me, anyway. I'm going out with Morgan."

Liz put her hands on her hips. "Wait, you're going out with the girl who dumped you ten years ago for some cowboy in Montana? Correct me if I'm wrong, but I thought she broke your heart."

I stopped fussing with the dress and turned to look at Liz fully, lips pursed. She'd been all atwitter when we'd opened Morgan's letters two months ago, but now she sounded—I didn't know what she sounded like, but she didn't sound terribly supportive. "Okay, Medlyn, spit it out. What's wrong?"

"Wrong?" Liz asked with an almost petulant tone. "Why nothing? Unless, of course, you count the fact that you've been hung up on this girl for ten years, even after she dumped you for some bloke. I just don't want to see you get hurt. That's all."

I squinted. It was a lie. "Well, thank you for the concern, but I'm all grown up now. I can manage my own heart. Besides, you said we're not attached, and no one should judge me for who I date."

Liz rolled her eyes and walked over, stepping deep into my space, almost nose to nose. "Cait, I know I said that. But she just showed up, and already you're going to dinner. Maybe you should spend some time with her first, coffee or something, see if she's how you remember, you know? Also, your lifestyle isn't really conducive to dating a mundane."

Her proximity made me flush, and I backed up a step. "A mundane? Wow. It's just dinner, Liz. It's not like we're going to hook up."

She raised a delicately shadowed eyebrow at that. "Oh, really? Just dinner, huh? So that's why you have a pair of Marcella's six-hundred dollar heels sitting there?"

"Those are my heels."

"That Marcella bought for you, and you've never worn."

I crossed my arms over my chest. "Okay, what the hell is going on? I figured you'd be happy for me. Are you jealous?"

"No, but I'll be happy when you're with someone who appreciates you." Liz shifted gears suddenly, turning all smiles, which was even more disturbing than—than whatever this was. "I just hope Ms. Kennedy is worthy of you."

"Liz! What is going on with you?"

Liz didn't answer. She just smiled and stalked out of the

room. I didn't know why I had bothered to ask that; I knew exactly what was going on, and I felt like shit about it. Did I know what I was doing?

I hung up the dress and set the ridiculous heels next to it. It was seven o'clock. Morgan wouldn't be there until eight, so I had an hour before I had to be ready. I headed down to the kitchen. Katie sat sipping blood and working on her math homework.

"How's it going?" I asked.

"Fine," she answered flatly, not even looking up.

"Hey, what's wrong?" I reached over and took her hand.

"It's Aunt Liz. She's acting weird. She was just down here giving me grief about studying without enough light."

I tilted my head and laughed. "What? But you're a vampire, honey. You can see in the dark. You can't ruin your eyes."

"Like I said, weird." Katie closed her book. "Can I ask you a question, mama?"

"Of course, honey, anything." I waited patiently as she seemed to think about how to ask. "Okay, just spit it out, honey. What is it?"

"Um, what's a ginger bitch?"

I blinked. "I'm sorry? What?"

"I said—"

"I heard what you said. I'm just confused. Where'd you hear that?"

"Aunt Liz said it, just a few minutes ago."

My eyebrows shot up. "What else did Aunt Liz say?"

Katie looked around. "Well—"

"Katie!" Liz snapped from the doorway. "Those were my private thoughts and not for public consumption."

I turned on Liz. "Don't snap at her like that. And if it's so private, don't flap your gums in front of our daughter." My stomach sank suddenly, realizing what I'd just said, and my hand flew to my mouth. I'd said, 'our daughter.' It wasn't wrong, Liz was spending as much time raising Katie as I was, probably more, but for Liz, the idea of having another daughter was too painful for her to consider. It was why she'd insisted on Katie calling her 'Auntie Liz' rather than Mama Liz and me, Mama Cait. The last time I'd said something to that effect, Liz had just burst into tears and run off to her room. After three hundred years, she was still traumatized by the deaths of her children. It had been the hunger, and it wasn't her fault, but she still blamed herself. "Oh, Liz, I'm sorry."

But Liz didn't react the way I expected. She didn't look upset or even angry. She looked uncertain, like she wanted to say something but didn't know how.

I stalked over and took her by the shoulders. "Liz, honey, do you want me to cancel? I can. It's okay."

"No, go on your date, have fun. I'm just in a bad mood. I'll be okay." She shrugged me off and headed to the elevator. I had half a mind to cancel anyway. I wasn't all that thrilled with this idea anymore.

"Like I said, weird," Katie repeated from the table.

The doorbell rang at seven-forty-five while I was still getting ready. *Shit, Morgan's early.* Liz had already answered it before I could finish putting in my other earring. The gnawing feeling of guilt in the pit of my stomach hadn't diminished, and something told me that I couldn't leave the two of them alone. More specifically, I couldn't leave Morgan alone with Liz. Liz was jealous. That much was apparent, despite what she said.

My earring in, I hurried to the elevator, not an easy task in four-inch heels, opting to exit on the second floor so I could see them. I reached the edge of the gallery wall, just before the handrail, and heard Liz's voice. So I peeked around the wall into the foyer below, hoping Liz hadn't noticed my approach.

Liz had Morgan backed against the foyer wall next to the door and was leaning in closely, intimidatingly so. I should have gone down there and rescued her, but I wanted to hear what was happening. I wanted to know how far Liz might go and how Morgan would react to her. Maybe it was wrong, but I felt I needed to see this.

"I can see why she likes you," Liz was saying. "You're pretty, strong, and have excellent taste in clothing." I grinned.

Liz wasn't wrong, not at all. Morgan was dressed in a custom-cut and mildly masculine black suit and a tastefully open white blouse, the collar of which Liz fingered as she spoke. A black wool coat lay on the floor next to them.

Though her back was to the wall, Morgan stood toe to toe with Liz and eye to eye. She didn't appear intimidated, wearing the cocky smirk she always did. "Um, thanks, I guess. Are you always this aggressive with Cait's friends?"

"Only the ones who might break her heart. Again," Liz replied, placing a hand on the wall and sidestepping, giving Morgan a little more room to breathe. It was a gesture meant to simultaneously give Morgan room and carry her just a bit closer in. Liz was playing with her. I frowned. This was not cool. But I couldn't bring myself to interrupt them, not yet.

Morgan didn't play into Liz's game. She stepped around Liz, placing herself between Liz and the door, guarding her exit. "Look, I don't know what you two have going, but we're just going out to dinner as friends. At this point, I don't have any intentions. But if I did, that would be between Cait and me." Then she added, with more than a bit of snark, "Three's a crowd. You know?"

I suppressed a snort. Fair play to you, Red.

"Going? We don't have anything going, but she's my friend, and I want to make sure you treat her right. Cait's had her feelings hurt many times, and I care what happens to her. Ride or die, you know?"

I jerked slightly at the sentiment, bumping the railing. Liz immediately moved back away from Morgan and turned languidly toward me. The jig was up, as they say, and I walked down the stairs, praying not to fall and break my neck in the ridiculous heels and long dress.

Morgan whistled. "Wow, Cait! You look fabulous."

I blushed. Liz, for her part, walked over and held out a hand at the last stair, helping me down. "She's right, Cait. You look lovely."

My blush deepened, and I was starting to feel self-conscious at all the attention. "Okay, you two, quit." I looked up into Liz's eyes for a moment. Even in the heels, I was still an inch short. "I won't be too late. We're just going to grab a bite to eat. There's a new French restaurant over in Back Bay." I looked around for Katie. I wanted to introduce her to Morgan. "Um, where'd Katie go?"

Liz gave me a guilty glance. "Probably swimming. She went down to see Kaja and Gretchen."

"Okay." I pursed my lips in annoyance. She'd sent Katie out on purpose. I wasn't going to argue about it in front of Morgan, though. "Ready?" I asked, walking toward the door and pulling Morgan along.

"Yup." She opened the door.

"Don't stay up too late," I joked as we walked out. Liz didn't even laugh.

"What's wrong with her?" Morgan said as we closed the door.

I put a finger to my mouth, saying nothing until we were safely in her car and on the road. "I don't know. She's been off since I got home last night. I have no idea what's in her craw. But you should know that vampires can hear and pick out conversations across a crowded bar with little to no effort, so she certainly heard you at the door."

Morgan pressed her lips together in irritation as we drove. The rest of the trip was spent in an icy silence that I didn't understand. Morgan gripped the steering wheel with white knuckles and blasted the horn at a few slow drivers along the way, taking the turns increasingly hard.

"Jesus, Morgan, slow down, will you? We have plenty of time."

She ignored me and downshifted as she pulled onto Storrow, weaving in and out of traffic. Fortunately, it was only another five minutes before we pulled into a street spot near the restaurant.

Before we got out, I put my hand on Morgan's arm. It was shaking. I wanted to ask if she was okay but thought better of it, waiting instead for her to speak. Instead, she let go of the steering wheel and looked at me with a tight smile that didn't reach her eyes.

"Come on, Kitty Cait. Let's eat. I'm starved." For just a

moment, as she exited the vehicle, she reminded me of Gabe, the way he would harness his lousy mood, holding it deep inside until it popped, and I had a sudden urge to tell her to get back in and take me home, but I didn't. Instead, I got out and followed to the restaurant.

Like most eateries in Back Bay, this one lay nestled in the basement of a three-story brownstone that served as a restaurant below, a clothing store above, and condos above that. On entry, the hostess greeted us in French, which I returned, much to Morgan's annoyance. When Morgan mentioned our reservation, the hostess found it swiftly and escorted us to our table. And there we sat, in uncomfortable silence, sipping at our waters.

I breathed an almost audible sigh of relief when the server came to take our drink orders. Morgan ordered a scotch, and I ordered a dirty vodka martini with blue-cheese olives. Then we sat and stared at each other again. I waited for Morgan to tell me what was wrong. But she didn't. She continued to watch me. Her jaw was working harder than a bench grinder.

When our drinks arrived, I took a sip of mine, and, unable to stand this bullshit any longer, I said, "I'm pretty certain Liz knew I was upstairs while you were talking, so that was probably her just showing off."

Morgan's jaw dropped open. Then she knocked back the rest of her scotch, raising her finger for another to the server as she passed by. "You left me down there with her on purpose?" Her tone was distrustful and accusing. The emerald of her eyes no longer looked lustrous and sparkling. They were hard, like jagged, piercing things that stabbed recrimination at me. "Jesus, Cait, she had me backed up against the wall. What the fuck?"

I was completely taken aback. I had obviously misjudged the situation, but I didn't understand where all the hostility came from. "You were holding your own. You certainly looked fine. I—"

Morgan's second scotch arrived, but she didn't sip it either. She snatched it up and knocked it back.

"For God's sake, Morgan, slow down. What is wrong?"

Morgan squinted and then leaned forward, hissing loudly, her temper long lost. "What's wrong? What's wrong? Your roommate is a vampire, and she's jealous that we're going out. That's what's wrong. She terrified me."

I recoiled. "Morgan, please, calm down—"

"Don't tell me to calm down," she yelled, launching to her feet and knocking over her chair. "I tried to play it cool, but before you got down there, she pressed in so close I could smell the blood on her breath. How can you live with that? Aren't you afraid she'd kill you one night in a fit of anger? And the smell of blood—"

I stared at her wide-eyed. "Please lower your voice. Why are you screaming at me?"

"Because—" she sputtered, red-faced, unable to force out any more words.

I kept my voice carefully level. "Morgan, I just said that I didn't realize that Elizabeth scared you. Please stop yelling at me. This was supposed to be our opportunity to get to know each other again. Besides, this isn't like you."

Morgan reined in her temper slightly and picked up her chair. Then she sat. Finally, she continued her rant, lowered to a dull roar this time, at least. "Cait, how do you know what's like me? We haven't seen each other in ten years. Of course, I've changed in that time. What did you think?" She turned to look at me more fully, eyes cold and penetrating. "Did you think that, after ten years, it would be just like old times? Two closeted dykes sitting on a Humvee looking at the stars, wondering if they were really in love? Afraid everyone would know?"

"No—I just—"

"Or maybe you thought I'd be so enraptured at seeing you again after the shit I just went through in Chicago that I'd want to hop in the sack and see how it goes?"

This wasn't the way it was supposed to go. I knew I'd had unrealistic expectations. Who didn't when meeting their first love again after so long? But the person across from me was a complete stranger, rage-filled and frightening, and I didn't know how to react, so I stared down at my bread plate, trying to figure out what to say. When I looked up, she was gone. I caught a glimpse of her retreating form storming out the restaurant door.

"Fuck," I muttered to myself and took a long sip of my martini, blinking back threatening tears. I wasn't going to cry over this shit. I hadn't done anything. I thought, *If Morgan can't handle my life, then fuck her.* Then I swallowed the rest of my drink and nearly choked on one of the olives.

As I spit the offending lamiale into my napkin, a velvety soft, vampire-cool hand came to rest on my left shoulder, and an arm brushed my right as another milky, white feminine hand offered me a handkerchief monogrammed with the initials HB in Cyrillic. Her soft words almost brought me to tears. "Are you alright, дорогая?"

I slapped my napkin to the table. "Of course not. I assume you saw all of that."

"Some of it. I only just walked in," Nastasia said as she moved around the table. "She doesn't seem to like us very much, I'm afraid." My breath hitched. She was in a deep red evening gown. A short blond woman in a ladies' cut tuxedo stood next to her. "I promise, Cait. I wasn't following you. It's not like I don't know where to find you if I need to—" Her voice trailed off with a wicked smile. Before, I probably would have been terrified or annoyed at the innuendo. Now I just snorted and shook my head.

"Miss, is everything okay?" The server had approached while Nastasia and I had been chatting. She had a concerned look on her face. "Do you need anything?"

I nodded and ordered another martini. Meanwhile, Nastasia whispered something in her companion's ear, and her tuxedo-clad 'friend' meandered to the bar.

"So, just like that, you're abandoning your date?" I asked, half-listening to the encouraging chutch-chutch-chutch of a martini shaker, my mouth practically watering for another drink.

"It's not like that. We're just friends. Not even, just acquaintances, really. It's a game of giving and taking. I'm sure you understand."

I understood perfectly. She was Nastasia's snack for the evening. "Consensual, I assume?" I asked flatly, now leaning back in my chair like the gorilla I was, one leg splayed out of the slit in my dress extended from under the table.

Nastasia scrunched up her face at the question but ignored it. "So, what was that all about? I only heard the last few words."

"A girl I knew as a kid. Kind of my first love. She works in the department now. This was supposed to be a date. You can see how it turned out. Liz scared the shit out of her, on purpose, I might add. I'm gonna stake her ass when I get home." Nastasia snorted in amusement, then laughed out loud before an odd woman approached our table, dressed in a three-piece suit with an impeccably tied double-Windsor at her throat. By her look, I suspected she was the manager or maîtresse d'hotel.

"Ms. Volkova, welcome back." She looked down at me, frowning, probably at my posture. Yes, definitely my posture. I knew this because she didn't stop staring until I sat up nice and ladylike. I thought to curse her mentally with a nice bitch or whore, but I didn't because my mother would have had the same reaction if she'd seen me sitting like that. "Would you like your usual?"

Nastasia smirked. "One Carson Special, please. And one for my compatriot, as well." At the maîtresse's puzzled expression, Nastasia added, "Just a bit of an experiment. Not to worry, she's safe."

"Very well, madame," the maîtresse replied and sped off.

My martini arrived a moment later, and I guzzled about half of it. I'd had enough of shitty nights, and I had decided that I was going to—intentionally this time—get thoroughly piss drunk. "So that you know, Nastasia. If you're sticking around, you're gonna be the one who has to take me home because it's either you or Lyft tonight. I'm going to get, as my mother would say, ar stealladh meisce—dead ass drunk."

"Perhaps you should eat something first, Cait." Nastasia didn't look at all concerned. As a matter of fact, she looked positively giddy at having caught me at a vulnerable moment.

Her face bordered between haughtily amused and almost affectionate, which made me feel none encouraged, nor did the pitter-patter of my heartbeat as I thought about what I might like to do to her. The pleasant warm buzz of alcohol finally began to set in, making my cheeks flush and my mind wander down naughty, dark paths.

"Are you even listening?" Nastasia said, pulling me from my now tipsy thoughts.

"Huh?"

Before Nastasia could repeat herself, the maîtresse returned with two dark crystal goblets, one of which she set in front of me. I raised an eyebrow at the immediate tang of blood that assaulted my nose. Nastasia raised her glass and drank.

My fingers worked involuntarily as the tips pawed at the table. The familiar sensation of bees rattled and jumped under my skin, my stomach jerked into a painful knot, and an unexpected emotion flooded my senses, joy. I looked down at the goblet before me and licked my lips before pressing them back together. I didn't want to drink it, did I? Of course I did. What was I waiting for, permission?

"It's okay, Cait. You can drink it if you want."

I tried not to. God knows I tried. But after only a few seconds, I couldn't resist. I looked around like a drug addict making sure no one was watching while she got her fix. Then I picked up the goblet gingerly and took a sip. It was everything I remembered, like sex in a cup. I breathed easier immediately as the shimmering, broken glass under my flesh stilled, and the shiver of a heroine junky pushing a spike into their veins forced my head back with a relaxed sigh. I took a long drink, draining the glass. I thought I'd get sick, but I didn't. I felt invigorated. That was not a good sign.

"Still think you're cured?" Nastasia asked, bright and arrogant triumph written across her damning smile.

CHAPTER TWENTY-FOUR

The buzz of my phone was annoying as fuck, though I hadn't been asleep. I glanced at my watch. It was two in the morning. There was only one person it could be.

Shit, I thought. *Liz. I was supposed to go through Schmidt's files with her tonight. How was I going to explain this?* I sent her to voicemail and got up.

I stood naked before the picture window, looking across the Charles River. The other side was mostly dark except for the lights of Memorial Drive and a few spots around the MIT rotunda. I watched a few of the scullers push a boat into the water. *Christ, they started early,* I thought, and a cold, pale hand slid under my right arm and cupped my breast, drawing me from my conflicted and admittedly meandering thoughts.

"Come back to bed."

Fuck it, I thought and dropped the phone back on the nightstand. *I'd deal with Liz later.* I turned and lifted Nastasia, allowing her to wrap her legs around my waist and giving her a gentle kiss. I lowered her back to the bed, and we made out for a while, but I was exhausted and now irritated by my inability to resist her. And I felt like a heel for being here it all. So for a little while, I just lay on the bed with her on my shoulder.

"I really should get going," I muttered.

"Schmidt's files will be there tomorrow night. Sorry I couldn't bite you, but you're low on blood. It wouldn't kill you, but you need to recover."

I looked down at the top of her head and ran a hand through her soft, jet-black hair. Nastasia's hair was naturally straight, and it reminded me vaguely of the hair of young Asian women like Maki, though Nastasia's was thicker, which probably made sense.

Central Russia was an interesting mix of genetic traits. I'd once seen an insurgent fighter who'd come to Iraq from Afghanistan. That kid looked almost Irish with red hair and freckles, so it shouldn't have surprised me. Ancient peoples, like the one currently lying on my chest and running a hand over my abdomen, tended to move around quite a bit. They got around, as Mike would say—hell, as Mike had. I wondered briefly in amusement if I had another sibling running around somewhere. I put that thought aside—my life was complicated enough—and lifted back off the bed, gently moving Nastasia's head to her pillow.

"I have to go," I said as I stood and flicked on the light. She gave me an adorable pout.

"I could make you stay," She threatened half-heartedly, quirking her lips into a comically evil half-smile.

"You could, but you won't. I have files to go through, and Liz will be worried sick as it is."

"So?" Nastasia said nonchalantly. "She's three hundred years old, Cait. She'll be fine in the morning."

I pulled on my panties and began fastening my bra. "Yes, but I don't want to be any more of an inconsiderate shit than I've already been. Liz is my family, Nastasia. I know you don't see things that way, but it matters to me."

Nastasia looked a little hurt, and it took me by complete surprise. I expected her to make some snide comment, but instead, she said, "Cait, you are my family, you, and Liz, and Katie, and even Marcella."

I scoffed skeptically. "Nastasia, you'd murder any one of us to further your designs. My ma didn't raise an eejit."

"No, Cait, that's not true. Everything I do is to protect us.

Including you. I know you don't believe that, but—"

"Nastasia, you locked me in a dungeon, starved me for blood, and then threw a kid in with me. You're ruthless, as you've said so many times. Speaking of, what was that deal at the restaurant? I drank blood. I didn't puke, but I'm still breathing. I'm still human."

"I was just satisfying my curiosity. Now, will you stay for the rest of the night?"

I sat on the bed and kissed her gently. "No, I'm going back to my own bed." Truthfully, I couldn't believe what I was saying. I'd been longing for her for months, and now, here she was, ready and willing to go yet another round, and I was leaving. "It's not that I don't want to, but I need to go back to my fam—to Katie and Liz. Besides," I said as I ran a hand through her hair and pushed a bit out of her eyes. "You know where to find me. And you even have a key."

"Is that an invitation?" Her wicked smile returned, and she became the real Nastasia again.

I smiled impishly and said, "Take it how you like." Then I got up and left to catch a ride-share back home.

Peeling off the ridiculous heels, I walked barefoot over the frozen sidewalk to the door as my Lyft driver sped away. Once inside, I closed the door softly and leaned my forehead against it. A deep depression settled over my thoughts. *Damn it.* I hadn't felt this way since the night Gabe had gone insane. Liz's behavior had been over the top, but so had Morgan's. Then Nastasia, holy shit. Morgan wasn't wrong, though; Liz was jealous. But this was my life, and we weren't a couple. She'd made it clear that we were just friends and should stay that way.

"Fun night?" Liz asked as she walked into the foyer. Then she saw my glare and jerked her head slightly in confusion. "What happened? We were supposed to go to the old Schmidt place."

I was so tired. I didn't want to discuss this, but it had to be done. So, I raised my voice and let Liz have it with both barrels. "What happened? You happened, that's what. You fucking terrified her. How dare you treat one of my friends like that."

Liz blinked and had the nerve to look surprised.

"What, Liz? No snappy comeback? You fucking scared her half to death, and she lost her shit. You ruined my date! Let's get something straight. I'm not your possession. You will treat my friends with respect. That type of behavior is something I'd have expected from Marcella but not from you."

Liz said something too quiet for me to hear.

"What?" I snapped.

"You're right." Her voice was low, regretful. "I let it get the better of me. I promise it won't happen again. I'll apologize to Morgan."

I studied her for a moment. I was still angry, but I couldn't think of anything else to say.

Liz walked over and took my shoulders. "I'm sorry. Let me fix you something to eat."

I shrugged her off, saying, "No, I'm not hungry." Then I marched to the elevator and went to my room to change into my pajamas. Liz wasn't the biggest thing bothering me, nor was my sudden addiction to Nastasia or even the blood, which was all kinds of fucked up. It was Morgan's temper that was weighing on me, which had been scary as hell. The way she'd screamed at me in the restaurant had reminded me of some knock-down drag-outs that I'd had with Tony, one of my previous boyfriends. Tony and I had been wrong for each other from the start. I didn't really like him, and he didn't like himself. Over about three months, we had a dozen fights. It had never gotten physical, but I think that was only because Tony knew I'd put his ass in jail or the hospital if he ever hit me. The way Morgan had shot from zero to a hundred in no time flat had been terrifying.

After half an hour of mulling over dinner, I decided I actually was hungry and went downstairs to find a snack. A post-it with an arrow pointing toward the kitchen stuck to the wall across from the elevator door. In the kitchen, another post-it arrow pointed toward the microwave. Attached to the microwave was yet a third post-it that read, "I'm an arse. Look inside."

My mouth twisted into a smile, and I had to blink back tears. I didn't know why the gesture made me cry, but there I was, wiping furiously at my eyes. I opened the microwave, finding a small dish with a roast-beef sandwich and some potato chips. It was even diagonally cut in half the way I liked it, and I could smell the horseradish. This would burn my vomeronasal duct, but it would taste so good.

"I promise I'll fix it," Liz said from the kitchen door.

I took the sandwich and poured some water for me and a glass of blood for Liz. Setting everything on the table, I sat down. "I know. I'm sorry I shouted at you."

"You're my friend, Cait. Maybe my only friend. I didn't want to see you hurt. I didn't realize it would frighten her like that."

"Yes, you did. But I forgive you. She knows what you are, Liz," I said around a mouthful of the delicious sandwich. My eyes watered from the horseradish, and I wiped them. "She knows you could snap her like a twig. She took what you said very seriously. She would have shrugged it off if you were human, but you're not."

We sat there in silence for a while, then Liz said, "Where did you go after that?"

I didn't answer for a long time, eating my sandwich instead. Liz kept looking at me patiently, face impassive, waiting for an answer. Then, after it was gone, I whispered, "Nastasia's."

"What?" Liz snapped. "Have you lost your mind?"

"She showed up at the restaurant right after Morgan left." I leaned my forehead against my hand and took a swig of juice. "It's not a crime."

Liz's voice turned gentle. "Cait, love, what are you doing? Do you know?"

I looked up at her, suddenly feeling very small and confused. "No. I don't think I do. Ever since Marcella left, I've been miserable. I've been trying to hide it with work, Katie, you. But I miss her, Liz. Why did she leave?"

Liz cradled my head on her shoulder while I cried. For the first time since the day Marcella had left, I let out my grief. Oh, I'd cried for her, but not like this. I wailed.

"Why did she abandon me?" Like a little girl, I begged for an answer to that one question.

"I don't know," Liz whispered as she held me, stroking my head.

Then I jerked as my stomach rebelled on me. I tore from the kitchen, just making the bathroom, where I threw up everything—the sandwich, my martini's, and the blood, black and thick.

"Cait? Are you alright?" Liz called from outside.

"Yeah, just nerves," I lied. I was definitely not alright.

After I was done, I flushed the toilet and washed out my mouth. I hoped Liz wouldn't smell the blood on my breath, or she might assume it was changed blood Nastasia had given me. She didn't need yet another of my issues on her head right now. "I'm okay," I said as I opened the door. "I'm going to go lay down."

"Okay," Liz said, and there was hurt in her eyes, but I couldn't deal with it right now. Exhaustion was dragging at me, and I needed to get some sleep.

A little while later, I brushed my teeth and was getting ready for bed when Katie entered my room. The light was out, but I was still awake, obsessing over how Morgan had reacted.

"Mama? Can I lay down with you?"

I smiled in the dark and turned over to the other side of the bed. "Sure, kid. Everything alright?"

"Yeah." She crawled in next to me and lay her head on my chest. "I just thought you could use the company."

I stroked her hair and was rewarded by the scent of dragon's blood with a hint of jasmine. "How'd you get to be so smart, huh?"

She kissed me on the cheek. "I have the two best teachers in the world, mama."

I rolled over, smiled to myself, and fell asleep. She was such a good kid.

A half-hour later, I woke, hearing the door open.

"Katie, come on," Liz whispered. "Let's let mama get some rest. I fucked up tonight, and I'd rather she wasn't cranky in the morning."

I smiled to myself but said nothing. Katie slid quietly off the bed, and I rolled over. Liz stood in the doorway for long moments. And while I couldn't see her eyes, she was definitely looking into mine, and I felt the tiniest brush of something in my thoughts, pained and bittersweet. I called out to her, but she had already closed the door, leaving me in darkness to ponder what had just happened.

After tossing and turning for a bit, I decided I couldn't sleep, so I wandered off to find either Liz or Katie, but the house was empty. I assumed they'd gone for a walk or to one of the camps. I ended up in the sitting room and poured myself some wine, turning on a small table lamp and feeling sorry for myself.

A few minutes later, there was a soft knock at the door. *Jesus Christ*, I thought, *who could be knocking at this hour?* I was already feeling pretty pissy about my night and wasn't in the mood for visitors. I jumped from the sofa and stalked to the door, throwing it wide.

"What the—mmph." Before I finished my sentence, Morgan grabbed my face and laid a lip lock on me. I backed away, but she pursued, holding my face and kicking the door closed with one foot.

I'm not sure how I got turned around, but I found myself pressed against the door with Morgan slathering my face and throat with kisses, drawing a harsh breath from deep in my chest. After I'd already come apart, I knew I shouldn't be doing this. This was the last thing I needed. Or maybe it was precisely what I needed. I guessed I'd find out.

She started tugging at her blazer, struggling with it. I dragged it down, pulling it from her arms and shoulders as we kissed passionately. I needed this. *We* needed this. Maybe it would go somewhere. Perhaps it would go nowhere. But we had to know. *I* had to know.

I hopped up, wrapping my legs around her waist, and she bore me into the sitting room, laying me back on the couch.

God, she was strong. Being carried by Liz or Marcella was so different. They didn't struggle or strain with my weight. But, with Morgan, I could feel the muscles under her shirt bulge and move with effort as she carried me, and it was sexy as all hell.

"Morgan. Please." I begged as she tore open my pajama top, sending buttons skittering across the rug. Every kiss burned like fire across my skin. She pushed her leg between mine, massaging me with her thigh as I fought to unbutton her shirt. Then I gasped, taken aback.

I couldn't help myself as I traced a long, straight scar that ran from her collar, over her right breast, ending just above her belly button. "Oh, Morgan, what happened?" I couldn't help myself. It was horrid.

She looked down. "What, that? Oh, my ex tried to gut me like a fish. I'll tell you later."

I couldn't let it go as fury and sympathy enveloped my thoughts. "Clint? Or Clay or whatever his name was? Did he do this?"

Morgan sighed and sat on the sofa beside me, running her hand through her sweaty hair. "Do we have to do this now?"

I looked at her, my jaw working. "We shouldn't have sex down here, anyway. Liz or Katie could walk in at any time. Let's go to my room." I gathered up the clothes and took her to the elevator.

"An elevator? Well, this is swanky."

"It's not like it's mine," I said as I stepped into the car and pressed the third floor. "Marcella owns this place, Liz and I just live here."

A few moments later, we were in my bedroom. I undressed properly this time and got into the bed, patting the mattress for Morgan to join me. "Come on. We have all night. Tell me what happened."

I knew she wanted me to ignore it, but I couldn't. The thought that someone had done this to her filled me with such painful emotions that the mood was gone anyway. Morgan undressed and crawled into the bed, placing her head on my shoulder. Then she began to talk, and I just let her go.

"To answer your question, no, Clay didn't do this. Clay was a sweetheart, and it broke his heart when I left, but you know how it goes."

I nodded. I knew exactly how it went.

"Anyway, I had a few off-and-on girlfriends in Chicago until about two years ago, when I met Andrea. I thought she was the one. At first, we hit it off. She took me out with her all the time, to friends' places, movies, concerts, you name it. And we liked a lot of the same things. Then, after a couple of months, we moved in together." She laughed mirthlessly. "We even rented a U-haul." She paused for a moment, and her face screwed up like she was reliving a painful, awful memory. "And that's when everything went sour. You really don't know someone until you live with them."

I snorted. "That's for sure. I thought—" I stopped myself. I had been about to talk about Liz. I'd thought Liz was a monster when I met her, but she'd turned out to be sweet and kind. I brushed the musings aside. "Sorry, this is your story. Go on."

"No, what were you about to say?" Morgan asked, turning to look up at me.

I sighed. "I was just agreeing with you. Keep going."

Morgan frowned briefly, and I had an almost irresistible urge to ask what she was thinking, but I let her continue.

"Like I said, Andrea was nice at first, but she changed. I think some people just lose their minds when they start to commit. She started complaining about my hours as a cop. Then we started fighting a lot. She had a lot of issues I hadn't known about, too. Her father had abused her pretty badly as a child. Nothing sexual, at least as far as I know, but he beat her and her mother. She drank a lot, too. That much I'd known, but I'd been so caught up in 'new love' that I'd ignored it." Morgan's eyes turned a little watery in the soft brownish light of my penshell lamp, and I swiped at a burgeoning tear with my thumb but said nothing.

"When she drank, she got violent, you know? Next thing I knew, we were fighting, and it got so bad that I started escalating, hitting back. Me, can you believe it? Anyway, about a year ago, we had a knock-down-drag-out that lasted almost a half hour. She was one of those LARPers and into swords. Had like a half dozen of them. She grabbed one off the wall during the fight and came after me with it. That's how I got these scars." She ran a finger the length of the scars, from brow to belly.

"Please tell me that she's in prison."

Morgan turned deathly quiet and closed her eyes. "No, Cait," she whispered, and her tears began to flow in earnest. "She's dead. I didn't wait for her to take a second swing. I managed to get to my piece, and I shot her."

I gasped, and my hand went to my mouth. "Oh, blessed mother, Morgan. I'm so sorry."

"A few weeks later, I got shot because I couldn't draw my weapon. I spent six months on the support squad before finally calling it quits and putting in for the job here. I was just —glad—" Morgan paused, and then her shoulders began to shake. Before long, her deep, mournful sobs filled the room. "I'm sorry—"

If she couldn't draw her gun, then she endangered herself and who knew how many others. In the end, as fucked up as it was, we were trained that our gun was our best and primary means to defend ourselves or the public from danger. And while I might wish differently, and even though a lot of cops used it when they shouldn't, sometimes it was the only answer. Morgan was lucky she hadn't been fired on the spot.

I kept her close, her hot breath on my chest and her tears sinking down my belly. We were just a fucked up lot. But this is the hand life deals us. Rutherford had checked out. I couldn't blame her for that, but I didn't want Morgan to go the same way.

"Oh, Morgan, honey," I breathed and squeezed her to my breast, stroking her head, hurting for her and ruing that I could do nothing more. "Have you, like, talked to anyone about it?"

She sniffed and stifled her tears. "I was assigned to peer support, Cait. It was required."

"I'm sorry, Morgan. I'm not trying to pry. It's just—" I

paused. What was I trying to say? "You seem so much angrier than you used to be. It's hard for me to—"

"To what?" She pushed herself up and looked at me, her expression stern, defensive, almost childlike in its indignance. "I remember how you were after Iraq? You were a basket case. Anytime I brought up the war or suggested you see someone about your PTSD or anything, you blew a gasket. So I don't understand why you're harassing me."

I pursed my lips, getting more than a little sick of her attitude toward me. I spoke quietly and kept my voice carefully level. "I was going to say that it's hard for me to see you like this. But I'm not harassing you. I'm just looking out for myself. I've been hurt multiple times, and while I can't imagine what you went through, I need you to understand that, just like you, I'm not the person I used to be. I grew up."

"Grew up? Lost your mind is more like. You're living with a blood-sucking fiend, Cait. They are dangerous. Can't you see that?"

More dangerous than a woman trying to cut you down with a sword? I thought, but I kept that to myself. It wouldn't help. But the casual way she spewed her ignorance pissed me off, and that was the last of it I was willing to listen to tonight. I pulled my arm out from under her and stood, grabbing pajamas from my chest of drawers.

"Now, you listen to me, Morgan Kennedy," I responded hotly as I dressed. "I was one of those blood-sucking fiends, as you call it, and I wasn't unhappy being one. Being a vampire is a condition. It does not define everything that they are. I didn't expect you to be a bigot. This is my life, now, for better or worse. More importantly, I like my life better now than I ever did before. I like myself better now, too. But if you don't like it, that's okay. You can hit the road." I pointed toward the door.

Morgan blinked. My furor had caught her by surprise. Her following words were a childish denial. She said, "I'm not a bigot."

I raised an eyebrow and put my hands on my hips. "Really? Not once have you asked me what actually happened. You haven't asked how I got here or why Liz is my friend. You haven't even asked me about Katie, my fucking daughter, and how that came to be. You have, however, been perfectly happy to cast aspersions on my entire way of life. If that doesn't smack of prejudice, I have no idea what does.

"As far as asking about your therapy, I'm trying to decide if we're a good fit, just like you obviously are. It's not unreasonable for me to know if you're working through something as traumatic as having to put a bullet in your ex. So, and I say this with all due care, I love you, Morgan, and always will, but I will not be abused or belittled in any way, nor will I let you do so to my friends."

"Shit," Morgan whispered. "I'm sorry. I—"

I stood there, stock-still, waiting for her to finish her sentence. For years, I'd put up with a lot of shit from a lot of people, but I was done with that. I never let Liz or Marcella talk to me the way Morgan had, and they could snap me in half on a whim. But she didn't finish. She just pulled the sheet up, covering herself.

I walked over and sat on the bed next to her. "Morgan, I can see you're in pain. It must be hard for you." I had a brief moment, wondering where all this compassion had been when Gabe had been wrecked, but that didn't matter anymore, did it? "I can't imagine what that must have been like."

Morgan burst into tears again, and I pulled her to me, letting her shake in my arms. I said nothing. I just stroked her head, shushing her gently. Her sobs of sorrow built to a crescendo of a heartbreaking wail, reminding me so much of my first night as a vampire, when I'd been blood starved and practically destroyed by all that had happened. I'd wailed just like this in Marcella's arms. A part of me couldn't believe that the woman I'd looked up to and leaned on for so long during the war was now such a mess, emotionally battered and broken.

After a time, her cries died out, and we lay on the bed. Before too long, physically and emotionally exhausted, Morgan drifted off to sleep in my arms, and I prayed for her to have some release in sleep, preferably dreamless.

Still, I lay there for a long time, gently stroking Morgan's hair in both sympathy and sorrow. Morgan was broken, and there was literally nothing I could do to help her. I lay awake for hours as I realized the truth. There was no going back, no fixing it, no starting over. We were different now. Ten years of experience had changed who we were, and, within that moment, I realized we would never know what we had lost when she'd walked out that door, when I refused to pick up the phone, and when I'd avoided reading a letter.

A light melancholy filled me the following morning when I opened my eyes. It was five and still dark outside. Morgan lay next to me, breathing deeply, fast asleep. I was relieved that I hadn't had sex with her. Truthfully, the desire to do so had fled almost as quickly as it had come. After ten years of wondering what if, I realized it didn't matter. There was no use in what-if. All that mattered was what I had now. I had a woman who, despite her hemming and hawing, loved me. I had a child I loved more than life itself, and she loved me the same. I had a good job and a wonderful home, even a stupid cat, who at the moment was curled up in the crook of my knee.

I had been out of control. Instead of managing my life and keeping my focus, I was all over the place, sleeping with whomever, questioning my sanity. And now, this morning, I had a deep sense of clarity.

I let Morgan continue to sleep, dressing quickly and quietly. I took one last look at her, and while it wasn't my place to have an opinion, I decided that the short hair suited her better. However, I was still momentarily struck by a memory of how it had smelled one night as she lay in my hospital bed after my seventh surgery. I let that go, though. There was no future for us and likely never would be. As Mike had often said, she wasn't where I was emotionally and might never be. I could finally exorcise that ghost of the past and focus on my present —the beautiful blond who'd rescued my mother, who had supported my every struggle since, and who had been there whenever I needed her. She deserved all the attention I could give her right now, as did our daughter.

Strangely enough, letting go turned out to be a great deal easier than I'd thought. I had been broken when Morgan left. Even if we'd stayed together, there was no guarantee that things would have turned out differently. At best, I would have broken Marcella's glamour, and Morgan would have been my first real relationship with a woman. From what little I knew, those rarely become happily ever after stories. We would have just as likely grown apart as grown together. Perhaps, in a few years, the stars might align. I just needed to explain all of that to Morgan, though I suspected she already knew this wasn't going to work.

Liz looked up from her crossword puzzle when I crept into the kitchen. "How is she?"

I stopped to look at her. The way she'd asked the question had been somber and concerned rather than a platitude, making me wonder briefly if she could read my mind. "Morgan? She's sleeping. Why do you ask?"

"I heard her crying last night when I got home. I wasn't trying to eavesdrop, but she sounded pretty distraught."

I grabbed some orange juice and sat, staring into my glass. "Yeah, it was a rough night. What are you doing up? I figured you'd be going to bed by now."

Liz placed a gentle grip on my arm. "I was waiting for you. I wanted to make sure you were okay, that's all."

I sighed and swirled the juice around, finally setting the glass down as the slow burn of more tears I hadn't shed the night before began to press at my eyes. I tried to squeeze them back, but they came anyway. "You can't go home again," I said as I wiped my eyes and sniffed. "You were right. For ten years, I longed for something that didn't exist. Morgan isn't who I remember, and even if she was, I'm not either. And I don't want to be with her anyway."

"Cait, first let me say that I'm sorry. It's a bitter pill. She's just not where you are in life."

I snorted and gave her a sad smile. "You sound like Mike."

"But you did nothing wrong by trying, and I shouldn't have been so hard on you about it. I ignored the one thing a vampire should never forget."

I downed my juice and looked back at Liz, genuinely interested in her meaning.

She gave me a soft, sympathetic smile, but it didn't reach her eyes. "Things have to happen in due course and naturally. Life has to be lived in stride, on life's terms, as it were. If you try to bend life to meet your needs, you'll end up miserable or dead. All things happen with time, or they don't. We don't control that."

She was right, of course. Marcella had once tried to tell me the same thing. Though, at the time, I had been in no space to hear it. "Thank you," I said and kissed Liz gently on the cheek as I got up to put my empty glass in the sink.

"For what?" Liz asked with a mix of tenderness and bemusement.

"For letting me go through this and still being here for me. I'm sure it wasn't easy."

Liz swallowed hard and coughed slightly, which was odd, given that she didn't have to breathe. "Not—ahem—not easy, how?"

"It's never fun watching a friend do something you know will hurt them."

"Oh! That." Liz waved her hand dismissively and picked up her crossword. "We're friends. Ride or die, darling. Ride or die. You know that."

"No, Liz. We're much more than friends, and I'm sorry if I've taken that for granted."

Liz opened her mouth to respond, but then she cocked her ear. "Morgan's tiptoeing down the stairs, love. Why don't you fix us some breakfast? I haven't eaten an egg in a very long time."

I raised an eyebrow but got to it. Morgan padded into the kitchen a few minutes later as the bacon fried and the grits cooked. She looked like hell. Her eyes were puffy and red. I walked over and pulled out a chair. "Come. Sit."

Morgan did as I bade, and I put a fresh cup of coffee in front of her. She looked up at me. "I'm sorry, Cait. I—"

"It's okay. I've been there," I interrupted and kissed her on the top of her head. "Let's get some food in you." I went back to cooking. "You want them fried or chopped?" It was an old army joke.

"Scrambled, please," Morgan said, sticking her tongue out at me. "Do you have hot sauce?"

Liz snorted. "Eww. I'll take mine fried if you don't mind, Cait."

"Uh, you're eating people food?" Morgan asked, looking confused.

"Just because I can't fully digest human food doesn't mean I can't appreciate it. I mean, it's not as tasty as, say, a six-foot redhead built for combat, but it's still a treat."

"Liz," I cautioned in my best motherly voice. I gave Liz a warning glance. I expected Morgan to get upset or scared, but she only looked taken aback. Liz winked at me, and I shook my head. 'Don't,' I mouthed. Liz stuck out her bottom lip at me but said nothing else.

Morgan swallowed a mouthful and looked across the table. "Liz, do you mind if I call you Liz? I'm curious. Does Cait know you're in love with her?"

I almost dropped the spatula in aggravation. Liz said nothing but gripped the table like she was about to snap the entire thing in half. Morgan just smirked. And though I had to give Morgan credit for courage, she got zero points for tact. It was time to end this.

"She does," I said softly and without inflection but loud enough for both of them to hear. Then I finished making Morgan's plate and set it down gently in front of her. "Eat that, please, and go home. You have work in a few hours."

I felt terrible for Morgan after last night, but I wouldn't deny what I knew any longer. And the thought of letting go and giving in to those feelings made me warm all over, even though I couldn't. Morgan scarfed up her food, army style, while Liz sat perfectly upright, eating in a very lady-like fashion. Both of them were scowling at each other. Finally, Morgan finished and stood. She reached for her plate, but I stopped her.

"Leave it," I said flatly, crossing my arms. "Now go home

and get ready for work, Kennedy."

I watched Morgan leave, head bowed and eyes downcast. That had been cruel of me, especially after all that had happened, but what she'd done had been just as shitty. It took a few moments for me to wrestle my feelings back under control, but as Morgan left, closing the front door behind her, the grin that had been threatening for the last few minutes finally split my face. "So, are you?"

Liz stopped eating and turned toward me slowly. "Am I what?"

My grin turned cheeky. "Are you in love with me?"

"Don't be ridiculous," she said, but her smile belied her words.

"Put down that fork, Liz Medlyn. We need to talk."

What ensued was a much shorter discussion than I'd expected. Liz's mouth pressed into a perfect, unreadable line. She quietly put the fork on her plate with the delicate precision of a finishing school graduate and carried the plate to the sink. She didn't take her eyes off mine as she set the plate down with the tiniest clatter of silverware. Then she stepped to me at the stove. She was very close.

"Yes," she whispered. "I love you. I—"

I pressed a finger to her lips. "I love you, too. But you were right. I'm not ready. I'm in a rathole of guilt and anger and misery. And I haven't figured out how to get out of it." Now I did drop the spatula on the counter, but it was so I could take Elizabeth's face in my hands, and I said, "Save this for later, maybe." Then I kissed her, hoping she might kiss me back.

And she did. And it was beautiful and wonderful and all the things a kiss should be. Her lips were cool and soft and light. Her breath was cold and tasted of her breakfast and a hint of blood. In the movies, I'd seen women pop a foot at being kissed like this and had always thought it was silly, but damnit if I didn't do exactly that.

Liz lifted me onto the counter by my hips, and there I stayed as she continued to kiss me far longer than I'd planned. I had promised myself that I would keep my heart in check and not fall for another vampire. I guess my heart had other plans. The fucking treacherous thing.

CHAPTER TWENTY-FIVE

Later at HQ, I saw Morgan briefly as I walked past the break room. I gave her a tentative wave, and she nodded, but there was no welcome in her eyes. I sighed, and tears threatened, but I didn't let them fall. She had her shit, and I had mine. And no one wanted to hear about mine, except maybe Maki or Doyle.

Doyle was back at work looking none the worse for wear since the bombing, but her eyes had a haunted look, and her usual bouncy demeanor seemed subdued and lost. I thought about asking her but decided she'd come to talk to me if she wanted to.

I said hello to Carol as I passed, and she looked up but didn't return the greeting, instead turning back to her work. Even Carlos seemed non-plussed to see me, so when I reached my desk, instead of sitting down to work, I took a moment to look around and wonder what had happened. Two months ago, this place had been my balm, my salve against a truly fucked up life. Now, all it did was remind me how alone I was. Carol, Carlos, and Morgan judged me for the company I kept, not even considering why I did it. I understood Doyle's obsession with vampires. Being in their power can be intoxicating and exciting. But she and I weren't in the same head space. I was a vampire, and she was just a groupie. And

Maki, well, she was a fucking enigma. I didn't know what she was, but she wasn't human, at least not entirely, and her aloof attitude said she didn't think much of anyone else, or so it seemed.

As I watched the other Detectives on the floor move about, I realized that these weren't my people anymore. I still loved them, but everything in my world had changed. And while I had begun to doubt that I'd been cured of my curse, it wouldn't have mattered if I had. Nastasia had been right all along. Vampires were my clan, my family. Nastasia had done me a favor. She had kept me close so that I would make this very discovery. Two months ago, I had been irrevocably changed into something different. That change had unleashed the darkness within me, and, cured or not, there was no turning back. I was someone else. And tonight, I'd be returning to where it had all happened.

"Hey."

I looked up as Morgan broke my train of thought, and I saw her with new eyes. There wasn't anything specifically wrong with her. She was wounded, that's all. As twisted up as I'd been over everything last night, she'd made me see the truth, and that was okay. So I looked up at her with kind eyes and said, "It's okay, Morgan. I still love you. I always will."

She blinked, looking somewhat startled. I suspected that, of all the things I might have said, that hadn't been what she'd expected. She stammered for a second, then said, "I just wanted you to know that I—"

"I'm sorry. I shouldn't have been so short this morning."

"Hey," Morgan said, tapping her fingers on her desk. "Will you let me finish?" Her tone wasn't aggressive or angry, but she clearly had something to say. So I pressed my lips together and stayed quiet, and she said, "I felt the same way. I had thought we'd find something we'd lost. But we're both different, and all I did was throw my shit on you. I'm sorry for that. Your friends scare me, I won't lie. But I'm with you to the end. I want you to know that."

I stood and gave her a quick hug. "I'm glad, Morgan. You were my best friend in all the world, and I want that back."

She smiled, but it didn't reach her eyes which glistened slightly. "Me too." She didn't say anything else and turned to go, but then she stopped, turning back. "Cait, there's something you should know—" She paused as if debating what she was about to say. Then she said, "Nevermind," apparently thinking better of it, and walked off.

Wow, I thought. *This is a pretty shitty New Year's.*

Doyle poked her head up, pulling me out of my sudden misery. "Hey, Cait, come take a look at this."

I walked around to find Carlos, Carol, and Maki all standing around Doyle's desk. "What is it?"

"These are four traffic cams from Lowell. That same SUV was parked at the club where Andrea was picked up, outside her apartment, and seen leaving the area, headed down route three back toward town. This is no coincidence. These are our guys. And this shot," she pulled up another picture. "It's from a gas station in Lowell. The camera is hi-def."

"That's a federal vehicle, FBI to be specific," Carol said. "Or one bought surplus. See the square spot with the four points on it? That's a directional tracking antenna. And that bump there," she pointed at a nub on the front left of the roof so small you'd probably miss it if you didn't know what to look for. "That's a two-way antenna. Only the Federal agencies hide them that well."

Carlos whispered what we were all thinking. "They're monitoring us. That's how they knew when to hit each lee— sorry, vampire. And it's why none of the vampires under surveillance have been hit. They're tracking where our cars are."

"We should probably go to undercover vehicles," Carol suggested.

"Nope," Carlos said. "It's business as usual until I say otherwise. Now let's get to it."

After we broke up with absolutely no direction from him, Carlos pulled me into the interview room and closed the door. As soon as we entered, we both noticed that the surveillance light on the camera had turned red. Carlos glanced at it briefly and said, "It was a shame what happened to Soledad. I had something perfect picked out for his birthday, too."

I furrowed my brow, then clued in. He thought there was a mole in the department, and he thought it was one of our team. More importantly, he felt they were listening right now. If we didn't converse about something that might seem private, it would look suspicious. Damn, he was good.

"Yeah, that sucks. So, what are you getting Carol for her birthday?"

He nodded almost imperceptibly and shrugged. "No clue. I haven't been able to pick out one for anyone on the team. Do you have any suggestions?" So he did suspect it was someone on our team or could be.

"What about Freyer's team? I mean, I should get something for Morgan and Freyer, too."

"Yeah, you should definitely get something for Freyer. You should keep looking for something for Morgan, though. I don't think she'll like what you picked out." *Okay,* I thought. *So he trusts Freyer and not Morgan.*

I said, "Well, I liked what I got for Morgan." *I trust Morgan.*

Carlos shook his head. "I'm telling you, it's not right. She's not who you remember. You should give it some more time before you pick something out."

"Point taken," I said flatly.

Carlos tapped his bottom lip. "I'm gonna see if we can get Freyer access to a new cruiser." *Undercover car for Freyer. Brilliant.* "First, I'm gonna see if I can ferret out if he'd like that." *He wanted to let Freyer in on the fact that we thought we had a mole.*

"Okay," I took out my pad and wrote two names on it. "I think Doyle needs something non-technical, don't you?"

"Yeah, she gets enough of that shit at work." *Doyle's okay. Alright.* "That just leaves Maki."

Carlos paused. "Let me think about it. I might have something in mind, though."

"Okay, I'll give that some thought, too." *We both thought Maki was on the level but weren't one hundred percent sure.*

"Sounds good. Make sure you tell me pronto. I don't want us getting the same gift for someone."

I rolled my eyes. "Of course. Duh." *As if I wouldn't tell my squad lead if I figured out who the mole was.*

We left the interview room, and I glanced to my right to see if anyone had come out of the surveillance room, but no one did. Whoever had turned on the equipment had hightailed it out before we'd left the interview room.

My anxiety flared as we rolled up to the Rodriguez place that night. The police tape was gone, and the house was still in a state of disrepair. Of course, the landlord couldn't fix it because that landlord had been Erik Schmidt, and he was dead. I wondered how many other places around Boston he owned and had kept in the same state of disrepair, forcing his tenants to live like Irish tenement farmers from the eighteen hundreds.

This had been the place that had changed my life forever. The place where I'd been infected by a parasite that should have killed me. The place where my life took a hard left turn, leading Marcella to take me to Bian to save me from, well, Marcella. Fuck, my life was weird.

We trudged through snow and ice across the lawn and down the half-destroyed driveway to the bulkhead doors. The old refrigerator still sat next to them, and the lock was still broken. Liz pulled open the doors with some effort; they were rusted shut, and one of the corroded handles broke in the process, but eventually, they groaned open with an awful screech that set my teeth on edge.

The basement was pitch black, but I'd brought high-powered flashlights this time. I paused at the top step anyway, though, a knot of fear sticking in my throat.

"It's okay, love. I'm here. Come on." Liz offered me a hand, and I took it as we descended the stairs.

Someone had been in the place. Most of the cellar was undisturbed, but there was paper strewn all about the floor, and two of the stacks of boxes had been tipped over, spilling their contents. Water had seeped in from somewhere as well, probably from the melting snow. It covered one corner of the cellar.

I cast a nervous glance at the file cabinet in the corner. It was turned on its side, and the steel plate on the wall over the old tunnel was pushed aside, just as Carlos and I had left it the night I'd been infected. Liz followed my gaze to the gaping black maw of the tunnel. Then she marched over, placed the steel plate back in place, and righted the heavy cabinet. I had a moment where I was certain the worm thing would reach out and grab her, but nothing happened.

Liz looked at me in sympathy. "Let's get started, shall we?"

"Yeah," I whispered. Then I took a deep breath and tried to put the tunnel out of my thoughts as we dug into the work.

It was slow going at first. We gathered up all of the papers on the floor and set them in neat piles, keeping the wet ones to one side. Liz swept a spot on the floor with an old broom should found stuck in the corner, and we sat down.

After an hour and a half, we'd managed to corral all of the loose papers by subject matter. None of them pertained to the hunters, but a few of them held account information and property locations for places Schmidt either owned or held via shell companies. There was also a fair amount of information on the old Council. Under a small pile, I found a photo that looked like it had been taken in the nineteen-twenties, maybe. In the photo, Marcella and Liz were standing in front of a large tent with a tall black man in a suit. Liz was in Marcella's arms, and they were cheek to cheek, like a couple, both dressed like late nineteenth or early twentieth-century British explorers.

"Hey, what's this?"

Liz looked at it and laughed. "Wow, I haven't seen this in a long time. I wonder how Schmidt ended up with it."

She took the eight-by-ten from me and held it in the light. "This was taken in the Belgian Congo in 1927. Marcella had dragged me there on a hunt for what we thought might be one of Bian's lost sisters. That man next to us we call The Maltese."

Dark and foreboding didn't begin to describe him. He was extremely tall, maybe a few inches taller than Marcella. Although very handsome, his ruthless black eyes and the firm set of his bearded jaw spoke volumes of his temerity and confidence. His tailored black suit and pin-striped, dark tie fit him well and gave him an air of professional menace, like an assassin or crime lord.

"Vampire? He looks scary as hell."

"Yes. And he should. None of us knows very much about him. We don't even know how he was branded with the appellation or who originally turned him. His birth name is Aremo Bakare. He was a revolutionary against Belgian colonial rule back then, but I don't know what he's doing today. Last I heard, he was making his home in South Africa and spending his time on charity efforts. I always found him friendly, but, make no mistake, he is more deadly than Marcella or Nastasia. If you ever end up on the wrong end of his blade, do not give him the slightest advantage. He and Marcella had quite the scuffle a few years before this was taken, and it was what I'd term a draw. He's powerful and immune to our ability to command others. Even Nastasia is scared of him."

I raised an eyebrow at that and whistled. "Okay. A scuffle over what?'

"A woman, what else?" Liz chuckled, and I laughed with her.

"Now that woman there," she pointed to herself in the photo. "Is not to be trusted. Word has it, her whole life is dedicated to relentless debauchery. She lures young women to her bed, then uses them as she sees fit. Sometimes she bleeds them dry. Sometimes she drives them mad."

I grinned. "I see. So which do you think she might do to me?"

Before I could stop her, Liz grabbed me around the arms and buried her face in my neck, biting gently and making silly munching sounds.

"You goofball," I said, batting at her playfully. But then she stopped playing and nibbled at my throat, sucking at the skin, and I gasped as gooseflesh rose on my arms. "Wha—what are you—" She bit into the skin of my neck. I didn't finish the sentence as she began to drink, overwhelming my thoughts with the soft, warm rush of pleasure that stole my breath. I twisted my head to my left, giving her more access.

She stopped just a moment later, kissing me, delivering just a little changed blood. The hunger followed immediately, crawling through my skin as my flesh knitted whole. I held her face and licked at her chin, then I pushed her head back and bit at her throat, wanting more. My blunt teeth did nothing but scratch her neck, but she made a soft pleasure-filled noise anyway. I pulled away, breath catching. I thought my heart might burst with the sudden rush of emotion that, in the end, only left me confused and lost. "But we said—"

"I know," Liz replied, halting my words. "I was caught in the moment. I'm sorry—"

"No!" I said quickly, startling her. "Don't apologize. I feel it, too. But we need to stop this."

Our eyes met, and it was electric. I almost leaned in, but then Liz leaned away with a sigh. "No. You're right. We need to stop."

I pressed my lips together, poorly suppressing my grin as I scooted away slightly. *God*, I thought. *This is fucking agony.* For the first time, I worried about what Liz would do when Marcella returned. If she returned. "Please don't leave," I whispered.

Liz stiffened. "Cait, I—"

I put a finger to her lips. "Let's talk about it later, okay?" I turned back to the papers, setting the photo aside and placing it in a dry file folder to take with us. "We have work to do."

We moved through the stacks of boxes for hours, looking for files on hunters, hunter families, vampire deaths, or anything that might give us a lead. We finally found it as my watch ticked over to three-thirty.

"Here," Liz said as she pulled a thick file from one of the boxes. She brought it over, and we both looked at it in the bright illumination of our flashlights. There were five separate dossiers in it defining each of the families. And each held at least one page with a crest or crests associated with each family. In addition to the De Medici, and Rognvaldr, there were the Rinaldi, the Saxon, and the Orsini. It was the Rinaldi that interested me most, though, as one of the crests in their dossier matched our calling card.

"According to this," Liz said, translating the German notes for me. "Schmidt's team tracked the Rinaldi to America and then west to Portage, Ohio. They followed the trail to Denver, but it went cold in Nevada. The researchers differed on whether they continued west or settled in the Utah-Nevada region."

"Huh," I grunted in interest. "Does it mention any aliases they might have used or name changes?"

"Yes, about a hundred." She flipped through several pages of names. "We'll have to research these, one by one. Let's do this. We'll pull the folders from each box that we haven't searched yet and see if they contain any relation to these surnames. They all start with R, so that should make it easier. If you find any, call them out, and I'll let you know if they're on the list."

We stood and rifled back through the papers and boxes. There were only a few files that contained family information with people's names. Only two of them were on the list of aliases: Ronald, which seemed unremarkable, and one that got my attention immediately, Reynolds.

"Are you fucking kidding me?" I said when Liz confirmed it was on the list. "I whammied a hunter?" No wonder Matt had taken such an interest in Marcella. And I'd glamoured the bejesus out of him. "Fuck! This is all my fault."

Liz pursed her lips in a crooked line. "No, Cait. This was going to happen eventually, as soon as they figured out we weren't all dead. So, let that go. We're making progress." She looked at the stack of hunter information we'd set aside and reached down, putting the files into one of the boxes we'd emptied. Then she stopped.

"What are—" I started, but she interrupted, shushing me hard. Then she hissed, "Do you hear that?"

I paused, holding my breath. At first, there was nothing, then I heard it, a scratching sound coming from behind the walls. All the walls.

"What is that?" I asked.

"It sounds like metal on stone." Liz started packing frantically. "You know what? I think we're done here. Grab anything vampire related and put it in this box."

"Yup," I agreed and started helping as panic chewed at my thoughts.

We scrambled to get the files into the box. On a whim, I snatched up the small pile of wet papers we'd yet to examine but dropped them when the scratching grew louder, followed by a horrid screech, like metal on metal, from the direction of the cabinet.

"Oh, shit!" I swore and pointed my lamp toward the cabinet; it was vibrating as the metal screamed louder. Something was scrabbling at the metal plate behind it.

"Okay, time to go," I called.

Liz grabbed the box and launched for the stairs. I pulled my weapon and backed out behind her, scope locked on the cabinet, which had moved several inches away from the wall. A thick gray claw dug out around the metal plate, knocking out chunks from the stone foundation. Another hole appeared to our left, too small to see any detail except for another claw-like finger-thing digging at the stone there as well. I recoiled in revulsion.

We topped the stairs, slammed the bulkhead doors home, and dashed for the car. It was locked. "Shit." I fumbled in my pocket for the keys, glancing back repeatedly.

The bulkhead doors shook with a massive bang, popping up about a foot and then falling back as if something massive had slammed into them.

"Oh shit! Oh shit! Oh shit!" I swore as I finally dug the fob from my pocket and unlocked the Jeep.

I jumped into the driver's seat next to Liz, started the car, and took off down Humboldt at a breakneck speed. Liz still had the file box clutched in front of her. Less than a block away, she screamed, almost causing me to drive off the road.

"What?"

She opened the window and swatted a small spider off the box and out of the car.

"Fuck, Liz, really?" I almost shouted. "You're a fucking

vampire. You nearly caused me to wreck the car!"

She looked at me indignantly. "I don't like spiders!" She shouted and shivered violently in disgust. "Blech."

I looked behind us. Nothing had come swarming out of the house to follow us, and I couldn't help myself. I started to laugh. "You fucking wuss."

"Hey!" She whined and pouted.

CHAPTER TWENTY-SIX

The doorbell rang at six in the morning, and I grumbled awake. I'd had all of an hour's sleep. I looked at my phone and checked the video doorbell. Outside stood four people. First, a patrol officer was the one banging on the door. I didn't know her. Next to her stood a self-satisfied-looking Jim Fincher and a terrified Anne. But what made my blood boil was the woman standing next to them. It was the Fincher's DCF caseworker. She looked like she'd been pinched at the head and feet, squeezing all of her body mass to the middle like a balloon and causing her crap brown skirt and undersized button-down shirt to bulge and strain against her belly. She also had the rather unfortunate name of Colewort, Ida Colewort. It sounded like a mean second-grade teacher. She held a clipboard.

The officer banged again, and I squinted as hot anger squeezed at my chest.

I snatched my badge off my nightstand and headed downstairs with the patter of Elizabeth's feet following close behind from the fourth floor. I stopped on the landing waiting for Liz as the officer banged once more. She started down the stairs, but I held her up. They could wait. They dragged me out of bed at six in the morning for this bullshit.

"Play this cool," Liz said as we walked down the stairs,

taking our sweet time.

Another knock. "Open up, please. This is the Boston Police Department."

I turned to Liz when we reached the front door. "You need to go get Katie up. They're going to want to see her. And have her pack a bag just in case. And call Philip."

Liz looked stricken. "You don't think—"

"Yes, I do. Now go, please, Liz." I took a deep breath to clear my head as she padded off to the elevator. Then I reigned in my boiling rage. Jim Fincher had called DCF. Like an asshole, he'd probably told them that either I'd kidnapped Katie or that she'd run away. The DCF officer had arranged a pickup. It was pretty standard stuff. Unfortunately, there was nothing I could do until I could arrange a hearing. If I didn't comply, I'd be in trouble with the department and possibly fired.

I opened the door, badge in hand. The officer was a little shocked when she saw me. "Detective Reagan?"

"Yes, Officer," I tilted my head, indicating that I didn't have the slightest clue who she was.

"Sorry, Ma'am, Aubrey, Ma'am. We received a report—" She looked pointedly over at Jim Fincher, her mouth twisted in the shape someone might get if they swallowed a shit-flavored lemon with a house fly garnish. "We received a report that a young girl had been kidnapped."

I smiled in vicious delight. "Well, technically, I think that's true. But not by us. The Fincher's daughter was found at the Elliot Norton Park incident. My partner, Elizabeth, and I have been caring for her. It took some time for me to figure out who the Finchers were, as Katie has amnesia, and, well, I couldn't find a missing person's report. And, as you know, Officer Aubrey, that was over two months ago now."

Jim Fincher shifted uncomfortably from one foot to another, and Anne Fincher looked as if someone had sucked all the blood from her head and shoulders. *You wanted this, assholes. Now we have to do it the hard fucking way,* I thought. At least my hands weren't shaking.

It was Ms. Colewort's turn to look like she had swallowed the shit-flavored lemon. "Detective Reagan, can we please see

Katie?"

"Well, she's become a bit of a night owl, so I'd rather you came back this evening when she's better rested."

"I'm sorry, Detective, that's not possible. Her parents are here to take her home."

I sighed heavily. "I see. That's interesting. Come in." I opened the door wider, and they all filed into the house. Jim and Anne looked around, somewhat stunned by the place, and I didn't blame them. I'd been impressed myself when I'd first set foot into the foyer.

"Nice place on a Detective's salary," Aubrey said, and I couldn't tell if it was jealousy or if she was digging at me, suggesting I might be involved in something untoward.

"Oh, Officer, it's not mine. It belongs to Marcella Carson. I'm sure you've seen her on TV, she's quite well known. Ms. Tyler and I live here with Ms. Carson, who is away on business. Why don't you come in and sit down?"

"Well, we can't—" Jim Fincher started to say, but I cut him off.

"Mr. Fincher, I expected you to come by after I contacted you a few days ago. Now, Katie's getting herself ready to go, and it will be a minute. So, please, come sit down."

"Detective, can I speak to you privately for a moment," Officer Aubrey said.

I turned to Ms. Colewort and the Finchers. Ms. Colewort still looked like she was sucking on the shit-flavored lemon. Anne Fincher still looked petrified. Jim Fincher's face had turned the color of a ripe tomato. If this kept up, I thought he might have a stroke. Good. His ass was grass.

They'd still probably take Katie. It was the law. But his butt was going to be up on charges after this. I was going to crucify his sorry ass. Bringing the social worker here had been a massive mistake on his part, especially under false pretenses. All it did was put me in the driver's seat to try and wrest Katie and, possibly, Leah away from them in the end. That was if I could somehow keep Katie from killing them first.

I said, "Please feel free to have a seat. We'll be right back." And I drew Officer Aubrey across into Marcella's library, closing the massive sliding doors.

The first time I ever entered the library had been one morning, not long after I was turned. I had been dumbstruck, much as Officer Aubrey was now, held in thrall like a child who had just entered her first candy store.

The room centered on a pair of oversized chairs, both comfortable and ornate. Rich leather, the color of aged whiskey, covered each seat, well coordinated with the polished bookshelves of beautiful solid cherry. Lovingly restored, the bookshelves, nonetheless, carried faded burn marks and discolorations that spoke of the trials and tribulations of each home they'd sat in previously.

Every type of book imaginable sat on the shelves. Most of the volumes were in languages I did not read, though some were in English and Latin. Sitting slightly withdrawn among them was one volume that had previously been secreted quietly at the end of one low shelf, an ancient printing of the Leabhar Gabhála, the Book of Invasions, reprinted from the original Old Irish.

There was nothing exceptional about the book itself. The binding was common, and the gold lettering all but rubbed away. But it had reminded me of stories my mother told me as an infant and a toddler, things I hadn't remembered until that moment. Memories that recalled what it was to love as a child loved her mother or a mother loved her child. At the same time, other kids in my neighborhood heard about Cinderella or Aurora. My mother fed me a diet of the world of the Morrigan and Badb and Macha, of the Battles between the Fomori and the Tuatha Dé Danann. I learned of the old Irish gods and their wars and the heroes they championed, scorned, loved, and cursed.

I once again picked up the book and clutched the cloth-bound book to my chest, looking for comfort, thinking of the same stories, which I now told Katie almost daily. "Book lover?" I asked.

"My mom's a librarian," Aubrey responded quietly. "Some of these books are almost impossible to find." She stepped over to one shelf and put her hand on one book. "This one here is a Great Expectations special edition put together by Dickens from scraps he'd gathered of the serialized version published in 'All the Year Round.' It's probably worth hundreds of thousands of dollars, and it's just sitting here on a shelf." At my amused expression, she added. "I tried library sciences, but it bored me, which is why I became a cop, but I can still appreciate this."

I smiled and spoke, pulling her out of whatever wild thoughts were spinning about in her head. "So, what did you want to discuss?"

"Oh, yeah. So this guy told Ms. Colewort that you'd kidnapped Katie and she was in danger for her life. I'm really sorry about all this. I can't arrest him for it, but—"

I shook my head. This would all come out in court, and Phillip would already be headed to the courthouse to file paperwork. Liz had seen to that. "I knew this was coming. Jim Fincher dug this hole, and now our attorney will bury him in it. We're doing this by the book. Just make sure you write a clean report, okay?"

Officer Aubrey nodded. "Just so you know, he gives me the creeps."

"You and me both."

We stepped back into the parlor and found the Finchers and Ms. Colewort in deep discussion.

Ms. Colewort was saying, "—you said she was in danger. I'm not seeing that here, Jim."

"I'm telling you," Fincher hissed. "These people are weird. Two women living alone with our daughter, maybe it's a sex thing."

I cleared my throat and glared in disgust at Jim Fincher. "Katie should be down any moment. Would any of you like coffee or tea? We need to discuss Katie's condition."

Jim Fincher looked up, face flushed in both embarrassment and anger. "We don't need anything from you. We just want to get our daughter and leave."

With perfect timing, Katie and Liz walked in. Katie was holding Vlad and carrying a good-sized suitcase. She had the look of someone who thought their entire life was over. For a moment, my dispassionate facade broke, and tears welled in my eyes.

"Oh, honey," I said. "It'll be alright. Don't worry." Then in the barest whisper only she and Liz could hear, I added, "Phillip is filing to have you brought back. You won't be there for more than two nights. Can you handle that?"

Katie nodded, dropped the suitcase, and threw her arms around me. "Please don't let them take me, mama."

Liz shot a hot glare at the Finchers that made them both shrink about three sizes. At over six feet, she could be genuinely intimidating when she wanted.

"It's just a little vacation," I whispered as the tears rolled, heavy and fat, from my eyes. "I want you to listen to me carefully. Keep it under control and stay relaxed, no glamour, no feeding. We'll be coming for you. Do you understand?"

Katie nodded again.

"That's my girl." I turned back to Ms. Colewort and the Finchers and spoke freely. "Mr. Fincher, I saw the bruise on Leah's face when I visited. If you lay a hand on Katie, there will be no place for you to hide. Also, given the circumstances, I expect we'll be in touch in a day or so."

Liz piped up. "Katie is carrying two bottles of oral medication that she needs to drink. She can manage it herself." Liz pulled out an official-looking prescription in her own handwriting and showed it to them. "It's her last two doses, and she needs to take them." No one looked too hard at the prescription. They just nodded. Jim Fincher no longer looked like a blustering asshole. He just looked small and petty. If I were a betting woman, I'd have put any amount of money he was rethinking this course of action.

That's right, I thought. *It's over for you and your wife. I gave you fair warning.*

"Katie, do you have anything you'd like to say?" Ms. Colewort asked.

I waited, holding my breath, unsure what she might say, but she surprised the hell out of me as the voice of a much more mature woman emerged. "I don't want to go with them. I don't remember either Mr. or Ms. Fincher. I've been happy here. I haven't been mistreated. Cait and Elizabeth have taken good care of me. Do I have to go with them?"

Ida looked away for a moment in discomfort. Her eyes flicked to the Finchers and back to Katie. "I'm sorry, Katie, you are their daughter, and they have a right to take you home."

I thought Katie would protest, but she said nothing else and just lowered her head, looking at the floor. I wiped my eyes and gave her a big hug, as did Liz. Then we watched as Katie, the Finchers, Officer Aubrey, and Ida Colewort walked out the door.

After they were gone, my careful composure finally failed, and I gave a wail of misery from deep within my soul. It was a cry of fury and rage and despair that I knew well and never thought I'd make. It was the desperate lament of a mother who'd just lost her child and had no words to express her sadness. Liz held me, keeping me from falling to my knees, suppressing her own grief, I was sure, to let me express my own.

She said softly, "We'll get her back, Cait. I promise we'll get her back."

I knew she was right, but nothing would assuage the awful pain that crushed my chest, so I clutched at Liz and continued to cry. But I knew, deep within me, in my rage-filled, horrible, darkened soul, I would kill Jim Fincher. I was going to murder him with my bare hands.

You, Jim Fincher, have just fucked with the wrong vampire.

CHAPTER TWENTY-SEVEN

My stomach roiled horribly, and my second cup of coffee hadn't made it any better. I stared at my screen, and the only thing I could think about was how best to murder Jim and Anne Fincher. Simplest and most likely to keep me from jail would be to make it look like a mugging. Buy a gun off the street and shoot the two of them as they walked somewhere. But that would be so unsatisfying. What I wished at that moment was to tear their throats out. I tried to quell the horrid ideations, but I couldn't. It was as if my emotions had total control. Eventually, the stress of it all became too much, and my stomach began to cramp. I squeezed my eyes shut, concentrating on my discomfort, which finally banished the tortured visions.

"You okay?" Carlos' words pulled me back to earth.

"They took Katie, Carlos," I whispered. "The Finchers came and took her."

Carlos frowned. "That's not good. What are you going to do?"

"I don't know yet. Philip is at the courthouse now, filing paperwork. We're going to try to get her back, but it's a long shot. On top of that, my stomach hurts, and I don't feel great." I wasn't in vomit territory yet, but I felt pretty close.

"You do look a little pale," Carlos said, then he sniffed

repeatedly and bent down, examining my face with an odd intensity, looking me up and down.

I leaned further back the closer he got. "What are you doing? Are you about to lick my face? 'Cause eww."

Carlos laughed, eyes twinkling with unbridled mirth. "Sorry, I caught a whiff of something. You may not know this, but every vampire has a distinctive—"

"Smell? Aroma? Odor? Yes, I know. Let me guess, cinnamon and burnt embers?" I raised an eyebrow.

Carlos squinted at me. "Yes. I was trying to put my finger on it. But that's it. We spent one Christmas at Lake George in New York when I was a kid. One night at the hotel, my dad got into it with another customer who assaulted him. The guy was a racist prick. Anyway, that's not the point. Afterward, we were all sitting around this big fireplace drinking hot apple cider, and I remember thinking that despite my dad's black eye, it was one of the happiest moments of my life."

"Is there a point to this trip down memory lane?" I said irritably. My stomach was starting to hurt worse now.

"I'm sorry, darlin', no real point. I didn't realize the scent was still on you or in you or whatever. I guess I just didn't notice it. It's pretty faint as it is. I was trying to be funny, lookin' for fangs or pale skin. I guess it fell flat."

I chuckled. "Nope, doing fine in that department. Thanks though. Hey! I forgot to tell you, Liz and I were at the old Schmidt place, and we think we got a lead. Oh, and we need to send the feds over there or something because there's something digging around in the cellar."

Carlos raised an eyebrow. "Digging around?"

"Yeah. Not sure what it was, but we heard scratching behind the walls, and something was trying to get out of the tunnel."

"Great, that's all we need. I'll call Schaeffer in a minute. Tell me about the lead."

"Well, one of the hunter families that's survived, according to Schmidt's research, was Rinaldi, and guess what family name that was changed to here in the US." I grinned, but Carlos just crossed his arms and waited. "Oh," I grumped.

"Fine. Reynolds. And who's gone AWOL from the Bureau?"

"Reynolds," Carlos said. "Huh. Not conclusive, but we need to run it down. I'll put out a BOLO on Matt."

"Nope. I'll take care of it. Not your job, Carlos."

I was about to say something else when my stomach lurched, and I snatched up my wastebasket, throwing up. "Christ, the stress is getting to me," I said as soon as I'd recovered.

"You alright? I thought you had an iron stomach or something."

"Usually I do, but I've been dealing with a lot lately, Nastasia, the murders, the Finchers, my mother." *The fact that I'm in love with a woman who's in love with me, and we both think that's a bad idea.* "It's pretty heavy stress, but it'll all pass eventually. At least, I hope it will. Meanwhile, I need to clean this out." I walked to Freyer's desk and grabbed a couple of antacids from the bottle sitting there, which helped. Then I went to the bathroom and cleaned out my wastebasket. *This sucks,* I thought as I headed back to my desk. I had almost sat down when Carlos' grabbed me.

"We've got our first request for PIU. A problem at Councilman Waller's house. Grab your gear and let's go, chop, chop. Patrol will meet us there."

"But my BOLO for Reynolds?"

"It'll have to wait. Let's go."

"Whatever," I said, following him out. "Five will get you twenty that Waller thought he saw a ghost or something."

Carlos laughed.

The scene around the city councilman's home was pandemonium.

Eight cruisers were spread about the brownstones on Worcester Square. Four officers were standing in front of one of the townhomes, weapons drawn. *Okay, so not a ghost sighting.*

We piled out of our cars and walked over to the supervising

officer. I stopped, though, when I saw something that made my skin crawl. One of the demonic spider things we'd fought in the gate chamber lay dead in front of the building.

"Is that?" Carol asked.

"Yeah." I looked at Carlos. "How'd they get out? I thought the feds had the gate chamber closed off and under guard."

Carlos scratched at his beard. "Beats me. Might have dug out? Or maybe there was another exit we missed."

"That's not good," Carol said flatly.

"No," Carlos responded. "It's not."

I turned to the supervising officer. It was Officer Best, who had responded to the Caldwell murder over two months ago. It seemed he'd been recently promoted. "So, what's the situation?"

Best's hands were shaking. "We tried to get into the building, but one of those things jumped out. Fortunately, Jackson," he pointed to one of the patrolmen guarding the house, "was quick on the draw and gunned it down. But it scared the shit out of all of us. We decided not to go inside until you guys got here."

I didn't understand. "Why didn't you clear the building?"

"See for yourself." He pointed toward the townhouse door.

The large oak door of the townhome had a few bullets lodged in it. Carlos and I took one side. Maki and Carol took the other. On three, we opened the door and moved in. We were immediately confronted with something out of a horror movie.

Thick black strands of cable-like webbing weaved from wall to wall, making advancement almost impossible beyond the foyer. The webs dripped in various places with a clear, viscous liquid that plopped wetly to the floor. My tongue flicked out, pulling in a thousand awful smells; most prominent were a decaying body, the unique scent of the spider thing, and something acidic that burned my mouth and nose.

"Oh, God!" I exclaimed as I pressed my nose to my arm. "That's fucking awful."

Carlos didn't say a word, keeping his eyes and weapon forward. His nose was as sensitive as my vomeronasal duct, and I had no idea how he didn't recoil at the odors. Even Carol and Maki were looking a little green.

Maki stepped in behind us, gingerly moving past the dead spider-thing out front. "Ogumo," she muttered. "Ick!"

I turned to Maki. "What's that?"

"It's what we call them in Japan. It literally means 'giant spider.' It's a demon. We have them in Japan in some more remote places, generally presumed to be haunted."

I raised an eyebrow at that. "You 'have them' in Japan?"

"Well, I've only ever seen one. It was a long time ago in the Fuji forest, also known as the—"

"Suicide Forest," I finished. "I've heard of it." Even though Maki looked in her mid-twenties, she talked like she was much older. She wasn't a vampire; that much I knew, but I still suspected she wasn't human either. It was the way she spoke to us, like she was ancient and we were all children. "So you've seen one of these things before?"

Maki put her weapon back in its holster. "This may not make much sense to you, but it was over four centuries ago. You should probably let me go first."

Carol snorted mirthlessly. "You'd be surprised, Maki. That's not the weirdest thing I've heard, this week even."

I even laughed at that.

Maki took point, taking out a short Bowie knife and cutting loose the strands of webbing. The living room was likewise covered in the stuff, but there was enough room to stand once we cut down the intervening webs.

Maki stopped at the living room entrance, grabbing Carlos' hand as he reached out to touch one of the strands. "Don't! They're covered with an acidic substance. It won't do serious damage, but it will irritate your skin, causing blisters, things like that."

There was barely enough space to pile inside the living room together. Along the far wall was a series of hanging pods of black leathery material that looked like nothing less than giant egg sacs.

"Are those?" I asked, gesturing at the sacs.

Maki made a grim face. "Eggs, yes. Do not disturb them

unless you want a million tiny versions of that thing outside crawling on us."

A thick, oily-black residue that looked like nothing so much as melted vinyl covered everything in the room: the walls, the furniture, even the ceiling. It anchored the black webbing in various places. We scanned around with our flashlights, looking for a way past the goo, when Carol spotted something.

"There's a DB." She pointed her light toward a desiccated hand protruding from underneath the sofa. "Is it the Councilman?"

I holstered my pistol and pulled on some gloves, peering beneath the furniture. "Maybe what's left of him," I said. The corpse lay stuffed under the sofa. Something had gnawed away a good bit of it to the bone. I'd never seen anything quite like it.

Gingerly, I tugged at the protruding arm to avoid disturbing the egg sac hanging just above it. On the first pull, the forearm came away from the body, and I fell backward onto my ass, my arm narrowly missing the egg sac. I held my breath as the sac moved slightly, quivering, then once more settling still.

I blew out the breath I'd been holding and slid the forearm to Carol, who looked about to barf.

"Maki?" Carlos chimed in, eyes locked on the egg sac.

"Yes."

"Will that thing open if Cait gets too close? Or does she actually have to touch it?"

Maki's reply didn't inspire a lot of confidence. "I don't know. I've never seen one of the eggs up close."

I looked to Carlos for any reassurance but found none. "Well, here goes nothing." I dropped to my belly on the floor and crawled forward, feeling clothing catch, sticking slightly to the viscous black residue. The egg sac moved again as I got closer, and I stopped. My hand was less than an inch away from the shoulder of the corpse. I could get it.

"Cait, stop. Don't move," Carlos hissed, and I froze. "There's something in the webbing on the ceiling."

I turned to look up, but a drop of caustic fluid fell onto my face, burning like fire as it trailed across my cheek, narrowly missing my right eye. I didn't dare move or speak. There, directly above me, was an ogumo hanging in the webbing. It had been curled up, camouflaged. Its six long legs, ending in steel-like talons, unfurled slowly as it aimed toward me.

Then, everything happened all at once. Carlos snatched me by the ankles, jerking me back from under the wretched creature just as the ogumo shot down, spiked legs driving into the residue coating the floor. Carol shot it several times, missing at least once and hitting one of the egg sacs, which exploded.

Hundreds of small skittering ogumo heaved out across the floor, immediately charging toward us in a mass of legs and razor-sharp teeth. Carlos yanked me off the floor and grabbed Carol in his other arm, pushing his way back through the hallway to the door.

I glanced back to see if Maki had made it out. She was standing, legs astride the hallway defiantly. As she drew a deep breath, a sparkling silver light glowed across her body. Nine bright-white, furry tails sprung from her back and fanned like peacock feathers. A jet of flame engulfed the swarm of demonic spiders, burning them to a crisp with a million tiny popping noises, like the crackle of searing bacon. From what I could see, it looked like Maki had just breathed fire.

Black smoke billowed from the burning room, enveloping us in a horrid stench like burnt plastic. Both Carlos and I gagged and vomited when we reached the portico outside.

"Fuck!" I exclaimed, stumbling further out of the black smoke. I called for Maki in a panic.

"I'm here," she coughed, stumbling through the door, arms in front of her. The tails I'd seen were gone. "I told you not to disturb the eggs." She bent over and puked in the bushes next to the door. Carol seemed the only one unaffected.

The fire engines arrived a few minutes later. Fortunately, the awful black goo that coated everything was more prone to smolder than burn, so the building was saved.

We waited for the firefighters to give the all-clear, then we went back inside. The entire building smelled horrible, and I wondered what awful form of cancer we'd get from just being here. Maki took point, obviously, with Carlos and I backing her up and Carol bringing up the rear. I desperately wanted to ask her what she was, but it wasn't the time for it. We needed to be focused in case there were more fucking creatures.

The upstairs was clear, and it looked like no one had been up there in days. The bed was unmade, but otherwise, it wasn't disturbed. The toothbrush was dry, as was the rest of the bathroom, so the victim had been stuffed under the couch for at least a little while. My best guess was that the vic had heard something downstairs and gone to investigate. From what I'd seen of the body before it had been incinerated, it had looked eaten, but that was all I could tell. It was impossible to know whether the ogumo had gotten him or he'd died beforehand.

We opened the cellar door and were greeted by what looked like about a foot of water at the bottom of the stairs, the runoff from the firehoses.

"Shit," Carlos said as we panned our flashlights around the black water. "I don't fancy walking in that."

"Well, don't look at me," Maki said. "You're the daring one, Reagan. You go in."

I shook my head. "Daring? More like stupid."

I stepped into the water and discovered it was far deeper than it had appeared, rising to my waist. And, fuck me, it was ice cold. I shivered violently as soon as I waded in. The cellar floor felt odd under my shoes, soft and squishy, not like mud, more like walking on a soggy foam mattress.

"Oh! This is so gross." I panned around with my flashlight and jumped. "Something just brushed my leg."

Freaking out, I turned back toward the stairs. It couldn't have been a second later when something wrapped around my right leg, jerking it from under me and pulling me beneath the oily water. Panicking, I pulled my left leg under me and shot back up, sputtering and gasping for breath, just in time to hear the noise of shattering concrete as the water began flowing violently toward the back wall, carrying me and whatever had my leg with it.

"Help!" I squeaked as it pulled me under again. Moments later, a massive clawed hand grabbed my shoulder, digging in deeply and jerking me to a stop. At first, I scrabbled at the cla, but then I realized it was Carlos, partially transformed, thick nails protruding from his fingers for purchase. Whatever held my leg released it and slipped away with the draining water. The ordeal left me heaving for breath on the nasty, spongy black surface that coated the cellar. "Holy shit!" I swore as I pulled myself back. "Thanks, Carlos."

"Damn, darlin', basements really aren't your thing, are they?" He said and pointed toward the back wall with his free hand. A large section of the wall had collapsed, revealing a shallow tunnel that sloped sharply down and away from the cellar and into the darkness. "Good thing I caught you, or you would've been on one hell of a water slide."

"Carlos, you're hurting me," I complained as my shoulder began to burn and blood ran down my arm. Carlos let me go, his hand returning to normal, and I crawled back to the stairs, cradling the two-inch gash in my shoulder blade as best I could.

Carol dropped to my side and ripped open the back of my shirt. "Let me look at that. Honey, this is going to need—" Carol gasped, and the pain in my shoulder vanished abruptly.

"What?" I felt around with my other arm, finding the flesh neat and whole. A burning, itching sensation flashed under my skin, and I shook slightly just before a wave of nausea and dizziness replaced the burning. I tried to get up and stumbled, clutching the handrail and Carol for support.

"Jesus, Cait, are you okay?" Carol helped me sit back down on the stairs.

"I don't know. I was just a bit dizzy. What happened? What did you see?"

"It just closed up all by itself, Cait. One second I could see the bone of your shoulder blade, then it was just gone." Her eyes were like dinner plates, and her expression inspired nothing so much as worry.

She shined her flashlight at me. "You look a little pale, too. What's going on?"

"Like I should know. I was fine until just now. Just give me a minute." It was the changed blood, for sure. Nastasia had given me a ton of the stuff. It was probably what made me sick earlier, too. I wasn't about to tell Carol that, though. She'd give me some bullshit lecture I didn't want to hear. I rubbed my hands across my face, wiping off the black gunk that had been in the water.

After I composed myself and Carol confirmed that the color had returned to my face, I looked at the hole in the wall with the rest of the team. The cavity inside sloped sharply down before dropping away about two feet into the rock. Carlos held my belt while I shined my flashlight down the shaft; it went on further than I could see. I had a moment of terror as I looked at the shaft walls that something was going to come groping out of the darkness to pull me to my death, but nothing did. I reached down and felt the sides of the shaft, finding it ridged. "Looks like they dug their way through solid rock to get in here. Anyone up for spelunking?"

Carol shook her head vigorously. Maki looked at me like I'd lost my mind, and Carlos just said, "Don't you remember the last time you crawled into a creepy tunnel under some house?"

"Oh, come on, Carlos, this time I have backup," I chirped, a little surprised at myself.

Carol looked around. "I'm sure you don't mean us."

I smiled, and there might have even been a bit of something naughty in it.

CHAPTER TWENTY-EIGHT

After some reasonably intense discussion, Carlos finally made a decision. We all left, cleaned up, and returned to the scene about two hours later wearing fatigues and armed to the teeth. Freyer and Kennedy volunteered to go down the hole with Carlos and me. Carol and Maki, who had no tactical training, were staying topside to continue working the scene with Doyle.

The fire and subsequent deluge of hose water had destroyed the electrical outlets, so generators were set up around the building. The houses on either side were evacuated, and we got started.

"Why are we doing this again?" Freyer asked as he loaded rounds into spare magazines.

"Because, Freyer, those things are crawling around under the city, and we need to see where they've gone. Also, whatever grabbed me wasn't a spider. It had a tentacle of some sort. Besides, you volunteered for this, remember?" It was a valid question, though. Larson had asked for the feds to be brought in, but the brass shut it down. The chief said the mayor wanted us to take the lead in investigating this. I didn't understand that decision, but it wasn't my call.

"Yeah, but why are we doing this?" Freyer repeated, clarifying the question.

"Because we," I gestured around," are who the mayor wants to do this. But look at it this way, we can shoot some stuff with impunity. It'll be fun." I grinned at Freyer, who shook his head, shrugged, and made a 'whatever' face.

"Okay, just remember how it turned out for the Marines in *Aliens*."

Morgan opened the case of submachine guns. "That's a movie, Freyer. This is real life." She pulled one of the weapons out and checked it over. "Ooh, sexy, I always wanted to use one of these." She fingered the MP5 SSD with near-romantic intent, one finger sliding down the integrated noise suppressor in an almost obscene manner. I couldn't blame her. Those weapons were used by the Navy SEALs and other special operations units. They were relatively light and short enough to use in close quarters.

Freyer scoffed. "It used to be Sci-Fi; now I file it on my shelves under educational films, just sayin'."

"And we have subsonic rounds! Hot Damn," Morgan said as she started helping Freyer with the magazines for the MP5s.

I stepped over to Morgan and helped load. "So, are we good?" I asked quietly.

She looked at me. I could see the hurt in her eyes but also resignation. "Yes, we're good. Just make sure she takes good care of you."

"For what it's worth, I'm sorry for what I said."

"Yep." She slid open the chamber on one of the side arms, eyeballed it, and then holstered it. "We'll be fine. It may take a while to get back to being good friends, but we're still way above starting over. Regardless, I have your back. I know you've got mine." She bumped a fist on top of my shoulder and moved on to the next weapon.

"You know I do, Red." And that was that. We were back in the suck, and we had a job to do. Our personal shit had no place. I didn't fool myself into believing there wouldn't be some hard feelings at some point, but that wasn't worth worrying about now. Either we'd be friends, or we wouldn't. But it didn't seem like we'd hate each other.

Once we were all geared up, I keyed my throat mic. "Radio

check." The others repeated it, and we all gave thumbs up. Freyer put on his helmet, clipped in, and Carol lowered him into the hole.

"See anything, Freyer?" I asked after the rope hit bottom.

Freyer's transmission was rife with static, but I could hear him. "There's a tunnel running northwest to southeast down here, no sign of the spiders. The southeast direction is pretty wet, but the northeast looks dry further down. It's safe to say the water ran south, which is weird because there's a slight incline before it slopes down. To the northeast, it's flat. The tunnel widens as it drops, but it's still pretty cramped. Enough room for the gorilla, though."

"Hey!" Morgan and I protested in unison.

"I meant Carlos. He looks like he ate one of you." We all laughed at Carlos' sour expression.

"It's alright, Carlos. I'm sure he meant your muscle mass." I tapped him lightly on the belly and clipped in when the carabiner appeared over the lip of the shaft. "Coming down."

"Hold up," Freyer called. "Contact."

My heart stopped as I heard the chunk-chunk of his MP5. "Freyer, status!" No answer. I waited for a second and tried again. "Freyer, talk to me."

After a few long, scary heartbeats, he finally responded. "I'm good. There was one coming down the tunnel. I capped it. Not sure how we're gonna get past it, though. The carcass is blocking the southwest. Looks like we're going northeast."

The vertical shaft ran down a long way, probably seventy-five feet. Freyer was on one knee and hunched over to my right when I landed. "All clear," he whispered, his weapon pointed down the southwest tunnel.

I crouched on one knee and jerked my weapon to my shoulder, covering the northeast tunnel. It seemed to run extraordinarily straight and uniform for something made by animals. I moved out of the shaft, covering the northeast tunnel as Morgan landed softly behind me and called back for Carlos to come down.

"You're so full of shit, Freyer; it's cramped as hell down here," Morgan bitched as she moved up behind me.

"Maybe you should eat less," I joked.

"Ouch," Carlos said as he landed. "That was harsh."

Morgan chuckled. "Kitty-Cait's just jealous of my stunning body, Carlos. She wishes she'd had it in Iraq. Now, she'll never know what she missed."

"What, the rash? I know about that." I shot back playfully, never taking my eyes from the tunnel.

Morgan whapped me on the arm. "Wow, Cait, when did you become such a bitch?"

"Okay, stow it, you two," Freyer ordered. "Let's get moving."

As I took them, I counted the steps in my head, measuring the distance. Moving was extremely slow, and we immediately lost radio contact with the surface. We were alone. We crawled along a cramped corridor, more or less frog walking, with no more backup than each other and no sound other than our labored breathing. It was also sweltering. Sweat dripped uncomfortably down my forehead and coated my face.

"I don't get the heat down here," I whispered. "It should be relatively cool."

"Maybe we're up against a boiler room for one of the larger buildings or something," Carlos suggested.

I was about to reply when I heard something, a skittering up ahead. I held up my fist to halt our progress and peered up the passageway. *God, I wish I was a vampire right now,* I thought as I strained to hear or see whatever it was again.

"What's the holdup?" Morgan asked.

"Shh." I hissed as the skittering started again. It was getting louder, accompanied by a huffing sound. I froze. It was breathing. My eyes shot wide in recognition and panic. "Oh fuck! Back, back, back!"

The others started scrambling behind me. At first, I followed, but then I stopped and turned. We'd never make it. "Get back to the shaft! I'll hold it off."

Morgan protested first. "No way, Cait! You're not doing it alone."

The thick, slimy, gray blob slid into view, pressed impossibly small in the tiny corridor, little taloned legs around its body, the white-worm, probably the one that had infected me. *Shit.* I squeezed off several rounds from my MP5. The chunk, chunk of the suppressed weapon echoed again and again. The beast slowed and screeched that same horrific sound. That's what had been in the cellar. That's what grabbed my leg. It just hadn't had time to sink its teeth into me before the water rushed out and washed it away down the shaft.

The beast darted forward again, much faster than I remember. I could see it clearly in my flashlight this time. Slime-like ooze dripped from its mouth, and its long snake-like proboscis threaded through its teeth, opening like a flower to show row after row of tiny backward curving fangs and a razor-like tongue that split three ways. *Fuck! Not again.* Fear squeezed at my chest. I couldn't go through that again.

I flipped the switch to full auto and held down the trigger. Chunks of the beast flew off in various directions. "Die, you fucking thing!" I screamed, but I had missed the proboscis, and it shot toward my face, latching onto my cheek. I felt the tiny fangs dig in, and I screamed. Stars burst into my eyes as something landed on me, knocking my head to the floor and jerking the god-awful thing from my face.

Moments later, my vision cleared, and I watched as the creature hurried back into the darkness, its metallic screech vanishing into the black. The disgusting tentacle-like tongue flopped on the ground in front of me, severed from the creature's mouth. Morgan lay on my back, chest heaving, her Bowie knife in her hand, dark ichor staining both. Blood ran down my cheek and neck.

"Here." Morgan snatched a thick pad of gauze from a vest pocket and pressed it to my cheek.

I jerked her hand away, and my voice rose in terror. "Look at it. Tell me if you see anything sticking out of the wound like a wiggling parasite. Quickly. Please, Morgan."

Morgan pulled out a pen light and shined it in my face. Long moments ticked past as she tugged at the skin. "No, there's nothing there. You have a couple of tiny marks here where it broke the skin, but I don't see anything wiggling or moving."

"Is there a circular wound in the center of the teeth marks?"

"No, there's nothing. It looks clean."

"You alright, Cait?" Carlos said, crawling up behind us.

Morgan crawled off me, and I propped myself up against the side of the tunnel. I put the gauze on my face to staunch the bleeding. The pain was excruciating, but moments later, it vanished in a wave of dizziness and nausea, which persisted for several minutes, causing me to gag and cough a few times before it passed.

"Cait? I asked if you were okay. Let me take a gander." Carlos pulled the gauze away and examined the skin. "There's nothing here. Just a little blood. Did it get you or not?"

"It got me, but it healed up. Don't ask. I don't want to get into it."

Carlos examined my eyes, making sure I didn't have a concussion. "Changed blood?" He asked in a whisper, eyes full of judgment.

I shook my head, ignoring his critical stare and wiping my face. "I'm okay. Let's keep going. We need to know how these things got here and where they've been."

"Are you shitting me?" Morgan exclaimed, her voice rising, incredulous and wide-eyed. "We were just attacked by that, thing, whatever it was. We do not need to be down here doing this. We need to call in the feds."

I shot forward and clamped my hand over her mouth. "Jesus, Morgan. Will you keep your voice down? We're not trying to bring every fucking monster under Boston down on us."

"We can't call in the feds," Carlos said. "Cait's right; we need to see what's going on. We've faced far worse than this. I'd rather kick a raging bull square in the nuts, but we gotta finish this. Why don't you and Freyer go back to the shaft? You didn't sign up for this. Cait and I can take it from here."

I took my hand off Morgan's mouth. "Sorry, Red," I whispered. "We just need to be quiet."

She nodded, her eyes wide and face drained of color. She was scared shitless.

Freyer poked his head around Carlos. "No way. We

volunteered to come down here with you. If you're going, we're going. Right Kennedy?"

Morgan didn't look convinced, but she sighed in resignation, nodding her head. "Okay, sure. But I'm registering my fucking objection right now, boss."

"Noted," Freyer replied. "Cait, you want one of us to take point? Or are you good?"

"Yeah, peachy," I replied softly. Morgan lay down and let me slide past her. As I reached eye level with her, I whispered in her ear. "Take a breath. Carlos and I are experienced with these things. It'll be okay. These things look scary, but they're not carrying AKs. They can't shoot us. I promise I'll keep you safe. I always have."

Morgan looked me in the eyes, searching for reassurance, then she nodded and pushed back, slapping me on the butt for my troubles as I passed. "You better," she said quietly.

I looked back and winked. "I hope you cover my ass as well as you slap it."

We continued on down the tunnel. After we'd gone maybe a thousand yards total, it sloped downward precipitously, and my hand almost slid out from under me as it landed in something wet.

"Eww. Watch it. There's blood or ichor or something here." I wiped the slimy shit off on my fatigues and continued, though it did little good.

"God, this shit is everywhere, Reagan. What is it?"

I felt a lot better hearing her use my last name. It meant she was back in the zone, viewing this as just another op. "No clue, Kennedy. Save your pants, and someone can analyze it."

"I just know I'm going to get some alien disease from this," Freyer griped from the back. I felt the worst for him. He'd been frog-walking sideways for almost a kilometer, watching our six. As exhausted as I felt, he must have been miserable. *God bless the man for his stamina.*

When we reached the end, it opened up into a wider passage that was clearly man-made and large enough to stand. I slid out of the tunnel and slipped on something, landing in an ungraceful heap on my ass. It was sandy material, a pile of it.

I stood and moved out to the left, sweeping the area with my weapon. I almost jumped out of my skin as I saw the awful gray worm in all its splendor, unmoving on the floor. In the light, just laying there, it wasn't nearly as large as it had seemed. It was about six feet long and maybe three feet in diameter. Small legs covered the entire body. Currently, they all lay limp, tucked against its body.

The mouth was just as I remembered it, round and full of long spiny teeth. The cut proboscis dangled from its mouth, still leaking ichor.

I pumped two rounds into it, but it still didn't move. Finally, I stepped forward and kicked the thick body. A spurt of ichor shot from its mouth, but it lay still. It was dead.

"Serves you right, you fucker," I muttered. "It's clear. Watch your step in here. There's a pile of sand at the tunnel edge." There was another tunnel, similar to the one I'd just exited directly across the passageway. Morgan, Carlos, and Freyer exited behind me. We were standing in some kind of concrete pipe or spillway that ran perpendicular to the ogumo tunnel.

Carlos went to examine the worm thing while I stood by the exit. "Looks like we found the source of the goo we just waded through."

Morgan stepped in and turned around, putting a hand on my cheek. "How's your face? Jesus, it's completely healed. How—"

I chuckled dryly. "Would you believe vampire spit?"

Morgan raised a questioning eyebrow.

"It has to do with how vampires feed and leave no trace on their victims." I could tell she wasn't getting it by her puzzled expression. "I'll explain later."

Before I could say more, an ogumo appeared in the tunnel behind Morgan. "Down!" I cried, and Morgan hit the deck. I hoisted my weapon, giving the ogumo a single shot, center mass. The creature made an odd hissing noise like a deflating balloon and died.

Morgan stood, looking thoroughly shaken and pale. "Holy shit—"

"Shh." I moved slowly toward the hole in the wall where it had emerged. I could see no more. "Clear," I whispered. The others were watching up and down the spillway, waiting for something to pop out. Finally, we all relaxed slightly. I could tell Morgan was just hanging on, so I pulled her aside.

"Now you listen to me, Kennedy. This is just another op. We faced down a dozen insurgents with nothing but M4s and our wits, and these things aren't nearly that dangerous, just numerous and strange looking. Now pull your shit together. Got it?"

Morgan looked back to the ogumo and its razor-sharp taloned legs. Then she nodded and took a breath. Again, she seemed to calm down and put herself back together.

Carlos sat down and pulled out his water pouch, taking a long swig. "Let's take a moment to get our bearings here."

Freyer looked around, taking in the passageway. "This is a seventy-two-inch standard reinforced concrete tunnel." He fingered the dust I'd slipped in earlier. "The concrete's been pulverized, and look at this." He held up a hand full of the dust, a mixture of a dark gray substance, the concrete, I assumed, and something reddish brown.

"What's that?" I asked, running a finger through the dust and uncovering some of the red material.

"That is rusted steel. This drainage tunnel is reinforced with steel rebar. Whatever dug these tunnels chewed through the rebar as well as the concrete and corroded the steel." Freyer brushed off his hands.

"How do you know all this?"

"My dad worked construction. He tried to get me in the business, but it didn't take."

Morgan gestured toward the hole in the northeast wall. "So where does this go?"

Carlos and I looked at each other before he answered. "My guess? The gate chamber. I don't fancy going back there, but we need to see what's going on."

It was my turn to get cold feet. "I don't know, Carlos. Are you sure that's a good idea?" I gestured to the dead ogumo with my weapon.

"No, but these critters have run of the city, and I want to know how they slipped right from under the feds' noses."

I thought about that. "I have a more important question. Why did the ogumo dig a tunnel straight from the gate chamber right to a specific cellar, kill the owner and take up nesting? Seems like a long way to go. Especially when they could go almost anywhere from right here. These drainage tunnels run everywhere, don't they?"

We all looked at each other. None of us liked where this seemed to be going. It was Freyer who gave voice to what we were all thinking. "They were after something."

"Or someone," I finished. "But they didn't act like they had any kind of intelligence when they attacked us in the gate chamber. They certainly didn't seem sophisticated enough to go after a specific person."

"Something is directing them," Morgan said flatly. "Most animals, intelligent or otherwise, explore their environment, assess where they are, and find a safe place to live. These things didn't do that. They just happily dug a kilometer worth of tunnel to one house. It's the only answer."

"Well, we're burning batteries. I want to get through this and get out." I walked over and shined a light down the hole. Seeing nothing, I climbed inside, and the others followed.

CHAPTER TWENTY-NINE

"So you did this in Iraq?" Carlos grunted as he scooted along behind Morgan.

I stopped for a second to give us a short break. "Yup. I was smaller than the guys, so I got to tunnel rat from time to time." I flattened against the tunnel so Morgan could cover downrange while I took the last sips from my water pouch. "Those tunnels were nothing like this, though. They were built for people. Many were positively roomy by comparison. Just hard to get into for a dude built to carry an M240 machine gun, kinda like you, Carlos."

"Gee, thanks for the reminder that I feel like a trout in a garden hose. You ever get stuck or claustrophobic?"

"Nope. Enclosed spaces don't bother me. I just don't fancy getting eaten in one." Morgan and I swapped, her drinking while I covered.

"Did you serve?" I couldn't believe I'd never asked Carlos that.

"Nope. Wanted to, but mama wouldn't have it. She told me if I didn't go to college, I'd be whupped, disowned, and if I were lucky, the family wouldn't use me for burrito stuffing. And you know how it works in that house."

I laughed. "What mama says goes."

Carlos nodded and turned to Freyer. "Anything?"

"Nope, clear so far. Honestly, it's fucking eerie how quiet it is. Given how hard we'd had to fight to get you guys out of the gate room, I'd have thought we'd see a bunch of the damn things in here."

I didn't disagree. It wasn't just eerie. It was downright frightening, and a sense of dread flooded me as I thought about what would happen if a crap ton of ogumo started coming down the tunnel. I shoved that thought violently aside, though. I didn't need to be any more scared than I already was. I talked a good game to Morgan, but I was on the edge of panic the whole way.

"Okay, let's move," I said, and we started again, but I stopped almost immediately as I heard a faint popping ahead of us. "Is that gunfire?"

We all listened intently but heard nothing else. We picked up the pace, and before long, I spied bright light ahead. About ten feet from what looked to be the end of the tunnel, my foot slid out from under me, and I scraped my cheek on the tunnel wall, opening a nasty cut. "Damn it," I swore softly. It bled for a moment and stopped, followed by yet another wave of nausea and dizziness.

"You okay?" Morgan whispered behind me.

"Yeah, just give me a second. This is getting fucking old, though." As soon as the discomfort passed, I looked at my boot. The sole was covered in the same slick black goo we'd seen in the cellar. That wasn't a good sign, but I'd expected it, so I huffed a breath and continued crawling.

The end of the tunnel opened into the gate chamber as expected. A thin, gray translucent film covered the exit. I nudged it with the barrel of my weapon. It was springy, almost like human skin. *Gross.* I pulled my knife and was about to cut it when a shadow skittered vertically across the opening, causing me to lurch backward, nearly toppling Morgan.

"Shit. What do I do, guys? One of those things just crawled across this—whatever it is."

Freyer spoke up. "Cut it open, Reagan. We've come this far. Let's get the hell out of this tunnel before I can't stand up."

I reached out and cut the film with my knife. "Ugh, it

stinks," I whispered as the intense smell of blood, decay, and ogumo assaulted my vomeronasal duct.

The film was smooth and even felt like human skin. I fought a wave of disgust as I pushed through the horrid stuff, feet first, feeling it slide disturbingly over my head and face. Once through, I dropped about three feet to the floor below, my feet, knees, and back aching. I stood and looked around. And my blood ran cold. "Oh, shit."

The gate itself was unchanged, sitting just as I remembered it, a yawning black sphere. Bright utility lights sat on stands around it, shining into the world beyond and limning the gate in a distorted halo. The interior of the sphere was now filled with billowing black fog hovering around a few feet of open volcanic dirt, but the chamber in which it sat? My heart rate jumped as I took in the spine-chilling changes.

The same slick, black, spongy substance covered the walls, floor, and ceiling. Great black webs dripping caustic liquid stretched around the chamber, and hundreds of ogumo hovered within them, occasionally moving about. A finger of panic ran down my spine as I moved gingerly to my left so the others could exit. In the light, the 'skin' over the tunnel exit pulsed with black, flowing veins, and I had to suppress a disgusted shiver.

Morgan slid out and moved to the left, sweeping the room until she focused on the gate. "Holy shit, what is that?"

I held a finger to my lips, silencing her, then pointed up to the ceiling where the ogumo lurked.

Morgan's eyes went wide, and her weapon flashed to her shoulder. She whirled around in a panic, not sure where to aim.

"Easy," I whispered, placing a hand on the barrel of her weapon. "They're not doing anything, so let's not disturb them."

Carlos tapped me on the shoulder and pointed to the floor on the other side of the chamber, indicating a massive trail of red blood. Too much for one person, it ran between the gate and the colossal steel doors that guarded the old subway tunnel. And even from this far away, I could see the doors didn't sit right. I switched to the tactical channel on my radio, telling the others to do the same. "Washington, you there?" I whispered.

Carol's voice, crackling with static, sounded in my ear. "Jesus, Cait. Where...hell.........were...... feds. I......read you."

"The tunnel let out in the gate chamber. But something's wrong. The main doors are ajar, and there's a huge trail of blood on the floor. Something bad happened here and recently."

There was a long pause on the radio, then nothing, only static.

"That's electromagnetic interference," Freyer said, pulling something from his pocket. "Here, look." He handed me an old-fashioned compass. The needle just spun.

I handed it back. "Shit. Okay, let's get out of here. We've seen what we need to see."

"Back the way we came?" Morgan whispered.

I sighed. Morgan was shaking like a leaf in the wind. *Damnit, Morgan,* I thought. *We've faced worse than this; what is going on with you?*

Carlos pointed to the doors and made a tip-toe motion with two fingers. We followed, single file, Morgan, and Freyer behind Carlos, me taking the rear. The ogumo above seemed to watch us. Though they had no eyes I could discern, their bodies turned in our direction, tracking us as we moved. My breath turned a little short and ragged as my anxiety elevated. *Please do not let them drop on us.*

"What are they waiting for?" Freyer whispered at my back. "I would have expected them to be all over us."

"I don't know. It's like they're afraid. Notice how they're all a uniform distance from the gate."

"That's comforting," Morgan said sarcastically. "What could they be afraid of."

"Watch it!" I said as I darted forward, shooting my hand out to catch a bit of dripping liquid just before it landed on Morgan's head. The spot where it landed immediately turned an angry red, then milky white, and then it went back to normal. Nausea returned with a vengeance, sending me to one knee for a second. No one bothered to say anything this time.

Carlos stopped as we reached the blood trail, bending down.

"Look at the doors," Morgan said in awe. They had several rents, some going completely through the thick steel, like claw marks. Something had torn its way out of here.

Carlos pulled a latex glove from his breast pocket and snapped it on. "It's still completely wet. This just happened." He held up a gloved finger, blood on the end of it, glistening in the light.

"Oh my God!" Morgan was staring at the ground near the door, the back of her hand over her mouth.

I walked over. She pointed toward the mixture of dirt on the floor. They were hard to see but were there, human scratch marks and a torn fingernail. Someone had been scrabbling at the doorway as they were dragged through. "There might be someone alive."

Carlos and Freyer joined us. "Let's get outside. Then we can figure out what to do next."

"Morgan took point, stepped through the wide gap between the savaged doors, and gasped. "Clear." Her voice sounded choked.

I stepped through behind her. The floor of the hallway was covered in blood and bits of gore. Weapons and bits of detritus lay strewn about the floor. I bent down and picked up a discarded M4, checking the magazine. "It's empty. They put up a fight."

Morgan checked the far door. "Same in this room here. There are some rooms back here. They look like torture cells or something."

My chest squeezed. I saw Katie lying on the floor, bleeding out, uttering her heartbreaking last words as a human being. 'I don't want to die.' I shook myself to banish the image. "That's exactly what they are, Morgan. It's where they kept me, me and Katie."

Morgan turned on me. "Where who kept you?" Her lips pressed together in a thin line of frustration and rage. It was like someone had flipped a switch.

"I can't talk about it. Let it go, Morg. It's a distraction. I'll explain later." At least she wasn't shaking with fear anymore. I was reminded again that she wasn't the same woman I knew. In Iraq, she'd been unshakeable, even in our worst moments. I'd leaned on her hard during that first year, and she'd gotten me through it with her can-do attitude and easy smile. Now, she seemed fragile.

Freyer motioned us to join him and Carlos by the door. "Okay, you two, sweep the rest of the facility and see who, if anyone, is left alive, then meet us back here in five minutes."

We did as ordered. The outer tunnel, the one that used to connect to the subway, had been converted for research. Several computers and scientific instruments lay strewn about, overturned, or broken. The scene was chilling, with plenty of blood but no bodies. Whatever had happened here had happened fast. There was blood splatter on the ladder rungs that ran to the surface hatch.

"That's new," I said, pointing up the ladder toward the hatch to the outside.

Morgan came over, glancing up the shaft. "What?"

"See the red display? They replaced the old maintenance cover with a computerized hatch." I looked around, finding a fat red button on the wall with a blinking display that read 'LOCKDOWN.' It was like something out of a sci-fi movie. "They must have been worried that something might escape into the city."

"Well, it was a valid concern. How did they miss the hole in the gate room, though?"

"It's covered with that filmy skin stuff, and it's on the opposite side of the gate. They probably couldn't see what the ogumo were doing." I looked at my watch. Three minutes had passed. "Two minutes. See if there's a laptop around here. Also, look for a USB cable."

"Why?"

"So Carlos can open the hatch if we need to. Right now, we're trapped in here, and the only way out is the way we came. I don't want to end up like these people, whatever happened to them."

We searched around and found a laptop with a cracked screen that seemed to turn on, and Morgan came up with a USB cable to fit the locking mechanism. We set them by the door and hoofed-it back to Carlos and Freyer.

"What'd you find?" Carlos asked when we returned.

"It's all the same, lots of blood, no bodies. The whole place is cleared out."

Carlos nodded.

"It gets worse," I said grimly. "They put in an emergency lockdown button and a reinforced hatch. Someone must have tripped it when everything went to hell. We're locked in here. But—"

"Shit," Freyer swore, interrupting me.

"But," I paused for emphasis, "the main unit for the lockdown has a USB port, and we found what looks like a semi-working computer. It boots, but the screen is a little cracked."

"I'll get to work on it," Carlos said and headed off for the lab.

Morgan gave Freyer a pinched look. "And what about the people?"

"What people? They're all dead. I mean, look at the blood?"

I sighed and shook my head. She was right. "No, they're not. At least one of them was alive when they dragged them out of here. We found human claw marks in the dirt and a torn fingernail at the door frame."

Freyer rubbed his face. "Shit. Come here. I want to show you something." He stepped through the doorway and back into the gate chamber, weapon at the ready, watching the ceiling. We followed suit. He bent down just at the edge of the gate, what my layman's mind decided was the 'event horizon,' pointing at an enormous clawed footprint. It was massive, easily two feet long, with three toes in the front and what looked like a fourth toe or appendage in the back. Claw marks capped each of the toe prints.

I stepped across the edge of the gate, my foot landing on the black basalt. I'd expected to feel something physical, like a wave of nausea or an electric charge or something. But all I felt was crushing anxiety.

"Reagan," Freyer hissed. "Get back in here."

I turned back. "Hang on," I whispered. But they weren't where I'd left them. I was standing almost ten feet away, entirely within the world on the other side. Thick black fog muddled my view of them, and from this side, with the spots on in the gate chamber, the gate itself looked like a beacon of hazy light rather than a globe of darkness.

I stepped back to the edge of the event horizon where I could see both Freyer and Morgan clearly and held up a finger, then turned around, searching the dirt. I didn't go too far. I didn't fancy getting lost out here if the lights in the gate room went out.

I immediately found tracks and drag marks heading off to my right. There was also a human footprint headed in the opposite direction. I guessed a woman's size six sneaker by the shape and size. I retraced my steps to the gate and found myself standing back next to Morgan and Freyer as soon as I planted my foot across the edge.

I looked at them both. "There are people alive in there, at least one."

"No, absolutely not," Carlos said firmly, a little later, when we told him what we planned. "We're not doing that."

Then Morgan shocked us all, speaking quietly but firmly. "I'm going whether you like it or not. Whoever she is, she's a federal agent. She's one of us. I'm not leaving her behind."

Everyone stopped talking. Morgan had been struggling with the alienness of it all, terrified of the ogumo, shaken by the worm-thing, wanting to get out of this place in the worst way. Now she was demanding we go into an alien world and rescue a single federal agent. The stalwart determination in her grim expression told me that she needed to do this. It dawned on me that, up until now, she'd felt helpless, up against threats she couldn't understand or cope with. But a rescue mission? That she could handle. It was something she could sink her teeth into. It had a measure of action and control.

I understood the feeling all too well and realized it was why I'd invited Nastasia to my bed. Giving my explicit consent to Nastasia had been my way of taking some control of our relationship. Where Nastasia had terrified me, making that decision freed me of feeling helpless, even if it hadn't really changed the dynamic. Illusory though it might be, doing something, even when it's pointless, hopeless, or downright crazy, can make us feel in control and give us the courage to endure what might otherwise break us.

Carlos pinched the bridge of his nose. "You do realize that this is half a bubble off plumb. We have no idea what's in there."

"That's not entirely true. Check this out." Freyer had been exploring the lab and returned carrying a large roll of paper. Unfurled, it turned out to be a plotted map of what lay beyond the gate, a hyper-accurate topographical survey with markers and a key. The feds had been very busy over the last two months. It's probably what got them killed, attracting unwanted attention from the denizens of the other side.

We pulled in a table from the lab that wasn't destroyed and used it to examine the map. There were several markers with numbers next to them. Freyer explained.

"This was created with a LIDAR-equipped drone. These numbers are frequency numbers for radio markers they've set up. It looks like they've explored almost fifty square miles.

"If you look here," he pointed to a circular marker on the map marked twenty-eight-bravo, "this is some kind of structure. Apparently, the last contact with the drone was this mark next to it. The red X closer to the gate indicates human contact with a hostile force. Most importantly, there are supply caches here and here." He indicated two green triangles. "My guess is these guys were making an exploration push to set up an advanced base when the drone went down. Their security detachment went to investigate, ran into something, and it tracked them back to the gate. And that was all she wrote."

I nodded, but I was still confused about something. "What about the ogumo? How did they get past them?"

Freyer dropped a brown lab notebook on top of the map. "According to this, the ogumo have been sitting just as they are for weeks since we left, doing nothing but scurrying around and laying those webs. One of the guys here was an exobiologist studying them. He noted that after a while, everyone just took their presence for granted, assuming they were more afraid of us than we were of them."

"Yeah, not so much," Morgan said, but she cracked a wry smile, and I saw even more of the old Morgan peeking out. I smiled back, and she winked at me, making me blush. Fortunately, Carlos and Freyer were intent on the map.

"Any idea what happened here and when?" I asked.

"Nobody writes 'argh,' Cait, they just say it," Morgan responded, referencing a mutual favorite movie.

We both chuckled grimly as Freyer looked at us in bemusement before continuing. "There are cameras, but the feed goes offsite. It's a good bet someone knows we're here. It doesn't matter, though. I think time is of the essence. If I were alone in a hostile landscape, I'd head here." He placed his finger on a cache marker, the one farthest from twenty-eight bravo.

Carlos looked at the map and then at us. "Guys, I'm not former military. I'm not sure I'd be much help if we do this."

I shook my head, gesturing around the blood-soaked room. "Huh-uh. We're not leaving you here, Carlos. What if whatever did this comes back?"

"Darlin', I can take care of myself." It was a fair point. "Besides, I need to get the hatch open. I don't want to crawl back through that tunnel, ogumo or no ogumo." He futzed with the map estimating the distance from the written scale. "Okay, the cache is about three klicks from here over flat terrain. You got two hours out and two hours back. That's four hours; then I'm crawling the tunnel if I have to and calling in the troops."

Freyer pulled a small black box out of his pocket. "This is a radio direction finder, RDF for short. I found it back there." He jerked a thumb over his shoulder toward the control room. "It keys a specific frequency and homes in on it. I've set it to the beacon at the cache." He gave us a quick tutorial, then we waved goodbye to Carlos without any more discussion and made our way through the gate.

CHAPTER THIRTY

I pushed aside a shiver of fear as we tracked the sneaker prints. It had taken a moment, but we picked up the trail, and the going was relatively quick, despite the lack of visibility. The compass was as useless here as it had been in the gate chamber, and the RDF didn't start working until we were some distance from the gate, long out of sight of it, and I wondered how we would get back.

We'd been walking for quite a while when Morgan broke the silence, speaking softly. "What is this weird fog, do you think?"

"It's fucking freaky fog," I answered glibly. "That's what I think." The fog swirled just out of reach, the empty space moving with us. "And where's this light coming from?" A strange ambient glow lit the space around us, sulfur-yellow and sickly, coming from nowhere. Morgan didn't answer, and we all fell silent again, listening for any movement.

We were about a kilometer from the gate when we lost the trail. The footprints were obscured by other tracks I didn't recognize. "What do you make of these?"

Freyer pawed at the prints. "These divots look like the spider things, but these other ones are new. They look almost human, except they have no definition, no toes, no tread, no nothing. It could be a boot track."

I wasn't convinced. "Let's keep moving, but keep an ear out. God, I wish I was still a vampire."

"Why?" Morgan asked, sounding almost accusatory.

I suppressed my annoyance at her tone. "Because they have bitchin' hearing, that's why. I told you. Marcella and I were at a crowded bar with loud music, and I could hear two women having sex in the bathroom fifty feet away. At least, I think it was two women."

Morgan snorted a laugh and opened her mouth to say something when Freyer raised his fist.

I tasted the air. Ogumo. We all heard the sound of skittering legs and shifting sand.

"Fuck," Freyer whispered, and we all dropped to one knee, back to back to back, bringing our weapons to bear.

Morgan's MP5 was the first to sound. The chunk-chunk of the suppressed weapon made me jump. A second ogumo launched from the fog. I took it down in a single shot, and it slid to a stop before me, dying with a hiss and splashing me with its foul-smelling ichor.

Another darted forward, stabbing Freyer in the thigh, and he cried out. I shot it point-blank, narrowly missing Freyer's knee in the process. Then I yanked Freyer back by his vest, pulling him between us. Arterial blood spurt across the sandy pumice. Freyer immediately yanked off his belt and cinched a tourniquet, growling through the pain and taking up his weapon again.

"Is that all of them, you think?" Morgan whispered as our eyes swept the fog.

"Maybe. Let's give it a minute. I say we hot-foot it to the cache if we don't have further contact soon. Freyer's hit in the femoral; he'll bleed out if we can't find medical supplies." I glanced at Freyer's leg. It had stopped spurting, but it was bleeding profusely. He wasn't going to make it long.

"He's okay, but he won't be." I grabbed the RDF as Morgan hoisted Freyer up in a fireman's carry, and we continued off toward the cache. A few minutes later, the fog ended like some kind of wall. One step we could hardly see, then the next, the blasted landscape spilled out before us. The sky was black and starless. In the distance, a low ridge rose in front of black clouds, periodically visible, as they pulsed with blue-black lightning and peels of chest-rattling thunder. The entire vision was surreal and beyond terrifying. Behind us, the swirling black made a long straight line as far as we could see, stretching hundreds of feet into the sky as if pressed against some invisible barrier.

"Well, that's not normal," Morgan grunted.

Freyer looked pale as a ghost. He'd lost a lot of blood, and black goo surrounded the wound. I wasn't sure if it was a splash of ichor or some kind of alien infection. Either way, it wasn't good.

We had to stop several times with the effort of carrying Freyer, but we still made good time. A pocket in the rising earth sat open at the bottom of the ridge slope. The RDF pointed right at it, the signal strong. "That's it," I shouted. "We're almost there."

"Uh, guys! Behind us," Freyer shouted moments later.

We looked back. Two roughly bipedal shapes were moving toward us. They weren't particularly fast, but they weren't carrying a wounded man either. We weren't going to make it.

"Take him, Morgan. I'll take care of them." Morgan picked up the pace. I turned, aiming my weapon at the monsters, and fired. Tight bulletholes opened up in the creatures, then closed. They didn't even slow down, still shambling toward me.

"Fuck," I muttered, firing a few more shots, this time at their legs. They stumbled but then stood as the wounds healed to nothing.

Finally, I dropped my weapon and pulled my Bowie knife. They were almost on top of me when one of them dropped to the dirt, an arrow in its torso. An arrow sank into the second one a split second later, dropping it, too. I spun in surprise.

Fifty feet behind me, silhouetted in the flashing lightning, stood what I can only describe as an amazon. She stood almost seven feet tall, if she was an inch, and wore a dark breastplate over a dirty white tunic. Her hair flowed in the wind behind her, cast in blue by the lightning.

"Dráti!" she cried, motioning for me to come toward her. I

recognized the word immediately. It was seared in my skull from my parasite-induced visions.

"Run, indeed," I muttered under my labored breath as I scooped up my weapon, charging away from the fog for all I was worth. I hazarded a glance behind me. A dozen more of the hideous man-things charged from the billowing fog. This time they weren't just shuffling along; they were galloping on all fours.

As I passed the amazon woman, she loosed two more shots quickly and followed me, her muscular thighs pumping, outstripping my shorter gait. She slowed periodically rather than leave me behind, though. "Dráti! Dráti!" She repeated in an urgent tone, pushing me to run faster.

"Fuck, lady," I huffed. "I'm dráti-ing as fast as I can." Flooded with adrenaline, I picked up my pace, rocketing onto the balls of my feet, suddenly able to easily keep pace with the taller woman. As we reached the cave, three women of similar stature to my rescuer dressed in the same black breastplates stepped out. One of them tossed me a strange, black leaf-shaped sword, looking for all the world like a Greek Xiphos. We all turned to face the oncoming creatures.

The monsters plowed into us, leaping with a ferocity I'd only seen in werewolves, clawing and scratching at us. My sword sliced through my first opponent like a scythe through wheat, felling it instantly, but not before its claws gashed me across the midsection. I dropped to my knees, holding my abdomen. Another of the creatures charged me. With brutal effort, fighting back pain, nausea, and dizziness, I raised the sword and impaled the monstrous beast, center mass. The black slimy creature tumbled over me in a heap, knocking me onto my back. The other women faired far better, cutting down the remaining monsters with ease, like practiced soldiers.

"Oye Konbom!" they cried in unison, raising their blades as they felled the last one.

"Oye Konbom," I repeated weakly, raising the sword before my arm fell to the dirt and everything turned black.

I woke inside the cave sometime later, a cold, damp cloth on my head. One of the women, in different attire, a light gray tunic and matching breeches, was tending to Freyer, wrapping his leg. He looked much better, certainly less pale. Morgan sat near the cave entrance, talking to a young human woman dressed like the others except for a black hoodie that read Stanford on the back. She was also wearing a pair of sneakers rather than the strange knee-high boots. The warrior women all sat around a small fire, deep in conversation. I didn't understand the language, but from the occasional glances my way, it was clear that we were the topic of discussion.

"Morgan?" I croaked and tried to sit up, but the woman in the tunic and breeches hurried over.

She placed a hand on my chest, pushing me back to the dirt. "Presht. Presht. Iani."

"She's telling you to rest," the woman in the hoodie said as she and Morgan approached. "I'm Erin, Detective Reagan, Erin Miller. And these are the Oşeni." Erin was maybe five-foot-six, dwarfed by everyone here except me.

"You can understand them?" I asked, pushing away the hand of the woman fussing over me. "I'm fine. I'm fine. Stop. Uh—Presht." The woman huffed but stood and walked back to Freyer.

"I learned a few words, then Grenha did something to me, kind of touch teaching, you know? Like in Zardoz. Now I understand them," Erin said. "Of course, it drained Grenha pretty heavily to do that, and she was in and out for almost two days. I've been camped out here with them for almost a week, local time. I'm guessing you're the rescue team?" For someone in this hostile, alien world, Erin seemed remarkably calm.

"Improvised rescue, but yes. Wait. A week? We just came from the lab—"

She held up a hand. "Time passes differently here, away from the gates. On Oşen, their home world, it's even more dramatic."

I looked around, seeing some empty crates near the back of

the cave. "Where are the supplies? This is supposed to be a cache for exploration."

"They're pretty much gone. There are a few gallons of water left, but not much else, just a first aid kit. There wasn't much here, to begin with; we'd only just started bringing them in the day before I got here. I ate most of the food. Even the Oṣení are running low."

I took a moment to get my bearings. Now that I could see them, I realized amazon didn't begin to describe the women who'd saved us. Every one of them towered over all of us, even Morgan. Their skin was gray but not sallow or unhealthy looking. On the contrary, it was smooth, lustrous, and beautiful. Long silver hair flowed loosely over their shoulders, dirty but magnificent nonetheless, and their ears were delicately pointed, elfin almost. In all honesty, they were stunning to look at, well muscled and fit, perfectly proportioned. Even the healer woman's arms were empty of fat.

While I observed them, they ate some kind of dried meat and spoke in hushed tones. They all looked, by human standards, to be in their early thirties, except the healer or priestess or whatever. She looked to be younger than the rest.

Erin stepped toward the group. "So, I guess introductions are in order." She walked around, pointing to each one as she named them. "This is Shiri, Arat, and Renna. The medhen, their healer, is Grenha." Erin pointed to the woman tending Freyer, who nodded. "And this is the Ánámensí—"

I immediately recognized the next woman, but my mind reeled; it was impossible. She had been a fever-induced dream, fighting in a basalt box canyon outside the black gate, a figment of my parasite-laden imagination.

"Déra?" I whispered, eyes wide. She'd been the one who'd rescued me from the first two creatures. I'd been so intent on survival, running from the things, I hadn't recognized her.

Déra's head snapped around, and she looked at me as I said her name. "Weidsí tuh emé?"

Erin raised an eyebrow. "That's an excellent question. How do you know her?"

"I don't know. Two months ago, I was infected by a bunch of these worm-like parasites. And I—"

Déra stood abruptly and walked over, kneeling and cupping my face, her black-gray eyes sparkling in the firelight. "Umbrá?' She asked softly.

"Uh, I don't understand," I replied.

Déra seemed to get frustrated and spoke in clipped tones. "Lehos? Umbrá?"

"I don't know what that is," I whispered, still staring into her eyes. It sounded like the Indo-European word Tlehos, but that made no sense. "In my tongue, that means messenger."

She released my face and made a wiggling gesture with her finger.

"Oh, yes, the parasite. It's in storage."

"Huweti?" She asked, her eyes bright and hopeful.

Sometimes, late at night, when I was little, my mother would try to teach me words of Proto-Indo-European. It bored me to sleep most nights, but now I was beyond thankful. She was asking if the parasite was alive. "Huwedi tuh," I confirmed. There was no PIE word for yes. I didn't mention that there was a distinct possibility that Bian had dissected it. I still didn't understand what the fuss was about.

Déra spent several seconds rattling off words I couldn't catch, so I gave up on this stupid back and forth. I looked at Erin, and she took the nonverbal queue, translating what Déra said.

"Tell me what you remember. Dreams or visions?"

Now it was getting creepy. "Yes, I dreamed of you, fighting those things and a blue-black fire—"

Déra pointed at me and shouted something to the others, again speaking too quickly for me to catch any individual words. The others chattered excitedly in response, patting Déra on the back and smiling. Erin beamed a smile along with them and hugged Grenha.

I immediately wondered if they were friends or maybe more. That made me think of Liz, which shoved a dagger of guilt right into my gut. I needed to get out of here and get home. This wasn't a fool's errand, obviously, but I had responsibilities to more than just myself. I needed to start thinking about the people relying on me and stop being so reckless.

"How are you feeling?" Morgan asked me before I could interrogate Erin further.

"Fine now, a little weak, but otherwise okay."

Tears glistened on Morgan's cheeks, and she sniffed, wiping her nose on her sleeve.

"Are you okay? Why are you crying?"

Morgan turned and scooped me into a hug. "Because there was no way you could survive your wounds. That creature cut you wide open. I was sure you were dying."

I looked at her in annoyance. "Cut me open? It was just a scratch. I'm fine."

"No, Cait!" She yelled, moving back and rocketing to her feet. The women around the fire all looked up. The one called Renna patted another on the shoulder, whispering to her and pointing to us while Morgan continued to yell. "There are parts of your intestines buried out by the cave mouth. I—" Her voice broke. "I watched them dig your grave. Then, suddenly your wounds just magically closed up by themselves. I saw it for myself. Now, tell me what—"

"Fine," I sighed, holding up a hand. "Sit, and I'll explain."

So I explained it all to Morgan, the bite, the changed blood, what vampires were like, all of it. I told her how I'd been turned, what Marcella had done, how the black gate had been opened, and what happened to my mother. I even told her about what I'd done to save Katie, why I had to take care of her, and why I was living with Liz. Finally, I explained about Nastasia and some of what had happened between us, keeping it somewhat vague because who I slept with was my business. The only other thing I left out was that Carlos was a werewolf. It wasn't my secret to tell.

When I was done blabbing almost every dark secret about the last two months, Morgan just sat there with a blank look on her face. Then she stood and walked to the cave mouth and looked out at the clouds rolling overhead until the healer, Grenha, pulled her away, motioning about the dangers of the falling lightning. In the meantime, I explained to Erin what might happen if she spilled any of what I'd just told Morgan to anyone. I didn't know if she believed me, but she said she'd keep it to herself.

"The storm will keep the emisai away," Erin said later, referring to the humanoid monsters that had chased us. "The Oşeni have been out here for months looking for someone, a girl named Umbrá. As I understand it, she's very important to Déra. Something you said has them all excited. They're starting to pack up." She didn't look too terribly thrilled by the prospect.

"You okay?"

"Sure." She said quietly and went to talk to Déra. Something in the way they spoke told me what it was about, even though I couldn't understand the words. The conversation was short, and when they were done, Erin looked positively ecstatic. *Good for you, Erin*, I thought. *I hope you find what you're looking for.*

I stood on wobbly legs and was promptly scolded by Grenha. Though I didn't understand a word of what she said except 'presht,' the meaning was clear, so I dropped back down grumpily. I grabbed Grenha's arm gently and pointed to Freyer. "How is he? Um, krem bis?" I hoped I didn't just call her mother a flatulent pig or something, digging so far back in my memories.

She waved dismissively. "Bis kohailus." Then she made a grumpy-faced imitation of Freyer, and I laughed. That sounded like him.

When Grenha finally sat at the fire to eat, I stood and wobbled over to Freyer. Grenha scowled at me the whole way, then said something to Déra. I didn't hear it, but she was probably cursing my stubbornness. He had some kind of cloth bandage on his leg that looked similar to suede.

"Hey John, how you feelin'?"

"Right as rain, Cait. That woman has magic hands. She just waved them over my leg, and the bleeding stopped. Then she stitched me up like a pro and put a wrap on it. It was impressive, kid."

"I'm glad. I thought you were a daisy for a minute. I assume they explained the time difference?"

Freyer nodded and yawned loudly. "Yup. I just need a few hours of rest, which should be about a minute back home. Maybe I'll take my next vacation here. A few years off would do me some good."

I laughed. "You and me both, my friend. You and me both."

Grenha gave me a bed roll, and I laid down near the smoldering embers of the fire. Morgan walked over just as I was closing my eyes.

"Cait?"

"Yes, Morgan," I said without opening my eyes.

"Do you mind if I—"

I smiled and pulled back the blanket. She lay down next to me and spooned up against my back.

"I'm sorry, it's just—it's a lot," she whispered.

I patted her hip with my free hand. "It's okay. I don't take it personally. I mean, who's really prepared for their vampire ex?"

Morgan laughed a little at that, then turned more somber. "Promise me that, if the time comes, you won't let me become one of them."

"One of what?" I asked, unsure if she meant a vampire or one of the awful things we'd seen.

"One of anything. I want to die human if it comes to that."

"That won't be a problem because you're not allowed to die. You get me, Detective?"

"I get you, ma'am," she whispered, and for the first time since she'd arrived, I thought I heard a genuine smile in her voice.

Morgan fell asleep almost instantly, but I lay awake for a long time, deep in thought about Morgan and the relationship that would never be. We'd had a shot at everything, but destiny had other plans.

CHAPTER THIRTY-ONE

A few hours later, Déra nudged me awake. She was kneeling next to us, two swords lying crosswise on her lap, each in exquisitely crafted knotwork sheaths. She motioned toward herself and then outside. "Gwemsí."

I extricated myself from Morgan's arm and shook myself awake. Déra was already headed toward the cave mouth, so I followed, wiping the sleep from my eyes. I stepped gingerly over Erin, curled up, asleep in Grenha's arms. Grenha was positively giant next to Erin, yet somehow, it was both adorable and seemed to work. Erin didn't need rescuing after all. She wouldn't be coming back with us, and we would likely never see her again. Something very intimate and personal had passed between her and these women in the week they'd been together. I sighed, silently wishing her godspeed.

Déra stepped out of the cave and sat on a flat crop of stone, patting the spot next to her. As I approached, she handed me a sword, and I took it, recognizing it for the sign of trust that it was. *Okay,* I thought. *This should be interesting.*

"The storm will be here shortly," she stated flatly, and I jerked my head around. Her English was American, lightly accented by our standards, and flawless.

"You speak English?"

"For several years now. If someone thinks you don't

understand their language, they're much more likely to communicate freely with their own people, don't you think?"

I nodded.

"I have watched all of you for several hours, but you especially. And I have listened. I heard your conversations with Morgan and Freyer. You're not like the others."

I gave her a crooked smile, impressed with her shrewdness and caution. "No, I am not like the others." I stuck out my tongue, wiggling it for her.

She laughed at my silly display. "That is not what I meant. You have a warrior's heart and leadership qualities. I can see why the others follow you."

I snorted. "Hardly. Freyer is in charge of our group. He's the Lead Detective."

Déra looked at me skeptically and turned her gaze back to the fog. "Freyer may outrank you, but he is following your lead, and you know it. He has tremendous trust in you. They both do."

I cocked an eyebrow. "How would you know that?"

"I can see the way they look at you. And I think Morgan likes you very much. However, Grenha sees a vast gulf of darkness in her. She is, what is the word, damaged?"

"She is." I didn't feel the need to elaborate. I did, however, note that Déra and the others did not share Grenha's abilities. Déra relied on Grenha a great deal, it seemed, but they didn't appear to be close. Grenha was the outlier, seeming to be there to help but not really part of the group.

"Yes. Perhaps she will recover with a good friend like you to help her."

"I hope so. Our friendship is very complicated and fraught right now. She and I once were very close, but now I'm with someone else."

Déra nodded and continued to scan the fog, then said, "That blade belonged to Feyla, a dear friend who died out here recently." She pointed to a mound of dirt near the cave mouth. "Treat it with care."

"I will," I said solemnly as I traced the knotwork on the sword sheath with my thumb. I was a little dumbstruck that she trusted me with the weapon, even for a few minutes. "Why let me have it?"

"A blade without a hand to wield it is meaningless," she said flatly.

It was cold logic I couldn't argue with, and it forestalled any more questions about Feyla or her sword. Besides, by Déra's somber tone, it was clear that she and Feyla had been close, friends perhaps, and I wanted to respect her privacy.

Sometime later, watching the roiling wall of fog, I asked, "Has something passed between Grenha and Erin? They seem very close."

"Yes, they have become intimate. It's not surprising, though. To teach our language the way she did, Grenha must connect with a person's spirit, their soul." Déra touched her chest. "It is an intensely intimate experience. They found a commonality of purpose. Grenha is—what is the word?—a bit of a nerd?" I laughed, and she continued. "But I think Grenha was a bit impressed with Erin to begin with."

I could tell that Déra spoke from experience. "And have you connected with someone that way?"

She didn't respond, choosing instead to change the subject. "You say that Freyer is the leader. I know it is common for men to command women in your world. In my world, it is the reverse, though it was not always so."

"Are your men smaller or weaker?" I asked, intrigued. A strictly matriarchal society had a strong appeal. I could see why Erin was so at home with them—well, that and Grenha.

"Not significantly so. We simply keep them in line, and we outnumber them two to one."

"Well, where we come from, it's a patriarchy, and it sucks."

Déra gave a rich bark of laughter. "I'm sorry. I assume that means it's bad?"

"Oh, yes. Men destroy things. They've ruined our world. At one point, it was a paradise, but unbridled greed has wrecked almost every natural habitat on the planet. Pollution of one type or another is rampant, so much so that the planetary temperature is increasing. I don't say much about it because there's no point. Nothing changes. There are more women than men, but men ensure they preserve their power, sometimes at all costs. In my country, the region—"

She interrupted me briefly. "Yes, I know what a country is, though we do not have them."

"Well, in my country, women do not have autonomy over their own bodies. In some parts, women are forced to carry out unwanted pregnancies, even when raped. You understand the word rape?"

She nodded. "I understand the word, and that is barbaric. It is not much different from our history in some ways, though it is ancient. Ten thousand cycles ago, our people were enslaved, if you could imagine. The Kaushkari Lords, a sect of very powerful men and women from another world, conquered our people. Our men failed us, making deals with the Kaushkari, appeasing them, worshipping them as gods, and even selling off the women of our world.

"That was until Avra—" Déra spat hatefully on the sandy ground, "That was until a slave, known to us now as Avra, a Kyliri woman, that is another race, came here and learned the secrets of this place. When she returned, she defeated the Kaushkari Lords and freed us from the yoke of our men. Since then, women have ruled. Afterward, something of a religion grew up around it all."

I found it strange that she spit on the ground as she said the name of their supposed savior, so I asked about it.

"She betrayed my people. I believe the same power that enabled our freedom has finally corrupted her beyond redemption. She summoned forth the creatures of this place a few cycles ago, and many of my people died defending our home. Işir, our city, was almost lost. This place is evil, Cait. Stay here long enough, and it will either kill you or turn you into something unrecognizable. Those creatures—" She gestured toward the fog.

"The emisai?"

"Yes. They were once like you or me, Earther or Oşeni or one of a dozen other races. Now they are mindless, bent and twisted to the will of Mother Darkness."

"I know Mother Darkness," I said softly, remembering the

power and malignancy I'd felt under the influence of the tablets. The wind picked up, blowing bits of ash and sand across the barren plain, and I pulled on a pair of shooting glasses I'd been carrying to protect my eyes.

"Can I ask you another question?"

"Of course," She smiled but didn't turn to look at me, her hawkish eyes still watching the vast plain for threats.

"It seems intimate relations between women are common among your people."

She chuckled. "Very, the men, too. I was surprised to hear from Erin that it is not as common or accepted among yours. That it is not common seems odd to me, but that it is not accepted seems unnatural. We have a saying, 'cordis wek cordis.'"

It needed no translation, but I echoed the sentiment. "The heart wants what the heart wants. We have that saying, too."

Then something occurred to me. "Do you think you could help us find the rest of our people? They were taken. Some might still be alive."

Déra shook her head. "They are dead, Cait. Or worse. There will be nothing to find. Aside from that, we have no idea where they were taken. And I must find Umbrá's lehos and return home soon. My world will enter a period of instability. Our gates will close for a time as the gravity of a nearby singularity we call The Eye of Şto slows time beyond its ability to compensate."

I snorted. "You know what a singularity is?"

She laughed at my ignorance. "Of course we do. We probably know a great deal more than your people about how the universe works, at least our universe, and probably yours as well. We choose our weapons, bow, and sword, and spear, because weapons such as yours are forbidden, but our academy of the sciences, Mens-Dhe, is very knowledgeable. We live simple lives because it is better for us."

I shook my head. "It sounds idyllic."

Déra laughed heartily then. "Hardly. We have the same problems: political squabbling, arguments of science and religion, and overarching ambition. The leaders of my world may all be women, but they can be quite ruthless. When you have a world where everything is organized and structured, you find a way to entertain yourselves, and the stakes can become very high."

"Ain't that the truth."

"Come, let me show you something," Déra said and stood, walking up the ridge without looking back. I shrugged my shoulders and followed.

"What about the others, aren't we supposed to be sitting guard?"

"Arat is awake. She will keep them safe. We won't be long, anyway."

The storm had long passed, and a hot wind blew across the plain below. The climbing was slow and far steeper than it had first appeared. Several times, one of us slipped and had to be helped by the other, and God, Déra was heavy. Eventually, we summited the ridge, dropping down a few feet on the other side so as not to skyline ourselves.

The view was both terrifying and breathtaking. There were no cities, no rivers, no towns, nothing but vast domed volcanoes that either smoked or erupted. Some of them might put Everest to shame. None of them was capped with snow. Of course, this land was a blasted desert with no water, so that wasn't surprising. Far in the distance, maybe twenty miles, my best guess without anything to compare for scale, sat a pinprick of red light.

Déra pointed toward it. "That is the Oşeni gate."

The thought was astonishing. Just a short hike away sat the gateway to another world, where women had complete autonomy of the self, a place where I could be myself without judgment or harassment, and where women never crossed the street when a man walked toward them. A place where there were no guns or school shootings, or threats of annihilation from global warming, or the fear of some idiot leader pushing a button and sparking a war that blew us all to hell.

It seemed as if Déra were reading my thoughts. "It is a hard life there for most, Cait. Many people live in poverty, and the wealthiest of us ignore them. Someone like you would be welcome, but your friend Freyer would not. And we have slavery."

I was appalled at her last statement. "Slavery?"

"Yes. It is reserved for enemies captured in battle, which has become more frequent lately as the Kaushkari have long memories and little sense, using other people as fodder to weaken our resolve. There are those who end up as slaves because of unpaid debts as well. The enslaved are not treated well. Many become sexual objects. So, no, it is not idyllic by any means. We simply have different problems." She let me stand there and absorb the landscape and all that she'd said, then she called me away, back down to the camp.

"How did you learn English?" I asked as we made our treacherous way down the slope.

"Occasionally, rifts between worlds open of their own accord in places where the worlds touch. In those places, the veil becomes very thin. People can fall through these rifts. I traveled with one of your kind for almost a year, a woman named Amelia. She taught me the basics, then I found a small enclave of humans, Earthers, in Centrus. There I learned more."

"So not the way that Erin learned yours." I slid on a loose rock and scratched my hand. Again, it hurt, bled slightly, and then healed. The inevitable nausea that followed stopped me in my tracks again. Déra was intent on her footing and didn't see it.

"No, Grenha can teach others only those things she already knows. And while there is a sharing of souls, knowledge is transferred from her to others. It is a rare gift, made even more rare in that Grenha developed it well into adulthood." Déra skidded to a halt about fifty feet from the cave mouth and turned. The sudden stop caught me by surprise, and I began to slip uncontrollably down a particularly loose portion of the slope. Fortunately, Déra caught me. Her body was unbelievably solid, and I felt the dense corded muscles of her thighs and buttocks as I scrambled to hold on.

Once I'd stopped sliding, I immediately let go, blushing furiously. "Oops. Sorry. I wasn't expecting you to stop."

Déra didn't seem to care, holding me in place by my shoulders. "You must never speak of Grenha's ability once you leave here. The priesthood firmly controls our entire society. For a high priestess such as her to have a way to express the entirety of their knowledge through such means would threaten our very way of life. They have many secrets. If the other priestesses knew, Grenha would be executed as a threat to my people."

"Who would I tell? I live in another world." I asked, shrugging my shoulders. "I assume the others in your party know."

"They do, and they are all sworn to secrecy. So, please, swear to me that you will say nothing." She searched my face with a desperate intensity.

"You have my word," I replied earnestly. "I will take it to my grave."

My word must have been enough because she released me without additional comment, and we returned to the shelter of the cave as the wind began howling outside. Morgan sat where we had been sleeping, drinking from a steaming cup of some sweet-smelling liquid. "Where'd you go?"

"We were just talking. Déra was telling me of her home. How are you doing? Did you sleep well?"

Morgan smiled more brightly than I'd seen since we'd reunited. "Like the dead, though I had strange dreams."

"And was I in those dreams?" I asked.

"Maybe." She blushed and raised her mug, hiding a mischievous grin.

"Uh-huh. Okay. Let's see if we can get some help finding the rest of our people."

Freyer was asleep, so I gingerly took the folded map from his pocket, unfurled it, and called Déra over. Morgan and I showed her where the gate sat in relation to the cave. Then I pointed to the spot marked twenty-eight-bravo. "We think this is where they took our people."

She frowned. "You're not going to let this go, are you?"

I gave her a stern expression, and she sighed.

"Okay, I will take you there so you can see, but only you. We need stealth, not brawn." She looked pointedly at Morgan. "We'll escort you to the gate first so that you can get your wounded companion back."

"No way," Morgan chimed in. "You're not going without me. Erin can take Freyer back through the gate."

"No, I can't," Erin said flatly and took a step toward Grenha as if she were afraid we might try to grab her. "I'm not going back."

Morgan's eyebrows shot up. "What? You can't be serious."

I put a hand on Morgan's shoulder. "She's serious, Red. She wants to stay with the Oşeni."

Morgan raised her voice as if volume would win the argument. "We came all the way out here to find her, and Freyer almost died. She has to come back. Otherwise, why did we do this?"

Grenha moved in front of Erin, and the other women moved up next to her, stern-faced and arms crossed. The discussion was over, and Morgan stalked out of the cave.

I followed and found her sitting on the same flat rock that Déra and I had occupied only a little while earlier. "She's in love, Morgan, and can you blame her? I mean, look at Grenha. Besides, I suspect she has nothing back home but her work. Something about her says she needs to find somewhere to be."

Morgan laughed sourly and shook her head, but her voice sounded more plaintive than truly argumentative. "But we came out here to rescue her."

"And she didn't need us. That's not her fault—or ours. We have no authority here. Besides, you saw the ladies. No means no."

Morgan laughed again at the ironic statement. "Okay, but I'm going with you wherever you go, and that's that. You're not the boss of me, Kitty-Cait."

I reached out and tucked an errant strand of hair behind her ear as I'd done dozens of times in Iraq. She looked up at me, her eyes flicked across my face, and she wet her lips. In the wan light of this place, the green of her eyes looked washed out, but the beauty of their placement and their depths was not diminished. Without thought, I stepped forward and pressed my lips to hers.

I'd have expected her to push me off, but she didn't. She returned the kiss and deepened it, parting her lips gently and putting her hands into my hair. The kiss was soft, deep, and lovely, and my entire body stuttered a bit as a flush of warmth and affection ran through me. We were like that for a long time as the hot wind blew across the desolate plain. In this dark and blasted landscape, we found a moment of heavenly quiet where the monsters and cares, both here and at home, faded away to nothingness. It was wrong, and I knew it, but she was here, and she wanted it. I wanted it.

When we finally broke the kiss, both a little breathless and, I think, lost in our twisting emotions, Morgan stood and took me in her arms, brushing a finger across her lips. "It's such a strange feeling."

It took me a moment to realize she was referring to my tongue, and I giggled ridiculously like a schoolgirl. "What's it like?"

"About like you'd expect, the tips of the fork brushing around tickle a little bit."

"So, like kissing a snake," I joked wryly.

She practically cackled. "Somehow, that sounds far less flattering than it should. But, truthfully, I was wondering what it must be like for you. We've been out here a while. My breath must be horrid."

It was my turn to laugh. "Actually, no. I can taste that weird seasoned Oṣeni meat you ate and the tea, but under that is your breath. It's—" I blushed slightly, unable to describe the pleasant feeling of her breath entering my lungs, filling me with longing.

Morgan ran the backs of her fingers across my cheek. "We should probably get some more sleep. We have a long day coming up. It is nice to think of what might have been, though."

I didn't argue as I let her lead me by the hand back into the cave, where we pulled our bedroll to the back, behind the empty crates, and made love as quietly as we could. This time nothing stood between us, not her scars, my curse, or even Liz.

And it wasn't awkward at all. It was beautiful.

We were both abysmally dirty in places, but that didn't seem to matter as we explored each other's bodies. I found sensitive spots along Morgan's ribs that caused her to jerk slightly, clenching her abdominal muscles under my hand. It was strange in a way. I'd never been with a woman with such fine definition and, for whatever reason, it fascinated me. I traced my finger around her muscular frame, stopping periodically to lean in and kiss a part of her body: her knee, a shoulder, a breast.

Morgan whispered, "You know we really shouldn't be doing this."

I giggled. "Because they might see?"

"No, silly. What if those things come back?" Then she said, "I don't want to be caught naked."

"I'm pretty sure some of these women have fought naked before, probably multiple times. I wouldn't worry about it. Our clothes aren't exactly protection."

She bobbed her head in acknowledgment and rolled us over, pressing me to my back. "I wish we'd done this in Iraq. To think, we'd had a whole trailer to ourselves, and we never —"

I pressed a finger to her mouth. "Shh. We're here now. Forget about what wasn't." I pulled her down on top of me, our legs entangled, and drew her face to mine. It was too dark to see any real detail, but I found her lips with my own and closed my eyes. *Am I really doing this? After all my pining and longing? Are we finally together after ten years? More than, really.* It seemed like a dream.

Morgan began kissing my neck, and I turned my head, giving her access to my throat almost out of habit. She nibbled and licked, drawing a noise of pleasure from me.

"God, I wanted this," I whispered into the dark. Morgan slithered downward, paying careful attention to each sensitive spot: my collarbone, the inside of my elbow, which made me giggle, and then she found my breasts. Her attentions were gentle, exploring me tenderly with her fingers and her mouth. She sucked at my nipples, causing ripples of pleasure to pool between my legs, and I let out a soft, passionate moan which I stifled with my knuckles.

And she laughed. *Laughed!*

I looked at her in total bemusement and not a little irritation. "What?"

"I'm so sorry," she said through almost uncontrollable giggles. "I was just thinking how glad I am that this isn't the first time for either of us."

I gave a snort of mock irritation and slapped her gently with the arm of my discarded shirt. Then I abruptly jerked her arm out from under her, rolling her over with a wicked smile, and plunged my face between her legs, taking her clit into my mouth. *We'll see who laughs now,* I thought.

Morgan gasped loudly then, her legs jerking straight, muscles clenching. "Hey," she protested between gasps. "That's—not—fair." The last word came out as more of soft exhalation of breath than truly voiced. I had her now. I was going to make her mine. I plunged two fingers into her, gently stroking upward as I now sucked furiously at her clit, feeling her body tense and jerk with pleasure. It was wonderful, all of it. She tasted both sweet and musky as I worked her toward orgasm.

She didn't grab or claw at me, instead drawing her hands above her head in supplication and breathing more and more heavily until finally, she came with a heaving gasp, stuffing an arm into her mouth to stay quiet. It was no use, and I continued until she begged me to stop, finally pushing me away from her with some effort.

"Oh, my god," she breathed. "Yep, definitely glad you've done this before."

I slid up and laid my head on her belly, and a soft sound echoed in the cave. It was a moment before I recognized it as gentle clapping. Then there was a soft whistle. "Good job, Reagan. About time, you two. I was sick of cutting the sexual tension in the office with my knife."

I groaned. "Shut up, Freyer," I called breathlessly, and there were several laughs.

Morgan wasn't done yet, though. She dragged us back on

the blanket and pulled me up until my clit was resting against her lips, then she began to nibble at it gently, sucking and pulling. It was all I could do not to fall forward to the floor on all fours.

I placed a hand back on her stomach to balance myself as I rode her mouth, rocking gently back and forth as her tongue worked magic. Sweat soaked my entire body now. I quit trying to be quiet and let her love me in a way that brought me to a passionate and beautiful climax. And it was lovely. It had taken ten years to get here. And now, in this alien world, we'd finally found each other, even if only for one night.

CHAPTER THIRTY-TWO

Morgan and I went back to sleep for the rest of the sleep period. Night wasn't the right word; it was always night here. I woke to a leaden and aching body which worsened as we prepared to leave. Grenha watched me closely, and after I'd stumbled the third time trying to move crates to the back of the cave in case we needed to return, she produced a flask of foul-smelling liquid. I tried to beg her off, but she was insistent.

"Urumé."

I sighed and drank the contents of the flask as quickly as I could. She laughed and shook her head. A few minutes later, my fatigue vanished as the powerful stimulant coursed through my body. My eyes were still tired, but my body was most definitely awake.

Freyer walked about, testing his leg gingerly. "There we go, all better." He walked around the cave competently but with a significant limp.

"Freyer, sit your ass down before you hurt yourself worse," I ordered. He complied, but his grumpy face made clear his thoughts on the matter. Déra then explained to him that Grenha had repaired the artery and much of the muscle, but she had reached the limit of what she could do. The rest was up to his own body, and he needed to rest as much as possible.

I was thankful that the woman was so tall, she seemed to intimidate Freyer, and it got him to shut up his griping while we worked.

When I asked, Grenha pointed me to Feyla's gear which I carefully wrapped in her bedroll. It turned out to be the one that Morgan and I had been using. That was mortifying. Finding some discarded rope in one of the crates to tie the breastplate and sword to the deceased woman's pack, I tried to treat it with as much dignity and reverence as I could, feeling it was the least I could do in return for all Déra's people had done so far. When it was complete, I handed it off to Déra, but she removed the sword and sheath from the pack.

"You keep this. I believe Feyla would find you worthy of it. The metal is black-steel. It is an alloy of iron and a special mineral from our world that has been worked by our scholars. There is magic in it."

"I—I can't take this—" I sputtered.

"Cait. When one of our warriors dies, it is common for their friend to find someone worthy of their weapon. It's a custom of almost ten thousand years. Do not insult me."

Her words were serious, but the corner of her mouth tugged upward. I suspected she was pulling my leg and playing on my ignorance. I smiled knowingly but took the blade anyway with appropriate solemnity. "I understand."

The sheath and belt were made of a soft, supple, gray material like leather, and the multi-colored embroidery of vines and flowers spiraled and turned in a complex design resembling a cross between a Celtic knot and a mandala. The craftsmanship was beyond beautiful, an art all its own. The weapon itself sported a grey and black teardrop Damascus pattern that seemed to shift and flow as I turned it in the dim light of Erin's emergency lamp, as exquisite and perfect as the women who wielded them.

"Oye Konbom, my friend," Déra said quietly as she patted my shoulder.

She hoisted her pack and turned toward the cave entrance. As I watched her assemble with the others, I thought about the phrase which Erin told me meant 'victory,' and it suddenly occurred to me that I had made a friend from another world.

Leaving our makeshift refuge, we split up. Morgan, Déra, and I headed toward the palace of Mother Darkness, the place where she believed Avra, the God-Empress of Oşen, had learned the knowledge that had both saved and betrayed them. The rest of the group would escort Freyer to our gate and then turn for the Oşen gate. My only regret was that I hadn't had time to get to know more of them, or Erin, for that matter. But in a way, I envied Erin and the tremendous leap of faith she was taking, both in going with the women and placing her trust in Grenha.

We traveled light, carrying no supplies or food and the barest of the remaining water. I'd managed to secure the sword sheath to my back, allowing an easy draw over my shoulder. Morgan and I were still armed with our weapons, and Freyer offered us half of his remaining clips to ensure we had enough ammo.

When we had suggested he might need it, the other Oşeni women scoffed and told him he might as well fight with his fists. I was pretty sure that Erin did not translate Freyer's rather colorful response.

Déra insisted that we send any electronics with Freyer and the women without explanation. It was her show, so I didn't argue. We dumped our comms. Morgan had her phone, so she passed that to Freyer as well. Finally, we pulled the batteries from our flashlights and the RDF and pocketed them.

As soon as we crossed the fog bank, Déra slowed her pace, walking with almost the preternatural grace of a vampire. Despite her size and physical bulk, she stepped lightly, leaving very little trace on the ground. As always, when I watched someone with that kind of step, a pang of jealousy stabbed at me as I felt myself clomp around like a bloody troll. I fingered the grip of my MP5 as we made our way along. After a short while, I moved closer to Déra.

"Do you know where you're going?" I whispered. She nodded and placed a finger to her lips, and then pointed directly ahead with her entire hand. The gesture was textbook US army style, and it occurred to me that her friend Amelia might have been military. I made a mental note to make some inquiries when we returned home. If we returned at all. Déra had made it clear that this endeavor could be a suicide mission.

My tongue began flicking out frequently in my nervousness, bringing in scents from all around us, but, so far, all I smelled was the foul, rotten-egg, sulfurous stench of this place growing stronger. It wasn't long, however, before I smelled something else, something alien and strange. I turned my head slightly, tasting the air again, then I grabbed Déra's arm. I pointed to my nose and then to our right, and the source of the odor, which I was certain was just across the bizarre fog line.

Déra raised her bow and pointed it in the direction I'd indicated. She had a second arrow tucked between her unused fingers in a style I'd never seen before.

Morgan and I held our breath as the amazon woman stood stock still, breathing slowly and listening. There was a slight scuff in the dirt ahead of us, and that was all it took. Before I could blink, Déra had shifted her aim and let fly not one but both arrows, resulting in two hits and a thick-sounding impact.

I shouldered my weapon and crept forward, each step seemingly ponderous as I moved with precision. Morgan had crouched, covering our six automatically. Excruciatingly slowly, a dead creature resolved itself from the fog, laying on its back.

As soon as she saw it, Déra relaxed and walked forward in quick steps, clearing the fog from around the corpse. "A koşant, one of the Dark Mother's assassins, a hunter of sorts. They usually move alone. They are intelligent but extremely rare. If one of them is out here, then the Dark Mother has designs on your world. That is—how did Erin put it?—no bueno?"

I suppressed a giggle, hearing the alien woman use the phrase. My mirth was short-lived, though, as I examined the creature. Roughly man-shaped and covered in mottled insectile chitin, the thing's face sat triangular, mantis-like, and rigid with a beak-like protrusion. The head swiveled impossibly around when Déra retrieved her arrows. It had no eyes or ears I could discern, but two large pockets covered a large portion of what might be considered its face. The legs ended in long, taloned toes, three of them in the front and one in the back, as did the arms.

I donned a latex glove from my pocket and examined the claws. They were beyond razor sharp, seeming made of the same stuff as the Oşeni swords and arrowheads. "Is this?"

Déra shook her head. "No, but I've been told it is similar. Those claws were the inspiration for the creation of our black-steel. Our people discovered long ago that ordinary iron-based alloys were as tissue paper to many of the creatures out here. It is unlikely that we'll encounter any other creatures anytime soon, and we can move more quickly. The koşant are the apex predators out here. We were lucky you smelled it before it was able to attack, or one of us would likely not have survived. They can leap incredible distances, and one swipe of their claws will easily cut a person in half. It's been said one of them can decimate an entire platoon—that's fifty women in our army—if it catches them unaware. They are incredibly fast and deadly."

"Will bullets kill them?" Morgan asked as she finally stood and examined the creature.

"Yes, if you can hit a vital place. The problem is this." Déra poked the chitinous shell. "It is almost as hard as my breastplate. Lead slugs have little effect. The best place to hit them if you are firing is here." She pointed to the two pockets in the head. "Those are sensing organs and unprotected."

I examined the creature from head to toe and flipped it over. There were gaps in the armor, but they were small. A skilled shooter would likely be able to take it out if it were standing still, but killing it on the move would be blind luck at best, more like a miracle. "But our swords will cut through it, right?"

Déra smiled. "Easily. Let's go."

After encountering the koşant, we moved more quickly. A few kilometers later, we passed several strange earthen mounds. I had just drawn a breath to ask what they were, but

Déra turned sharply and grabbed my face, planting her hand over my mouth. We all froze. Then we heard it, like the scrabbling of a million legs across the dirt. It was distant, but that didn't diminish the alarm I felt at the sound. A few cautious, slow steps forward, the fog cleared, revealing what had to be the place we'd been looking for. If I'd thought the fog was frightening and creepy, this was beyond horrifying.

It was as if we were standing in the eye of some malignant storm. The fog swirled, rotating around a vast open caldera, and my mind ran immediately to the dreams Carol had been having.

Thousands upon thousands of ogumo moved about the crater floor, crawling over each other, stabbing at the ground, then lowering themselves down. A dozen monstrosities, roughly oblong and easily twenty feet tall, made almost entirely of black muscle and armor on a dozen legs, moved about them, occasionally picking an ogumo or two with the stab of a leg and stuffing them into their great maws, which opened like flowers. At the head of each behemoth was a great, heavy-lidded, red eye.

Above them circled beasts on insectile wings of black and gray filament. The flyers had massive claws compared to their short bodies and small, long-snouted heads. The sight was made even more terrible by the sickly light that emanated from the center of the caldera, in which moved a great palace of translucent crystal, glowing eerily from within. Its insides swirled with strangely vibrant purples, blues, and blacks. Atop a center spire that rose two hundred feet into the black sky sat two enormous black spheres that seemed to move of their own accord, swiveling left and right.

Periodically, a portal would open within the lower portion of the palace, and one of the emisai creatures would slide forth, covered in horrid slime. Riding the moving palace's center spire were easily twenty of the koşant creatures similar to the one Déra had capped an hour or so before. More terrifyingly, though, at the top of the spire sat a figure with iridescent-white, shimmering skin, the woman that Carol had seen in her visions. *Jesus,* I thought. *Oh, Carol, what is going on?*

"That," Déra said, "is Mother Darkness."

She guided us down behind a small earthen mound for cover. We had no worries of being overheard. The skittering of the ogumo below was deafening.

I was trembling with awe and almost insanity-inducing fear. "The person atop the palace? I—"

"No, Cait, the 'palace,' as you call it, is Mother Darkness. The figure at the top is Avra."

I was stunned and further terrified by the revelation. "That thing is alive? Dear God, it's the size of a small city."

"Yes," Déra said impassively. "It is alive."

"That Avra lady looks asleep," Morgan said, pulling a small set of binoculars from her face, which she handed to me.

"Or meditating," I added as I gazed through the field glasses. Behind her sat an octagonal obsidian black surface, like a mirror. Reflected within it were shifting dim images. With horror, I realized the images were of Earth and very close to home: a view of my old apartment veranda in the north end of Boston, the inside of someone's office, the Bunker Hill Monument, and others. The images flashed by too quickly for me to make much sense of them or see much detail, but even so, some of them were obvious and panic-inducing: the exterior of Marcella's home, Schroeder Plaza, Elliot Norton Park, the inside of the gate chamber.

"This is where they brought your people. Either as food or to be raw material to create those." Déra pointed at the emisai. "You're people are dead, Cait."

"She's right," Morgan said. "Let's book. We don't need to be here."

I didn't disagree. Carefully, we threaded our way back into the fog, Déra leading the way. I pulled out the RDF unit, but Déra put a hand on mine. "I told you, no electrical devices. The flying ones will sense it. They can sense almost any electrical discharge at this range."

Morgan looked at me. "The drone."

I nodded, then my eyes grew wide. "Shit!" I scrabbled at my watch, tearing off the band and casting it aside. "Your watch, Morgan. Get rid of it." She looked down at her glowing smartwatch, working to peel it off her arm and throw it away, when a screech exploded in the distance that sounded like nothing so much as a steel drill on hardened metal. It was immediately followed by several others.

"Run!" Déra cried, leading the way.

"We can't lead them back to the gate!" I shouted as a sound like giant dragonfly wings buzzed overhead. "Morgan! Follow Déra! Get back to the gate! I'll meet you there." I peeled off the group and charged off into the fog, weaving as best I could through the field of earth mounds, popping the battery into the RDF and flipping the switch. My breath heaved, and the exertion began to immediately take its toll as fatigue rolled over me. *Fuck. Not now.*

The buzzing wings grew closer, zooming low and loud overhead, just out of sight. With tremendous effort, I threw the RDF as far as I could and dove for the ground. The buzzing continued on, following the tumbling RDF unit, then there was another horrible screech as the beeping of the RDF was silenced with a sickening crunch. I screamed in agony as a spike of pain drilled through my head, and a hissing voice shattered my thoughts.

Cáitlín, I know you are here. I can feel you. Come to me! Do not resist.

I clamped my eyes shut, trying desperately to summon any thought or emotion to drown out the terrible voice and the sudden and powerful compulsion to obey, but nothing worked. I couldn't think. I could scarcely breathe for the crushing pain.

The buzzing of wings sounded above me. Something ponderous and heavy landed near me, but I couldn't move. The ice-pick pain driving through my skull intensified. Warm blood ran over my neck and down my cheeks as blood leaked from my ears and eyes. An indescribable fire burned within me. I was going to die right here, right now. I finally managed to force open one eye as a monstrous claw half the size of my body hovered over me.

Then I heard a scream and the chunk-chunk of Morgan's MP5. Ichor and bits of chitin rained down upon me as thick gray arms scooped me off the ground. Déra pulled me onto her shoulders and ran, Morgan firing behind us somewhere. Slowly, the agony within my head dimmed. My eyes burned like liquid fire in the dull, vague light of the gate. Déra breathed hard, hauling me on her shoulders as she ran. She stumbled, and we both spilled to the earth. I rolled through the fog.

"Morgan!" I shouted as Déra began hauling me up again. "We have to find Morgan."

I jerked at Déra's grip as she dragged me across the ragged ground toward the gate. "Stop," I cried. Tears mixed with blood stung my eyes. "Stop, please. We have to get Morgan." I raised my head, yanking with what little strength I had left, trying to see.

We crossed the threshold into the gate chamber, and Déra tumbled to the dirt floor, rolling to a stop in front of Freyer and Carlos. I tried to rise, but my legs and arms would barely hold my weight, and I retched over and over. Moments later, to my relief, Morgan stumbled through the gate and turned, dropping to one knee, weapon raised, to wait for whatever might follow.

My breath came in ragged gasps as I tried desperately again to pull myself up. Morgan still knelt in front of the gate, waiting patiently for the next thing, whatever it might be, to come flying, skittering, or leaping through. Déra stepped in front of me, her bow drawn like the avatar of Artemis herself. But nothing appeared, and even the ogumo, tucked away within the caustic webbing around the gate chamber, lay still.

Unable to believe that we'd made it back without being torn to shreds, I finally rolled over onto my back. After a few more minutes, Morgan stood, slung her weapon over her shoulder, and turned, walking over and pushing her arms under me. She lifted me gingerly off the floor, carrying me out of the gate chamber, her face a mixture of relief and absolute rage.

For long moments as she set me down on the table we'd moved into the hallway, she said nothing. Emotions warred in her expression as her jaw worked, tears tumbled down her face, and her bottom lip quivered. "What were you thinking?"

She asked finally before she bent over me and sobs wracked her broad frame.

I struggled to speak through the migraine that pounded in my skull. "I—I just wanted to protect you. Oh, God—" I turned on my side and retched again. Finally, with no relief from the pounding headache, I curled up into a ball and squeezed my eyes shut, praying for blackness to take me. Eventually, after a time, it did.

CHAPTER THIRTY-THREE

I stand at the cave mouth, looking across the broken, cracked, deserted plain. A figure resolves itself from the fog, decrepit and stumbling, zombie-like. I think it's a woman by the shape of her, but it is hard to tell. She's staggering toward me; at first, I'm revolted by the site. The skin is thin, almost translucent. Her head is nearly bald, and a few thin, dry strands of blond hair hang down into her face even as she staggers ahead.

Her face. Marcella's face. Oh, God. Figures emerge behind her, but they are not the horrid creatures I expect. They are soldiers in black fatigues; one of them, a tall woman, has short red hair. Morgan? What the fuck?

I charge out of the cave at full tilt. I'll never make it in time. Morgan raises her weapon and shoots. The bullet rips through my leg, but I neither feel it nor stumble.

"Morgan! Stop! It's me!"

She fires again. This time the bullet tears into my shoulder. Impossibly, I'm almost to Marcella. She says something, but it's muted, strange. The words seem to reach me after she speaks.

"Find me, Cait. Help me."

Then she is gone, vanishing in a swirl of dust. The soldiers are gone. Morgan is gone. I turn around, looking about. A door appears, standing impossibly on the windswept basalt desert, steel with a crossbar. She's there. I know it. I don't know how, but I don't question it. I race to the door. There is a thick lock on the crossbar. I don't have a key or any picks. I can't open it. I look through the view slot. Marcella huddles in the corner, lost and alone. My heart breaks, and I pound on the door, crying. I have to get her out. I have to save her.

"Get away from the door, Cait."

My eyes fluttered open. The relentless pounding in my skull had become more of a dull ache, but my heart still thrummed from the dream. I was in a concrete room with a single dim recessed light in the center of it. It was one of the cells of the gate facility. Anxiety squeezed at my chest, and an involuntary shiver ran through me before I realized that the cell door was open a crack, admitting a sliver of crass, fluorescent light from the hall beyond. The stink of blood and death floated all around me. I heard light snoring and a mild whimper as I moved. An arm tugged at my midsection and the day's events filtered back into my groggy, sluggish thoughts.

"Morgan?" I croaked through parched lips. God, when was the last time I'd had water?

Morgan's reply sounded as tired and sleep-fogged as I felt. "Hmm?"

"What time is it? How long was I out?"

The arm around my waist slid away as Morgan glanced at her wrist. "Oh, yeah. I left my watch in the bowels of hell. I don't really know."

I moved to sit up, but the room spun. "I feel terrible," I muttered hoarsely and lay back on the floor. Every joint in my body hurt, my muscles ached, and my head felt like it was in a vice. "I need some water. I think I'm dehydrated."

"Hang on." Morgan extracted herself from around me and left. She returned a few moments later with a bottle of Evian. "I have some good news and bad news."

"Okay, enough preamble," I said as I sipped at the water slowly.

"The hatch is open, so we are outta here. Unfortunately, the

FBI has arrived, and they look none too happy about our presence. Some woman named Schaeffer, she's talking about quarantine with Carlos."

"Fuck. Yeah, we probably need to go into quarantine. Though they've had people in and out of the gate for two months, and no one has gotten sick yet, as far as we know. Besides, Erin would have been sick by now. They're going to want to debrief us, too." I was wracked by a coughing fit and took another sip of water.

Morgan's brow furrowed as she began checking me over, looking into my eyes and checking my lymph nodes. "Speaking of quarantine, you don't look so good."

"I don't feel so good. Something's wrong, but something's been wrong for days."

Morgan just nodded, accepting the explanation. "I think some idiot tried to take Déra's weapons. The guy's bleeding and bruised on the floor, out cold. We should probably get out there."

I was glad that Morgan had changed the subject. I knew it wasn't the changed blood. Nastasia had done something to me. I was sure of it, and I was deeply worried. But I was also tired and run down. I hadn't had five minutes to catch my breath in a week. A few days of quarantine would be just fine.

Morgan supported me as we walked into the lab. Carlos was nose to nose with Special Agent Schaeffer, who stood in a gray suit and white blouse. I'd always found Carlos extremely intimidating when he looked down on me like that, but I had to hand it to the lady; she didn't back down.

"Special Agent Schaeffer," Carlos growled. "I need my team on the street tracking down the ogumo, those spider things. They can't be sitting around at BMC twiddling their thumbs all week."

"Detective Ramirez, you're team has been in contact with an unknown." Schaeffer pointed at Déra. "I'm sure she's fit as a fiddle, but we have diseases for which she likely has no immunity. And she may be carrying some for which we have none. So, like it or not, you go into quarantine for seven days."

Carlos opened his mouth, but I interrupted. "Carlos, you

need to stop. The Special Agent is right. We can't risk an outbreak of a foreign contagion. I know Erin was with them for some time and seemed fine, but we need to be sure. She may be an exception, not the rule."

Carlos' jaw worked as he stepped away from Schaeffer.

"Thank you, Detective. Now, will someone please tell me what the hell happened here? And where are the survivors? Where is Erin Miller?"

Morgan spoke up. "Erin Miller was the only survivor. The rest were—I don't know, eaten, I think. They were taken to some giant beast as food, or raw material, or something."

Déra had been quiet up to this point, tending to the man she'd knocked unconscious. Now she looked over. "They were taken to Mother Darkness, a monstrosity the size of a small city. They are all dead. There's nothing you can do for them, um, Schaeffer, is it?"

Schaeffer turned toward Déra, mouth open. "Where did you learn to speak English?"

I related what Déra had told me about her friend Amelia.

"Well, that certainly makes things simpler. Welcome to Earth." Schaeffer turned back to Morgan. "And Miss Miller?"

Again, Déra spoke, finally rousing the Agent on the floor in front of her. "Ms. Miller chose to stay with my people. She has bonded with one of them."

"Bonded? She was only in there for a couple of hours." She turned toward me. "Did you at least get a statement?"

I snapped. "We spent most of the time either running for our lives or in abject terror, so fucking excuse me if we didn't follow police protocol in the extra-dimensional fucking space! Now, can we please just get to the quarantine? You'll have to go in with us, given your proximity to Déra. We can brief you on what we found once we're there. I'm exhausted and not feeling well." I held up a hand to forestall her questions. "Before you ask, it's a condition I've had for some time, not contagious."

Thankfully, everyone agreed, and we had time to get our situations in order, all of us making phone calls once we returned to the surface. I called Liz and gave her a brief rundown on what had happened, my condition, and the plans for quarantine. She promised to see me soon and get me clothes and other supplies. I didn't see how she would make that happen, given that we'd be in isolation for a week, but I left it alone.

"Cait," Liz said before we hung up. "Please try to be more careful. We need you here." There was a long pause. "I need you here."

I tried blinking away tears, but I was just too tired. "I know. I'm sorry. I'll see you soon."

"And Cait," Liz said, her voice just a whisper. The phone got very quiet, and it seemed as if all of the other conversations had ceased as the silence on the line stretched.

"Liz?" I prompted, waiting for her to say whatever was on her mind.

"Nothing. I'll see you tonight." She hung up.

I sighed and sat down in the dirt, waiting for the van that would take us to quarantine. Fortunately, Schaeffer had selected the closest facility that could handle high-level quarantine, Boston Medical Center, only a few minutes away. So, as the van pulled up, I cajoled Déra into giving up her weapons. In the end, she only relented because I promised they'd be returned, though I suspected she knew it was out of my immediate control. Immense guilt tugged at my heart as I passed the blade Déra had given me to a man in MOPP gear, and we all piled into the transport van.

The quarantine area sat in a disused corner of the hospital that had once been converted for COVID patients. Once in my room, a nurse wearing protective gear came and took my clothes, leaving me chilled in the air-conditioned unit. The nurse pointed to my bathroom, suggested a hot shower, and left, handing me a dressing gown. I sat down on the floor, unable to stand any longer. I was beyond exhausted. My emotions were churning chaotically. Ripples of broken glass tore up and down my body, just under the skin. I recognized it for the full-blown case of vampiric hunger that it seemed to be. I couldn't keep a thought in my head. A blond doctor covered almost head to toe in protective gear came in, hauling a sizable

Louis-Vuitton duffel bag.

"Oh, Cait, let me help you up."

"Liz," I gasped weakly. I didn't ask how she'd gotten in; I didn't care. I raised my aching arms, and she pulled me up, helping me to the bathroom. "I was worried they might redirect you to Hanscom or some other military facility where it would be much harder to get to you."

"That only happens in the movies," I said, then collapsed into her arms, crying. "I'm so sorry. I'll never do that again. I shouldn't have gone through the gate. It was—" I couldn't say anymore as a wheezing, coughing fit stole my breath.

Liz turned on the hot water, set my dressing gown aside, and retrieved a purple scrubby, anti-bacterial shampoo, and soap from the duffel. Then she stripped and pulled me into the shower. "Dear Lord, Cait, you stink to high heaven. What the hell have you been up to?"

I leaned against the wall of the shower, letting the hot water flow down over my head and shoulders as Liz began washing me. Moments later, my knees gave out, and I crumpled to the floor. "Cait? Are you okay?"

I sat there in the hot spray, unable to summon the strength to move. "No," I whispered hoarsely. "I'm not. Something's wrong, Liz. It started after Nastasia and I—"

Liz nodded, wiped the grime from my face with the washcloth they'd left for me, and kissed my lips gently. "I think I know what's going on. As far as the hospital knows, I'm your private physician. I may or may not have glamoured a few folks to get in here."

I laughed weakly. "Are you really a doctor?"

"Of course I am. Elizabeth Tyler, MD. I graduated from medical school in Paris in 1874."

I gave a snort and rolled my eyes. "Of course you did."

"I also have recent medical credentials. I'm even board-certified. Don't ask. In any event, I have a theory as to what is wrong with you. I'll leave orders for you that will probably leave you feeling right as rain, at least for a while." Liz continued to bathe me like that, sitting on the floor until all of the ichor, bits of chitin, dirt, and God knew what else was off of me, leaving me smelling like a hospital room.

"Liz, I have a confession to make. It's about Morgan. I—"

She placed a finger to my lips. "Are you in love with her?"

I looked up into Liz's eyes. "No. I'm in love with you."

"Then I don't care." There was no judgment in Liz's eyes as she dried us both off and carried me to my bed.

"Why are you so good to me?" I asked meekly as she helped me into some pajamas, tossing the shitty hospital gown into the laundry bin.

She paused again, saying nothing for long moments, just looking at my face with a searching gaze. "Because dear," she replied finally. "For whatever reason, I've fallen for you."

Those words, 'fallen for me.' They would have made me feel all tingly inside if I didn't already feel so shitty. "Yeah," I said quietly, almost to myself.

I reached up and hugged her, then fell back to the bed. My head was still throbbing, and fatigue wracked my body. "God, my joints hurt. Maybe I do have something."

"I'll be back shortly. Not to worry." Liz dried her hair furiously, then dressed and left the room. A few minutes later, a woman and a man came in. The woman carried an IV, and the other had a phlebotomy kit.

"You here to take my blood?"

The man laughed. When he spoke, I could barely understand him through his mask and plastic visor. "Of course. And no vampire jokes, please. I've heard them all."

"Not unless you're planning on taking it from my neck," I joked. *If he only knew.*

"Not bad," the phlebotomist said. "That's a comeback I haven't heard yet. Good for you. Now give me your arm."

"Your physician has ordered some bloodwork. I also have to send your blood down to the lab to make sure you don't have any little nasties running around in your body." He wrapped a rubber tourniquet around my arm and pushed on the inside of my elbow. "I'm guessing you haven't had anything to drink in a while."

While he tried to find a vein, the woman took my vitals and hung the IV. Eventually, they finished fussing over me and left me alone, though the nurse returned a short while later and hung a second IV. This time, it was a bag of A-negative blood. My heart skipped a beat. "What's that for?"

"Your doctor ordered it to help with your condition. She says you have hemolytic anemia."

I had no idea what that was, but I played along. "Yes, diagnosed for a while now."

She nodded and squeezed the blood into my vein. Immediately the headache started to subside. "Well, you need to watch your condition better."

The nurse also pulled out a hypodermic needle.

"What's that?" I asked, eyeballing the needle with semi-serious suspicion.

"Something to help you rest."

"Liz ordered a sedative?" *Yay, Liz,* I thought.

"Dr. Tyler said it was your choice, but she thought you might need to sleep."

I snorted a laugh. "Yes, please." I probably sounded a little too excited about the prospect, but I didn't care. The idea of being knocked out seemed perfect right about now.

CHAPTER THIRTY-FOUR

As our quarantine clawed its way into the third day like a sloth on Valium, I was crawling the walls with boredom. My TV was broken, only tuning in two channels. Quarantine sucked ass.

I kept a loose grip on the semi-broken TV remote, trying to decide which of my options was worse. On Fox News, the talking heads were decrying the 'monsters' of Boston as beasts ready to eat your children. Opposite that, ironically enough, was *Twilight* on TNT. I sighed. At least Bella was somewhat open-minded, even if Edward was way too old for her, the cradle robber.

Hell, I didn't know shit at seventeen. I certainly wouldn't have been old enough to handle Marcella, and I still wasn't. And as cool as the van scene at the beginning was, I couldn't help but laugh. The laws of physics still apply to vampires. In real life, Edward would have been severely injured for at least a few minutes, and Bella would have been chunky salsa.

I sighed as I flipped back to the Dwight-Walkers on Faux News, as I liked to call it. Some idiot with big hair was talking about how a mermaid had eaten her husband, and I shook my head. Although, it was undoubtedly a real possibility. Even great white sharks steered clear of mermaids, and with good reason. A single mermaid can swim fast as a mako shark, and, in their element, they were beyond lethal, with teeth like razor blades and claws like a harpy eagle, not to mention their big brains and opposable thumbs, just like us. I flipped back to *Twilight*; at least it had Kristin Stewart.

"Pack your shit, darling. You are out of here," Liz said as she barreled through the door, leaving it wide. "Infectious disease has come up fuck all on everyone's blood, so you're clear. Schaeffer tried to fight it, but I raised a stink and threatened to sue, and it seems the FBI doesn't want everyone to know about the gate, so they agreed to let you 'quarantine' at home." She lowered her tone to a conspiratorial whisper. "They think it might cause a panic."

My mouth dropped open, and I hopped from the bed like a bug running from a can of Raid. "Thank God, I was going out of my mind. What about Déra?"

"She's released into your custody. It pays to have a friend in the Mayor's office."

"Marcella?" I asked hopefully.

Liz snatched up my duffel bag and started stuffing things in. "Nope, the Mayor."

"The Mayor? Who called her?"

"No clue. Have you been screwing Mayor Kim on the side or something?"

"What? Eww. No. She's a politician. So did you bring the Jeep?"

Liz zipped up my bag after stuffing everything in it. "No, Nastasia has it. Running some errands, she said."

"You let Nastasia drive my Jeep?" No one was allowed to drive my Jeep except Liz.

"Cait, it'll be fine. She's bringing it back tonight. I didn't want to leave it at the police station in a snowstorm. They'd tow it to plow the lot."

"Hold on a second," came another voice from the doorway. "You may be free to go home, but I still have questions, a lot of questions. I need to debrief you." Special Agent Schaeffer stood defiantly in the doorway.

Liz donned a crooked smile and looked the agent up and down. "Love your suit, dear. And all that hair pulled back into a tight bun reminds me of how Cait used to dress. If you take my meaning."

"Hey!" I protested. "I wasn't that uptight."

Liz continued as if I hadn't spoken. "If you want to have a chat with Cait, you could always come back to our place. I'm sure you'd have a blast."

I gave Liz a warning look as she slunk over to Schaeffer, whom I was dead sure was straight. But Liz ignored me.

"Wha—what are you doing, Ms. Tyler?" Schaeffer stammered slightly, backing into the doorframe.

Liz closed to a hair's breadth and reached up, tucking a stray strand of hair behind Schaeffer's ear, speaking with a voice that oozed sensual promises. "Oh, you know, just wondering who the gorgeous brunette is trying to push my friend around."

When a vampire stalks prey, depending on the vampire's temperament and mood, they can make others see them as absolute sex objects, and Liz was stalking Schaeffer. I wondered what feelings she'd engendered in the conservative FBI agent in the bland gray suit, plain brown shoes, and cream-colored blouse. Because she looked both terrified and aroused. I was willing to bet that she was hella confused right now.

"Liz, leave the woman alone," I protested half-heartedly, thoroughly enjoying the show.

Liz didn't even look my way. "Stay out of this, Cait. I'm playing. So, Special Agent Schaeffer, maybe you can come by the house for your—what did you call it—debrief?" Liz made the mundane activity sound terribly lewd, and I pressed my lips together in suppressed amusement. After Nastasia, I thought the poor woman would have at least some idea of what she was up against. Apparently not.

Schaeffer tried to straighten up and look Liz in the eye. *Good for you, Schaeffer,* I thought sarcastically. *Except that was the absolute worst move.* Liz had her. I could see it in the shift in Schaeffer's posture as she leaned forward slightly, eyes dilated, nostrils flaring, a dreamy expression on her face. Schaeffer said nothing and began opening her blouse as Liz caressed her face and leaned in. They were just about to kiss when I stomped my foot. "Medlyn!"

At the sound of her last name, Liz pulled back slowly and looked over her shoulder. "Yes?"

"Time to go. Ms. Schaeffer, if you'll excuse us. You may join us at the house for debrief, or you may meet me at Schroeder on Wednesday. Which would you prefer?"

Special Agent Schaeffer shuddered slightly and looked around for a minute as if she wasn't sure just where she was, then finally straightened her jacket. She looked down at her shirt and flushed, quickly buttoning up. "The—" Her voice broke, and she swallowed loudly. "Schroeder would be fine, Detective." Then she exited with as much dignity as she could muster, which wasn't much, replaced moments later by Déra standing in a set of ill-fitting hospital scrubs, holding her tunic, boots, and breastplate.

"Where are your weapons?" I asked Déra, wondering the same about the sword she'd given me. "The man, Carlos? He said he would drop them off this evening at your place. He assumed I'd be staying there."

Liz just raised an eyebrow and smirked. "Sure, the more, the merrier, especially now that Andrea's gone back to her own place. And, love, your feet will hang off the bed."

"The floor will be fine," Déra said flatly.

Of course, it will, I thought. *She probably sleeps on a bed of spikes at home.* Then I shook my head and turned to Liz. "Did you have to do that to Schaeffer?"

Liz continued to smirk, eyes crinkling with amusement. "You know I did."

"You're getting so good at the whammy."

"Aren't I, though?" Liz replied, and we all headed for home, thank God.

As soon as we got home, Liz went to her room and crashed, but not before finding some loose drawstring pants and a t-shirt for Déra. The pants fit her waist but were tight in the thighs, and the t-shirt might as well have been a midriff. I had to cut the sleeves off to make room for her arms. I showed Déra to the spare bedroom. She seemed in awe of the place, commenting that in her city, the houses are all made of stone because of violent storms every year, or every cycle as she called it. They measured time on a different scale, something to do with a large planet in their solar system called Áregos. She also mentioned that her world had no moons, so after we had some real food, Déra followed me up to the roof to watch the moon rise.

I was shocked that she didn't seem to mind the freezing temperatures in the limited clothes we'd found for her. I was in a t-shirt, sweater, heavy pants, winter boots, gloves, and my yetiesque parka, and I was still cold. She was barefoot in only what we'd given her.

"Doesn't this bother you? The cold, I mean."

Déra shook her head but didn't explain. I let it be, though, because she seemed enraptured by the massive glowing sphere rising into the sky, and I didn't want to ruin the moment for her. We stood there for about forty minutes, watching a wonderful harvest moon creep up over the harbor.

"Truly beautiful," Déra whispered, awestruck, as she watched it rise, then she frowned. "Where are the stars?"

"Light pollution," I explained wistfully, "from the city. When I was a vampire, I could see all the stars regardless, but now I'm back to being just me."

Déra said nothing else, but after a few more minutes of shivering and teeth chattering, I complained of the cold and promised the moon would still be there tomorrow. So we retired to the sitting room next to a roaring fire, where she finally spoke.

"Do you miss it?" Her voice was low and inquisitive. "Being a vampire?"

I took a sip of my wine to think about how to answer her. "Yes. I miss it. I didn't want to admit that to myself for a long time, but I do."

"It seems an odd thing to miss, feeding on people. Amelia told me of vampires, but she believed them to be fiction and myth." Déra sniffed her wine, then finally drank it and smiled, relaxing on the sofa.

"Yes, I'm sure she did. So did I until I met Marcella. Their existence is widely believed to be nonsense here, born of folklore and legend."

"What is she like?" Déra seemed insatiably curious about us, not humans in general, but us. And while I knew that curiosity is what had prompted the question, I couldn't help but feel irritated. I took a few moments to quell my sense of loss before answering.

"She's a warrior like you in many ways. She's tall, powerful, and far better with a sword than I will ever be. She's also fifteen hundred years old. But she's also very lonely. She fills her life with helping others to avoid it, and sometimes she makes awful decisions because of it." I sipped my wine and looked into the fireplace.

"I would like to meet her. She sounds fascinating. It's also clear that you love her very much."

I looked down and squeezed the rug with my bare toes, then quietly said, "I did. I want her to come home, but I'm not sure I want to be with her anymore." Then I laughed without humor. "Of course, that's if we can find her. She's missing. Someone has kidnapped her."

"Kidnapped?" Déra looked puzzled. It seemed we'd finally found an English word she didn't know.

"Taken against her will and held."

"Ah." Déra sipped at her wine again, staring into the fire. "That happened to Umbrá at one point. The priestess caste of my society took her while I was away. I broke every rule to free her. We were about to go on the run when our city was attacked. On the lamb, I think you call it."

I laughed out loud. At Déra's bemused and irritated expression, I explained. "The phrase is 'on the lam.' A lamb," I said, emphasizing the 'b,' "is a small wooly domesticated animal. Lam means to run away."

Déra grinned at that, probably thinking of sitting on a small wooly animal.

The conversation stalled, and we sat there for a bit. I started feeling a little warm from the wine and a little drowsy. I looked over. Déra seemed lost in contemplation. "Can I ask what you are thinking about?"

"That it's unlikely I'll ever see home again."

I decided I liked this woman. She was an open book. No nonsense, no bullshit. If you asked her a direct question, you got a direct answer, and that was refreshing. I didn't have to guess at anything.

"Why didn't you go back as soon as you got me back through the gate? You could have, you know."

"Yes, I could have. But that is not the most important thing to me."

"Umbrá?"

"Yes."

"Will you tell me about her? I'd really like to know who she was."

Déra laughed loudly. "I believe you would call that irony." At my puzzled expression, she continued. "You knew my name, Cait. That means that her lehos was in your head. Not just in your body, but in your head. You shared minds with her. I find it amusing that you are asking me about her."

I shrugged. "Maybe so, but all I got were a couple of strange visions, and then I died. Her memories were mixed with my own, so it is hard to understand."

Déra nodded politely and said, "The first thing you need to know is that Umbrá is my sister after a fashion."

"Um, you mean a blood relative?"

"Not as such. A few cycles after my birth, my mother gave birth to a young male child who was not everything she hoped for. She was aging, and her reproductive organs were reaching the end of their usefulness."

"Ah, I said. Old eggs. I get it."

Déra tilted her head. "I'm not sure what that means, but I'll assume it's similar. My younger brother, at the age of three, still did not speak or walk. He could not handle even the simplest tasks one might expect of a child of six months. Then the sages of Mens-Dhe came and offered a possibility. They would implant a small creature in my brother that would change him physically and mentally."

"I don't understand. Was it an experiment?"

"Yes. My mother chose to have this done in the hopes of

having a normal child. I was very young at the time and didn't understand what was happening. When my mother left and returned alone, I assumed that she had killed my brother."

"Killed him? That's barbaric." I caught myself, reminding myself of my chat with Nastasia. Déra was from a different culture.

"To some, maybe. But to us, it is a mercy. Life in Işir is harsh and unforgiving. The infirm, especially the impoverished, often die horrid deaths. A child like my younger brother would normally have been killed as soon as the signs of such debilitating birth defects were known. We were relatively wealthy, however, so there were options."

"I'm sorry for interrupting. So what happened to him?"

"The sages of Mens-Dhe placed Umbrá's legos on his face. It entered his head through the eye, and then the transformation began. It consumed his brain and replaced it, then it reformed his entire body, turning him into a physical, genetic clone of Umbrá as she had been when she died. But something went wrong. Normally, the Kylir, Umbrá's people use the recently deceased. And there is a complex ritual that accompanies the process. As a result, Umbrá retained none of her memories. Thousands of years of living memory were lost."

I finally understood, and the implications were bizarre. "So, the lehos used your brother as raw material to create a clone. And then, what, your mother just accepted it into her home as her daughter?"

"No. Because the process resulted in a Kyliri baby, she chose to make her a slave to the household instead. But there were things she did at the time that seemed odd. When Umbrá began to show an almost prodigious talent for the Xharpras, a harp-like instrument with black-steel strings that makes music you can scarcely imagine, my mother hired one of the most renowned players to teach her. Umbrá became a virtuoso with the instrument, a phenomenal talent."

"I take it they don't typically teach slaves to play music in your culture."

She chuckled. "No, they don't. But it's an abominable practice, to begin with—the slavery, not the teaching of music.

Unfortunately, there is no way in our law to free a non-Oşeni slave. Once a slave, always a slave, unless sold to someone off-world."

"That's horrible. Is it intergenerational?"

"Yes."

"God, that's even worse."

"Yes. Umbrá is not like you, or Liz, or anyone I've met here. She is prim and proper. As a maidservant, she kept our home perfectly in order. When I—" Déra paused oddly as if rethinking her words and then finished her wine before proceeding. "When my mother finally passed, Umbrá kept our finances managed. And to say that I liked her from an early age would be quite an understatement. But she rebuffed my every advance. Women who sleep with their servants are considered unseemly among the great houses. And Umbrá was never unseemly."

I laughed. "Yeah, that's literally no one around here. The closest would be Marcella, but even she has quite a naughty streak. We're all pretty unseemly."

"As am I, Cait. I was what you might refer to in your language as a cad of sorts. I took many partners. Another reason that Umbrá refused me."

"So what happened? How did it come to where it is now?"

"That is a years-long story, and for another time. For now, I am tired, and I think I'll go to bed for the night. I did, however, appreciate the conversation. And thank you for showing me the moon." With that, Déra stood and left the room before I could even return the pleasantries. It was so abrupt that I wondered if I might have said or done something to offend her, but then again, that might just be her.

CHAPTER THIRTY-FIVE

Two months. It has been two months since I last fed. My body will fail soon, sending me into torpor to save my soul from the ravages of the curse. The hunger's hold over my mind vanished days ago, and now I am a broken thing, a dried husk, bald and faded and gaunt. My skin is like paper, my bones brittle, easily broken. And yet, I cannot die. Deep within my core resides the last reserves of my soul, locked away, a tiny reserve of energy—waiting to spring should the living come near. I fear for that time, for I will kill whoever approaches. Even after sundown, I am weak, but it is okay. I won't go down without a fight. I still hold out hope that the bond was not broken, that she will find me. The woman with the auburn hair and fabulous eyes, whose name I can no longer remember, will never love me again, not as she once did, but she will not let me die if she can help it. I have faith in her.

My mind wanders, and I am in the park again, lying in the warm sun. I adjust my skirt, leaving the slit just a bit slack. It's silly. She may not even notice, but we do odd things when we desire someone. I see myself, the woman with the auburn hair, through the slit of my eyelids, walking toward me. This feels so surreal, remembering this moment, our lunch date in the park, as seen through Marcella's eyes, through Marcella's thoughts. She thinks my body is impressive, and dimly as if through a cottony, gauze-like film, I feel a sense of pride. I've worked hard for that body. She wants to see me naked one day, but it has to be my choice, well, mostly my choice. She smiles inwardly at that thought, playfully, not maliciously.

The image twists, though, and I am in the gate room. I see myself again. She thinks I hate her now. She thinks she was so short-sighted.

The dream is so confusing. Marcella's thoughts and my own fuse and twist, but I mentally scream into the turbulent eddies. I do not hate you. I never could. I still love you. A glimmer of hope appears almost there, but it flashes away, like a candle vanishing into dense smoke. No! I will find you! I will save you! But she cannot hear me, and I am sucked back down into the river of chaotic, restless baubles of reminiscence.

I wait for Liz. I am handcuffed and gagged. That idiot Schmidt is pontificating. Part of me laughs. He will die unceremoniously very soon. I recall the prophetic words of Marcella's maker, a goddess of death and magic, lingering and waiting, but it all slips away save one, Maerta. It is Marcella's true name, her birth name, inscribed among three others in a ring of red marble.

The scene shifts again, and I am crawling with one good arm across the dirt. Both of my legs are broken. I cannot feel them, but I know that they are. My left eye has been plucked out, and my right arm is mangled, the hand missing. I hear massive, soft wings beating in the dark, and I hope it is the valkyrie come to take me to Folkvangr. I took down four of the bastards, and I pray it is enough. Did I die honorably? I tried. I don't want to go to Valhalla and battle sweaty men for the rest of eternity, but then again, there may be women like me there. Inwardly I smile at my humor. Mother Freyja, please come for me. I was never in life as I was at my death. I wasted my time with many distractions, but I tried to die well.

"Freyja cannot hear you, child," a gentle tenor voice says above me. "She has long gone, and Folkvanger is closed. But I am here to give you eternity and vengeance. Before I do so, though, you must swear to fulfill one duty."

I look up, one good eye, bleary and unfocused. It is a woman, raven-haired, with deep mossy colored eyes and black hair. Marcella does not know her, but I do. Mother Morrigan. "What duty?" Marcella's words are garbled and unintelligible, but the Morrigan seems to understand.

"There will be, in the distant future, far from this place a child, my

child, one of two. You will know her when you see her. You must protect her, for she will bring back the magic that once was and finish the work that my sisters and I began. When she is ready to receive my dark gift, she will be a battle-hardened warrior who has seen death. You will give her this gift that I give to you now. And at the moment in which she is her most powerful, she will also be her most vulnerable. You must be there, Maerta. In a single strike, my child will end him. You must be there to save her. Swear it, and I will give you such power as you may vanquish those who committed such a heinous breach of trust. You will have your vengeance in the cold of a winter night. Do you swear?" This dark angel above me, raven-haired and, now, raven-winged, stares down at me, hands on her hips, and waits.

At first, I see the humor in the request. I half expected a riddle. But I do not even think about the request itself. "I swear," I mutter through my broken jaw. She does not smile, only nods. Silky darkness, syrupy and caustic-looking, spills from her hands and coats me like a blanket, flowing over me, through me, into my mouth and my nose, burning my eyes, choking away my breath. The darkness covers me and steals my senses. And thus, I float alone.

Is this all there is? I think as the terror of eternal isolation floods through me.

My eyes open with a gasp. The pain is gone, and I am whole. The nighttime sky above swirls with a million stars that I've never seen before. I look to see my village, a smoking ruin. The snow is falling thickly, but I feel no cold.

I stand. My arms and legs feel powerful and strong. I lick my now-pointed teeth and have a moment of fleeting horror as I realize I have become draugr, one of the walking dead. My stomach churns, and I vomit the contents across the freezing mud. Gods, what is this? The hunger runs across my body, driving across my skin like spikes. I smell the blood on my body, heavy and sweet. 'The old legends tell truth,' my mother had told me. I have become death, and death I will bring. I turn to the North. I will kill them all.

The rage is all-encompassing, as is the desperate need for blood.

"Marcella! It's Marcella!" I hissed as I awoke and tumbled almost out of bed, gasping for air. The pulse of the hunger raged through me. I clamped my hands to the side of my head as the thump of my own heart banged in my ears like a rifle shot. Every noise, every sensation was agonizing: the soft movement of the covers as Liz slid over to me, the whoosh of the heating vent, it all stabbed into my head. The hunger was like I'd never felt before in my worst moments captured by the council. It felt like a million bees stinging my skin, stabbing in and out repeatedly, and I shook uncontrollably, closing in on myself and rubbing my arms. *God, help me. Make it stop.*

Shivering and sweat-soaked, I turned on the light and dragged myself up from the warm bed into what felt like frigid air.

"Why is it so cold?" I groused. Jabba was curled in his bed next to the heating vent, watching me with shining eyes as I staggered across the room. I was starving. I needed to eat.

Finally, in the kitchen, I stood in the cold air of the refrigerator to cool my now-burning skin. I reached for the orange juice, but my eyes lit upon the bags of blood sitting there.

"You're not a vampire anymore, Cait," I told myself. "It won't help."

I licked my lips, though, and, unable to stop myself, grabbed the blood and tore open the bag. I upended it, letting the cold syrupy blood pour down my throat and across my chin and chest. I gasped at the salty taste, like heaven, feeling it press the hunger down like a hammer. My senses returned, and the crawling of my skin and spine vanished. I sighed and laughed almost maniacally as I sat with my back to the refrigerator. My stomach growled a few times in satisfaction. Then a horrible cramp doubled me over.

"Oh shit," I muttered as I puked blood all over the floor.

"Cait, what the hell are you doing?" Liz stood in the doorway looking at my blood-covered face as I heaved more sickness onto the floor.

"I—I don't know," I said with a desperate breath before heaving up the rest of the contents of my stomach. "I couldn't stop myself. I couldn't—" I began to cry. "What's wrong with me, Liz?"

Liz doused a washcloth with warm water, wiping the blood off my chin and breasts. "I think we know what's wrong with you."

"I can still feel it, riding under my skin like insects, clawing to get out. And my stomach feels like ground glass and fire."

"You're definitely turning again, but I've never seen anything like this." She said it softly as if I might break.

I nodded through a cough. "It has something to do with what Nastasia did. And it's Marcella, too. She's reaching out to me from wherever she is. She's locked in a cell and starving. It's not a dream." I pawed at Liz's arm desperately. "It's not a dream."

"Okay, love. Okay." She pulled me off the floor and set me at the table, then grabbed her phone, shooting off a text message. A few minutes later, she looked up as her phone dinged. "There, I've texted Bian. She'll get to the bottom of this."

I coughed, and a little more blood came up; I swallowed it back down. "Let's just get this over with, now. We can go upstairs—"

"No, Cait. I don't think that will work. You already have the curse. Trying to turn you in this state might just kill you."

I hung my head and rubbed my arms, trying to make the pins and needles on my flesh stop. Shivers ran up my spine as I looked at the blood on the floor.

"When do we leave?" I asked

"As soon as I clean up this mess." In a matter of minutes, she'd mopped the floor, and then she scooped me up.

"I can walk, you know."

Liz hit the call button on the elevator. "I know, but I like doing this."

"Are you okay to drive? I mean, aren't you tired? I don't want you wrecking Marcella's Audi or killing me."

"Cait, love, I've been driving since before the Hansom. I'll be fine. I'm old enough to stay up for days without feeding if need be."

An hour and a half later, we were once again clean and trudging through the old Cambridge Subway tunnel to the camp three surface entrance. Liz knocked, and a lamia I didn't recognize answered the door.

"Hi, is Bian here? We have an appointment."

"You must be Cait," the lamia said with a broad grin, looking at me weirdly.

I looked at her askance. "Yeah, I'm Cait. I don't think we've met."

"Oh, I'm sorry, I'm Kara. I apologize for staring. It's just, well, they told me that you transformed into one of us at will. I just think that's so cool."

"It was an accident, and I don't think at will is a fair assessment. But, I have to say, it was interesting." I tried to smile back, but my discomfort and the rushing hunger overwhelmed me. I started leaning on Liz, who finally just picked me up again.

Kara opened the door, and we entered the camp. Liz followed Kara through the facility with me in her arms, past the temple and the various private chambers. I looked around to see if my mother was about, to no avail. Our journey ended in a hospital-like area where Bian stood looking at a computer screen, one hand on her hip. The screen displayed a microscopic picture. "I think that might do it," Bian said to no one in particular. "The only thing to do is test it."

"Bian, ma'am, your appointment is here."

Bian twisted around. "Cait, how—oh, you look atrocious. Liz, honey, put her on the gurney."

Liz set me on a gurney in the middle of the room, and Bian glided over. Well, more like she just moved her torso over. Most of her sat perfectly still. Sometimes I forgot just how large she was.

"So, tell me what's going on. Open up and say ahh." I opened my mouth, and Bian pulled on my jaw, causing it to unhinge. "Oh, my. I think I see your problem. Have you been having problems handling food? Craving blood? Feeling vampiric hunger from time to time?"

My eyes popped at how accurate she was. "Yes, how did

you know?"

"Have a look at your teeth." Bian handed me a mirror, and now that she'd said something, I could see what she was talking about. My fangs were almost back. It was subtle but noticeable.

"Well then." I handed her the mirror. "How long do I have?"

"Hard to say. Lie down and close your eyes."

I did as she asked and felt her cool hand slide under my shirt, coming to rest over my heart. Bian closed her eyes and cocked her head as if listening to something. I gasped as an otherworldly hand reached within, as into a secret pocket within my breast that I didn't know existed. The hand traveled still further, silken scales brushing past every nerve, every thought, every emotion like coarse sand filtering through a funnel, all shushy and swift, leaving chaotic visions and feelings in its wake like mental turbulence.

My eyes ran with blood and tears in deep despair and joy and a thousand feelings for which I had no names. Then the hand withdrew, leaving loneliness and loss in its wake. I turned on my side and curled up, quaking with tremendous, painful, hiccuping sobs.

Liz wrapped her arms around me as best she could, turning accusingly on Bian. "What did you do to her?"

"I touched her soul," Bian said as if speaking to a child, then she eased me out of my fetal position. "You are turning again, Cait. That's certain, but the curse is in a state of flux I've never felt before. It's truly novel." Bian pursed her lips and leaned down next to my face, flicking her tongue out.

When my feelings finally began to settle, and the sense of desolation finally faded, I spoke, my voice tiny. "How is this possible? I was cured."

"No, you were never cured. I do have a theory about why you reverted. Magic is energy. It's like electricity, light, or other types of energy. It has many forms, but it can be transmuted from one to another. When you activated the tablets, you were bound to them by the energy they took from you and the energy they channeled through you. Had you been human at the time, it would have killed you instantly and likely destroyed your soul in the process. But, you had a second source of magic."

"The curse," I mused, almost to myself.

"Precisely. In simplest terms, think of it as a battery. You touched the tablets, and the energy of your curse began to discharge into them, like starting a car. Once the gate was opened, that line of energy fed into the gate. Eventually, over the course of a few minutes, the curse was drained of magic, and its bond to your soul was weakened to the point of being almost non-existent. But you can't remove a curse once placed. It must either be subsumed by another curse, or it must be non-sustaining, meaning it simply dies after completing a preset function. But, this seems to be accelerating dramatically. When did this start?"

I thought about it. "I don't know, maybe a week ago, I guess."

"Did something happen? Have you been in contact with a heavy source of magic?"

"The ritual the other night. There was a lot of magic there."

Bian shook her head. "That's earth magic, different stuff entirely. That wouldn't do it. This would be contact with a fae creature's magic or perhaps being given energy from another vampire."

I pursed my lips in aggravation, looking at Liz. "She knew. She fucking knew this would happen."

Liz frowned. "I told you that everything she does has a purpose. Don't be shocked, Cait."

I shook my head. "I'm not. Just fucking irritated." At Bian's bemused expression, I explained. "Nastasia fed on me recently and gave me a lot of changed blood. I mean way more than normal. Since then, I've been healing like a vampire. Each time I heal, it's immediately followed by a wave of nausea and dizziness."

"That's blood loss," Bian said. "Blood rushes to fuel the curse, taking it from your brain."

I jerked in surprise. "Well, that's not good."

Liz put a supportive arm around me. "Seems like all we

have to do is wait."

"No," Bian said, crossing her arms. "You can't wait. Cait, you have a larger problem at hand. You need to complete the change soon. The slow nature of your turning is going to drain your soul of its life-giving essence. The same thing that vampires feed on, that is constantly replenished in the living, will run out for you. The blood can be replaced, but your soul cannot. In the meantime, your body will grow weaker for lack of food, it has already begun consuming its own blood in larger quantities, and eventually, you'll likely die from the strain of the change. I do assume you want to live."

"Of course I do."

"Good. Blood transfusions will keep you going for a while, maybe a month." Bian looked back to Liz, eyes alight and wheels of her mind very clearly turning. "But in that time, we need to figure out how to complete her change. Cait can't take this forever. If she dies before being turned, there'll be nothing you can do. And don't bother to try turning her, Elizabeth. She's already cursed. It would just kill her faster."

I withdrew from Liz's arms and looked into her eyes. She held my gaze. "I don't want to die, Liz."

She hugged me close. "I know. We'll sort this out." Then she turned to Bian. "I'll call if anything changes." Liz lifted me off the gurney and set me on the floor. "Let's go home, love."

I tugged at Liz's shoulder. "Hang on." Then turning to Bian, I said, "Where did you put the parasites?"

"They're here with me."

"Are they all intact?" I asked hopefully.

"Yes, why?"

"Don't dissect them."

Bian looked aghast. "Cait, those things are, as near as I can tell, complete people contained in a genetic template. I'd never hurt them. I just don't know what to do with them."

"Okay, so there's someone at the house who can help with that. I'll have Carlos bring her over. Liz, could you ask Mother Lamia if that's okay?"

Liz nodded.

Bian raised an eyebrow. "Who would he be bringing?"

"You'll see," I said with a smirk. "She'll blow your mind, and I promise, it's worth the wait to find out."

Bian looked at me skeptically and with not a small amount of irritation. As much as she liked to dish it out, she couldn't take it. I looked back toward Liz and the door and gasped.

My mother perched in the doorway, then she slithered over to us, performing a full turn along the way as she did. "Well, what do you think? Good enough?"

I wrapped my arms around her in a long hug. "Perfect. I'm so glad you're doing well."

"What brings you here?" My mother asked as she pulled away.

"I'm turning back into a vampire," I said quickly. "We were just confirming some things." I didn't want to worry my mother. Of course, having me turn back into a vampire might worry her plenty.

"Oh, thank goodness," she said, clutching her hand to her chest.

I looked at my mother in total confusion. "Thank goodness?"

"Lamiae live to be thousands of years old, dear. I didn't want to bury my own child. This saves me having to ask—" She trailed off strangely.

"What is it?" I asked, looking her in the eye.

"I was thinking today about your sister. I don't know how Aoife is going to handle all of this."

I raised an eyebrow. "What's with that anyway? I told her you were sick and she wouldn't make the trip over. She won't even talk to me right now. It's starting to piss me off."

My mother slid down a little and coiled her tail, sitting on it. "Cáitlín, dear, you need to understand. Your sister has been through a lot, and she's not you. She never had your temerity or your tenaciousness about family. And I wasn't there when she needed me half the time. I left her with Donny, and he was largely useless. She thinks you got the better end of things."

I had considered that she might be jealous, but I thought my mother's assessment of her personality was way off. Aoife had always been the crazy one, always trying one thing or another.

She hadn't been afraid of anything. If my mother was right, I wondered what happened that might have changed all that. I shook my head, unable to understand it all. Mom had spent more time over in Ireland with her than with me during the two years after Mike died, too. Maybe I needed to have a heart-to-heart with Aoife about it all.

"Ma, I'm sure she'll be fine with it. The three of us just need to sort things out. And we will. I have faith." In what anymore, I wasn't certain.

"I hope so, dear," Ma said softly. "I have to get back to my lessons. I'm learning how to use these today." She opened her mouth and popped out two vicious-looking fangs as long as my middle finger. Then she put them away and grinned wickedly. "We're using them on grapefruits, but it's kind of neat. Now, enough fooling about, child. I'm sure you have things to do. See you later this week?"

"Of course. Are you really doing okay with all of this?" I waved my hand around.

"Yes, dear. I'm learning so much, and I feel like I have a new and very interesting lease on life." She put her hand on my arm, squeezing gently. "You did well. Thank you."

"Thanks, Ma." I kissed my mother goodbye, and Liz and I left.

CHAPTER THIRTY-SIX

Thursday, January 6th
   One week before my murder. . .

I was back at work the next day, full of new blood and feeling a little better, but not much. My chest ached, and my joints hurt. I was also tired. But Bian had said that would pass quickly as soon as my body adjusted. In the meantime, I slumped in my chair in Larson's office while he read us the riot act.

"I didn't expect you to burn the fucking place down!" Larson shouted as we stood in his office. As he paced behind his desk, he reminded me of a target duck in a shooting gallery. Unable to control myself, I barked a laugh which turned into a wracking cough that dropped me to my knees.

Maki rushed over, turning my face to hers. "You're white as a sheet and ice cold. Here, sit down. Are you okay?"

"I—I'll be okay. Just give me a minute." Carol rushed out and back in moments later with water as I sat down in a chair. A sudden flush of warmth crept up my neck into my face, and I took the water, gratefully downing half the glass.

"That's better," Carol said. "You alright?"

"Jesus, yeah, yeah," I said, shooing everyone back. "I'm fine."

"Cait, have that checked out," Larson said, concern and pursed lips, wrinkling the scar on his cheek.

"I'm fine, Bill. Just get back to chewing us out," I croaked and downed the rest of the water.

Carlos spoke up, though, jumping to our defense. "Bill, you weren't there. There were a million of the damn things. It was beyond creepy. It was fucking scarier than the boohag."

"It was pretty awful, Lieutenant," Maki said in a small voice. I raised an eyebrow. In the apartment, she'd breathed fire, and now she sounded like a scolded schoolgirl.

"And you," Larson barked, turning on Maki. "I asked you to join them because of your expertise, not so you could be a portable flame—"

"Hey!" I shouted, interrupting Larson, startling everyone, even myself. "I get that we set fire to a building in a swanky neighborhood, but we were under extreme threat. Maki did what she should have done—whatever it was." I looked over at her. What had she done exactly? I lowered my voice. "The mayor has made us the squad to deal with the fucking unknown. That also means that unexpected things will happen." Four weeks ago, I wouldn't have dreamed of taking on Bill in front of the team like this. I guess Carol was right; I had changed.

Bill finally sat down and began rubbing his neck. "Get out, all of you. Next time try not to commit arson during your investigation, especially in my last week."

I shot Bill the bird as we walked out the door, and Larson called out. "Reagan! Get back here."

I flinched and shuffled back in, and closed the door.

"What the fuck was that for?" Larson demanded, both hands on his desk. "I'm not the bad guy here."

"I know, Bill. I don't know why I did that. I feel—off." I did indeed feel weird. My emotions seemed to be tumbling end over end, and a bizarre rage was building in my chest. I took a deep breath to tamp it down, but it just sat there, simmering.

"Okay, go get checked out before you go home. And find out who died in that building."

"Okay. But, Bill, and I mean this in the nicest way and with all due respect. You need to ease up. The mayor and the commissioner just assigned us all to the most fucked up detail, and we don't really have a playbook for this."

Bill tilted his head and stared for a moment. "Huh," he said thoughtfully, scratching his head.

I squinted at him. "What?"

A slight smile cracked his face, but he shook his head. "Nothing, I'll tell you later."

It was my turn to shake my head, and I left.

Back at our cubes, Carlos, Carol, and Maki were standing around waiting for me. If I hadn't known better, I'd have sworn they were placing bets on something.

"So, that was rude," Maki said indifferently. "I mean, he was out of line, but, gods Cait, did you have to flip him off?"

I dropped heavily into my chair. "I know. I don't know what got into me. I'm not feeling great."

Carlos leaned back and put his feet up on his desk. "So, did we get a confirmed ID on the victim?"

Carol walked back to her desk and returned with a printout. "It's Councilman Waller, alright. He's lived in Boston since seventy-four and owns a dry cleaner over on—wait." Carol pulled out her phone, thumbing through the map. "It's a block away from Elliot Norton Park. Tell me that's a coincidence."

Carlos leaned forward, taking the paper from Carol. "You gotta be shittin' me. Hang on." Carlos pulled up a map of the area around the park and sent it to the printer. A few minutes later, we were huddled around his desk as he began marking lines on it with a ruler, finally circling an area of roughly a city block next to the park. "This is the park, and this circle is roughly where the gate chamber sits." Carlos marked an ex on the map, dead-center of the circle. "And that's the address of Waller's dry-cleaning service."

"So," I said, looking at the map. "Let's assume it's not a coincidence. We should probably check out the dry cleaners."

Maki looked at her watch. "We should wait until daylight. If it's at all like Waller's home, it's probably not a good time to go down there. Besides, we'll want to give some thought about how we can best defend ourselves without lighting up the place."

"About that," Carol said, chiming in with a shit-eating grin. "You're a Kitsune, right?"

Maki sighed. "Not exactly. One of my ancestors was tenko, a kind of celestial spirit, I guess. The legend is that every few generations, she possesses one of the women of my family. I'm just the lucky one this time around. It's not all that great, to be honest, having weird thoughts intruding on your own or seeing visions of the awful things that happen to people. Basically, it sucks."

I shook my head. "I know how you feel on that count, having something messing up your brain from the inside."

"Oh?" Maki looked intrigued. "Do tell."

"Oh, lord, where to start?" I explained the parasites and how I'd stupidly gotten infected, and the strange visions I'd had during that time. Maki sat and listened, intently absorbing everything I said and even taking notes.

I snickered at that. The girl had a voracious appetite for all things preternatural. "So, what's it like for you?" I asked after I'd finished.

"What, having an ancient spirit running around inside me? Not as weird as it might seem. Okay, no. That's a lie. It's really weird and super annoying. Occasionally she just appears out of nowhere to point out things that I've overlooked. One time I was looking for my keys all over the house, and then I catch this movement out of the corner of my eye. This little white fox is standing on the dining room table where I'd just looked and is pointing out that I'd walked right by them."

"Sounds handy," I said with a laugh. "I wish I had someone to point out shit I missed."

"Yeah, but when I was sixteen, she appeared while I was in the shower, and I was umm—" she stopped and turned about six shades of pink.

"Oh," I said, then my eyes went wide, "Oh! How rude!"

"I know, right?" She said with a conspiratorial giggle. "And one time, I was with a boyfriend, and she didn't appear to me, but I could hear her making a tsk-tsk sound. Of course, only I could hear it, but it totally spoiled the mood, you know?"

"Does that still happen?" I asked, shaking my head in both amusement and disbelief.

"Not as much. We had a chat one night where I threatened to call a priest and have her ass put to rest permanently. I didn't know if that would work, but she started being a little more discrete after that. She's kind of a bitch, though, always critical of shit I do."

"I'm sorry," I said. "You should be allowed to have privacy in your own head."

She shrugged. "I wouldn't trade it for the world. She's taught me so much. I have generations of knowledge and experience, and I get to help save the world."

"I'm sorry? Save the world?" I looked at her in total confusion. "What do you mean?"

Maki covered her mouth for a second, looking for all the world like Katie after she spilled the beans on something. Then she leaned over, whispering, "I'm not supposed to tell you. Let's just say we're in it together. And it'll get harder before it gets better, but it'll all be alright."

"Uh-huh," I said. "Well, I don't know what dear old granny's been telling you, but so far, I've done nothing but fuck up the world. So, unless you're here to put a stake in my heart, I think you and your granny are betting on the wrong horse."

"I don't think so," Maki said with a weird kind of cheeriness. "You doubt yourself too much, Cait. "

"So I've been told." I tried to ask more, but Maki dodged any more questions about 'saving the world.' So we got back to work. If she'd been trying to make me feel good, she'd done no such thing. I was now officially fucking terrified of Maki Imai.

CHAPTER THIRTY-SEVEN

"You look fabulous," Liz said as she adjusted my dress uniform. "And don't worry about Katie. I'm going to take her out tonight after we're done if I have to glamour Anne and Jim Fincher into murder-suicide." Then she added, "Joking, Cait, I'm joking," when she saw my glare.

"Not funny. By the book. This is important to me."

Liz huffed. "Fine. But I could make this a lot easier."

"After what happened to Gabe and Reynolds, I don't want to chance it. Leah's in that house. If Jim loses his shit, he could kill her."

"I understand. And I promise. I won't do anything unnecessary. But I have to take her out every two to three nights so she can feed." She fidgeted, straightening my collar. "You'd have looked much better in a dress." She picked up my jacket off the bed and ran a lint roller over it. Jabba meowed in protest at having his latest lounging spot removed. I shot him a disdainful glare for getting fur on my uniform, but he just yawned and settled next to my pillow, the lovable little asshole.

"I can't wear a dress for this. You know that. Besides, I can't hide my Xiphos or the Sig under a dress."

"Yes, you can," Liz said with a smirk.

"Why do I feel you speak from experience?"

"Because, my dear, I've slipped amazing things from this bodice." She gestured toward her chest, which, in her dress, sat with fantastic cleavage.

"I bet you have," I replied with a naughty grin.

"Hey!" She said, snapping her fingers at my lingering gaze. "Eyes up here."

"Oh, sorry." I grinned as I slid my sig into its holster at the small of my back and slipped the straps of the Xiphos sheath around my shoulders. Then I put on my jacket and looked in the mirror. You couldn't tell I was armed to the teeth, and since this was a gala function and we were cops, we got to bypass the metal detectors. However, I wondered momentarily if the Xiphos would even set it off, given the weird metal.

It lay awkwardly against my back, and I'd be sitting bolt upright all night, but the hilt was facing down to hide it and to make it an easier draw. Liz had given me the Sig and a spare clip. It beat our service weapons for reliability. I just hoped I didn't need it.

She handed me a small case with spaces for a dozen earwigs. One was empty. "Put one of these in your ear, and give one to each of the other squad members. That way, we can keep in touch if we need to. This will be the perfect ambush opportunity with the two of us together." She stuffed the case in my pocket.

"Where'd you even get this sh—stuff," I amended. I was trying to clean up my language a little, at least for the evening. It was probably a lost cause, but I wanted to present a good image for the brass.

"The armory downstairs. Now, how do I look." Liz twirled around, causing her dress to shift and flow like liquid as the removable silk skirt spun behind her, finally coming to rest with her leg slightly splayed through the high slit.

I gave her a salacious grin. "Like sex on a stick."

She laughed and cuffed me on the shoulder. "Thank you, I think. Cait, let me say that you look rather dashing in your Class-As with your hair braided up like that."

"I know," I said cheekily, tugging at my cuffs. "The name's Reagan—"

"Stop! Don't do that. You don't hold a candle to Daniel Craig, so let's dispense with that silliness."

"What? I'm so much hotter than Daniel Craig."

"Now," she stepped in and brushed the back of her fingers against my cheek, "If you were English, maybe. But your just a mick."

"Ouch!" I said with a laugh, clutching my heart in mock hurt. "That's rough, you tight-ass brit wanker."

She just smacked my ass and started for the door. "You coming?"

"Yes, Ma'am." I replied and followed her as she said, "That's better. Now come along."

While we waited by the door, I looked Déra up and down. She was in a pair of leggings, sneakers, and a t-shirt with her breastplate over top. Her Xiphos was at her hip, her bow unstrung in one hand. She had a large bag of potato chips and a cell phone we'd given her clutched in her other hand, and I just made an amused expression. She'd been eating practically nonstop since she'd arrived.

"You know what to do?" I asked, handing her one of the earwigs.

"I do. If I see anyone attacking, I kill them. Seems simple enough."

I put my hands on my hips at the flip response. "We'll call if we need you. Just stay with the car until needed. Hopefully, it will be a boring night."

Déra held up the cell phone. "I have this to keep me occupied. I want to see if Arya escapes King's Landing."

I laughed, and Liz said, "Well, don't get so engrossed that you forget to show up when we call."

"That won't happen. I'm not some néwosi." Déra said indignantly, giving Liz a hard look.

Liz looked at me.

"A less than flattering term for a cadet," I translated automatically, though it definitely wasn't a word my mother had taught me, more likely a leftover from my time with Umbrá stuck in my noggin. I had given up trying to figure that out.

We started loading into the Limo, which had just pulled up. As we all sat down, I turned to Déra and said, in all seriousness, "Do not get attached to anyone in that show."

Liz smiled knowingly, and Déra looked at me with a puzzled expression. "Why not?"

"Just trust me."

Liz and I had gone back and forth about renting the limo, but I finally gave in and let her do it after we realized that Déra barely fit into the Audi. I felt almost naked not having a car to use to get out of there quickly if things went south.

Even though there'd be two dozen cops there besides mine and Freyer's teams, I still had a bad feeling about it. It was something elusive and weird that I couldn't put my finger on. I trusted that feeling. Something about this whole thing seemed completely off. Carol, surprisingly, had agreed and had been plenty happy to have Liz there. It had been quite the about-face and had honestly caught me off guard. I supposed that her time with Mother Lamia had done her some good.

The hotel wasn't the buzz of activity that I'd expected. As a matter of fact, it was eerily quiet. Then again, this wasn't exactly the Oscars. This was a thank-you dinner for a dozen cops and some commendations. But the number of cops outside was easily half what I'd expected. And why had they recommended formal attire? It was just odd. My unease only grew once we entered the Hotel.

The main lobby of the Liberty was a vast open floor surrounded by three levels of wrap-around balconies. The ceiling above was supported by large rafters that appeared to be dark wood, but more likely, that was a facade for steel struts. The wall sconces and overhead lighting was all turned down low, giving the large space a more cozy ambiance.

A group of about twenty round tables covered half the lobby, directly in front of the bar. Each was set with a simple flower arrangement and seating placards. Apparently, Freyer and Carlos would be sitting at the mayor's table from what I could see.

News crews were floating around, as were a small number of local business leaders and the city council. The mayor was currently in deep conversation on one side with Sesi.

Above, all the balconies were empty except the top floor, where three SWAT officers overlooked the entire room with sniper rifles. Everything about the security setup seemed wrong, especially the presence of the snipers. I mentioned it to Liz.

"I thought you might just be paranoid, Cait. But now that we're here, this looks pretty fucked up. Go get a club soda and find the rest of your team. I'm going to take a look around."

I spotted Carol and Carlos by the bar, so I joined them. They were chatting away from the largest throng of people, so we'd be able to talk at least semi-privately.

"Well?" I asked as I walked up and ordered a coke.

Carlos took a sip of his soda water, but his eyes were scanning the room, as were Carol's.

She said, "See? What did I tell you?" Then she turned to me. "For what it's worth, I'm sorry I ever doubted your vampire friends. Though, Nastasia still gives me the creeps."

I laughed. "You and me both. Here, these are for you." I pulled out the case and handed them their earwigs.

"Let me guess, goodies from the gun runner?" Carlos asked with a wry smile.

"Marcella's not a gun runner, Carlos. Carson Logistics is a legitimate humanitarian business, but since you asked, yes, they're from Marcella's collection. Try not to lose them. They cost a couple of grand a piece, I'm sure."

Carol looked at it briefly, then stuffed it in her ear. "Mic check," she said.

"Loud and clear," I responded in a whisper, and she gave me a subtle thumbs up, as did Carlos.

"Where's Maki?" I asked, searching the room.

"Wow," Carol said. "Right there." She gestured to the front entrance. Maki was not wearing her uniform as she wasn't being honored. Instead, she was in a high-slit, black, buckle-fastened evening gown topped with a pleated white bodice that seemed to flow around her. Her feet were clad in low black heels. But there was something about her that was mesmerizing, and it wasn't the clothes or the way her long black hair was styled in a complex beehive of braids and curls. She seemed to exude an aura of confidence and beauty. It felt something like a brush in my head, but it wasn't like vampiric glamour. It was more like a wave. And it wasn't sexual, more like I just wanted to be close to her.

"Easy there, tiger," Liz said through the earwig. "That's Kitsune glamour right there."

"Liz is here?" Carol asked, looking around.

"Yup. She's my plus one."

"I heard that, Cait. I'm your bloody date, not just your 'plus one.'"

"Sorry, dear," I said and rolled my eyes.

"I saw that," she replied.

I stuck out my tongue, though I had no idea where she was. By that time, Maki had approached the bar.

"Holy shit, Maki," Carol said, a little starstruck. "You look—"

"Thank you," was all she said as she took the earwig I offered. Whether it was to me or Carol, I couldn't tell.

Carlos was the only one of us not affected at all. He was still scanning the room. "This is all wrong. We're short about a dozen officers."

I looked over toward the Mayor, whose conversation with Sesi seemed to be getting heated. "I know. And it doesn't look like Detective Williams is thrilled about it." I gestured to the pair.

"So which of them thinks there's not enough?" Carol asked.

"Detective Williams," came Liz's voice in our ears. "She's asking why the Mayor chose to call off half of the special detail for this event. She also wants to know why the Chief and Commissioner aren't here."

I took in the room. She was right. Neither the Chief nor the Commissioner was present. Morgan strode up, dressed in her uniform, though she was likewise not on the list of honorees. There was a bulge at her back, and she had a touch of right foot drag. But damn, she looked good in uniform, and I smiled broadly.

"Hey! None of that," Liz said in my ear with a little chuckle.

"Can it, Medlyn. We're not attached," I said, and I heard mock tears in my ear.

"Cait, how could you?" Then there was a brief chuckle.

"Alright, you two," Carlos hissed. "Knock it off. That's distracting. We're here on business."

I handed Morgan her earwig and gave her one for Freyer, too. "What's this?"

"Private chat room," I said with a wink, and she stuffed the earwig in her ear.

"Mic check," Morgan said, and I gave her a thumbs up just as Liz said, "Hey there, Red. You look fabulous in uniform."

"Fuck you, Medlyn," Morgan replied. "You don't get to call me that. It's Detective Kennedy to you." I snickered at Morgan's red cheeks, and Morgan made a snide expression before rolling her eyes.

Morgan looked around. "Where the hell is she?" I just shrugged.

Sesi's heated conversation with the Mayor ended, and the Mayor returned to hobnobbing with the business folk, a smile plastered on her face. Sesi, on the other hand, looked like she'd swallowed a rather large stinkbug. I caught her gaze as she followed the mayor. "Oh, yeah, Sesi's not happy. Not at all."

"So it would seem," Liz replied.

"Okay, where are you?" I asked, finally wondering where my date had wandered off to.

"Look up," she said, and we all looked up, scanning the balconies.

"Oh, Christ," Liz snapped. "Not all of you. One at a time. Maki first, since I suspect you have the best eyes for the dark. Above the top floor."

Maki glanced up toward the ceiling, snickered, then went back to the bar, leaning next to us. "Above the top floor, opposite the entrance. Rafters. How she got up there, and in heels, I'll never know."

When my turn came, I glanced at where Liz perched. I could

barely see her, the black dress blending well in the flickering shadows left by the wall sconces. She was over fifty feet above the ground, standing on a narrow rafter that hid her rather well from view. But if she looked, she had a view of every floor, every landing, and every balcony. "Holy shit," I whispered. "How the fuck did you get up there?"

"Ancient vampire secret," Liz said cryptically. "What I've seen so far has been interesting. "The doors on the right side of the room are all locked, including the fire doors. I just watched one of the protection detail checking them and calling on his radio. He didn't seem happy.

"The elevators are only going up to the second floor. There are three snipers on the fourth-floor balcony, two to my left and one to my right. They look bored, just sitting there watching the floor below. They are way more still than I'd expect. Wherever they trained, they got some solid discipline knocked into them. The locked fire exit bothers me, Cait. It's there to allow people to get out in case of fire, you know?

"There are four other exits, but two of them lead to the same part of the hotel to the rear of the lobby. There's the front door at the bottom of the escalators and a side door on the left that's not locked. It's the one farthest from the event. If there was a fire, a lot of people might die. Something's not right about this at all."

I looked away. "How are you going to get down?" I asked but got no reply. I moved back to a corner of the massive room, out of sight of the snipers and the other officers, and looked back to where Liz was. I got my answer.

As I watched in total disbelief, Liz launched herself into a head-first dive from the rafter, right between two of the snipers and just out of sight of the third, who wasn't looking that direction anyway. Then almost forty feet below, as she reached the second-floor balcony, she neatly grasped one of the wrought iron supports and landed without so much as a whisper. It was one of the most graceful and terrifying things I had ever seen. "Fuck me," Morgan and I both whispered at exactly the same time.

"What?" Carlos asked over the comm.

Morgan answered first. "Nothing, Ramirez, we'll tell you later. But you just missed the most incredible thing I've ever seen in my life."

Liz's laughter echoed in our ears. "Why thank you, Red. I try." Moments later, she exited the elevator and strode toward me, looking just as she did when we'd arrived, hair, makeup, dress, everything perfect.

We weren't in the hotel much longer before we were all hustled into the main ballroom. It was pretty much the typical hotel ballroom affair, but the Liberty had tall windows on either side, and a portable stage had been set at one end with a podium. A dozen or so chairs sat on the stage. There were probably twenty people in attendance in the audience, not including the mayor's security detail, led by Sesi.

I watched as Sesi scowled at everyone, including the mayor. So before we started, I walked over to talk to her.

"Rough day?" I asked in greeting.

"Shit day. The boss is interfering with my job. She said she didn't want as much presence as I requested. Too many cops would spook everyone."

"Well, this is a short ceremony and dinner out on the main floor, right? It's not like we should expect anything."

"That's not the point, Cait. She's never gotten involved in my event security planning before. It's just pissing me off. I don't know what she's playing at."

"She's the Mayor, Sesi. She can do what she wants. We work at her pleasure to some extent, you know."

"Oh, go take your seat, Reagan," Sesi said irritably, ending the conversation as she went to go bark at one of the other Detectives on her team.

I laughed and went to sit down at my seat on the stage. I hated these things because they were boring. And this one was no different. At least we got to sit down for most of it, which constituted a short speech from Mayor Kim.

I kept my face neutral, but everything about this seemed shitty. Something fucked up was going on. Next to me, Carol coughed and shook her head.

I pulled out a handkerchief and made a show of leaning

over to give it to her. "You okay?" I whispered.

"No. Something's wrong."

One by one, the Mayor introduced each member of Carlos' and Freyer's squads and gave us each a commendation medal for meritorious service. Then we stood there while people clapped and the press took photos. Then we sat again as the Mayor began a short closing speech. I really just wanted to slouch in my chair, but that wouldn't be very professional, and the Xiphos at my back didn't let me anyway, so, like everyone else, I sat bolt upright. Except for Carol, who was now leaning forward like she wanted to jump out of her seat.

"What are you doing?" I asked out of the corner of my mouth.

"We need to get out of here," she hissed. "They're coming."

The Mayor's eyes shifted in our direction. She was clearly irritated at the noise and our lack of decorum. It didn't matter, though, because she didn't get any further into her closing remarks before there was a strange pop in my earwig, and I heard a car door slam. This was followed by several grunts, each of which was, in turn, followed by a strange twang that it took me moments to understand was the singing of a bowstring.

Déra announced that all holy hell had broken loose outside with the calm words, "Cait, we have a problem out here. I think the word you would use is 'incoming?'"

None of us waited for the ceremony to continue any further. My team rushed to the escalators, Carol way ahead of us, while Freyer's team stayed behind to guard the Mayor with Sesi and her protection detail, all except for Morgan, who had been closest to the door and had bolted into the lobby already.

"Lock the door," I shouted to Freyer as we exited the ballroom. "Sesi, see if you can get one of those emergency exits in the back open."

When we reached the escalators, we could see Déra backing her way into the lower portion of the lobby, followed by a small horde of ogumo. Carol and Morgan were firing down the escalator shaft. Liz blurred past me, tackling Carol as a gunshot sounded from above. Liz came back up first but stayed on one knee, cradling her shoulder. Carlos immediately scooped her up and ran behind the bar with her.

"The fuck?" I glanced up. The snipers fired at Liz. Other officers on the floor with us were rushing forward, weapons drawn. As soon as they saw Déra backing up the escalator and, more importantly, what was chasing her, they started firing down at the inbound ogumo. I was terrified that Déra was going to get hit, but everyone seemed to know she was a friendly and looked to be avoiding her. The rest of the lobby turned into fucking pandemonium, with the few civilians left there running for cover behind the bell desk, the front desk, tables, and the bar, anything they could find, really.

"Pull back!" I shouted as Déra reached the top of the escalator, her quiver empty but for one arrow. The officers fell back into a line with us.

Another shot sounded from above, and Déra jerked as a neat hole appeared at the left edge of her black-steel breastplate. In a single swift movement, Déra rolled with the momentum of the hit and then felled the shooter with her last arrow, sending him tumbling back onto the third-floor balcony. Then she turned and stumbled toward the back of the lobby.

I rushed over. "What happened?"

"The projectile must be black-steel or maybe something harder. I think I'm okay, but I can't see what it was."

Blood, very dark and deep red, flowed from the hole. I grabbed a napkin lying nearby and wiped it away. "If your organ placement is anything like ours, I think it's just a flesh wound." I pulled a handkerchief from my breast pocket and stuffed it under her breastplate. "Where would they get black-steel shells? We don't have that metal here."

Morgan and I pulled Déra up, and we scuffled her toward the bar and the only real cover from the snipers. "I don't know where they got them, but it doesn't matter. The emisai are coming, and there's only the two of us."

Liz waved toward us to move faster as we approached the bar. Another shot rang out, just missing Carol by inches and sending splinters flying out of a nearby chair. I saw that blood still leaked from Liz's shoulder when we rounded the bar. At my concerned glance, she said, "It's healing, just slowly. It's something about the bullets they're using."

"Why are the fucking snipers shooting at us anyway?" Morgan asked.

I looked up. The snipers had taken cover after a few of the protection detail began firing at them. "I don't know. None of this makes any sense."

The ogumo began clamoring over the top of the escalators, right into withering gunfire. But then one of the officers dropped from another sniper shot. "Shit. We're boxed in." I put my hand to my ear and looked around. Carlos was standing at the edge of the escalator shaft shooting ogumo with his forty-five. His uniform had a couple of holes. At least the black-steel didn't seem to affect him. "Carlos, kill those fuckers up top, or we're all gonna die."

There was a blood-curdling howl, and Carlos shot from where he was standing, transforming into his hybrid wolf-man state in the air. Bits of his dress uniform tore away and floated to the ground as he launched himself up the balconies, one by one, faster than I could have sprinted the distance on a flat surface. Within seconds he'd torn through both remaining snipers.

I looked around to find Carol. She was at the corner of the escalators, not far from the bar, firing at the remaining ogumo and retreating just as the first emisai topped the escalators. I took off at a dead run, calling for them all to fall back and drawing my xiphos. The creature turned toward Carol right off and dove right for her. I wasn't going to make it.

Carol put her hands up, and I screamed, certain that my friend was about to be rent apart as they went down in a heap. But a guttural moaning noise filled the room, and it took a second before I realized that it was coming from the emisai. The sound was horrible and chilling, deep and groaning as if the thing was in terrible pain. Everywhere, people were covering their ears, but I kept running forward. Blue fire spewed down Carol's arms and engulfed the thing. Moments later, it was nothing but so much ash.

Another emisai leaped into the air, again towards Carol. But

I was there by then, and this time I didn't misjudge its tactics. I stepped inside the swiping claw and took it across the midsection, sending it to the ground and unmoving, splattering both Carol and me with dark, black ichor. A third leaped forward, but Déra was back up and neatly dispatched it, kicking it off her blade and down the escalators. I took out the next one that appeared. Three more were bounding up from the entrance, claws crunching into the cement of the escalator shaft as they lept along the walls.

Carol lay unconscious, her breathing shallow. I checked her over quickly, but she didn't appear injured, so I picked her up and hauled her back to the bar. Two emisai topped the escalator and turned toward us, trying to chase us down, ignoring everything else.

And then Maki appeared, bless her. Nine tails were fanned out behind her, and cute little fox-like ears topped her head covered in white fur. She was holding a ball of what I could only describe as liquid fire in each hand, which she bobbed nonchalantly like she was bobbing a pair of volleyballs. Then, with a graceful, dance-like spinning motion, she threw them with perfect accuracy, tearing massive smoking holes within each of the emisai. They both dropped in heaps of black smoking ruin, stinking of sulfur and acrid acidic smoke.

I set Carol on the floor and then stood, scanning the lobby. Four officers were down. Two of them dead for certain, having been torn open by ogumo or emisai, I didn't know which. Déra stood over the dead corpse of the last emisai, and the rest of the ogumo were dead. I lifted my blade and cried, "Oye Konbom!" in unison with Déra.

"Um, Guys, after you're done with your Klingon celebration, you need to come up here and see this." It was Carlos. He was back in human form and waving, half-naked, from the top-tier balcony.

"What the fuck is that?" Morgan asked after we'd joined Carlos. She stared at the thing wearing the Boston SWAT tactical gear lying next to its rifle.

I fished through the pockets and found a wallet. "I think that's Sergeant Meyer from SWAT."

The thing on the ground in front of me resembled a human being in size and shape. It had a head, arms, legs, and fingers, and after I took the time to fish off one of the boots, I saw toes. It wasn't quite an emisai, but the skin was all oily looking and black, like latex, just like the emisai. The face still looked human, discounting the latex-like skin around the edge of the jaw and hairline. The eyes, though, were utterly liquid black, with no pupils, no irises, nothing, like the descriptions of demons of old.

Next to the body pooled a dark mixture of blood and ichor, red and black, that swirled together but never truly mixed. It was like oil and water. As if the blood wanted nothing to do with the black viscous stuff.

I glanced at Maki, but she just shook her head, her mouth covered, clearly horrified. Then looked at Déra. "You ever see anything like this?"

She shook her head. "No. This is something new. But the fact that they seem to be a hybrid of humans and emisai is probably why Carlos was able to kill them so efficiently. Whoever they were before, they became minions of Mother Darkness. That much is certain."

We all looked at the creatures with the same mix of revulsion and fascination. The black skin still seemed to be spreading, even though the creature appeared dead. It didn't last long, though, as Déra stabbed it neatly through the chest, and the spreading goo simply stopped.

I considered that for a moment. Vampires take energy from the soul, but the curse is something else, something dark. The black-steel blade seemed to suck the energy that fed the black skin covering Meyer's body. That skin originated on the other side of the gate. Black-steel also slowed Elizabeth's healing. There was a connection here somewhere. It could be that black steel just suppresses magic. At least, I hoped that's all it was. In the end, I kept those thoughts to myself. If there was a connection between the vampire curse and Mother Darkness, no one needed to know that.

CHAPTER THIRTY-EIGHT

We were all freaked out about the incident at the hotel, but the feds had come in and taken over. We all gave our statements, and that was about it. Schaeffer, per usual, was leading the show. She spent a fair amount of time hanging with the team, drinking coffee, and bitching about Boston suddenly being a weirdness magnet. But she also spent a lot of time grilling us about the hotel incident, especially Déra and me. So, I was thrilled when, two days later, my day off came, and I could finally get a break.

I would have liked to have spent it running errands, doing chores, and working out, but there was nothing doing. It was court day, and Liz and I sat in the Family Court building with Phillip. He'd prepped us, but the odds were not in our favor. It was a rarity for a child to be placed in the custody of a non-family member when they had living relatives. Our best bet was to prove abuse and that it was in Katie's best interests that she be in our care. He explained that this was just a party hearing, an opportunity to discuss things with the judge and see if a pre-trial agreement could be arranged to forestall going to court. We would sit in a room with the judge, Phillip, and the Finchers to discuss the unusual filing we had made to take custody of Katie. Ms. Colewort would be there, too, along with a legal aid lawyer for the Finchers. My only hope was that the

Finchers would see reason and let Katie stay with us until we could have an official hearing. Unfortunately, Massachusetts has no minor emancipation law, so that was out.

In our favor was the Finchers' history with both Leah and Katie. That and the fact that they had falsely accused us of kidnapping, and God knew what else to their daughter. Also in our favor was the fact that Phillip and the Judge, Kimberly Watson, knew each other. Phillip had practiced family law for a time before working for his current firm. According to Phillip, they had a good relationship, and she didn't see Phillip as the type to file a frivolous action.

Against us was the most basic of tenets of family law. People often wonder how children can end up back in the custody of abusive parents. The reason is simple. It is the view of the courts, rightly or wrongly, that a child is best raised by their own parents. Also, the fourteenth amendment's implied right to privacy generally trumps the opinion of the state unless it is proven, typically through clear and convincing evidence, that the child would be harmed by remaining with family. Getting custody of Katie was a long shot.

Also working against us was the fact that I'd been on the news holding a sword, fighting a bunch of monsters, side by side in the company of a kitsune, and what people were calling Lady Wizard on Twitter, that being Carol. Amazingly, neither Carlos nor Liz was ever mentioned, thankfully. Then again, all the news caught was Liz getting shot, and somehow, they'd completely missed Carlos' transformation. Interestingly enough, the Vestry was completely silent on his breach of the accords in front of so many people. I just hoped it stayed that way.

The Finchers arrived at the courthouse just a few minutes after we did. Standing so close to them, knowing they were, for all intents and purposes, the enemy, was awkward, so I spent most of the time glaring at them. Then their attorney arrived. He looked familiar, though I couldn't place where I'd seen him. It had certainly been in court at some point, I was sure. But I spent a lot of time in the various courts around town, and he could be from any one of them. Oddly, he didn't introduce himself to us. Instead, he spoke briefly to the Finchers, saying something that made Jim give me a hateful smile and Anne breathe a sigh of relief. That, in turn, made my stomach sink. I wondered what he had up his sleeve.

Katie and Leah stood next to them. I was surprised at how awake and alert Katie looked in the middle of the day. *Good girl*, I thought. *She really had been practicing.*

Leah had her hands folded and her head down, occasionally casting a furtive glance at me from under her mop of black hair. She only looked at me, not at Liz, not once, which I thought was interesting. Katie also looked at us from across the hall, but only for a moment, as if deciding whether it was okay to come to us. Ultimately, she must have decided it was alright because she stalked away from the Finchers, shooting two fingers over her shoulder when Jim hissed for her to return. I pressed my lips into a thin line and forced the corners of my mouth level to avoid showing the absolute glee with which I watched the exchange. But as soon as Katie was within reach, I scooped her to me, and Liz wrapped her arms around us both.

A social worker took Leah to another room where she could color or read a book with other children. Before she walked away, she turned her gray eyes toward me, and my heart stuttered at the abject misery I saw there, that pleading look I'd seen during our first encounter at the Finchers' home. I gave her a solemn wink. I didn't know why. Maybe it was because, already, in the blackest reaches of my heart, I was ideating on the best way to kill the Finchers and steal the girls back to my home. Also, at that moment, I realized that Nastasia might be having more of an effect on me than I'd realized. But I brushed that aside. I didn't care about that. My family and their happiness were all that mattered. *I take care of my own*, I thought, echoing Nastasia's very words.

My musings stopped when Philip finally stepped up, accompanied by a woman in a tan skirt-suit, and said, "The judge is ready for us."

We were ushered back into a small conference room. I made to enter first, but Liz snagged my arm gently and held me back as the Finchers, their lawyer, Ms. Colewort, and the judge entered, followed by Phillip, and Liz, leaving Katie and me to go last. I had a flash of annoyance at being last, but then I remembered my training. In large groups, people tend to enter based on their seniority. The effect can be devastating in some cases. It allowed Katie and me to grandstand our entrance and had the added benefit of making everyone else wait on us.

I turned Katie toward me at the door. "Are you doing okay? Are you ready for this?" I asked gently, more for the Judge's benefit than hers. I knew she'd be fine.

She nodded and smiled and threw her arms around me, squeezing me hard enough to make my breathing falter. *God, this kid is smart,* I thought.

Finally, I put a protective arm around Katie's shoulders, pulled her to me, and we walked in side by side. *That's right,* I thought. *Take a good long look, you wankers. This is my little girl, and no matter what happens, she always will be.*

Once we were all settled and the judge had made the perfunctory offer of water or coffee, we got started.

"Phillip, I didn't think this was your kind of law," the judge began.

"No, Kim—" he caught himself, "I'm sorry, your honor." *Nicely done,* I thought. He was flexing in front of the snot-nosed kid from legal aid. "It's not typically my area of practice. But as you know, I worked in your court for over a year before moving into corporate law, and I honestly believe in this case. Neither Ms. Tyler nor Detective Reagan is paying for my services here."

"I see." The judge didn't smile or make any other expression for that matter, and I realized abruptly that I'd be hard-pressed in a game of poker with her for all my training. She turned toward the Fincher's counselor. "And you, Mr. Carrigan, what's your story?" And it finally clicked. His name was Lee Carrigan. He had interned just a couple of years ago in Judge Bates' office in criminal court. He must be fresh off the bar exam.

Carrigan looked a little taken aback by the question. "Your honor?"

"Well, why are we here?" Judge Watson gave Carrigan a firm and somewhat motherly stare.

"Your honor, the plaintiffs have asked for something extraordinary. Katie Fincher is my clients' daughter. They have taken lawful custody of her from the plaintiffs. As a result, the plaintiffs have filed an action claiming that Mr. and Mrs. Fincher are unfit. DCF has had ample opportunity to evaluate the Finchers' relationship with their children and has seen fit to keep them with their parents. As a result, the law is clear. Ms. Tyler and Ms. Reagan have no standing to file for custody, so I am moving to dismiss the case." Carrigan reached into his briefcase and pulled out a set of papers, sliding them to the judge. Jim Fincher leaned back in his chair and put his hands behind his head, a self-satisfied smile on his face. It didn't last long, though.

"Hold your horses, Lee," Judge Watson said, pushing the paper back toward him after a brief glance. "There is precedent here, and this is just a parties conference. I'm not planning on ruling on anything today." She looked down to the end of the table where Colewort sat. "Ms. Colewort, what are your thoughts on this?"

Ida Colewort looked even more pallid than usual. "Your Honor, it is DCF's position that a child is best raised by their parents. Now, I have the paperwork showing that Mr. Fincher has been attending the requisite anger management courses that your honor required from our last visit to your courtroom. Given that Mr. Fincher is abiding by the court's orders, we have no choice but to recommend that Katie stay with her parents."

Katie made a noise, but I gently squeezed her leg under the table, and she composed herself.

"I have a sworn document from Detective Reagan that she witnessed a bruise on Leah's face. How did that occur?" Judge Watson turned hard eyes toward Jim Fincher, who immediately looked extremely uncomfortable.

"Mr. Fincher—" Carrigan began, but Judge Watson interrupted him.

"I was asking Mr. Fincher, Lee."

We all waited as Jim cleared his throat and sat bolt upright like a kid suddenly realizing that he needed to behave lest he be punished by mom and dad. Then he delivered an impassioned plea that sounded genuine but, I was certain, was rehearsed. "It was an accident, your honor. Leah and I were playing around. It's true that I did it, but it wasn't intentional. Please, we're just trying to do what is right for our daughters. You can ask Leah. She will tell you that it was an accident."

Katie snorted derisively, and I turned a warning eye on her. The judge caught it, though, and said, "Something to add, Katie?'

Katie looked up at me, and there was something in her eye I couldn't understand, regret. Then realization dawned, and my eyes went wide with panic for just a second.

"Um, I don't believe Mr. Fincher. And I love ma—Cait and Liz. But, I think the best thing would be for me to stay with Jim and Anne, if I could see Liz and Cait still, too, please." Then she turned and looked up at me. "Mama, I'm sorry," she whispered.

My heart jumped into my throat and then plummeted through the floor. The shock on everyone's face was clear. Carrigan almost choked on his water. The judge's eyes went wide, and even Jim and Anne Fincher looked dumbfounded. I wasn't confused at all, though. She was protecting Leah. *Son of a bitch*, I thought as I fought back tears. I pursed my lips, then I sighed and put my hand on Katie's cheek. "Are you sure, baby? You don't have to do this."

"I'm sure, mama," she said, then she looked at Liz's stricken face. "I'm sorry, Auntie Liz."

At first, Liz just looked at Katie with a mixture of absolute affection and abject misery, then she said, "You have nothing to be sorry for, Katie. I look forward to our visits."

The Judge scratched her head for a moment, then looked to the Finchers. "Mr. and Mrs. Fincher, do you have an objection to Katie spending time with the Detective and Ms. Tyler? I would hate to have to take this to trial."

Fincher opened his mouth to speak, but Lee got there ahead of him. "Given that Ms. Tyler is an MD and that Ms. Reagan is a decorated police officer, I'm sure my clients will have no objection. Can I have a moment to confer with them outside?"

Judge Watson nodded, and they left the room.

Once they were gone, Ida Colewort looked at me. "My hands are tied here, Detective. I know you mean well, and while it would probably be better for Katie to stay with you, it's just not the law."

I frowned, but my opinion of Ida Colewort changed at that moment. Before, I'd seen a negligent case worker. Now, I realized she was someone who was hemmed in by bureaucracy and legal requirements. "Thank you for that."

The judge glanced down the table at Katie. "Ms. Fincher? Why would you want to go back home?"

"I don't," Katie said flatly. "But Leah is my family. She needs me. And Cait and Liz taught me that we have to take care of our family. This is the best thing I could think of."

The judge responded immediately. "That is very kind of you, Katie, but you do know it's my job to look out for you here."

"I know that. But, please, your honor, this is better. I don't want Leah to be alone anymore."

And as heartbroken as I was, I couldn't help feeling a deep sense of pride at how much Katie had grown and what she'd learned from us. Liz, I was sure, was proud, too, but I could see in her eyes the rage and hatred that was building. It wouldn't be apparent to anyone else, but I knew her better. She was planning a double homicide in her head.

The rest of the conference was short. When the Finchers returned, Jim and Anne were very quiet. The Judge ordered that the Finchers would retain full custody of Katie pending the following: they agree to allow Liz and me to take Katie out three times a week and that she could spend two weekends a month at our place if she so chose. Katie was, of course, ordered to return to school, which Katie was thrilled by. Liz and I, not so much. Honestly, I was terrified of the entire situation because of Katie's regressions, but there was nothing I could do. Philip, Liz, and I sat in the conference room with Katie for a moment longer after everyone else filed out. As soon as they were gone, Liz finally spoke.

"Katie, what are you thinking? What if you have an episode?"

Katie looked at Liz squarely. "Auntie Liz. Jim drinks at night. When he does, he gets angry, and Leah has to hide. Someone has to take care of her. You taught me that."

"But, Katie—" Liz started, but I put a hand on her shoulder.

"Liz. It'll be okay. This buys us time. We won this round."

Liz shook my hand off. "How can you say that?"

Phillip interjected. "Ms. Tyler, this is what winning looks like in family court. Detective Reagan is right. And honestly, I'm impressed with Katie that, at such a young age, she understands what's important here. Leah needs protection right now, and Katie can provide that in a way that few others could. This is not a bad compromise."

"But, Phillip," Liz said, and her voice choked. "She's our baby."

Katie stood and walked over to Liz and put her arms around her. "I still am. Don't worry, Auntie Liz. I promise it will be okay."

We all stood and hugged each other while Phillip waited. We talked for a few minutes, and Liz gave Katie some last-minute instructions on things to do and to avoid. She also told her to be careful at school and remember to keep her head about her. I didn't waste those precious moments on advice, though. I just hugged my daughter and cried. Then Liz and I stood in the corridor and watched as Leah, Katie, and the Finchers left. Liz and I even managed to keep our composure until we reached the car, then we sat there, wrapped in each other's arms, and cried until it hurt.

"How could you let her do that?" Liz shouted as we walked into the kitchen.

I waited patiently, letting her lose her temper, in as much as Liz ever did. She ranted and raved for a few minutes, leveling curses at the Finchers, DCF, the Judge, and even Phillip. When she finally slowed down, and I thought she was close to getting spent, I said, "Liz, this is the best outcome we could hope for."

Liz glared at me. "Nastasia and I both told you something like this would happen! But, no, you insisted. Now she's gone. This is your fault. You should never have gone over there. If you hadn't let them know she was living with us, she'd still be here." It was true, but it was also a low blow, and it pissed me off.

I burst in on her tirade, literally screaming at her. "This isn't the nineteenth century, Liz. There are fucking laws. On top of that, do you have any idea how much trouble we would have been in if I hadn't made the effort? I'm not interested in upending my life to go on the fucking run with you. I love you and think you're great, but in the end, I have to live here. I have a career to think of.

"All of this is great, but nothing in this house is mine except my clothes. You can at least go back to the UK and do whatever you did before you came here and helped turn my life to ruin." Liz whirled on me, but I wasn't finished. I was too angry, too full of rage and guilt and hurt because Katie was gone, and it was my fault. I wanted someone or something to take it out on, and unfortunately, Liz was the only one there, so I said something truly awful. "Besides, the only reason you do all this is that you feel fucking guilty, not because you actually care."

Liz's shock was palpable in the air, and my gut sank with instant remorse, but it was too late. The words were out, like knives from my hand, and I couldn't call them back. I couldn't unsay them. And for a few seconds, Liz's mouth opened and closed as if she were about to say something, thinking better of it, then about to say something else, then thinking better of that, too. Finally, voice low and filled with hurt, she said, "You fucking bitch."

I jerked as if she'd slapped me. But she didn't stop there. And what she said next hurt like nothing anyone had ever said to me before, not because it was harsh, which it was, and not because her tone was accusatory and nasty, which it also was, but because it was all true, and I knew it.

"I do everything for you! I cook for you. I clean this house from top to bottom. I make sure you have clean towels. Where do you think those come from? Huh? The only fucking domestic duties I don't do here are wash your clothes and wipe your arse. In addition to that, I'm filling in for Marcella, keeping the goods flowing to the camps as best I can, given the state the company is in.

"I have helped Katie. No, I am spending more time with Katie than you are. While you've been fucking Nastasia and fucking Morgan and traipsing across an alien world, I've been teaching her." She held her hand up, stalling out my angry retort and growling at me, "I'm not finished. I'm not just teaching her to feed. I've been teaching her Maths and English. Proper English, I might add, not that rubbish you speak here. I've been attached to her hip while you sleep away the night hours, and then I get to watch as you get the easy job. You get to love her and comfort her and kiss her better. I have to be the bitch and make her do things she doesn't want to do. On top of all that, I paid for your mother's rehab, arranged her transport, and worked with Bian to convince Mother Lamia to help her. I've sat here and listened to you wail about every bad thing in your life.

"You are right, Cait. I did it at first because I felt guilty. I felt bad that you and Katie got caught in the middle of a fucking vampire war. But guess what? That's not why I do it now. I do it now because, regardless of all the ungrateful dross that you almost constantly spew at everyone, I love you. God knows why."

Liz's eyes turned glassy and wet, and when I moved toward her, she held out her hand again, halting my steps. "I'm still not finished. You know why I won't sleep with you. Because I can't. I already love you. I don't want to get any deeper than I already am. Because you're doing what new dyke's do, Cait. You had your first. Now you're bedding everyone you can. But most of all, because," her arm shot out, almost violently, pointing toward the foyer and her voice rose, "as soon as Marcella comes through that door, as soon as we find her, you'll run back into her arms, and I'll be left to rot." She was crying now, tears free-flowing. Then she dropped her arms and turned her back on me. "You fucking bitch," she said again.

I approached her gingerly, placing my hand on her shoulder, and she stiffened. "I'm sorry, Liz. I didn't mean it. I don't know why I said that."

"I do," Liz said quietly. "And that's the hardest part, Cait. I know exactly why you said that. I know what it's like to feel lost and confused. I know what it's like to be off the rails. I've been there. It makes it very hard for me to stand my ground with you because I see so much of what I've been through and what I've done in what's happening to you now. And all I want to do is make it better, but I can't. So, I sit here and wait until you come to your senses and see what's right in front of you."

I grabbed her then, spinning her around and putting my arms around her, holding on for dear life. God, I was an idiot. At first, she didn't respond. She didn't lift her arms or lean on me. I pleaded with her. "I'm so sorry, Liz. Please, hold me or say something."

"Let go of me." Her words were a knife driven under my ribs and straight into my heart. I dropped my arms and turned back toward the hallway. I didn't cry. I was past tears. I'd been a fool. What's worse, I had hurt Liz in the process. Liz, who had saved my mother's life. Liz, who had rescued Marcella and me. Liz, who'd stopped me from killing Marcella when I'd been under the influence of Mother Darkness. I was beyond horrible. I struggled to understand how I'd gotten this way as I pressed the elevator call button.

Liz still stood in the kitchen, back to me. I watched as she wiped her nose and eyes. Then she put her hands on her hips and looked at the ceiling. Then she sighed, and I wondered what she was thinking. Was she thinking of leaving? Would she throw me out? I thought maybe to ask her, but the elevator dinged. Besides, I'd done enough damage already.

I rode up and was glad that Katie wasn't here and that Déra was sorting out the lehosi with Bian. No one was around to hear our argument, to hear my shame. And I was ashamed. Liz had not only cared for Katie and me but opened her heart. Katie had been right; I was an idiot.

Oppressive darkness shrouded my room with the curtains drawn. I pulled them back, but the low clouds and overcast sky only made things worse, reflecting the sickly orange-yellow light of the early evening city. I closed the curtains again and got ready for bed.

Every movement, every action seemed ponderous and slow, as if I were moving through some viscous substance made of my own despair. I stripped out of my clothes, not bothering to shower. I'd clean myself up in the morning. As I brushed my teeth, I noticed the care with which Liz had hung my towels, perfectly even. The mirror before which I stood was clean, not a speck of toothpaste or a water spot. No dust lingered on any of the furniture in my room. Even the bulb in my lamp was clean. Everywhere I looked lay examples of the tenderness and attention that Liz had taken in making this a home for me.

I turned out the light in the hall, calling a soft "Goodnight, Liz." Then I slid between my sheets, doused the table lamp, and curled up almost fetal, letting the water slip from my eyes to wet my pillow with the tears of my self-disgust and self-pity.

Moments later, the covers drew back, and Liz slid into my bed without a word. I thought I might be imagining it for a moment, but her arm slid across my midsection, and she moved closer, spooning up next to me and stroking my head.

"I am so sorry," I whispered.

"I know. I am, too."

Stillness settled between us for a long time before she said, "I love you, Cait. I tried not to, but you make me laugh, and I know you love me too, and for all of your faults, you try so hard to care for everyone. And in all of that, you just want to be loved. And I know you'd lay down in traffic for us, Katie and me."

Slowly I unfolded, her words coaxing me out of my shell like the bloom of a flower. And as I did so, I turned to face her. The room was utterly black, and the darkness blinded me, but

I knew she was there. Not from her breath. She did not breathe. And not from her touch. She no longer touched me. And not from the heat of her body. She was cold. But somehow, I could feel her. She was so close, the barest inch away, and all of my denials, and fears, and defenses just melted away.

A soft hand rose to my face, caressing it in a way that made my heart thunder in my chest. "Oh, fuck it," Liz whispered, then she placed that gentle hand on the back of my neck and pulled me into a fabulous, toe-curling kiss that I didn't deserve. Gooseflesh rose all over my body in anticipation of what she would do to me, her hands on my flesh, her mouth on my throat, her tongue between my legs. She didn't need glamour to make me surrender. It was what I wanted and what I'd been denying myself for months.

For a moment, I worried about how unfair it was to her and how rent asunder my heart would be when Marcella returned. But I reminded myself that she was a big girl and knew what she was doing. So I pulled her close and let her tongue slide through the barrier of my lips as she pressed my wrists to the bed, eyes alight with love and want.

CHAPTER THIRTY-NINE

My phone rang at nine-thirty in the morning, yanking me violently awake. My arms and legs were trembling with fatigue as I scrambled for my phone and hit the answer button. God, I needed to get a full night's sleep at some point.

"Homicide, Reagan."

"Cait, It's Carlos. I need you to stay calm, but I need to know where you were last night." His voice was steady and dispassionate, like he was interviewing a suspect.

"What's up?" I asked, my voice tired and raspy.

"I'll tell you in a second. Where were you last night?"

"I've been home all night, Carlos. What's going on?"

"You sure? You haven't been out this morning at all? Can someone confirm that?"

"Yes, Carlos, I was here with Liz. Now, what the fuck is happening?" My heart thudded in my chest. Something was definitely wrong.

"The Finchers were attacked early this morning. Jim Fincher is dead."

"Katie?" I screeched. "Where is she?"

Liz shot up in bed and looked at me, eyes wide.

"She's not here."

"She didn't—" I couldn't finish the sentence, terrified of the answer.

"No, they were both shot in the head. Anne is in critical condition and is headed to BMC. We think they took Katie."

"Oh, God! What about Leah?"

"She's okay. She hid in her room while it went down. We're taking her to the station. She's in shock and not speaking to anyone, but she did ask for the detective who had taken care of Katie."

I took a deep breath and scrabbled my brains back together. Freaking out right now wouldn't help me find Katie. She needed me level-headed and professional. "Any leads? Was there a calling card like the others?"

"No. No calling card. We don't need you down here right now. But Leah saw what happened. The best thing you can do is get to HQ. Leah will probably need a change of clothes. She's covered in blood."

"Yeah, I can bring her what she needs. I think I can find something warm to fit her from Katie's closet."

"I'll grab something for her at the store," Liz whispered. "You get yourself ready and go to work. I'll meet you there. Find our baby, Cait."

"I'll see you this afternoon, Carlos. I'm headed in."

"Okay. I'll see you when we wrap up here."

My tone turned deadly serious. "Carlos, whoever did this, when I find them, I'm not bringing them in. That's my baby."

"Now, Cait—" Carlos warned, but I hung up before he could finish.

Liz glanced up, and I could see the worry in her eyes. Whether it was for Katie, or for me, or for both, I didn't know. I grabbed Liz and pulled her into a quick hug. "I'll find her, Liz. I promise." I launched out of bed and stalked for the shower, calling over my shoulder, "And we will find who did this. I'm done playing by the rules."

I found Déra in the Kitchen rooting around in the refrigerator for something to eat. She had a hunk of blue cheese in her hand, pulled off a piece, and tested it before frowning and running to the sink.

"Blech," she said as she spit it out, followed by something in her language, which I assumed meant 'eww, that's awful.'

We'd managed to get Déra some clothes that fit. They weren't stylish, jeans and long-sleeved shirts. But she looked okay if you were into seven-foot women who could bench-press the front end of a car and put an arrow through your eye at a hundred yards.

"I have to go to work. My daughter is missing," I told her as I scooped up my keys. "I know I told you I'd take you back to work with Bian, but I can't right now."

Déra walked over and put a hand on my shoulder, still working her tongue as if that would take the taste of the cheese from her mouth. "It's okay, Cait. Do what you have to do. Your family is more important."

Overwhelmed with a hundred emotions, I gave her a quick hug. "Thank you," I said as I grabbed the keys to Marcella's Audi and ran out the door.

"I heard a crash and went to see what was going on. There were three of them. One of them was really big, and he growled a lot. The other two were dressed like him." Leah pointed to Carlos.

Blood still caked Leah's neck and one of her forearms, but we'd gotten it off her face and hands, at least. When Carlos had shown up, Leah had looked like an extra from a horror movie. Blood stained her hand, and there was hair stuck to two fingers where she'd tried to hold Jim's head together. Her mother was at BMC undergoing surgery for bullet wounds to the head and chest. We didn't know if she'd make it.

"In a suit?" I asked. "A jacket and pants like that?"

"Yeah. Daddy told them to get the hell out, and then Katie told me to get under the bed, so I hid. Katie went out into the living room and told them to leave Mommy and Daddy alone, and they killed her."

I blinked, taking a moment to remember that this was a twelve-year-old who didn't know Katie was a vampire. "This is very important. How did they kill her?" I asked hopefully, my heart ready to rend my breast in two.

"They shot her. They shot her in the head."

I sighed in relief. Then I did something I might regret later, but I didn't want Leah to think her sister was dead. "Okay, Leah. I want you to listen to me carefully. You can't tell anyone, but Katie is special. They can't kill her by shooting her." I squelched my building rage. It wouldn't help. They wanted Katie alive. I didn't know why. But if my visions were right, they had Katie and Marcella. That meant Liz would be next if I didn't miss my guess.

"She's not dead?" Leah asked tentatively. "Is she like a zombie or vampire or something?"

"What makes you say that?" I asked.

Leah took another sip of the water we'd given her. Her entire body shook like a leaf in the wind, poor girl. "Her skin is all white, and she sleeps all day, and you just said they couldn't kill her with a gun."

I leaned in close and took her hand. "Does that scare you?"

"I guess—if she was a zombie. Daddy watches this show where zombies eat people and they shoot them. I don't watch it because it scares me."

"What about vampires? Do they scare you, too?"

"The good ones don't. I saw *Twilight*. Edward was good, and so was his family."

I snorted in amusement. Well, thank the world for small favors. Those fucking books had done some good. I leaned in close and whispered in her ear. "You're right. The good ones aren't scary. Can you keep a secret?"

Leah's eyes went wide. "Really?"

I put a finger to my lips. "But you can't tell anyone. It's an important secret."

"I promise," she said quietly. Her hands were right in front of me, and I glanced at them to make sure her fingers weren't crossed. Kids were funny that way.

I leaned in and whispered, "Katie's a vampire, now. But don't tell anyone. Detective Rodriguez here knows, and maybe a few others, but it's a big secret, and no one can know."

"Okay," she whispered back, and she looked at Carlos, who smiled and winked at her. She didn't smile back.

"Now, is there anything else you can remember?"

"Their shoes." She said. "The two men in suits wore shoes like policemen wear. Not the regular police, the ones with the big guns."

"Like soldier boots?"

"Yeah. They weren't Corcoran's, though, but they were black. I know what those look like. My grandpa had a pair of those."

"Anything else?"

"One of them smoked. Cigarettes, not Cigars like my daddy."

I was impressed. The kid had a good head for details. She'd make a good cop one day. I glanced over at Carlos, who was writing everything down.

"Okay, now this is important. Can you think of anything else about how they smelled or what they had with them?"

She shook her head.

"Did you see the guns?"

She nodded and pointed at my Glock. "They were like that but different. More like the black lady Detective carries back here." She gestured to her lower back.

Carol carried a Sig Sauer as a backup to her Glock. It was against department regulations, but only a few of us knew about it.

"Did you see their faces?"

She shook her head again. "No. I'm sorry."

"Leah, that's okay. You did really good. Carlos and I are going to step out." I stood, and Leah grabbed my hand.

"Please don't leave. I want to come home with you. Katie said you protected her and took care of her."

I sighed and looked at Carlos, who shrugged. "Leah, I'm not going home yet, but we need to get you to a safe place, and my home isn't safe right now, okay, honey? But I promise, no one is going to hurt you. Now Detective Rodriguez and I need to tell the rest of the police everything you said so we can find your sister, alright? I promise we'll be back."

Leah seemed mollified for a moment, and Carlos and I left the room. I glanced at my new watch, and I said, "Where the fuck is their DCF caseworker? She should have been here by now."

"No idea, darlin', but this whole situation sucks. I'm going to take her to your place."

"It's not safe," I said.

"You've got a vampire and a muscle-bound elf at your place. Where else is safer? Besides, if we have a mole in the department, we can't send her to a safe house."

I sighed. "Fuck, fine."

There was a noise from the conference room that drew our attention. Five of the detectives were standing around the television. The mayor was holding a press conference.

I grabbed the remote and turned it up slightly.

"—so, given the recent events at the Liberty Hotel," Mayor Kim said. "I am announcing the formation of the Preternatural Investigations Unit." She gestured, and there were at least twenty patrolmen behind her, all of them wearing nice shiny red badges. *Fuck.* "As you can see, they have new badges. With this evening's resignation of both the Commissioner and the Chief of Police, I have appointed decorated Detective Sesi Williams to oversee the department until suitable replacements can be found."

"You hear about any of this?" Carlos asked.

"No," Maki and I said in unison.

One of the detectives, Shira Silverman, shushed us. "We need to hear the rest of this."

"Also, in an emergency session, the new city council has passed a new ordinance, which I have decided not to veto. All preternatural creatures, especially those of near human stature and appearance, must register themselves with the city within thirty days or face incarceration until registered. In addition, all creatures of a preternatural nature are to be limited to the existing camps now in place around Boston. It is my duty to protect this city, and we will.

"Finally, rumors abound that the disturbance around Elliot Norton Park was related to the events at the Liberty Hotel. At this time, we do not have clarity on whether that is true. However, as it is within the city limits, the Boston Police

Department, in conjunction with the National Guard, will be taking sole jurisdiction of the facilities erected by the federal government. Frankly, we have lost confidence in the Federal Government's ability to manage this crisis. Thank you. I will take questions now."

There were a dozen questions, mostly around the camps and about what constituted a preternatural creature, which, as it turned out, was anyone they suspected might be. Then Shandra Clark asked the magic question. "These are sentient creatures with feelings and intelligence, Mayor. Don't they have rights under the constitution? Are you just going to incarcerate them without due process?"

"Ms. Clark, that is a question for the courts to decide. As it stands, and I have conferred with the District Attorney, the constitution is only interpreted to apply to humans, no one else."

My mouth dropped open, and then I snapped it shut to hide my tongue, not that everyone in the room didn't know exactly who I was.

Detective Silverman marched out of the conference room and straight into Larson's office. I followed and peeked around the corner. Silverman threw her badge on the desk. "I quit. Go tell the Mayor that this Nazi shit doesn't fly, and I won't be a part of it. Also, tell her I said fuck you while you're at it." Then she stomped out of Larson's office without giving him a chance to respond.

I looked at Carlos, the emotions flashing in rapid succession across my face as I wondered if it was better for me to be inside or outside the department. He shook his head and gave me a glare. "Don't," he mouthed. So, I collected Leah from the interview room and went back to my desk. I sat down quietly as the weight of everything I'd just heard suddenly landed on my chest, making it hard to breathe.

Maki was ashen-faced as she sat down next to me. She didn't say anything at first. She just stared at her computer screen. "My grandfather was born in America. Did you know that, Cait?"

"No, Maki, I didn't."

"When World War II broke out, he and his parents were placed in an internment camp. My great-grandfather died of pneumonia there for lack of effective medical treatment. My great-grandmother moved back to Japan with my grandfather after the war ended." She turned toward me, and there were tears streaming down her face. "Why? Why is she doing this?"

"I don't know, Maki. I just don't know."

"This is the time that we should pull together. There's a hole straight to hell under Boston, and they need us. The Mayor knows that. If we hadn't been at the hotel, she would be dead right now."

I took a moment to think about that statement. My eyes went wide. "Carlos!" I shouted, and he came running.

"Where's Carol?" I asked, my panic and alarm growing.

"Still at the crime scene, I'm sure. Why?"

"Call her and tell her to get herself and Janelle over to my house right now. No questions, no bullshit."

"What are you thinking?" Maki asked.

"Why would the emisai storm the hotel in the first place?"

Maki shrugged. "We already know they're under someone's control. I assumed they were after the mayor. She was the most important person there."

"Exactly. To us, she was the most important person there. But they didn't go after the mayor. The first person the snipers shot wasn't me or Carlos or even one of the other officers. It was Liz as she'd knocked Carol out of the way. The first emisai up the stairs jumped at Carol. And even after Carol went down, the remaining emisai still pursued her."

"Why Carol?"

"I don't know, but I think she can sense them somehow. There's more to this. Can you go to my place and stand guard when she gets there? And take her with you." I gestured to Leah, then said, "Leah, Maki's going to take you to my house. I'll be there soon, okay?"

Leah nodded. I looked at Maki for a sign that she understood.

Maki took a deep breath. "I'd rather do that than go to some registration office or get stuffed in one of the camps."

Ain't that the truth, I thought. *Things were going to get very ugly for all of us.*

CHAPTER FORTY

When I got home, the garage door still wasn't working, and the sky had opened up, dropping heavy snow and blowing in a miserable nor'easter. Fortunately, I found a spot on the square. But of course, it had to be all the way across the park again.

Nastasia was bitching to Liz to get the garage door fixed when I walked in the door. I blanched, and Nastasia turned to me.

"Oh, good. Come with me, Cait." Nastasia held out her hand. "I want to show you something. You'll want to leave your coat on."

"Hold on a second, Anya. Where's Carol?"

"She went home. Maki is staying with her and Janelle," Liz said. "The three of us spent a few hours chatting in the sitting room. I think Carol's coming around."

I raised an eyebrow. "Really?"

"Yeah, I think her time with Mother Lamia helped, and I'm pretty sure I was able to convince her that we're not all blood-guzzling fiends out to dominate the world. At least most of us, anyway." She threw a glance at Nastasia as she said that last and I chuckled.

Nastasia put her hands on her hips and pouted in a very uncharacteristic manner. "I am not out to dominate the world.

Don't encourage her, Liz. She thinks little enough of me already."

"Oh, yeah, so I've heard. She hates you so much she can't keep her hands off of you."

"Hey!" I barked. "I'm right here."

Liz walked over and put a hand on my cheek. "It's okay, dear. I'm just playing with you." Then she kissed me deeply, and a soft sigh escaped my lips.

"Liz, darling," Nastasia said snidely, "if you're done spraying your territory, Cait and I have business."

I held up a hand. "Just a second, Nastasia, for Christ's sake. Where's Leah?"

"Watching TV," Liz said, jerking a thumb upward toward the media room.

Nastasia tapped her foot, and I squinted at her, then sighed and followed her outside. We pushed our way against the wind and through the drifts to my Jeep, half-buried in the blizzard-like conditions. The wind had to be blowing at forty miles an hour, pelting my exposed face with stinging ice crystals and making the freshly running snot from my nose freeze in streaks.

I headed for the driver's side, but Nastasia waved me off. "Around here!" She shouted over the wind. Nastasia unhooked latches from the hood and lifted it, barely catching it and stopping it from jerking back into the windshield when the wind caught it. She pulled a small magnetic box off the interior of the engine compartment, maybe three inches on a side, before closing the hood again. It was a GPS tracker unit like the ones we used for surveillance at work. I looked at it closer. It was exactly like the ones we used at work. The only thing missing was a BPD property marker.

"What the fuck!" I exclaimed. "How did you know this was here?"

"Come on. I'll show you," Nastasia shouted back, and we marched down the street to the camp two entrance. As we walked, I related some of my dreams about Marcella, specifically the one I'd had after I'd returned from the 'bad place,' as I'd come to call it, and the one in which it seemed

Marcella was begging me for help. I wanted her opinion on them, was it just my overactive imagination, or were they really the visions they seemed?

When we entered the lee of the buildings on Mt. Vernon, she said, "Vampires often form a special bond with those they turn, so it is possible. When we have fed on a human, we can sense them when they're near and sometimes when they are in danger. But turning someone is a deeper bond. It has a more—intimate nature. So these visions may be exactly what you think they are. Let me think on it for a bit."

I felt much better. That meant that Marcella was still alive. I was going to find her.

It took a few minutes, but we were able to clear off the street elevator doors, and even though they were iced over, Nastasia yanked them open with ease.

It was fabulously warm and a bit humid inside the warehouse below. Immediately, though, I smelled cigarette smoke and a whiff of body odor, werewolf body odor. I went to draw my weapon, but Nastasia stayed my hand. "It's okay, Cait. Follow me."

Instead of heading into the camp, Nastasia brought me around the far side of the warehouse to the refrigeration unit. Salloweye, the redcap, sat quietly, reading a book outside the unit on a small three-legged stool.

"Finally," Salloweye said grumpily as we approached. "It's well past my dinner time, Nastasia."

"Sorry, Salloweye, things to do, you know. How is our guest?"

I raised an eyebrow. "Guest?"

Nastasia just smiled wickedly as Salloweye walked over and pulled out a ring of keys like you might see on the hip of any public school custodian. He unlocked the fridge and opened the door. Inside, bound to a pole with strong steel cuffs, the kind I'd use to cuff a vamp, sat the werewolf I'd smelled from the other room. The guy was in his mid-thirties, beefy, with a balding pate and scruffy beard. He looked rough, shivering in the cold, and puffy-eyed as if he'd been crying. There was a bullet hole in his right leg that oozed blood slowly.

"Oh, poor baby," Nastasia began cruelly, kneeling in front of him. "Did the big bad vampire lock you in the freezy?" She knocked him on the side of the head. "Well, that's what you get for putting a tracker on my car, you little shit. And in my purse." Nastasia gestured a couple of feet to the right, where two tracking units sat, both crushed. "So, do you want to tell me who put you up to this, cub?"

"Fuck you, you fucking leech!" The man growled, and I could see the gold flecks in his eyes. He had a southern accent that sounded like maybe rural Alabama, but I wasn't sure.

Nastasia ignored his taunt. "You dumb ass, I checked with the Vestry. You don't exist as far as they're concerned, so you're ours to do with as we wish. If you don't tell me what you're doing here, I will feed you to the mermaids alive. And with that silver bullet in your leg, you won't be able to shift. Won't that be delightful? Now, who are you working for?"

The werewolf turned his face away from us. "Go take a flying fuck at a rolling—"

Nastasia kicked him in the groin hard, and he slumped forward, groaning. "Watch your mouth, mutt. It may be against the accords, but I'll feed on you happily if you piss me off. I can keep you alive almost indefinitely until you fucking spill you're prom date's twat size. Do you understand?"

The man snarled and snapped his teeth at Nastasia; she backhanded him, rattling his jaw.

I stepped forward, knowing when to play good cop. "Hey, take it easy, Nastasia. You're not going to get anything out of him that way. The Vestry is going to kill him anyway. Unless, of course, we speak up for him."

"Go fuck yourself, Reagan," he snarled at me, baring fangs. "Yeah, I know who you are. And I can't wait to get a piece of that little girl bloodsucker."

I turned back and looked at him, shooting him a dangerous glare. It had been the wrong thing to say. Nastasia reached into her purse, pulled out a twenty-two pistol, and handed it to me. I checked the magazine, nine rounds, all silver. I knelt. Rage scoured my conscience away like the wind blowing sand off a board. This was the kind of man who raped me, raped Nastasia. This man thought he could do whatever he wanted to women and get away with it. I looked closely at him, and all I could see was Holley. He was so fucking confident in his own superiority. Maybe he thought I wouldn't hurt him because I was a cop. He was totally fucking wrong. I was going to dig out what he knew, and then I would put him down like the fucking mongrel he was.

"You know," I said as I chambered a round in the twenty-two. "A man can take a lot of bullets from a twenty-two if you know where to put them, and they hurt like a motherfucker. You can relax about the mermaids; you won't make it that far." I placed the gun against his right ankle, and fear swept through him. He stank of it. Then he screamed as I pulled the trigger. His hot blood splashed across my chin and lips, and I licked it off.

"Who fucking sent you," I demanded as I placed the weapon against the side of his knee, carefully aiming to blow off his patella while missing all the vital blood vessels.

"Go," he said through heavy gasps. "Fuck—"

I pulled the trigger again, and he howled in agony as bone and blood spewed across the floor. "Tell me what I want to know, and we'll get you patched up. I'm sure the Vestry will help you. Otherwise, they'll be calling you the three-legged dog for the rest of your short life."

"Jesus! Stop! Please." He said between guttural noises. "I'll tell you."

I lifted the weapon, aiming it casually away. "Well, speak up. Don't leave us in suspense. Where is my daughter? Who hired you, and where did you get those?" I pointed to the crushed GPS units.

"Your daughter is at Disney World. The Jolly Green Giant hired me," he said through a half laugh, half groan. "And I got those from the fucking tooth fairy."

I shook my head. "Wrong answer, asshole." I pushed the weapon against his shin, and he jerked away. Nastasia grabbed his leg and yanked it straight, stealing a scream from his throat. I aimed again and shot straight through the bone.

"You dumb fuck," I shouted. "I don't know what you think you're going to accomplish by holding out. All it's going to do is get you killed slowly. I don't want to do this." It was a lie. I definitely wanted to do this. Nastasia had been right. I had a dark side, and it felt damn good to have this fucking monster to take it out on. I'd do whatever it took to find Katie, and this motherfucker was going to give me something.

"You can shoot me wherever you want, but I'm not telling you shit. You've hit a major artery; I'll bleed out soon."

I yanked off my belt and cinched his leg, slowing the bleeding. "Not before I blow your dick clean off." I aimed the weapon at his crotch, and his eyes bulged. "Let's get this straight. I know what I'm doing. Your knee is starting to heal, and so is your leg. I just have to keep you alive long enough for the artery to stitch itself back together. After that, I've got days before I have to return to work. Nastasia and I will take turns."

Nastasia reached into her purse and pulled out a spare magazine, also loaded with silver bullets. "I can get more," she said offhandedly with a twisted, evil smile. "What we need here, Cait, dearest, is something nice and hot to cauterize the wounds. No point in blowing off his dick if it will just grow back."

I turned back to him, giving him the same wicked smile. "You can face the Vestry, or you can face us. Your pick there, my friend." I turned to Nastasia. Something in her unabashed glee gave me a moment of pause. I looked back at our prisoner. *Could I do this? Is this really what I've become?* I pushed the thoughts deep down. What else could I do? They had Katie.

I turned back to Nastasia, standing and holding the twenty-two nonchalantly. "You know, what we actually need is a decibel meter. We can take wagers on how loud he screams with each shot. I mean, we're fifty-feet underground. No one will hear him." I knelt down again and shot him between the legs.

Ten minutes and eight shots later, he finally caved. His name was Matt Churdin from Minneapolis, a Marine grunt whose life had never gone according to plan. He'd been a good

Marine for a time, but then he'd gotten into drugs, and everything fell apart.

"I don't know his name," Churdin said, coughing bits of blood and tissue. "I used to work for Black Eagle Consulting."

I gave him a drink of water, and he continued, everything he knew spilling from his lips in a torrent. He couldn't get it out fast enough.

"But I got fired. This guy just paid me to keep tabs on the four of you. Tall guy, brown beard, brown eyes, brown hair. Wears mediocre suits and smells of cheap cologne. He was scruffy, you know? Looked like he'd been living out of a cabin or something. Now, get me some help."

I stepped out and rummaged through a few boxes in the warehouse. I found bandages and a pair of forceps lying about in one of the medical kits. "What else?" I asked when I returned and began probing at one of the bullet wounds.

Churdin spoke through gritted teeth. "Nothing else. He drives a black suburban, like the ones the feds drive. Everything about him says he's serious about taking you guys out. I overheard him talking to a woman on the phone." He howled as I dug out one of the bullets, but the wound started to close. The nice thing about silver slugs is they don't fragment like lead. I could get them out in one piece and patch him up for the few minutes it'd take him to heal. "That's all I know. Oh, one other thing, he said he already had some of you 'in custody.' Talked like a cop, you know?"

I paused, the forceps over another bullet hole. "What do you mean some of us? You mean he captured a vampire?" I looked up at Nastasia.

"Yeah, man. Yeah. He said he had a vampire captured. I think he said the place was called bluehill or something."

"Bluehill what?" I demanded, pointing the gun at his shoulder. "Bluehill what?"

"I don't know!" he screamed. Then his screams turned into sobs. "Please don't shoot me again. Please!" Tears flowed down his face. "I've got a sister. I only did it for the money. Really. I needed the money. The Vestry has obviously disavowed me. I haven't been able to find any other work, and my sister is an addict. I'm trying to get her straightened out. I'm as good as dead if he finds out I told you all this. You said you'd put in a word for me. But please, for the love of all that's holy, don't shoot me again." His begging was pitiful, and I sighed, rubbing my forehead with the back of one hand.

Nastasia motioned me to step outside, and I followed. She closed the door. "We can't let him go."

"What? Why? He told us everything he knew, I'm sure of it."

Nastasia blinked. "Cait, the Vestry will kill us if they find out."

"I thought you said—"

"I lied. He needed to believe he was in this alone, that no one would help him. The Vestry would likely punish him, but he hasn't actually broken the accords. Putting GPS units on cars isn't a violation. On the other hand, they'll kill us for torturing him like this."

Torturing. The word stuck in my head. I'd tortured a man. After all of my high horse ranting about Abu Ghraib and CIA black sites, I'd just tortured a man. Werewolf or not, I'd just shot a man a dozen times to get him to talk. I'd wanted to be the monster in the dark; this was it. And it wasn't sitting well with me. At all.

"Cait?"

I looked up at Nastasia, horror, I was sure, plastered across my features. "You mean we have to kill him."

"No, Cait. Not we. *You*. You have to kill him."

My mind rebelled, and I backed away. "No, I can't do that. I won't. Please don't make me. I'm a cop, Anya. I swore to protect people, not torture them. This isn't me."

"No, Cait. It is you!" she snapped. "You are a vampire. What did you think? That life would always be filled with hot women, drinking your fill of their blood? Right now, you have one foot in the human world, but that won't last. We are always on the edge of discovery or, worse, extermination. I'm sure you saw the news. Your Mayor has declared open season on all of us. Your loyalty has to be with us first, period. With Katie and with Liz." Her voice softened suddenly, and she put a hand on my face. I flinched but didn't pull away. "With me," she whispered.

I stood there for a long moment, staring at the door. "Do you think he was telling the truth?"

"Yes. They hired him—"

"No, about his sister. Do you think he was telling the truth about his sister?" I looked into Nastasia's eyes for some comfort, some redemption, some compassion. I found none.

"I don't know," she said blithely. "But if it makes you feel better, we can ensure she's taken care of if she even exists."

And there it was, clear and plain as the nose on her face. Nastasia was a sociopath. She had no empathy for anyone. She pretended well, but everything in that brain was cold calculation. Whether she'd been born that way, which I suspected, or she had grown to be that way, it didn't matter. I closed my eyes. Nastasia had seen my darkness and had begun to nurture it, but I couldn't be the monster. I couldn't just murder people. Of course, I liked the power that came with being a vampire, but even when I'd been with Pauline on my first feed, I'd never wanted to kill her. I'd just wanted— I let the thought die. "No. We're not murdering him."

"Oh, for heaven's sake." Before I could stop her, Nastasia snatched the gun from my hand, charged into the refrigeration unit, and shot Matthew Churdin in the heart, silencing his pathetic cries for mercy. I put a hand on my head as salty tears filled my eyes. Salloweye just watched it all impassively. He didn't judge or comment or stare in disbelief or horror. He just watched, but his gaze felt like damnation. *What have I done? What have I become?*

CHAPTER FORTY-ONE

Salloweye tidied up the mess we'd left, carting away Matt's body. *Matthew,* I thought. *Matthew Churdin.*

I'd tortured a man. I didn't say anything as we walked back to the house through the snow. This wasn't me. It couldn't be. Nastasia had to be doing this.

"Why?" I asked when we finally reached the front door.

Nastasia gazed at me with her liquid brown eyes shifting, searching my face. "Why what?"

"Why did you do that to me?" My voice was quiet, low. The wind hadn't quite blown itself out, but I knew she could hear me.

"Me? I didn't do anything to you. It's what I have been trying to tell you. That was all you. I didn't glamour you or influence you in any way. It's what you are, what *we* are. You're not sweet like Elizabeth, or twisted with a messiah complex like Marcella, or power-hungry like Schmidt was. You did what was necessary to protect your own, just like I do."

"Necessary." I turned the word over in my thoughts. "Was it? Necessary?" I couldn't believe that this was what I had wanted. I wanted the power to protect Katie and Liz and my mother, sure. But torture?

"Cait," Nastasia's voice was gentle, and she reached out to touch my cheek. I flinched. But she didn't pull her hand away.

"What were we going to do with him? Turn him over to the vestry for a slap on the wrist? They would have made him promise not to do it again, that's all. And we'd have no more information than we walked in there with. At least now we know the SUV you've been looking for belongs to whoever is hunting us. We know there is more than one perpetrator. They're organized. We know they have a vampire, Marcella, most likely. And we know that at least one of these men, at minimum, has a background in law enforcement. Finally, we have a lead on a location. We'd know none of that if you hadn't forced it out of him."

"But Nastasia, shouldn't we be abiding by the rules? You know, the accords? Doesn't this power come with some responsibility?"

"Don't be naive. We are the apex predators. We are also the creatures who have the longest sense of history and the longest vision. The pandemonium of the past is over, and we need to reconstitute our numbers. But this world is ours. It's time for us to save it."

Her words sank in deeper than I would have liked, but they didn't excuse my actions or hers. I had to wonder, was the vampire culture she represented worth saving? At what point did the argument of self-defense ring hollow and become the justification for evil? I didn't know the answers, but I knew I'd crossed a line tonight from which there was no escape. Somehow, what I'd done was worse than Iraq. There, I'd had to save the lives of my patrol with no time to think. This time, I was sure, there had to have been a better way.

Nastasia wrapped her cold arms about me and pulled me in close. I didn't fight her, but neither did I return the embrace. I stood there numbly, and she said, "Cait, you have the potential to be the greatest among us, and you are correct. That comes with responsibilities. Chief among them is the responsibility to protect your own. Sometimes that means doing things we'd rather not. Now, I need to get back home. Give me your keys."

"What? Why do you want my keys?" My voice sounded far away, lost in the blowing wind and numbness of my own scarred heart.

"Because Cait, I'm taking your Jeep. They're tracking it, and I might be able to catch another one of them. They don't know I caught their spy. Let's see what they do next, yes? This is me protecting you." She smiled and kissed me on the cheek. "Despite what you might think, I care about you, Liz, and Katie, even the new vampires, some of them anyway." Marcella's absence in that statement was noticeable.

"The only difference between you and me, Cait, is clarity. I have clarity of purpose. We will get to the bottom of who is killing us and make sure it stops. And that, my dear, is the end of the story." She cupped my face. "One other thing. Unlike you, Cait. I've never killed a vampire. I have never forced a vampire to kill another, nor have I torn the head off one as you did in your cell."

"Y—you tried to do that very thing to me once."

"That was different. I was fighting for my life. You're a better fighter than I am, Cait. I had to end it quickly, or you would have killed me. Don't bother to deny it. Now, give me your car keys."

"But—" I began to protest, but it died on my lips as she kissed me and reached into my pocket for my keys. She pulled the Jeep key from the ring and handed the rest back to me. I didn't say anything else, not even goodbye, nor did I watch her leave. I stepped inside the house, shut the door, and slid to the floor to cry uncontrollably.

Liz came and knelt beside me, putting a hand on my shoulder. "God, Cait, what happened?" She leaned in and sniffed at the blood covering my hands and wrists. "That's not human blood. Oh, God, honey, What did you do?"

"Liz—" I struggled to finish my sentence as the sobs poured forth. "I'm a monster."

Liz and I sat at the table as I quietly lifted a glass of bourbon to my lips with trembling fingers. The burn of the fiery liquid did little to soothe me. Nothing would. I related everything that Matt had said, especially the bit about a captured vampire. I couldn't close my eyes without seeing the man scream. After all the work I'd done to process the guilt from my time in Iraq and the struggles with nightmares and the horrors of war, I'd done this. It took me a moment to realize that Liz was talking to me.

"Huh?" I couldn't meet her eyes.

Liz spoke softly. "You're not a monster. Now, I want you to look at me."

I looked up, and Liz's mind brushed against mine. It was the barest of touch, but I felt it. "No, Liz, you can't take this from me. I don't deserve that." I tried to stand, but Liz grabbed my arm.

"I'm not. You're in shock. You need calm, so we can discuss what happened. You need to talk about this and process it so it doesn't fester. So, sit and look at me."

I sat back down, and Liz cupped my cheeks, holding my face in place. Then she kissed me gently on the lips as I fell into her gaze, her will washing over me, softening the hard edge of guilt and remorse that had threatened to overwhelm me. My body relaxed as she snatched away my thoughts. I felt as if I were floating in a warm pool of water, and my eyelids fell shut.

"Can you hear me?" Liz's voice filtered in, resonant and echoing in my head but soft and gentle.

"Yes."

"I want you to show me all that happened."

An errant thought slipped past as I remembered the trek through the snow; Liz had been practicing, and she was getting much better at this.

"Yes, I am. Now focus, stay in the memory," she said, drawing out my thoughts and memories like a string of pearls.

"Go fuck yourself, Reagan," Matt snarled at me, baring fangs. "Yeah, I know who you are. And I can't wait to get a piece of that little girl bloodsucker."

Rage tumbled through me again as I was forced to relive the entire event. Liz blunted the emotions, giving me some clarity, though I still felt a sense of horror at my actions. And despite Liz's efforts to keep me thinking objectively, I was trembling and dripping with sweat when it was all done.

The kitchen seemed to materialize around me as Liz withdrew her influence. "I suspected as much," she said as she stood and stalked to the refrigerator. "I'm sorry, Cait. I should have known she'd do this to you."

"Do what?" I asked, hoping she'd tell me that Nastasia had glamoured me.

"Turn you toward her way of doing things? However, I'm not sure I disagree entirely with the methods this time."

"Wait, what? You agree with torture?"

Liz sighed and pinched the bridge of her nose. "You should already know the answer to that question. I helped kidnap you. I let Schmidt keep you in a concrete cell and starve you, all in the service to my own debts to both Schmidt and Marcella."

I was flabbergasted, not by the admission itself—I already knew that—but it certainly wasn't anything I expected her to say, the farthest from it. My mouth worked, but nothing came out, and the shock was, I was sure, readily apparent on my face.

"You knew that," she said flatly, misreading my expression.

"Yeah, but I thought it bothered you to some extent. Otherwise, why else—"

"Of course it did. I don't like hurting people. But, honestly, to me back then, you were just another vampire that Marcella had turned. Tell me something. Do you feel bad because you tortured that man or because you think you should feel bad?"

That pulled me up short. *Did I feel pity for him?* I sat and thought, trying to be sober and sanguine about it. Ultimately, I realized that, no, I did not feel one bit of pity for him. The man was an animal, and his poorly veiled threat to rape my child had sent me over the edge. He'd had a shitty turn, but hadn't we all? It harkened back to the night that Blackman had attacked Marcella and me in this very house. I hadn't felt bad then, either. But that brought up Liz's other point. "Shouldn't I?"

"I saw the look in his eyes, in your memory. There was no other way you were going to get the answers we needed. And we need answers. Katie is missing, and I'd do anything to get her back, wouldn't you?"

I sat back in my chair, dumbfounded. She was right. We were running out of time. Katie had been missing for two days, and that man—I refused to think of him by his name; he didn't deserve that—had given us our first solid lead. I pressed my mouth into a thin line and squinted my eyes. "Yes, I would do anything," I said quietly. "Go through anyone to get her back. So what do we do next?"

"You're the cop, you tell me?"

"Okay, we need to get a bead on who these people are, and we need to research this 'blue hill' whatever it is. Blue Hill is a common name for a ton of shit around here, but only a few places come to mind where they might stash someone. If they have Marcella somewhere, they'll need to have her in a secure location like the council had us, out of the way and private."

"Do you think the FBI has her?" Liz asked. It was a valid question. The vehicle we'd seen in the cameras and Churdin had described was definitely a fed car. But this wasn't the way the Bureau did things.

"No. And as for the CIA, they might do some of the things that we've seen, but the Agency is more competent at it, and they're not allowed to operate on US soil. I think we've got a rogue agent or something here."

"You don't think Schaeffer could be involved, could she?"

I thought about it. All of my interactions with Schaeffer had been above board. She was a career agent. You could see it in her eyes. "No, I don't think so. She's too much of a straight arrow, and Nastasia scared the shit out of her. You know, if Nastasia weren't so fucking evil and was just a little bit under control, she'd be useful. Reese and Reynolds are a different story. I could see Reese doing this, and if Reynolds has regained his faculties, he might. "

"Speaking of which, I have an idea what to do about Nastasia. Give me some time to work on that. In the meantime, let's focus on keeping you safe from her and solving this case so we can get back to some semblance of stability."

I leaned over and hugged Liz. "Liz, you're—"

"A good friend, I know." She smiled.

I snorted a laugh. "I was going to say wonderful, and I love you, and I like being with you. Please don't go anywhere."

Liz looked at me strangely for a moment, then hugged me back. "Let's just live in the moment, okay?"

It wasn't the answer I'd hoped for.

CHAPTER FORTY-TWO

My conversation with Liz ended abruptly as an explosion sounded, rattling the entire house and bringing with it shouts and the sounds of tinkling glass. I vaulted from the chair, nearly tumbling to the floor as my foot caught on the table leg, but I recovered and charged outside.

A pillar of smoke rose from across the other side of the park. "Holy shit!" I rocketed across the snow-covered park as fast as my now bare feet would carry me, vampire-fast. Liz was on my heels the whole way until I lost my footing and toppled down the concrete stairs on the other side.

"Cait!" Liz called, but I was already up.

The scene on the other side left me speechless. Windows were blown out all around the blast zone. One corner of a house nearby was sagging, likely to collapse any minute. And at the center was a mangled, twisted wreck in flames. Almost unrecognizable, a burnt, mutilated form tried to pull herself out of the burning vehicle, *my* vehicle.

"Nastasia!" I ran to her, feeling the heat scorch my flesh, burning my eyes, and raising angry red welts on my face. My fingers and feet blistered and burned horribly as I heaved on the twisted door, foot planted on the car frame. With a massive groan and a pop of twisted metal, the door tore loose, and I tossed it aside. Then I pulled Nastasia from the wreckage, backing away quickly.

"Nastasia, say something, please!" I didn't get any further, as three things happened at once. My entire body spasmed, wracked with pain, nausea, and dizziness. I puked up everything in my stomach, almost dropping Nastasia to the asphalt.

"Oh my God," Liz shouted from somewhere in front of me.

I couldn't speak as my body convulsed again, and my vision blurred and tunneled to nothing. "Is she?" I grunted through the shaking seizure. Somewhere I thought I heard car tires squeal.

"I'm sorry, Cait. She'll be okay, but I need to get her out of here before the paramedics arrive. I'll be right back."

I heard Déra's voice. "Go! I've got her." Strong arms scooped me off the ground, whisking me off, away from the carnage.

I screamed as I lay on the bed. Anything that touched my arms and legs seared like the fire they'd just come out of. My eyes wouldn't open. I couldn't feel my hands or feet. Both forearms and calves hurt with a scorching pain I'd never imagined in my worst nightmares, as did the right side of my face and neck. This was bad, I knew, third-degree burns or worse. I struggled, moaning in agony, unable to pass out. It was unbearable.

A voice cut through the torment. "Cait? Can you hear me?"

"Yes," I grunted through blistered lips. "Where—"

"You're in my bed, love. I've got you."

"Liz?"

"Yes, sweetie, I'm here."

"Is she—Is she okay?"

There was a brief pause, and I thought the worst.

"Is she dead?"

"No, Cait. She's not dead, but she's in a right strop. You saved her. She'll be fine. Now I just need to get you fixed up."

Fire lanced through my chest and throat as I coughed

violently. "Liz, it hurts so bad."

"I know, and it will hurt a lot worse before it stops. I'm sorry." Liz grabbed my head and neck and lifted me off the bed. I groaned through gritted teeth as Liz bit into the unburned side of my throat, opening the artery. I barely felt the pinch through the horror that was my limbs. As Liz drank quickly, the burning eased, barely able to cut through the magic of her bite and glamour. It wasn't pleasant by any stretch, but it was better than it had been.

Moments later, Liz's lips pressed to mine as she pushed the transmuted blood back into my mouth. I swallowed quickly. There was a moment of nothing where even the burns seemed snuffed out.

Then I screamed. The burns had been excruciating, but the torment I endured as the nerves in my limbs flared back to life had no words. My attempts to stifle my screams did nothing. I bit into my hand, but Liz pulled it away.

"You'll hurt yourself." Liz practically sat on top of me, trying to hold me in place. But even with her strength, the lack of leverage made it almost impossible.

Over the ensuing hour it took for the nerves, muscle, and skin to regrow, I begged Liz for mercy, help, and eventually, in a small, broken voice, death. I prayed for the bliss of unconsciousness, but it never came. The agony was indescribable as I breathed howls through my teeth, trying desperately to spare Katie my screams, but then I remembered she wasn't here, but Leah was. *Fuck*. My eyes felt like needles were being pressed into them from every direction as they reformed, and the swelling around them vanished.

Eventually, the burning in my face and eyes faded. Then, inexorably slowly, the pain in my limbs faded as well, and I could breathe easily once more.

Finally, I opened my eyes to find Liz hovering over me, her face a mask of impassivity. At first, I was a little put out by her lack of concern, but I realized she knew she had it covered. She knew she could help me. She could heal almost anything if I had enough blood and could swallow.

"How do you feel?" She asked, gingerly checking my hands

and feet.

I closed my eyes, exhausted. "Can I have something to drink?"

She pressed a water bottle into my right hand, and I drank heavily.

"Easy, the water will—"

"Taint the changed blood," I finished for her. "I know." I set down the bottle on the nightstand. Despite the healing, my muscles hurt, and I was developing a headache. "I need acetaminophen or something for my head, and I feel dizzy."

"No, Cait. You need blood. I've sent Déra down to fetch some A-negative from the fridge." Liz then scooped me off the bed, and I yelped.

"You don't need to do this," I protested half-heartedly through trembling lips. A flash of Marcella washing me in the shower made my stomach turn over, but I reminded myself that this was Liz. This was different.

I tucked my face into her neck.

"You comfortable?" Liz joked half-heartedly and gave a humorless laugh.

I nodded into her skin. Beneath the odor of soot, gasoline, and smoke, I smelled the dragon's blood scent that lightly permeated her hair and skin. Her arms were blissfully cool under my legs and back, countering the remembered burning. Soft, pleasant emotions began playing about my heart as she set me down on one of the chairs in the palatial bathroom. My first instinct was to squash it, but I brushed that away. This was okay. *I* was okay.

Liz returned moments later, having stripped naked, and hoisted me from the chair. My laugh was probably inappropriate given the circumstances, but it bubbled up anyway as she carried me to the shower and set me on my feet in the warm water.

"Now, love, let's get this off you." She spoke softly as she gently scrubbed the dead skin, pus, and soot from my body. I giggled slightly as she scrubbed my feet.

"Feet too? Oh, my." Liz said with a mischievous smile.

"Umm, Liz?"

She looked up. "Yes, darling?"

"Should this—I mean, with what just happened, should I—I mean, I feel kind of giddy."

She looked into my eyes. "You're a little blood drunk."

I held her gaze for a moment, searching for something, but I wasn't sure what. Maybe some sign of reassurance. She didn't look away. Then she smiled a kind, gentle smile. "What is it?" Her voice was soft, almost intimate.

"Nothing," I answered, suddenly feeling extremely vulnerable.

We didn't speak much after that until Liz finally said, "Do you think you can manage the rest on your own? I need to check on Nastasia."

I nodded. "Yeah, I'll be fine." I took her hand and held it for a moment as she stepped from the shower, feeling that if she left, she might never return.

"Not to worry, I'll be right back." With that, she grabbed a towel and exited the bathroom.

The shower was comforting, but by the time I was finished, the shock of what had happened had worn off, and exhaustion suffused every bone and muscle. My head was pounding, and I needed rest. Somehow, someway, all of this was going to come down on me hard back at work, and I needed my wits about me. I piled myself into bed and waited, head still throbbing.

Liz returned a short time later and hooked up the blood infusion.

"Where's Nastasia?" I asked with a grimace as Liz pushed the needle into my vein.

"She just got a lift home. She's leaving town for a bit. She should have left weeks ago when the first body turned up, but she's fucking stubborn. Now you get some rest."

The blood was still pretty cold and chilled me, making me shiver. Liz crawled into the bed, and she was oh so warm with my stolen body heat. And with her wrapped around me, I decided it was a hell of a way to give it back. Then I passed out.

CHAPTER FORTY-THREE

"Shit just happens around you, doesn't it, Reagan?" Sesi asked. It was probably rhetorical, but I answered anyway.

"I guess so." I sat in what used to be Larson's office, arms crossed, waiting for newly minted Acting Chief of Police Sesi Williams to finish telling me whatever it was she wanted to say. Hooked to her belt was a shiny, new, red badge.

"You've been blown up, attacked by monsters, and now someone has bombed your car. What the hell is going on?"

"I wish I knew. Your guess is as good as mine. I don't have any enemies that I know of. No one who'd have the skills or go to this kind of trouble to get to me."

Sesi stared at me with wolf-like intent, looking for something, the big fat lie I'd just told, probably. In some ways, she reminded me of Carlos. But she wasn't a werewolf. She couldn't smell out a fib.

"Fine. It's just a good thing no one was in the car when it happened."

"Yeah," I lied again and felt not a bit of remorse for it. "Good thing."

"You seem a bit glib about having this close of a brush with death, Detective."

I shrugged. "Sesi, this isn't my first and probably won't be my last. As you said, shit just happens around me. Besides,

Larson was like family. And now, here you are in his seat, head of the fucking Gestapo."

Multiple emotions warred across Sesi's face in the span of a second. First, there was hot anger, then sadness, then a firm fixity, a stony expression, then finally something almost pleading before she returned to the hard expression. "Cait, we are not the Gestapo. Please don't be dramatic—"

Oh, fuck no, she was not going to do that. "Don't you dare gaslight me, Sesi. You heard the Mayor. Registrations, confinement, loss of civil liberties—"

"Civil Liberties that don't apply to them," Sesi interrupted with a voice sweet as honey and nothing like the woman I remember as a rookie, the one who pushed me to shoot for Detective. "But, Cait, if you don't like your job anymore, you can always resign. Unfortunately, a transfer isn't an option right now."

I screwed up my face in disdain. "You've changed, Sesi. And not for the better. Just remember, it won't be long before they find a boxcar for you, too." I stormed out of her office, slamming her door hard enough to rattle the floor and walls. Then, I darted to the ladies' room to puke up my breakfast.

At the counter, I looked in the mirror. The skin of my face had gone almost sheet white, and I felt cold. The room began to spin, and I clutched at the counter as my gums flared with pain. I felt the teeth descending. *Fuck.* Bian said I had a month. Of course, that was before I'd broiled myself rescuing Nastasia from my burning jeep. Liz had given me more changed blood. It probably accelerated the process. I was royally screwed, but I'd been here before. We'd find a way to fix this.

Slowly, with extreme effort and concentration, because I was so out of practice, I pulled my fangs up into my aching gums and lowered my head between my knees.

Eventually, my color returned, and I felt a little better, but I knew I didn't have much time left. A week, maybe two? Maybe less? I heard the squeal of someone's radio from one of the stalls.

"Shotspotter report, more than two dozen shots fired at Monument Square."

"Oh shit." I shot out of the bathroom. Son of a bitch, they'd gone after Liz, the bastards. Leah was there, and Déra. As formidable as Déra was, Liz wasn't a fighter, and Leah was only a child. *Damn it.*

I flew down Tremont, lights blaring, and cut across past the science center. When I finally rounded the corner onto Monument Square, the cruiser was practically on two wheels. There were a few tourists lying flat in the park who glanced my way as I squealed by. No one was gawking at the blackened buildings and the remnants of the street where my jeep had exploded.

Flanking the front of Marcella's building sat two cruisers, both occupied, so I slowed, ready to pull directly at the doors. As I passed the first of the cruisers, my relief turned to complete horror as I realized the driver was slumped over the wheel, blood leaking from a head wound. He wasn't breathing. I glanced at the other cruiser, facing the opposite direction. The driver was also slumped forward, but she was moving slightly, one bloody hand pawing at the driver's side window. The left side of her face was a catastrophe of blood. *Shit!*

I opened the door and stood up, the radio mic in hand. "Victor 8-9-4."

"Victor 8-9-4. Go ahead."

"Dispatch, I have two officers down, southeast corner of Monument Square. Code 105. Request Backup."

"Victor 8-2-9 Responding. We're on the way, Cait! One minute out." It was Morgan's voice, and something in me relaxed slightly, but I didn't wait. I opened the door of the second cruiser and grabbed the officer's hand. She was mumbling something unintelligible. Her wound was bleeding profusely, and I pulled out my handkerchief and pressed it to the wound as best I could, unsure if it was the right thing to do. On the one hand, I wanted to keep blood in her body, but on the other, I didn't want to cause her to stroke out or something. "Hold on, honey. I got you."

Sirens sounded in the distance, both ambulance and police. Freyer's cruiser flew down Monument Square from the opposite direction I'd come, blocking off the corner as he, Morgan, and one of Freyer's men, Detective Mark Adrian, exited the car. Freyer and Morgan armed up. Adrian, a short, squat fellow with a bit of gut, grabbed an aid kit and rushed over.

"I've got her, Detective. I'm a trained EMT and a combat medic," Adrian said with a gentle smile, peeling my shaking hand away from her head. He looked at the wound. "Jesus, she's lucky."

"Lucky?" Part of her face was missing. I didn't think that was terribly lucky. But then again, she was alive.

"The bullet passed through her temple to her eye," Adrian said. "She's lost some vision, but her brain is uninjured. She'll live to draw her pension. In this instance, I call that fucking lucky. A good plastic surgeon can fix this. I've seen a lot worse look a lot better when it was all done." Then he spoke to the officer. "You hear that, honey. You just stay conscious with me, and you'll be on the cover of *Vogue* in no time, I promise." The officer didn't respond, but her right eyelid fluttered open.

I wiped my hands on my pants, getting as much of the patrol officer's blood off as possible, and snatched up the mic from the cruiser. "Victor 8-9-4, making entry." Then I checked my weapon and rushed to the door, which had been forcibly opened. A split-second glance at the pattern of splintering told me that they'd used a tactical entry tool. The B team may have been handling the lesser vampires, but the bad guys' A team was on this one.

Judging from the horror show I found inside the foyer, it almost hadn't been enough. Three men in military-style black fatigues were dead, one decapitated. My black-steel Xiphos was stuck into the marble at an odd angle. Blood covered the entire floor in a spreading pool. I had to step lightly to avoid slipping on the marble. Déra had put up a tremendous fight. "Good girl," I whispered. "Make 'em pay."

"Holy Shit!" Freyer said with a whistle. "What the fuck happened here?"

I cleared the library and the sitting room before I answered. I was beyond fear and sadness now. They'd taken my baby and one of my most beloved. They were all going to die for this if it killed me. "Déra was here. That's what happened."

Then I caught myself and shouted for Leah. There was no answer. Outside, sirens approached with the peel of tires. The sheath for my xiphos was on the stairs, so I grabbed it and strapped the sword to my back. Fuck evidence. If any more of them were around, I was going to gut them.

I glanced around as Morgan headed up the stairs with two tactical officers that had just arrived. There were a few bare footprints in the blood, but they were definitely Liz's size. "Holy shit," I breathed. "This wasn't Déra. This is Liz's handiwork. Just because a vampire doesn't have their superhuman strength during the day doesn't mean they're helpless. She got three of the fuckers. There's a pretty heavy blood trail leading out the door, too, so she likely took a chunk out of a fourth." Liz had always told me she was a better lover than a fighter. I'd obviously misunderstood what she meant by that. "But where the fuck are Déra and Leah?"

I started for the stairs to follow Morgan, but something caught my eye. In that shitty little wooden bowl on the foyer table sat Liz's keys to the Audi, but underneath was the gleam of a red circular key. I snatched it up.

"I have to go get Leah. I think she's in the sub-basement. Clear the rest of the house, please."

I ran to the elevator, and I heard it trundling up from the basement then the doors opened. There was blood in it, too. Not as much, just Déra's gigantic sneaker prints. I stuck in the key and turned it, and the elevator started to descend. *Fuck, this thing is slow,* I thought. *Come on.*

Nothing prepared me for what I saw when the doors opened. Six men lay, either bullet-riddled or cut to ribbons, all down the hallway. I checked each one as I went along. They were all dead. When I reached the steel door, I knocked three times and called, "Leah! Leah! It's Cait. I'm here, honey."

There was a click, and the wheel spun. I pushed the door open. Leah was inside, sitting in the corner, holding a small .22 caliber pistol in shaking hands. Déra sat next to her, holding a wound in her shoulder and a bad wound in her thigh.

"Hey, honey, let's put that down, okay? I got you."

She tossed the gun aside and jumped up, running into my arms, where she bawled. "They came in the front door. We were in the kitchen. Liz sent us down here, but she didn't follow us."

I looked at Déra, and she nodded. "They followed us down here through the stairwell in the equipment room, but I managed to kill them. Then I did as Liz had told me. I closed the door and locked it."

I looked back. The door to the elevator equipment room was propped open, and I thanked my lucky stars no one had been there. In my rush to get to Leah, I'd forgotten it was even there.

Leah spoke up again. "I heard a lot of shooting and screaming. Is Liz okay?"

I closed my eyes and blew out a breath. "Yes, honey. For now. They wanted to take her, not kill her. I'm going to find her and Katie, I promise. Come on."

I picked up Leah and held a hand over her eyes as I took her upstairs and outside. I took a blanket from the EMTs who had just arrived and sat on the steps with Leah, both of us shivering with both cold and adrenaline. Carlos, Maki, and Carol arrived a few minutes later, just as they were bringing Déra out the door on a gurney. "No blood products," I told the EMT, and he nodded.

I pulled my phone and shot a text off to Nastasia to let her know what was going on. She didn't respond.

"How bad is it?" Carlos asked when he walked up.

"I don't know, Carlos. Liz took out three of them before they finally brought her down. Déra killed six in the sub-basement before she retreated to the panic room. But Liz isn't here. They still managed to grab her. That means she's probably still alive. They've taken Marcella, Katie, and Liz. Whoever it is, they want to hurt me specifically."

Carol frowned at me. "We don't know that."

"Yes, we do. I did something bad, Carol. I mean, really bad. This is my fucking fault." Then I shouted, "Fuck!" The word was filled with pain and fury and self-recrimination. I had been arrogant and stupid. "Right before Schmidt's crew kidnapped me, I did something I thought at the time was simple and innocent. I was angry and full of myself. I was also sick of being pushed around.

"I was about to discover that Elizabeth had come into the country on Marcella's passport, glamouring her way past passport control. FBI Special Agents Matt Reynolds and Carter Reese came to me and said that they knew that Marcella and I were vampires. So I glamoured them both and told them there were no such things as vampires and to go away."

Maki gasped, but Carol looked confused. She said, "So. So what?"

"Carol, Reynolds went insane, just like Gabe. It can sometimes happen when vampires use glamour and make someone believe something too far outside their worldview; think Renfield from Dracula. Matt had a psychotic break and murdered his wife. No one knows precisely what was in his head at the time, but afterward, he disappeared.

"I pulled Reynolds' file. He was EOD in Afghanistan, disposing of bombs and shit. He had military and private military contractor contacts all over the world, and the Rinaldi family is a hunter family. He drives a black suburban SUV, and Rinaldi is one of the origins of the name Reynold's in the US. It all stacks up pretty neatly." I put my head in my hands. "I fucked up in a moment of fucking pique and set all this off, getting four people killed so far. If you don't include the nine guys lying dead in my home here."

Carol shook her head. "Jesus, Cait. Are you sure?"

"Pretty sure. The mark on the cards we found is the Rinaldi family's hunter mark. Liz and I found that out in a file at the old Schmidt place on Humboldt. The place where I got infected. The place that led to me becoming a vampire."

Carol put her hands on her hips and stared up at the gray, snow-filled sky. "Good God."

Maki just watched me with her fox-like eyes like she often did. There was no judgment there, only sympathy. Then she knelt and said, "I have been where you are. It is not your fault. You did what came naturally when threatened. Now you need to pull yourself together, and we need to find where they are keeping them."

I looked at her, drawn in by her soft brown gaze. There was a gentle power there, and I realized that I wasn't just speaking to Maki but to her ancestors. "How? We have no idea where they are other than a lead I have on a place called Blue Hills. There are a lot of blue hills around here. There's Blue Hill Avenue, which would fit their MO, given the number of fucked up buildings in that area. There's the Great Blue Hill. There's the Blue Hills reservation. Shit, even WGBH is named for Great Blue Hill."

Maki looked up at Carol. "I think you can help us with that. What do you say, Wizard Lady? Do you want to give it a whirl?"

Carol raised an eyebrow. "I don't know how I can help."

Maki snorted. "You're a witch, Carol. I'm sure you can help. Come on. Let's get this scene worked and get to HQ. Cait, we'll see you there."

Carol watched Maki throw on her booties and step into the house, then she glanced at me, and I thought it was for support, so I said, "Sorry, Carol."

"What for?" Carol asked, a puzzled look screwing up her forehead and eyes.

"Opening the gate and getting you dragged into this shit."

She pursed her lips, working them back and forth in concentration as if fishing for the right words. Finally, she said, "I was too hard on you, Cait. You've had it pretty rough. No, I didn't want any of this, and I would have been plenty happy to watch from the sidelines, to be honest. And, no, I didn't need to be seen as a 'preternatural creature' of, how did the mayor put it, 'near human appearance?' In addition to being a black woman, that is. But I know bigotry when I see it, and it may take me a minute, but I know it when I perpetrate it, too. It wasn't fair for me to blame you or to judge your relationships with Liz and Katie."

"Thanks for that."

"No, Cait. I'm not finished." Her face turned serious and almost solemn. "You're one of the bravest people I know. You always run toward danger while other people run away.

Freyer told me how you faced down those things with nothing but a bowie knife to give him and Morgan time to get to safety. Then you did it again at the hotel, for me this time. I saw the footage; you dragged me to safety."

I didn't know what to say, so I did what I always did when people complimented me. I said, "I just did what anyone would have done."

Carol stared at me then she put her hand on my shoulder. "You need to stop telling yourself that. It's not true. Nobody does that, Cait." She headed inside.

I sat there for a moment. It didn't make me feel much better, but it helped some. At least my friends didn't blame me for everything, even if *I* did.

CHAPTER FORTY-FOUR

Carlos stayed at the crime scene to provide oversight. He also made sure the armory was locked up tight and the techs stayed out of there. We were going to need that stuff, and none of us needed to answer questions about why we had enough ordinance for a Marine battalion in the basement. Carol, Maki, Morgan, and I met at the office. Morgan had grabbed an old paper map of the city.

I'd stopped by evidence and collected a few things from the recent vampire murders. I also grabbed Vlad from Katie's room before I left the house. I had an idea.

We threw it all on the table, and I said, "Okay, Wizard Lady, do your thing." I was really joking, but I wanted to see what she'd do. To my surprise and everyone else's shock, Carol didn't argue. First, she pulled a latex glove onto one hand, using it to move around the items and sort them: things belonging to the bad guys, things belonging to the victims, and miscellaneous junk spread out at one end of the table. The axe, she laid away from all the other items. She reached down and took each hunter calling card in hand, one at a time. As she touched each one, her forehead puckered as if she were in pain, then she frowned.

"These have nothing useful that I can glean," she said flatly and set them down. She moved slowly around the table as if trying to decide what to grab next. She avoided the axe we'd recovered from the Hyde Park bombing. "The axe is no good. The terror of the dead will make it impossible to get anything useful. Strong emotions seem to be a problem."

I tilted my head, both impressed and confused. "When did you become an expert?"

Carol didn't even glance at me. "I've been practicing a lot. I mean a lot. After that first time at the Wilson crime scene, I sat with my mother. She doesn't have a gift like this, but she's read some books and suggested what to do to manage it. Mother Lamia helped as well. Psychometry, they call it."

She passed over Vlad and Cynthia's coat. Instead, she looked closely at a piece of burnt, mangled plastic that I'd grabbed on a whim. It was the GPS unit we'd found under the hood of my Jeep, recovered from the explosion. The magnetic case was fucked, but the unit inside was probably largely untouched. She picked it up and frowned. Then she looked at me. "Cait, put on some gloves and get this open, but don't touch it. You'll contaminate it."

I nodded. "Yes, Ma'am." I did as she asked, and after a lot of jimmying with a screwdriver and a pair of pliers from Morgan's toolbox, I was able to coax the plastic into a few pieces. Though, it would probably be better to say that it fell apart. Inside, in almost pristine condition, was the GPS unit. Those cases were designed to take one hell of a beating.

Carol took the GPS unit in one hand, and then she froze. When someone says that a person freezes, they just mean they stop moving around, no longer walking and talking and such. Carol froze in a way that suggested she might have just been petrified. She stood stock still. She didn't even breathe for long moments. Then she took in a deep breath, and her face screwed up. She turned to her left like she was looking at something from behind her closed eyes.

"This was handled by a werewolf," she said at first, and I held my breath, heart pounding. If she sussed out what I'd done, this was going to go bad in a hurry, but I said nothing, waiting.

She spoke again, her voice completely monotone. "He is

dead. Nastasia killed him, I think." I raised an eyebrow, and my heart pounded harder. But then Carol said, "It was given to the werewolf by a man in black fatigues," and I let out a breath I hadn't realized I'd been holding. I glanced around. Maki and Morgan were both watching with rapt attention as Carol continued.

"The man in black fatigues is in the back seat of a black SUV. He is placing the unit into the case. The driver has brown hair and is wearing a brown suit, but I can't see his face well. I think he has a beard. He is on a dirt road in the woods. There is a door leading underground, like a bunker, or maybe a utility tunnel in a park. There's a red and white sign, 'No Trespassing, Cameras in Use.'" She set the unit down and opened her eyes. "That's everything."

"That—that's remarkable," Morgan said, eyes wide. "I need to bring you back to Montana one day and have you check around for buried treasure."

We all looked at her, astounded that she could be joking at a time like this. Her eyes darted across all of us, then she said, "What? We were all thinking it." At our irritated looks, she added, "Oh, come on. It can't be only me."

I shook my head in disbelief as I stripped off my gloves. "Jesus, Morgan, have some respect, will ya?" Then we all broke out in laughter, happy to have just a moment to break the tension.

Carol passed over Cynthia's jacket and picked up Vlad with a gloved hand. She looked at me as if for permission, and I nodded. Carol closed her eyes and placed her ungloved hand on it. This time, she wasn't calm. She sucked in a gasping breath, then she said, "Don't worry, Auntie Liz. Mama will find us. It won't be long."

I had never told Carol that Katie called Elizabeth Auntie Liz, and despite everything Carol had said about her visions, things she'd known that she couldn't possibly have, I'd still been a touch skeptical. But now I knew. This was real. Carol was for real. Her visions were real.

Carol's hand shot out and grabbed my arm, pulling my hand to her face. I gasped as magic shot through my entire body like lightning when I touched her cheek. The world dissolved around me, reforming into a darkened concrete cell, maybe four feet on a side. Katie sat, her back to the door, right in front of me.

"Katie!" I cried.

"Mama?" Katie shouted.

There was a bang on the door and a gruff man called from the other side with a voice like rock-strewn dirt. "Keep it down in there, leech."

"Katie! Can you hear me? I love you, baby. I'm coming."

"I hear you, mama—"

Then the vision vanished as Carol collapsed to her knees. I knelt, holding both of her hands. Her breathing was labored, and her eyes were closed, but she was conscious, and I was sobbing with tears of relief. "She's alive. They're alive."

Carol looked up at me, her own eyes wet and glistening. "Yes. They're alive."

"Um, what just happened?" Morgan asked.

I didn't answer. I pulled Carol to me. "Thank you. Oh, God, thank you."

"I've got you, sister," Carol whispered. "I'm sorry I ever doubted that she loves you and that you love her. I felt it."

I cried even more.

We were still tossing ideas for recon when Carlos and Doyle arrived. They both looked exhausted. They'd been on site for hours. We were tired, too. We'd been going over the map for all that time, looking for possible matches to Carol's visions.

We thought about Blue Hills Reservation first. It was a large state park and facility outside of town, holding transmitter towers for several organizations, most notably one of the nation's largest public radio and television outlets, WGBH. But we couldn't find any place in the park that could support an underground facility. Otherwise, Marcella would have leased it from the state and used it for a covert camp.

Having dismissed the reservation, we were buried in our

computers, looking up other places around Boston that carried the name Blue Hill. There were just too many to go through, and my eyes were starting to get red. My cough had gotten worse, too. My handkerchief was stained with blood. And my head hurt. I popped four ibuprofen, but it didn't help. What I needed was another unit of blood, but that had to wait. Then I heard Carol and Doyle talking.

"They're in Blue Hills Reservation," Doyle said flatly. She walked over to the map of Massachusetts and, leaning down, marked a small X with a sharpie. "They're right there. I've been there before. There's a geocache nearby. A friend and I used to do it. I know it's a nerd thing, but I only did it so that I could spend more time with—"

"Doyle," I snapped. "Focus. How do you know that's the place?"

"The description Carol gave me of the entrance is dead on. In the fifties, the 8th Air Force Command Operations division created a bunker out west, south of Amherst—"

"Cut to the chase," I said impatiently.

"Fuck, Cait, I am cutting to the chase, but you need to fucking know this," she snapped, her usually ebullient smile gone, replaced by a laser focus. My eyebrows shot up in surprise, and I clamped my mouth shut, stunned by the rebuke. I hadn't even known she knew how to yell at someone. She was always so sweet. Then she smiled again like she'd flipped a switch and continued, eerily reminding me of Katie when she turned from cold-hearted predator to sixteen-year-old sweetheart in an instant.

"There's a Post-Attack Command and Control System bunker under Bare Mountain that was discontinued by the Air Force and is now used for library storage. But most people don't know there is a second PACCS bunker under the Great Blue Hill because it was never finished. They built part of it but then abandoned the project when expansion plans were deemed unsafe because of an area of unstable rock." At my annoyed expression, she said. "My point is, they used the exact same internal floorplan as the bunker under Bare Mountain, well, a third of it, anyway."

"How do you know that?" I asked, now thoroughly interested.

"Don't any of you ever watch PBS?"

"But—"

"Cait, you're wasting time," Doyle said, taking my shoulders. "Trust me." Then she smiled and bounced off to her desk. After ten minutes and twenty sheets of printer paper, we had a shitty taped-together map of the underground facility at 'the notch.' Doyle then marked roughly the areas she believed weren't finished. I could have kissed her right then and there. I said, "Gold Fucking Star, Jess. Gold Fucking Star."

True to form, she beamed, then said, "Can we go kill the fuckers now?"

"We can; you are staying here with Carlos. It's going to be Morgan and me on reconnaissance first. That's it."

Carlos and Doyle both opened their mouths to object, but Morgan shut them down. "This is a quiet operation, and we need to be smart about it. Yes, it would be nice to have a werewolf on the team, but we're not expecting an army. Besides, it's just recon."

Before Carlos could even suggest going with us as a wolf, I said, "Carlos, they know werewolves exist. There are no wolves around here, so if they spot you, the jig is up. So you get to stay here. Also, guys, this is on the DL. After what the Mayor said, we can't be caught, and no one else can know."

I looked at Morgan. "Thanks, Red."

"What is it, your girl says, Cait? Ride or die."

"Yeah," I said, then I added softly, "That's what she says. But she's not my girl, Morgan. We're just good friends. And, also, we're roommates," then I winked.

We all laughed at the joke except for Maki, who just looked confused, which made all of us laugh even harder.

"I'm going with you," a voice said from behind, startling the lot of us. It was Special Agent Schaeffer. "I spent two tours in Afghanistan. I've seen action."

Morgan and I looked at each other and grinned, then Morgan said, "Welcome to the club, Angela. But I have to ask, why? This is an awful risk for a Bureau Agent."

"Nastasia's told me to help you in whatever way I could."

I balked. "Where is Nastasia anyway? I texted her, but she didn't answer."

"She went to DC for something, but she said to tell you she's on her way back. If a Bureau agent is involved in this shit, they need to be dealt with. I swore to uphold the constitution, and until someone says otherwise, that includes any sentient creature in the US, not just human beings."

I patted her on the shoulder. "Well then, welcome to the team."

CHAPTER FORTY-FIVE

"Holy shit," Schaeffer said in awe as we entered the armory. "You've got enough in here to invade a small country."

"My ex moved arms for the US Military from time to time. She likes to be prepared."

Morgan gazed around at all the weapons. "Prepped is the word, Cait. Except there's no food. Where are the MREs?"

I laughed at the irony. "We're the food, Morgan. Vampires, remember?"

"That's comforting," Schaeffer said sarcastically and looked pointedly at the bag of blood attached to my arm. "Remind me why we're going to rescue them?"

I scowled at her, moving the IV stand behind me. "Because it's my family, and the bad guys are murdering people. Cynthia was pretty benign. She worked a normal job, paid her bills, and had a kid living with her ex-husband in Denver. She didn't deserve to be tortured and murdered."

"Ease up, Cait. I was joking," Schaeffer said. "I didn't mean to hit a nerve."

I blew out a breath. "Sorry, we're so close to finding them that I'm having severe anxiety that we won't be in time. You know?"

Schaeffer took my shoulders. "Hey, we'll get there in time. Nastasia said that it's you they want. They won't kill them until they find you."

I took a deep breath and calmed myself. "Right. Okay. Let's get what we need."

The armory was beyond loaded with everything we could possibly want except, maybe, a bazooka. There was even a fair amount of cold-weather gear. I wondered at that, given that vampires didn't freeze, but then again, they might need to look human, and a couple of folks walking around in their skivvies in thirty-below weather would probably look odd.

Morgan jerked her head at the locked door at the back of the armory as she tied up her boot. "Where does that go?"

"To a street exit and a long tunnel that dead ends. It's unstable back there, so don't open it."

Morgan raised her eyebrows but continued getting geared up. By the time we were done, we were armed to the gills and looked ready to go to war. Each of us carried an MP5, similar to the ones we'd used in the ogumo tunnel, but they weren't SSDs, no integrated suppressors, which was kind of a bummer. I'd liked those. They were cool. We also carried Sig Sauer nine millimeters in shoulder holsters. In addition, I'd grabbed two clips a piece for the MP5s and sidearms, a .308 sniper rifle with a dozen rounds, a spotter scope, and two pairs of field glasses. Under the parkas, we were all wearing bullet-resistant vests. I had told the rest of the team we were just doing reconnaissance, but we three knew that was a lie. We were ending this bullshit today.

"You know, you have to wonder where they got all this shit. Who supplies the hardware and manpower? Reynolds is in the wind and left the Bureau, so he can't be doing it."

Morgan and Schaeffer kept looking through the field glasses, watching two men mill around in front of two double doors buried in the side of the hill. We'd only had two pairs in the armory, so Morgan and I shared.

The entrance to the tunnel at Blue Hills was very different from the notch at Bare Mountain. 'The notch' was a completed facility with a nice entrance, a control room with pretty screens, and indoor heating. This place was a dump.

"You know," Schaeffer whispered. "I'd give my left tit for bad guys to hole up in a tropical volcano base once in a while rather than these creepy-ass old tunnels. This is going to be like that shit under Elliot Norton, all oozy, mildewy, and cold."

"Amen to that," Morgan agreed, then she said, "Cait, you remember that time we found those two dudes in that bombed-out house in Mosul?"

"The gay guys making out?"

"Yeah. They were so scared we were going to rat them out publicly that they surrendered. That was fucked up."

I pressed my lips together to keep from laughing and giving away our position. "Yeah. You know what—"

Morgan finished the thought. "I felt bad for them."

"Yeah."

"Truck on the dirt road," Schaeffer said. Morgan handed me the field glasses. I watched a green Ford F-150 roll up to the facility, and I noted the license plate on a small pad lying next to me. It was a local plate, probably not stolen.

"You know, Red, these guys may have been good at killing vampires, and they may have been good at tracking us down, but they seriously suck at OPSEC." She nodded in agreement. The place they'd picked for their base was surrounded by trees, yes. But the trees were bare and far enough apart that we could sit and watch it from a small rise on the other side of Washington Street, almost a half mile away. We even had the high ground in relation to the entrance at the base of Great Blue Hill. Old brambles and a fat log concealed our position well. "This would be a good spot for a sniper nest."

Morgan smiled a wide, mischievous smile. "Why yes, Cait. Yes, it would. How's your aim these days?"

"Still phenomenal. I was trained by the best."

Morgan took the field glasses again and watched the guards. "Yes, I know. Paid for in bad sex and worse beer, as I recall. I miss McCall. He was cool."

I sighed, remembering his easy smile and near-constant dad jokes. "Yeah, me too. He was the best."

"No." She dragged the word out. "I was the best. You just didn't know that."

"Don't start, Morg. We've already talked about this." I knew she was fucking with me, but it was still a little raw.

"I don't know, Kennedy," Schaeffer said. "She's hemmed in by two gorgeous blondes. I saw a picture of Marcella. She and Liz are both fucking hot."

I snorted in amusement, still watching the facility. "Yes. Yes, they are."

Morgan moved slightly, adjusting her position to get comfortable. "Well, at least you're not hurting for dates. Just don't forget about us while you're playing ham and cheese in the vampire sandwich."

"Morgan!" I hissed. "Honestly."

She hissed back. "Seriously. I mean it. What else are you going to do? You're in love with two women, Cait. I mean hopelessly."

"I am not in love with two women. And it's certainly not hopeless."

"Hey, you see that?" Schaeffer said, handing me her field glasses.

I gazed at the entrance. "No, it looks the same, two idiots walking back and forth like a fucking metronome."

"No, in the trees, dummy, about halfway down in the branches."

I looked again at the spot she indicated.

"You're right about the hopeless part. It most certainly is not, but you are in love with Liz. We all know it."

"Shut up, Red," I growled. "I'm trying to concentrate."

"We all hear you on the phone with her. 'Oh, Liz, how's our baby?'"

Schaeffer grunted. "And the way she just marched right into quarantine to give you special treatment. One of the nurses said she gave you a sponge bath."

I started to blush. "Okay, you two, quit."

Schaeffer said, "Now we're out here freezing our asses off doing surveillance because of her, Katie, and Marcella. I don't know how they knew, but they hit you right where you live."

After a moment, I saw it. Several cameras were poorly camouflaged in the branches. "Hang on," I said through chattering teeth. "Slide that spotter scope over here."

Morgan handed me the scope, which had a much higher level of magnification. Each of the cameras—there were several—had an antenna on it, no cables. They were wifi cameras. "Oh, I have a delicious idea," I whispered. "Leave the cameras to me. I know exactly what to do about them. And stop fucking with me. Yes, I admit it. I'm in love with both of them. So, will you two stop now?"

"Yup," Morgan said with a grin. "I just wanted to hear you say it. Now, what are you gonna do about it?"

"Can we please talk about my love life when said people are not being held by nutjob vampire hunters?"

I backed my way away from the brush and pulled out my burner, dialing Celeste.

She picked up on the first ring. There was a strange crunching sound, then she said, mouth full, "Hi, Cait. I thought you'd forgotten about me. What the fuck? You get me in trouble with the university, then ghost me?"

"Celeste, I didn't ghost you. I was up to my neck in my own shit. Now, I need your help."

"With what?" Crunch. Crunch. "And why is it you only call on me when you need something? You never just stop by to say hi." Crunch. Crunch.

"What are you eating?" I asked.

"Prawn Cocktail Pringles. My friend Callie brought some when she came back from England. They are too good. Betcha can't eat—"

"Celeste, focus. My girlfriend's been kidnapped, and I need your help."

There was a pause on the line and the sound of a Pringles can landing loudly on a desk. "Sorry, what can I do?"

"This place I'm in front of has wireless cameras. Can you do your wizardry and, like, I don't know, hack into them or something?"

"Where are you?" She asked, and I heard the clack of her keyboard.

"Blue Hills Reservation, just off Washington."

Another pause. "I'm not magic, Cait. There's nothing out there."

"Okay, it was just a thought. I was hoping—"

"Hold on. I didn't say I couldn't help; I just said there's nothing out there. I'll have to be closer. What's nearby?"

I scooted back up to our hide, looking down to the road below. "Well, there's a Dunkies between us and the facility. Washington runs right between us and the entrance. It's a way up Great Blue Hill."

"No problem. Got a directional, two-mile range." Whatever that meant. "So, give me an hour, and I'll call you back. Easy-peasy."

"You're the best."

I thought that was it, but then her attention deficit took over, and I chuckled inwardly. "Hey, did you see the Mayor? What's that about?"

"No time to chat, Celeste. I'm on an op."

"Oh, right. Got it." She hung up.

"What was that about?" Schaeffer asked.

"Dealing with the cameras. So, what do you say? We go in about ninety minutes?"

Morgan and Schaeffer both lowered their field glasses and glared at me. "That's why you had us pack all that shit," Schaeffer said and looked back at the facility. "Well, there are only two guards. If there aren't too many more inside, we'll probably be fine."

Morgan snickered. "Yeah, you aren't kidding. Did you see that pudgy dude on the left? He looks like he joined a militia 'cause the US Army makes you run."

"Just nobody get injured going in," I said, then cringed. *Fuck.*

Schaeffer cuffed me on the shoulder. "Way to jinx it, Cait."

"Yeah, Cait," Morgan said, piling on.

"Sorry, guys." Chagrined, I slid back down the back side of the rise and waited for Celeste to call. About thirty minutes later, though, Schaeffer hissed at me to come back up.

"What?" I asked as I reached the edge of the brambles.

"Four more guys just showed up and went inside, followed by the two who were at the entrance, replaced by two more. One was in a hat and trench coat. And there's our SUV."

I snatched up the spotter scope. Sure as shit, the black SUV we'd been tracking was sitting right in front of the facility. Pudgy-man was gone, and the entrance was flanked by two guys looking far more professional. "Son of a bitch. That sucks."

Morgan pursed her lips in thought, then said, "That's the lot of them. There might be five or six inside."

I scowled. "How would you know that?"

"Okay. So, two men got out of the truck to cover the entrance. Pudgy-man and his buddy went inside, replaced by the A-team. Also, one of the guys who went in had his arm in a sling. He looked rough. I'm betting that's the other guy that Liz got a piece of. So two stay, and five go in, including the dude in the trench. It's almost sundown; they wouldn't leave a guard alone inside, but they can't leave the outside unguarded either because they have to suspect we're going to find them, and more importantly, Nastasia's still running around. If I were them, I'd split my forces the best I could and put some guys in ambush positions. But if I were short on manpower, I'd leave two men outside as canaries and keep my remaining men inside where there's cover."

"Okay, but what if they're just stupid?" I asked. "I mean, there could be a dozen in there."

"Cait, that place isn't that big. What are they going to do with twelve men? And if they're stupid, I'd say that works in our favor, wouldn't you?"

She had a point. I really preferred stupid bad guys. Just then, my phone buzzed. "Hang on; it's my contact."

"Who?" Morgan asked.

"Our ace in the hole," I replied with a grin and slid back down the embankment to answer the phone. "Where are you?"

"Sitting at the Dunkin' Donuts, like you said."

"Okay, sit tight. I need to bring you something."

I heard a strange squishing in my ear then Celeste said,

around what I assumed was a donut, "These guys have shitty security. The cameras are all unpatched." She hung up.

"That was fast," I said and realized I was talking to myself. Fucking kids. Never know when to say goodbye.

I made my way down the hill to the truck, where I dug the earwigs from the back. Once we went inside the building, I'd lose contact with Celeste. The bunker's structure would absorb the radio signal. Fortunately for us, the earwigs also came with a repeater, a handy little device that could relay signals around a blockage, like big steel doors. It wouldn't go very deep, but it would give us some coverage once inside.

After grabbing the earwigs, I made my way down to the Dunkin' and just wandered into the building like any customer. From a distance, I probably looked like any basic snow bunny. I even ordered a latte at the counter before I sat down next to Celeste. "Hey there."

"Come around here often, hot stuff," Celeste said. The shit-eating grin on her face told me all I needed to know.

I scooted around to her side of the booth and looked at the screen. She had control of every one of the exterior cameras. There wasn't much to see, though, just the two guys out in front of the building.

Celeste waggled her eyebrows. "So, we have the two neckbeards outside with M4s. I'm pretty sure there's an internal camera system as well attached to these because they're transmitting to a private router."

She popped a screen on her laptop, and a bunch of text scrolled past. Then she looked at me. "You want me to go low and slow, or just take it all as fast as I can?"

I raised an eyebrow. "I assume faster is better."

"Do these guys have good intrusion detection?"

It occurred to me that she might have asked that before she took control of the cameras. "I have no idea, but given what we've seen so far, they're not what I'd call top-grade."

"Yeah, figured." She typed something on the screen, and I looked at it and then immediately wished I hadn't. It said she was starting something called RouterSploit, whatever that was.

I dug the earwig out of my pocket and stuck it in her ear.

"Hey? Jeez, Cait, if you wanted to get frisky, you didn't have to go to all this trouble."

I laughed. "It's an earwig, dummy," I whispered. "So we can keep in touch. Now, do your stuff, but be quiet about it until you hear me say go."

She nodded. "What are we doing here?"

"I and two other former soldiers are about to break into that facility up there and rescue my girlfriend, my ex, and my daughter."

Celeste's eyes went wide. "You have a daughter?"

"Yes, I'll explain later. Now please, time is a factor here. It's almost sundown."

"Okay," she said and turned back to her computer.

I waited for her to say something else, but she just shooed me away. I took my coffee, walked around the back of the Dunkin', and climbed back to our hide.

Morgan reached for her sidearm as I crawled up the back side of the rise but relaxed when she saw me. "Jesus, Cait. Where the fuck did you go? Wait, did you go for coffee and get none for us? Asshole."

I grinned. "I told you. Ace in the hole. Now, we ready?"

Both women slid down the ridge, and Schaeffer grinned, "As ready as we'll ever be, I guess."

We walked down to the truck and piled in. The drive was short. Hopefully, the tinted windows would keep anyone up there from getting too suspicious since we had to drive down Washington to get to the turn-off for Summit Road. Morgan couldn't help but use the field glasses as we drove by, but she couldn't see much, which was great because it meant they couldn't see us, really, either.

We peeled off Summit Road just as the sun dipped below the horizon. I didn't see it drop. The sky was overcast, but I felt it. There wasn't the burst of energy I'd normally have gotten, just a subtle awareness and a slight shiver. I found a place to park and placed a police parking placard on the dash before we exited. In minutes, we were geared up. I gave Schaeffer and Morgan an earwig, and we did a radio check.

"Shit, that's loud," Celeste hissed.

"Who the fuck is that?" Morgan asked, giving me a hard stare.

"Our ace in the hole, Red. Now chill."

"Oh, Cait, is that Morgan? I can't wait to meet you. I've heard so much—"

"Celeste, Stop!" I interjected. "No talking."

There was a long pause, then, "Sorry, guys." I shook my head in exasperation.

I grabbed the .308. As much as the far side of the road would have been awesome for a sniper nest, I didn't want Schaeffer and Morgan going in alone. Neither of them had any experience with starving vampires, and even if we were successful, they'd probably get killed without me, if not by the bad guys, then by Marcella for sure.

We checked all of our gear and vests and made sure our shoelaces were well and truly tied. Then we headed off.

CHAPTER FORTY-SIX

We found a clump of brambles, prickers, and assorted sticky things all wound up together just down the hill from the entrance, giving me a perfectly covered peephole through the snow. The angle wasn't perfect, being side-on, the biggest downside being a slightly narrower target. The upside, though, was that Kevlar didn't usually cover the side of the body well, and if you were really lucky, you could sometimes get a two-for. Both men were standing side by side in typical military fashion. At that range, my shot would likely pass through one and hit the other. How much damage it did to the second guy was up in the air.

I hadn't done this in ten years, but they say once you learn, you never forget, which is probably true, but then again, muscle memory dims over time. I slowed my breathing: In, two, three. Ready. In. Two. Aim. Half-in. One—I blinked. In a matter of a second, both men had turned and run through the entrance.

"Did they see us?" Morgan asked.

"Nope," Celeste said. "They have bigger problems. Something really bad is going down inside. Cait, you might want to get in there, or there won't be anyone left to question."

"What do you mean?" I asked, ditching my hide and slinging the .308.

"There's something down there, but four of the cameras just went out, and the lights are flickering or broken."

"Jesus, Celeste," I snapped. "Define something."

"God, Cait, I don't know. A monster or something. It tore a guy to shreds. Fuck, I'm glad it's in black and white."

"Are you still in the donut shop?" I asked gently.

"They think I'm playing a video game," she whispered, and I shook my head. *Fucking kids.*

"Okay, thanks. Let me know if you see anything. I need you to guide us in."

"Guide you in? Uh, okay. How do I do that?"

"We go in, and you tell us left or right as we reach each junction. We need to go to the monster, not away." *Marcella must be loose,* I thought, *and as starved as she must be, she would be tearing through them like tissue.*

"Guys—" I turned to the others as we all reached the entrance.

"Nope," Morgan said flatly. "We're coming with, right Ange?"

Angela seemed to waffle for a second. "I guess so. Let's go."

"I'll take point," Morgan said, but I held my arm out.

"No. If it is Marcella, I should be in front."

As we entered the facility, I activated the repeater and dropped it at the entrance. It would give us some reception inside, at least for a bit.

The small set of doors was deceiving. The main entryway opened into an enormous round chamber, maybe forty feet in diameter, with a domed ceiling. The walls, the floors, everything was bare concrete. None of the normal military emblems were ever put down. Somewhere above, there must have been a crack in the dome as water dripped into a thin layer on the floor. Hastily assembled lamps, similar to the ones the feds had used in the gate chamber, illuminated the room with a wan flickering light that died periodically, leaving the entire room in darkness. We flipped on the flashlights attached to our MP5s and moved forward.

"Okay, Celeste, we're in the entryway. Which direction?"

"Shit, if I know," she said. "That's what I was trying to tell you. I can see some of the cameras, but I don't know—wait. There you are." Above us, an electric whine sounded as a camera turned toward us. I waved briefly.

"Celeste, online there is a map of a place called 'the notch.' You can use that. This facility was built identically, just not finished."

"Oh. Hang on." Celeste said. "Okay, straight ahead. There will be two junctions."

"Some ace in the hole, Cait. She's gonna get us killed."

"I fucking heard that, Kennedy," Celeste snapped, then more jovially, "And not a word from you, Angela."

I turned to Schaeffer. "How does Celeste know who you are?" Gunfire sounded in the distance, cutting off her answer, followed by a scream that ended abruptly.

"That's not good," Schaeffer said.

"Which way," I said as steadily as my terrified nerves would allow.

"Okay, straight ahead, and turn right at the third junction," Celeste said finally. We started moving forward in a chevron formation, me on point.

"I told you, fucking eerie and oozy," Schaeffer whispered as we moved forward. "Maybe I'll take an assignment in Puerto Rico or Hawaii."

"Yeah, with the gate open, you might want to wait on that," I whispered back.

Schaeffer balked at that. "Why's that?"

I held up a fist for quiet, and we all stopped. I smelled blood, a lot of it, and something else, a weird scent like Japanese Agarwood or potpourri. "Fuck!" I swore.

"What?" Morgan hissed. "What is it?"

"Unknown vampire."

"How can you smell a vampire?" Schaeffer asked.

The reflection of her light on the wall was shaking, so I turned around and put my hand on her arm, and said, "Take a deep breath and slow down. Remember, most of what's down here is either friendly or mortal and easily killed with that weapon. Leave anything else to me. That's why I have this." I pulled out my Xiphos. "I can handle a single vamp."

Schaeffer did as I asked, and I sheathed the Xiphos. The first two junctions were clear, the side passages not going very far. The third junction, however, left us speechless. There were five bodies, all in military fatigues, including pudgy-man. They were all gray. Their throats had been ripped out, and they'd been drained of blood. But that wasn't all. There were claw-like gashes across their torsos, and one was missing an arm.

"Oh, shit," Morgan whispered, looking at the carnage. "What the hell happened?"

I looked at the bodies and tilted my head. "I don't know. This is wrong. A vampire did this, yes, but this seems like rage or mindless—oh, shit!" This looked like the work of a revenant. It wasn't something I'd seen, but based on descriptions that both Liz and Marcella had given me, it seemed to fit. But revenants shouldn't be possible anymore with the gate open. "Come on. We need to get down there and see what the fuck is going on. Keep your eyes and ears open. No talking anymore."

The overhead lights in the hallway had all been smashed, and glass lay strewn about the corridor. Blood drops accompanied every busted overhead lamp, and bare bloody footprints with a staggeringly long stride led deeper down the tunnel.

About sixty feet down, there was another junction that split in three directions. Ahead, there was a large steel door. To our left was a tunnel that led off into the darkness. To our right, another tunnel continued on about thirty feet, then turned left. From that direction, a harsh white light glowed. We took the right-hand tunnel, and after making the left turn, we were met by a grisly sight. A hallway, maybe sixty or seventy feet long, was flanked on the right by a series of alcoves enclosed in steel frames, each had bullet-resistant glass viewing ports.

Inside each alcove was a person strapped to a steel frame. All of them were dead, and each looked like they'd died slowly and horribly. The first was half covered in that same black goo that had been on the snipers at the Liberty Hotel.

"Reynolds, what the fuck were you doing down here," Schaeffer whispered, her voice a mix of horror and disgust.

The second alcove contained a woman strapped to another steel frame. This time only her arms and legs were covered in the goo, but her face, pulled back in a horrid snarl, held a series of vampire-like fangs, too many fangs. Every tooth was a razor's point. Long IV tubes tunneled into each of her arms, one containing a blue mixture, the other containing blood. The bag of blood was marked with a large, handwritten 'M' in marker.

The third alcove contained something that couldn't be described as having been remotely human. The arms and legs were twisted at impossible angles, and the black skin of the emisai covered almost all of it. Only a single uncovered human hand, fingers twisted and broken, suggested it had been a man.

The corridor ended in a laboratory with another steel frame. The door was ripped from the hinges, and three people lay dead inside, the two soldiers we'd just seen outside, whose heads had been torn from their shoulders, and a man in a lab coat who was missing most of his abdomen, as if something had eaten it.

"Oh, God," Schaeffer whispered. "That's Mark Franklin, one of the biochemists working at Elliot Norton. What the fuck was he doing down here?"

"Playing God," Morgan said as she flipped through a chart she'd picked up off a steel lab bench. "They were using some kind of serum to combine vampire blood with that black shit that they harvested from the ogumo in the gate chamber. And from the carnage here, I'd say it worked."

I looked over Morgan's shoulder at the mixture of gobbledygook and chemical equations I didn't understand. "How do you know that?" I asked, one eyebrow raised.

"Unlike you, Cait, I got a degree in something useful."

I squinted at her. "Such as?"

"Agriculture."

"And that qualifies you to read that medical chart how?"

Morgan scoffed. "Yeah, that's what everyone thinks, dumb farmer's degree. I had several years of organic chemistry. I won't lie, it's not a STEM field, but it's still a fucking science.

Also, I got my master's in biochemistry. I can't read all of this, but most of it."

I blinked, unable to process what she was saying. Morgan had always been the dumb jock between the two of us, or so I had thought. Now I felt stupid, for several reasons, not the least of which was underestimating Morgan's intelligence. She was a fucking genius. *Why the fuck do all these brilliant women hang out with me anyway?* I wondered. *I'm an idiot.* I moved over toward the door, watching down the hallway. "What else does it say?"

"Not much," Morgan replied, grabbing another chart. "Except that three of the subjects died because the black goo, which they called morphic-gel—rather unimaginative—had an adverse reaction to something in the serum. There's a bit in here about werewolf blood being incompatible with it."

I turned back to her slowly. "Does it say where they got this so-called serum?"

"Not that I can find."

I looked at Schaeffer. "Angela, what haven't you told us about what your team has been doing at the gate chamber?"

"It's classified, Reagan. I can't talk about that. TS-SCI, you know the deal."

I turned my weapon on Schaeffer. "Angela, you have until the count of three to tell me where they got this serum. One—"

Schaeffer tilted her head, giving me an incredulous look. "You know where they got it, Cait."

"And what else did they take from Bian's lab?"

"Nothing that I know of. There was a refrigerator, but it was empty of everything except the serum when they got there."

"Fuck. God damn it, Angela, do you have any idea what you've done?"

"Hey, guys—" Celeste said, the reception was scratchy and hard to hear, so we only caught part of it. "Something's—."

"Say again," Schaeffer said, pressing a finger to her ear.

"There's a thing co—" then Celeste's voice dissolved into static.

Before I could turn around, Schaeffer brought up her weapon and fired. Bullets whizzed past me. Eyes wide, I dove to the side, about to fire at her, when I realized I wasn't the target. Morgan was now firing into the hallway as well.

I turned. Something—I couldn't rightly call it a person—stood in the doorway less than a foot from where I'd been standing. It jerked repeatedly from the gunfire but didn't go down. The thing was about six feet tall, roughly humanoid. The body was covered almost head to toe with the emisai skin, but its face was still mostly visible. The mouth had fangs, but they weren't vampire fangs. They were huge, sticking down over the chin. Its hands ended in six-fingered claws that scrabbled at the air as it took the withering fire.

I jerked up my MP5 and fired, but it still didn't drop. Nice neat bullet holes appeared in its skin, but they closed just as neatly. It started toward me, glaring sightlessly at me with swamp-green human eyes, mouth gaping open and unhinged. We emptied our magazines quickly and slammed another one home one by one, still firing. I scrambled backward and stood next to the other women. We fired until we were out of ammunition, and Morgan drew her Sig, firing again.

The beast launched through the air toward me, swiping down with a claw. It was insanely fast, and I barely avoided having my head taken off. Before I could bring myself back up, it backhanded me with bone-shattering force, breaking several of my ribs and throwing me into the wall.

Morgan stepped between us, firing her Sig again, but it simply batted her aside as if she weighed nothing, and she slid across the bloody floor to the other side of the room. Schaeffer came forward and sliced an arm with her trench knife, but the thing ignored her as it scurried forward and grabbed me off the floor, throwing me through the air again into the steel door.

Schaeffer tried to tackle the thing, managing to knock it off balance, but it simply grabbed her by the arm and threw her across the room, where she landed hard with a loud crack and a groan.

The creature turned back, marching with deliberate steps toward me. It wasn't moving quickly, and why should it? I was on my hands and knees, barely able to breathe. I came up on my knees and went for my sword, but I was too late. It was already above me, the killing stroke dropping. And it stopped.

A delicate-looking, pale hand with pretty red fingernails had ahold of the monster's wrist. The thing flew against the far wall with enough force to rattle the entire room and drop dust from the ceiling.

"Sorry I'm late. Traffic was a bitch," Nastasia said, then she snatched the Xiphos out its sheath on my back. "Mind if I borrow this?"

It was really no contest after that. The thing swiped at Nastasia, but she met each strike with the blade, removing both of its arms. It didn't scream or roar or howl in pain. It simply kept trying to come at her until she chopped it neatly in half and took off its head.

She wiped off the blade on a nearby towel.

"Do you know it took me almost an hour to get my bags?" She griped as she walked over to Schaeffer, then she sighed loudly. "Oh, Angela, let's get you up. I think that's enough playing around."

Nastasia bent down and went for Angela's throat, but I didn't see anything further as I doubled over.

Morgan's boots came into view as she limped over. "Cait, you okay?"

"Yeah," I wheezed. "Give me a second." My head throbbed in time with my ragged pulse, and the hunger barreled across my skin, sinking down to my bones and making my joints ache. My stomach felt like it was full of razor blades. My fangs descended painfully, and I began to have trouble thinking.

"Look around," I said desperately as I dropped to my hands and knees. "Is there any blood? Like human blood. Check that refrigerator." I pointed to an overturned cooler in the corner.

Morgan ran over and opened the refrigerator. "I don't see any. It's just that blue shit and the black shit."

I finally rose and staggered over to the fridge, digging through it. I found two units lying on their side amid the mass of other IV bags. They were both stolen from the Red Cross by their markings. One was A-negative, and the other O-negative, thank God.

I grabbed one, cut the top of the bag with my utility knife, and upended it, dropping the blade with a clatter. Cool blood ran down my chin, the hunger started to ease, and my whole body relaxed. I grabbed the second bag and opened it as I breathed out a relieved breath. "This sucks."

"There you go, all better," Nastasia said as she helped Schaeffer up, who looked disheveled and stunned, her eyes wide and searching. A trickle of blood leaked from Schaeffer's mouth. Nastasia shook her shoulders gently but practically shouted at her, snapping her fingers in Schaeffer's face. "Come on, Angela, Wake up."

I reached out with a handkerchief and handed it to Nastasia.

"Good God, Cait, how many of these things do you have?" Nastasia asked as she took it.

"I buy them in bulk. The monogram costs extra, so I save those for special people." I replied and winked. She glanced at the monogram, wiped Schaeffer's cheek, then handed it back so I could wipe the blood off of my own chin.

Schaeffer seemed to get her bearings, picking up my sword and handing it to me before she finally spoke. "What did you just do to me?" Schaeffer asked.

Nastasia frowned slightly. "I bit you, honey. It saved your life. Do try to keep up. And try not to get hurt like that again. You're running low on blood. Diminishing returns, you know?"

I turned to Nastasia. "What are you doing here?"

"I came to help. I told you, Cait, I protect my people, that includes you. I can, of course, go if I'm not welcome."

I made a wry, 'quit being an asshole' face, and she smirked.

"How did you find us?" Morgan asked, squinting at her with undisguised hatred.

Schaeffer held up a hand as she rubbed her neck with the other one and said, "That would be me. I called her before we left."

"Well, thanks," I said to both of them.

"Don't get all mushy, Cait. I thought about not coming at all, but then I remembered that everyone loves a good redemption story. So save that for your memoirs."

I rolled my eyes, but I suspected Nastasia knew I thought of her as far from redeemed. "So, how was DC?"

"Political," she said, then added, pointing at the thing she'd killed, "What is that, anyway?"

"That is someone called Special Agent Wilsher," Morgan said. She'd holstered her weapon and picked up the chart again.

Schaeffer gasped. "Gerry Wilshire? Oh, Jesus."

Morgan flipped a page in the chart and continued. "Looks like he volunteered. There's even a signed waiver here. Who the fuck signs a waiver to be turned into that?"

I shook my head and gulped down the second bag, wiping my chin on my sleeve. The hunger still hadn't vanished. We needed to hurry. I couldn't keep this up. I sheathed the Xiphos. "Let's go."

"Uh, Cait? They used your DNA," Morgan said, looking up at me slowly from the medical file.

"What? Where the fuck did they get my DNA?" I charged over to Schaeffer and jammed her against the wall. "Huh? Angela? Where—" I was overwhelmed by a fit of coughing that stymied anything else I might say.

"I don't know?" Schaeffer said, backing away from me.

"Your blood, Cait," Morgan said, still flipping through the file. "The blood they took while you were in quarantine. It seems they felt your blood was best as a catalyst for the transformation." She glanced at the dead thing on the floor. "Looks like they were right, sort of."

Nastasia strode over to Schaeffer. "Angela, honey, is there something you want to tell us?"

I pulled myself back up to stand and waited.

Schaeffer looked at all of us. "I had nothing to do with this place. I didn't even know about it."

Nastasia locked eyes with Schaeffer. "You wouldn't lie to me now, would you, Angela?"

"No," Angela replied mechanically, her eyes taking on that far-away, glamoured expression, then she recovered abruptly.

"Right answer," Nastasia said, then started for the door. "Now, let's go, ladies, the villains won't wait forever, and I should know."

"Umm, wait." Schaeffer pointed at the blood bag I had just finished. "Are we gonna talk about Cait's blood habit?"

"No," All three of us said in unison, and we started back out of the lab. Schaeffer shrugged.

We stopped trying to be stealthy as Nastasia walked ahead of us. When we reached the steel door at the end of the main corridor, it was locked. I looked at the knob and pulled out my picks, but Nastasia pushed me aside and kicked it. The dent she left was impressive. She kicked it again. And a third time. On the fourth kick, the door finally flew open.

Inside was a room with five cells. One each on the right and left walls, which were open, and four straight ahead. I pointed to Morgan and then to the open cell on the right. I checked the one on the left.

"Clear," I called.

"Look what I found," Morgan said as she hoisted a terrified-looking Special Agent Reese from the right-hand cell.

"Mama?" Katie's voice called from the middle cell on the far wall. "Is that you?"

"Yeah, baby, it's me." The cell door had a thick steel crossbar and a heavy lock. I yanked my picks and went to work. "Morgan, watch our six. Matt's in here somewhere."

Reese chuckled. "Matt? Matt is MIA. I haven't seen him in weeks. Oh, wait, you thought—" He snorted in amusement, then laughed out loud, almost doubling over. "That's just too precious. This is why women suck as cops. Too much emotion. Matt and I are half-siblings. My mother wasn't born in the church, Cait. She married into the Reese family and converted. Not that it matters. None of you are getting out alive. Oh, and Schaeffer, you're fired."

Schaeffer stared at him, disbelieving. "I'm sorry, I think you've confused me for the guy doing unsanctioned and illegal human experiments in an underground lab. You should be worried about your own ass, Carter."

"And I'm already dead," Nastasia added with a smirk. "Now here, let me frisk you and see what you've got."

I turned back to finish working the lock and jumped as I heard a crunch and the sound of a falling body. Then Morgan said, "Get away from the door, Cait."

I bowed my head and sighed inwardly. I hadn't wanted it to be her. I had *hoped* it wasn't her. I had prayed. But there were only three people it could be. Maki, whom I barely knew but was just as much under the gun as the rest of us. Carol, whom I'd known for years but had hated vampires, or Morgan, who'd just joined the team and was terrified of the preternatural. It really could have been any of them, but that was the way of my luck with women.

I glanced back. Schaeffer pointed her weapon alternately at Morgan and Reese, unsure what to do. Nastasia lay with a thin stake in her back. And Reese was bending over to retrieve his weapons. The tumblers in the padlock released, and I turned the tension wrench, gently and noiselessly opening the padlock. The fucking thing wouldn't budge, it was a tight fit, and it would take some fiddling to pull it loose. "Why, Morgan?" I asked, turning all the way around, trying to stall.

She didn't answer. Instead, she pulled the trigger. The shot burned through my right leg, and I staggered, barely holding on to the open lock and the crossbar. "I said get away from the door." Another shot rang out, and I jerked, expecting it in the chest, but nothing happened.

Morgan stumbled back against the wall, hands scrabbling to stem the flow of blood pouring from her right thigh. A third shot erupted from my left, and Schaeffer staggered back, hit in the chest, dropping her piece. Reese had retrieved his weapon.

"Reese?" Schaeffer gasped, tugging at her shirt. There was no blood. Her vest had stopped the bullet, but if she wasn't seriously injured anyway, she was making a good show of it. He turned the gun on me.

"I've been waiting for this," Reese said. "After what you did to Matt. Ever since I saw you on the Internet, running down the street after Blackman, I knew what you were. My grandfather had warned me and prepared me. 'One day,' he said, 'they'll come back. They're not gone.' I thought he was crazy. But the whole time, he was right. You bloodsuckers have to be stopped."

I snorted. "Us? Why, because we're different?"

"Because you're evil, Reagan. You and your friends, you're demons. You drove Matt crazy with a thought, and I know you're turning back into one of them. She told me." He gestured at Morgan.

"At least we don't turn on each other," I shot back hotly as I slid a little to my right, trying to stay upright, my right hand behind me jimmying the padlock still stuck in its slot.

Reese raised his eyebrow and laughed. "How do you think I got to Marcella?" He gestured at Nastasia. "She told me everything I needed to know. Heck, it was her plan, using credentials to snatch Carson before security."

I would have liked to say I was surprised, but I wasn't, so it wasn't hard to hold my expression in check at that admission. Nastasia had been trying to use Reese to get Marcella out of the way and take over as queen or regent or whatever—disappointing but not shocking. Looks like it backfired. *Nastasia, you idiot,* I thought. *Why would you trust a man, especially a man like Carter Reese?*

Reese pulled the hammer back on his weapon. "Get away from the door, Detective. I'd rather not kill you like this. You want to stay alive as long as possible, don't you? You might still have a chance to save them." He waggled both eyebrows, taunting me. "Besides, you need to watch as I kill them all: Nastasia, Elizabeth, Katie, and most of all, the queen herself, Marcella.

"Vampires have no place on this earth. The book of Leviticus says, 'You shall not partake of the blood of any flesh, for the life of all flesh is its blood.'"

Great, now he quoted scripture. He was a fucking zealot. It didn't matter what I said. He was going to kill us all.

"You know, Reese," I said. "Your God wasn't a God at all. He was just some malignant narcissist from another world. The Greeks called him Zeus, the Romans called him—"

"Shut up, Reagan. Your blasphemy won't save you, no matter how desperate you become."

I leaned back casually against the door, fighting back the surging gorge in my throat and the burning ripples under my skin. Then I smirked. "Reese, do I look desperate to you?"

"Yes, Detective, you look very desperate." He laughed again and shook his head. "I have been waiting months for this."

"One question: how did you get Morgan to betray us?"

"He kidnapped my sister," Morgan said through gritted teeth as blood flowed freely between her fingers into a quickly spreading pool on the concrete floor. Morgan wasn't going to make it, no matter what I did. "I'm so sorry, Cait. He took Caileigh. I didn't have a choice."

"Did that feel good? Kidnapping a young girl with her whole life ahead of her? Where is she? What did you do with her?"

"Shot trying to escape, I'm sad to say. Just last night."

"No!" Morgan screamed. "You fucking bastard, I'll kill you." She turned on her side, trying to reach her lost weapon, but she was too weak. Reese kicked it aside. Then he said, "That was a good shot, Angela, right in the femoral, just below her vest."

He trotted over and kicked Schaeffer in the face as she reached for her weapon. "Now, now, none of that." Reaching down, his gun still trained on me, he tossed Schaeffer's gun over next to Morgan's. "Now get away from the door, Reagan, or the next bullet goes in your head, and we'll see if you come back from that."

I raised my eyebrows and chuckled. "Sure thing, Reese. You're the boss."

"What the heck are you smiling about, Reagan?"

"Because you're an idiot." I cackled malignantly as I stepped to my right, holding up the steel padlock I'd been weaseling out of the crossbar for the last two minutes. "Here you go," I said as I tossed the crossbar at his feet with a resounding clang. "You can come out now, Katie."

Reese's eyes went wide, and I saw a moment of indecision in them as he glanced at the crossbar and back to me, costing him precious milliseconds. Then he tried to say something, 'Oh fuck,' probably. But then again, he was Latter-day Saints, and they didn't swear much. I thought it might have been 'Oh, fudge,' like Ned Flanders on the Simpsons. But it didn't matter. He didn't get that far, nor did he have time to pull the trigger as the cell door exploded open with an ear-splitting boom, and Katie shot out, grabbing Reese and hurling him against the far wall with a bone-shattering crack that made me flinch. Reese slid down the wall, a thin line of blood trailing from his head.

"Help her!" I told Katie, pointing at Morgan.

"But mama, she—" Katie protested.

"I said help her!" I snapped. "Baby, please. It's not her fault."

Morgan looked at Katie, then at me, terror twisting her features, then back to Katie. "No," she said weakly.

"Do you want to die?" Katie asked as she bent down and gently lifted Morgan. "If I don't do this, you will."

Morgan seemed to think about it for only a moment, and then she closed her eyes. "Will it hurt?"

"Just for a second," Katie whispered and tore into Morgan's throat. Morgan gasped in pain and then sighed, wrapping her arms around Katie, jerking slightly with Katie's long pulls. Tears welled in my eyes as I heard Morgan gasp again, this time in ecstasy as Katie's glamour rolled over her mind and twisted the pain into pleasure.

Morgan didn't have enough blood for Katie to give any back. Katie had been starved too long, and most of Morgan's was all over the floor. As I watched, the tears spilled over my lashes. Morgan would never be the same again. She may not die human, but for now, she would live.

Morgan's arms grasped at Katie's back, hanging on until she had no strength left. I couldn't watch any longer. The room spun, and my head started to pound. I dropped to my hands and knees, trying to keep from retching up the blood. The bullet in my leg finally worked its way out and fell to the floor with a metallic clink. Amid my heaving breaths, I saw that hot blood still trickled from the wound. It hadn't healed all the way. I took several long gasps of air as I looked back up at Katie and Morgan.

Katie opened her throat, allowing drops of her blood to trickle into Morgan's mouth. Morgan's eyes flew open, and she slapped a hand to the back of Katie's neck, pulling her close. Those beautiful emerald eyes were devoid of any human presence, so fully was Morgan consumed by the flourishing curse as it wrapped itself tightly around her soul. And, for just the briefest moments, I was worried that perhaps she had become a revenant as Katie had been. But Morgan's pulls slowed, and Katie pushed back, lowering Morgan gently to the floor.

The change was almost instantaneous. Morgan's skin turned milky and pale, her fangs descended, and ever so slowly, her breath ebbed until it stopped. She lay there, staring at the ceiling. Her lips moved as if she were saying something, but the words had no voice.

"I'm sorry, Morgan," I whispered as I pulled myself back to my feet on trembling legs. I limped over and yanked the stake out of Nastasia's back, tossing it to Katie. "Watch her." Then I dug through Reese's pockets, finding the keys to the cells. At least I wouldn't have to pick the rest of the locks.

I opened Liz's cell first, and Katie ran to Liz as she walked out, throwing her arms around Liz's shoulders. The third cell, probably meant for me, was empty. But when I opened the fourth cell, I was almost pushed back by the stench of decay and death that assaulted me.

The cell itself was bare but for a wooden bed with a moldy mattress. In one corner sat the desiccated body of Daryl Cummins. He'd been dead for months. I shook my head. He deserved better than this, and, as in the vision I now knew to be from Marcella, I wondered how Reese had known about him. But it didn't matter anymore. Reese was a dead man.

In the other corner lay Marcella, huddled and desiccated, appearing almost mummified. The few remaining strands of her hair sat plastered flat against her pale skull like brittle, white filaments.

"Marcella? It's me, Cait. I've come to take you home, honey." At first, she didn't move, and I thought perhaps she was truly dead, but with a rasping sound like dried paper, her body moved, and she spoke. All that remained of her velvety voice was that sandy fry I'd first noticed the day I met her.

"I knew you'd come. But don't come any closer, Cait. I don't want to hurt you. I haven't fed in months."

Heedless of her words, I closed the distance and bent down. Her skirt was in tatters, and her shirt hung on her like a drape, torn and smeared with Goddess only knew what. Gently, so very gently, I slid my left arm under her back and my right arm under her legs and lifted her off the ground. She weighed almost nothing, and her face had become skeletal, her lips drawn back, exposing her teeth. I sat down on the ratty bunk with her in my arms and rocked her. She made a strange, raspy sound, almost like a hiss, and I said, "Take what you need. It's okay."

A gentle and resigned calm settled over me as I made the choice to give myself to her. I wouldn't say I believed it was what I deserved, but I had caused all of this when I'd glamoured Reese and Reynolds. This was my fault. And if Marcella needed my blood to survive, she could have it.

"No," Marcella growled defiantly. "Take me home. I can make it."

I didn't argue with her. Either we would make it, or we wouldn't. And that was okay, too. I had found her, and right now, that was all that mattered.

I kept her head tucked neatly under my neck as I cradled her tenderly in my arms. She was so cold, so much colder than she ought to be. She was dying. Her curse had responded to my presence and lifted her out of her torpor. But because she refused to feed on me, it also meant the curse was depleting the last vestiges of her soul. I finally understood what vampires were—what *we* were. The curse, as bestowed by the Dark Goddess on Marcella, Nastasia, and the others, was a gift for the vengeful to exact justice as she saw fit. But, like many gifts, it came with a price. The gift consumed the energy of our souls.

Because of that gift, vampire souls did not replenish their light and thus could be drained away until they died. So, we consumed the energy from others to sustain us. If starved long enough, we went into dormancy, which kept the last little bit of our soul intact so that, should another victim pass near, we could attack and drain them and recover. A simple but effective defense mechanism. But this time, I was the victim, and Marcella refused to feed, refused to kill me. She had little time, and she needed live blood.

Nastasia stood in the doorway beyond the cells. "Bring her to me, Cait. She can't be allowed to live. She'll be the ruin of us all." Obediently, I walked toward Nastasia and her gorgeous brown eyes. *What was I even doing here?* I wondered. *Anya was all I wanted, after all. Marcella was nothing to me.* "As you wish, my love," I whispered. But the glamour vanished abruptly as Katie punched Nastasia square in the jaw, knocking her back against the wall.

Nastasia recovered and struck out at Katie with her left. Katie dodged under the blow, snatching Nastasia's arm and jerking it out straight. Then she backhanded the stake right through Nastasia's ribcage and right back into her heart. Nastasia's features froze, and she crumpled to the floor. And I saw it all, not as a blur but in real-time, and I couldn't have been prouder. *Good girl.*

"And that's how it's done, Auntie Liz," Katie said, dusting off her hands and kicking Nastasia in the side for good measure. "Stupid bitch." Then Katie turned to me as I gawked, and she said, "I told you she leads with her left and leaves herself open."

I continued to gawk.

Finally, Katie said, "What? You said to watch her."

I grinned at Katie, beaming with pride, and snatched her into a firm hug. "That's my girl." Then I looked at Liz. "Can she hear me?"

Liz nodded. "Her eyes are open, so she can see you too, though you might be blurry. She can't focus." Then she went to check on Morgan.

I bent down and hovered over Nastasia's face. "It was all bullshit, you know. You weren't looking out for all of us. Maybe you told yourself that, but that's not a self-delusion I think you suffer from. You're just too sadistic to be in charge."

"What about him?" Schaeffer said, pointing to Reese's unconscious body.

I frowned and thought for a moment about what to do about him, then set Marcella down and knelt next to him, slapping his cheek. "Wake up!"

Reese seemed to come around, dazed. One of his pupils was blown, indicating a severe concussion or, more likely, a brain bleed. "Where is Caileigh?"

Blood trickled from Reese's mouth as he muttered, "She's dead. I told you."

"Then where's her body, you lying sack of shit?" I shouted.

He just grinned with a bloody smile. I shook my head and put my hand on my sidearm but then thought better of it.

"This is for taking my family, you fucker."

I picked up Marcella and lay her so that her face was close to his neck. And that was all it took. Marcella latched onto Reese's throat. He screamed in agony. He'd starved her, and she had no energy to glamour away the pain, not that she would have, anyway, I suspected.

He beat at her and clawed and tried desperately to dislodge her, but it was too late. Less than a minute passed before Marcella, looking far more herself, though not fully recovered, rose on wobbly legs. She said nothing, but when she looked at me, I saw her gratitude and sorrow, so I scooped her up again and then marched out, calling back, "Katie, do bring the trash with you, won't you? Liz, can you gather up Morgan, please? There's blood in the truck."

Schaeffer stared after us, horrified, and I heard Liz tell her, "Welcome to our world, Angela. Do come along now."

Angela hesitated for just a moment, then obediently followed, a blend of dismay and awe painted across her face. Katie carried Nastasia's inert form, careful not to dislodge the stake, and Liz supported a very confused and pained-looking Morgan.

CHAPTER FORTY-SEVEN

When we returned, Liz took Marcella to her room and fetched blood for her. I wanted to do it, but Liz told me Marcella didn't want me to see her like that again, so I waited. Katie unceremoniously dumped the staked Nastasia on the floor in the middle of the foyer and scowled at her. I reached down and closed her eyes for her and said, "I think this is more mercy than you deserve for what you've done."

"That's for sure," Katie scoffed and went to the kitchen to get some blood. "I'm starving," she called as she opened the refrigerator. "Anyone else want anything? Never mind, the fridge is pretty much empty. Who ate everything? All they left was a hunk of blue cheese."

I looked at Morgan. "Go with her. I'll be in there soon."

Morgan stared at me in shock as she tottered slowly into the Kitchen, and I heard Katie say, "Whoa, slow down there. Let me open the tube first."

There was a bit of rustling, then Katie's voice. "That's it, slow sips. It'll be okay." I closed my eyes and hung my head in both sorrow and silent empathy as I heard Morgan's quiet sobs filtering from the kitchen. *This is what happens*, I thought. *My shit gets all over everyone I love.*

I pushed the thought aside violently, though, admonishing myself. *It's not all about you, Cait. These forces were set in motion over a thousand years ago, and you're not allowed to blame yourself anymore.*

I knelt down next to Nastasia, kissed her gently on the cheek, and spoke softly and intimately. "I'm not going to let anyone hurt you. And you should know that I paid attention to your lessons. Never waste a good resource, which is why you're still alive. Never leave an enemy alive if you can help it, which is why Reese is dead. Sometimes you have to be ruthless to protect your people. And, I won't lie, the sex was amazing, so there was that."

I paused and pushed a stray strand of hair from her face, admiring it. "You really are the most stunning of us. God, you're beautiful to look at. And for being so smart, you're also an idiot. Love matters. Family matters. Loyalty matters. I'm loyal to my family, and I love them. That's why Katie would risk her life to stick this chunk of wood in your chest. That's why I offered to give Marcella my blood if it would help her survive, even though it would surely kill me.

"I can't imagine what you have suffered over eight hundred years or what you've had to do. But it hasn't made you stronger. It's made you bitter and spiteful and petty, just like them, those humans you hate so much. You turned on your own kind in the name of protecting us. And that's not only ironic. It's also sad. So I pity you. But I won't leave you like this."

"She is very pretty, mama. Can I keep her? Maybe mount her on the wall?"

I glared at Katie, who was standing in the doorway looking pointedly at Nastasia. "Katie, honey. Nastasia almost undid us all, and you wouldn't be here without her efforts to find you, so show some respect."

I expected her to roll her eyes, but she had the decency to look chastised and returned to the kitchen and sat down next to Morgan.

I reached down and pulled the stake from Nastasia's heart. There was no following gasp or any kind of response really for long moments. Nastasia simply blinked and sat up.

"Mama! Why?" Katie said, stalking back into the foyer.

"The same reason I'd do it for you, baby," I replied. Then I turned back to Nastasia and raised an eyebrow. "You're an asshole. You know that."

Nastasia didn't say anything at first, and Katie scowled at her. "Well, you could at least say thank you. God."

Nastasia quirked her lips in a soft smile. "Thank you, Cait."

I nodded, then said, "Leave Schaeffer be."

"Can I ask why you unstaked me?"

"Because you weren't wrong. There are nine other vampires out there with no self-control to speak of who were hanging on Schmidt's every word. Your task will be to bring them back here, so we can see if they are worth saving. Now, leave Schaeffer be. She's under our protection, and so is her daughter. Imperium Personae."

"Well done, Cait. Finally, a smart declaration."

"I mean it, Nastasia. She's our friend now."

Nastasia nodded, then left. I suspected she had a lot to think about.

Schaeffer had gone into the sitting room, so, having nothing else to do, I joined her. "Hey, you okay?"

She sipped at a glass of scotch and stared at the bare fireplace. "Nope. Not even a little bit."

I nodded. "You get used to it."

"What if I don't want to get used to it? You—" She swallowed. "You murdered an FBI agent."

"Did I? How?" I said flatly.

"She drained all his blood, and you made sure she did it."

"Can I ask you a question? What wouldn't you do to keep your daughter alive and safe?"

"Nothing, but—"

"So it would have been better if I'd shot him? Which, by the way, I was about to do."

"Yes—I—no—I don't know. You're a cop. You're not supposed to kill people in custody."

I tilted my head, trying to decide how to put my next words so that she would understand. "That wasn't a law enforcement operation, Angela. It was an assault on an urban stronghold to rescue my daughter, my girlfriend, and my ex from hostile forces."

"Jesus, Cait, you make it sound like a war," Schaeffer said, looking at me in shock.

I spoke softly, but my tone was deadly serious, so there was no question I meant every word of what I said next. "The Mayor is rounding us up and giving us a number like the Jews of Nazi Germany. Just so you know, I do not intend to go out like that."

She gave me a horrified look and grimaced. "I think that's a bit of a harsh comparison."

"Is it?" I said impassively. "Haven't you studied the holocaust? This is how it starts." I reached over, pulled my red badge off the end table, and tossed it to her. "What does that say?"

"Special Unit Detective," she replied as she fingered my shield, rubbing her thumb slowly across the metallic red surface.

"That's right, Special Unit. Why do we need a special unit dedicated not to a specific type of crime, which is normal, but dedicated to a specific kind of person? And why are the badges red? What kinds of special authorities are red badges going to have?"

She didn't answer, still fingering the badge. Then she raised an eyebrow. "You really think it'll come to that?"

"It already has, Angela. In less than a week, the Mayor has taken advantage of an attack on the Liberty Hotel and turned half the country against us. She's eyeballing higher office, and she'll get there by stepping on our backs. Anything we do to defend ourselves will be seen as terrorist activity or some bullshit like that. She wants us to go downtown and register ourselves. What do they need a registry for?"

She returned my badge and stared back into the empty fireplace, her gaze distant and contemplative. "What's it like?"

I tilted my head in puzzlement. "What's what like?"

"Being a vampire. Being one of them."

I raised an eyebrow. "Why do you ask?"

"I'm jealous."

That took me by complete surprise. "Jealous of what,

exactly? I just said—"

"I know what you just said. But I wish I had what you all have. I mean, Nastasia's a heartless bitch, and there's drama, but you, Liz, and Katie are more than a family. It never occurred to me, had I even believed in vampires, that they might love each other. I figured it was like the movies, all backstabbing and politics. But you all take care of each other. My daughter is about to graduate college. I live alone, and all I have is my job."

Ah, I thought. *So that's it. Empty nester.* She was sad and lost, so I tried to be gentle. "Becoming a vampire is not a cure for missing your kids, Angela."

She gave me a thoughtful glance and a knowing smile before responding. "I know that. But, Cait, I'm alone. I've been in the bureau for seventeen years. It's cost me two marriages and strained my relationship with my daughter. I'm eligible for retirement. And, honestly, I'm tired. If nothing else, this little adventure has shown me how hilariously vulnerable I am. And, honestly, I don't like that, either. I was wondering if Liz might—" She trailed off.

I nodded in sympathy. I understood how she felt. "Yes, she probably will. You'd make a good addition to the family, I think. But, you saw how it is. You better make sure you're ready for that. And it's a one-way trip. Once you've been turned, there's no going back. Not ever."

"I figured as much. I'm not afraid of that. And from what Liz told me, you don't have to take lives."

"No, but—" I stopped. She wasn't really listening to my arguments. She'd already made up her mind. She just wanted someone to say it was okay. But I had one last consideration she needed to think about. "You need to think about your daughter. Do you really want to have to bury her?"

She snorted. "No, but she doesn't talk to me. She hates me. I really have no one, Cait."

I pursed my lips. "Angela, it's your decision. You don't need anyone's permission to do it except the vampire who turns you. But you need to know that we're a pretty ruthless group regarding our own survival, as you've seen. And while we do love, we love differently."

"How so?"

"We don't have much, if any, empathy for those we don't love. So, it's easy for us to treat others, humans especially, as objects rather than people. Liz is pretty much the sole exception to that. And for the people we love, it's a possessive thing, almost territorial."

"And the feeding? The—drinking—"

I laughed at Schaeffer's discomfort. "Drinking blood is like sex on a stick, I won't lie. And there's a strong draw to the power that comes with it. But there's a dark side. You're stealing something very intimate from someone without their consent. You have to be okay with that. And if you're not, you have to get okay with it."

"And did you?"

I nodded. "Yes. I realized what all vampires do. We're predators, and this is how we survive. Being a vampire changed me—permanently. As I said, there is no cure."

"So why do you seem so human?"

"My curse is just fucked up, malfunctioning."

"What do you mean?"

"I'm likely going to die. I'm going back to being a vampire too slowly. My body will give out before the change completes. We're trying to find a way to solve that, but so far, bupkis. What's worse, if I get fatally injured before then, it's probably all over. My leg still burns from the bullet wound, so the wonderful healing I've enjoyed the last week or so seems all but over."

Schaeffer shook her head in sympathy. "Fuck, that sucks. The tablets Nastasia mentioned?"

I nodded, realizing Nastasia had told her more than I'd thought. "Speaking of which, don't worry about Nastasia; we won't let her hurt your daughter."

"I saw that you let her go."

"Yes. We don't kill other vampires unless there's no other choice, Angela. It's a rule. And she saved my life and the life of someone I care for very much. I owe her a great deal. But now that Marcella's back, she won't be any more trouble."

She paused and finished her scotch. "Do you think Marcella or Liz would be put out if I slept here tonight?"

I blinked. "Of course not, but can I ask why?"

"I haven't felt safe since Nastasia threatened me. I might feel better if I stayed here. Just for the night." Schaeffer looked beyond tired. I could see her bloodshot eyes and the dark circles beneath. I moved closer to her and placed a gentle hand on hers.

"You can stay here as long as you like. You'll have to share a room with Déra, but she sleeps on the floor. I'll be honest, though. I don't know how long we'll be safe here, what with the new city ordinances."

She sighed and patted my hand. "I know. But they won't come here tonight; we have a little time." I looked at her in sympathy, noticing how she'd pointedly said 'we.'

"I need to check on Morgan," I said as I stood. "Will you be okay for a bit?"

"Oh, sure. What other option is there?"

I chuckled, knowing exactly what she meant. Morgan, on the other hand, was not okay in the slightest. She sat with her head bowed, crying. I walked around behind her and put my arms around her, hugging her in earnest.

"I don't deserve this," she whispered.

I frowned to myself. "No one deserves to be turned without consent, but I couldn't let you die."

"No, Cait. I don't deserve to have you here, comforting me after what I did."

I sat down and gestured toward the door where Katie had just left to go check on Liz and Marcella. "What wouldn't I do for that little girl, Red? I don't blame you. You did what you thought you had to. And it wasn't like you were thrilled with vampires, to begin with."

"Yeah, but you were right. That was ignorance. You guys are no different, stronger maybe, and," she raised her cup of blood, "with an odd diet, but you take care of each other."

"Angela just said the same thing," I said, trying to be as gentle and soft as I could. I could see just how awful she felt.

"But it doesn't matter now. Caileigh's dead." She broke

down into sobs, and I stood and hugged her again.

"We don't know that," I said.

"No," it came out as an agonized squeak, "Reese had no reason to lie. I just want to find her body and take her home to my parents. My parents, God, how will I explain this to them?"

"You're a cop. Until you have evidence, you don't give up hope. Sadistic bastards like Reese lie all the time to cops and family. We've both seen it."

That seemed to quell her misery a bit, and her tears slowly died off.

"That's better," I said, grabbing a tissue and wiping the tears from her face. "Now, keep your hope alive. Reese was dismally prepared for us to break into the facility. Obviously, you didn't warn him."

She shook her head. "No."

"So, he needed her alive—"

Katie appeared in the doorway to the Kitchen and interrupted us. "Mama, Aunt Liz is packing."

My head whipped around. "What?" I turned back to Morgan. "When you're done, go upstairs to my bedroom and grab a shower. I'll bring you some clothes to sleep in."

Katie and I marched upstairs, and Katie guided me to one of the third-floor bedrooms where Liz was rapidly packing two heavy suitcases. My stomach fell. "Elizabeth Charlotte Abigail Medlyn," I said, using my best mom voice that I typically reserved for Katie. "What do you think you're doing?"

"What does it look like? I brought my stuff down from Marcella's room, and now I'm packing. Honestly, you suck as a detective, Cait." She smirked, but I could see the disappointment in her eyes. Then she stopped for a second and took my shoulders. "I'm going back to London. Now help me with all this."

I stood there stunned until Katie, standing with Vlad the Bat clutched to her chest, said what I was thinking. "Auntie Liz, why are you leaving?"

Liz looked toward me briefly, giving me a warm smile before she looked back to Katie and cupped her face. "Because

I did what I set out to do, honey. And I'm not leaving forever. But now that Marcella's back, I have things that need sorting back home in London. You'll be coming to visit me soon."

"But you don't have to leave just because Marcella's back," I whined. "I don't want you to go."

She turned to me and closed her last suitcase. "Yes, Cait, I do. I have a life in London. I never intended to stay here, but you and Katie needed me. Marcella's here, and now I have to go home."

"That's crap. What's the real reason?"

"Because I don't want to be here for this. I love you. I do. But I told you. We just can't. I can't. And it'll hurt too much to see you with Marcella. It's okay. I'm not angry at you or anything. I need time to get my feelings and world in order."

I frowned as Katie gave Liz a deep, long hug. "Can we go to Soho when I visit?"

Liz laughed. "Oh, Cait, you've created a real monster here. She'll be snacking on the girls of Soho."

Katie laughed, too, and it sounded—adult. "I like girls. They taste way better than boys." She said it with a naughty smile and a hungry expression. Then she saw my horrified face and added, "Mama, I'm fucking with you."

I screwed up my face in a pantomime of irritation and gave her the finger.

"I think you're number one, too, mama," she said, that same impish smile plastered on her face. Then she gave me a V-sign.

Liz said, "You know, Katie. You can be truly terrifying sometimes."

Katie grinned even wider and stuck out her tongue. My eyes went wide in surprise. At the end of it, just barely visible, were two little extensions reminiscent of a fork, and her tongue was darker, more purple than pink.

"When did that start?"

Katie stuck her tongue out even further, absurdly far. "I don't know. One day I just noticed it. I think it's because you turned me, mama."

"I could figure that one out for myself, strangely enough. I just didn't expect it. Have you noticed a difference in your sense of smell or taste?"

"No, but there's holes in the roof of my mouth."

Liz glowered at her. "It's 'there are holes in the roof of my mouth' not 'there is.' Use proper English. You didn't think to tell us?"

Katie just shrugged. "There was a lot going on. You were busy."

Liz made a disapproving face at Katie but said nothing else.

I turned away and pouted at Liz's suitcases. "I wish you weren't leaving." I didn't bother to try to blink back my tears.

Liz wiped at one with a thumb and showed it to me. There was the barest hint of pink in it. Then she kissed me on the cheek. "My flight isn't until tomorrow. I'm not leaving forever, Cait. You don't have to cry."

"I'm just going to miss you." Then I paused and brushed aside the fear that had stymied what I was about to say for weeks. "I love you, you know?"

"I know, Cait. And I love you, too. But Marcella is home, and you should work things out with her."

"You're not hurt or angry?"

She tilted her head in a look of understanding and sympathy. "Of course, I am a little hurt. But, three hundred years, Cait. I know people. And I like to think I know you well. Go, be with her. She loves you, and you love her. And I love you both, so it doesn't hurt too badly. You two were meant to be together."

"Are we?" I said absently, not expecting an answer, and I wondered for a moment whom I meant. Then I sighed. "I guess I'll go check on her."

"Yes, go *check* on her," Liz said with a sly smirk. "Don't forget to look under the hood and make sure her fluids are full."

I snorted joylessly at the ill-timed joke and walked out. As I left Liz and Katie, the two of them started planning Katie's first visit, talking about all the places Liz wanted to show her.

I took the stairs slowly, unsure what I would say to Marcella. When I exited the stairs, I found the curtains open and a single lamp lighting the room. Marcella sat in bed, sipping on a blood bag and reading a book. Though entirely bald, she looked as beautiful as she had the day I met her. Then she looked up, and a million emotions swept through those fabulous, ice-blue eyes: love, sadness, fear, but most of all, remorse. They stopped me in my tracks as my own feelings sought to overwhelm me, a twisted mix of rage, betrayal, hurt, and love. But I didn't turn away.

I crossed my arms and examined the delicate frost-colored skin of her face, watching the light shimmer in her tears as they began to fall over her beautiful black lashes and across her sculpted cheeks. And I traced the line of her ruby lips as they formed a soft plea. "I'm so sorry, Cait. I should never have left you. I love you."

God, I had missed her. The anger that had trailed me like a bloodhound for months surrendered to my wounded heart and its needs. Every kind moment with her: when she scooped me from despair on her bathroom floor, that first kiss that seemed to go on forever and for too short a time on the beach, the kindness with which she drew me from my animalistic state desperate for blood at Bian's, it all came roaring back into my head.

I walked over and sat on the bed with her. I gave myself over to feelings of forgiveness and kissed her on the cheek. But forgiveness isn't trust, and trust isn't love. I still cared for her deeply, but our torrid affair had been just that, something built and burdened by planning and awful choices made both recent and long past. I was done blaming myself and being everyone's doormat.

"Marcella, I don't want to hurt you, but this," I waved my hand between the two of us, "can't work. I'm—"

She placed a finger on my lips, shushing me and smiling. "She's an idiot," Marcella whispered. "And I'm not stupid. I know what I've done. It was wrong, and I have apologized, but all I can do is make up for it and try to rebuild some trust and loyalty between us. Now, go get her. We can talk later."

I nodded, then said, "Before I go, I have a favor to ask." I went into her closet and returned with some PJs for Morgan. "I need you to take these down to my room and help my friend.

Morgan is in a rough state. Katie turned her to keep her alive, but she's pretty broken all the way around."

Marcella nodded. "I'll take care of her." She placed a hand on mine. "And Cait, I think this will work out for you and Liz."

"It has to," I said gently, feeling unexpectedly choked up at her grace and dignity.

Something broke within me, but not in a bad way. It was like a weight of obligation, and fear had been lifted. I hugged her and kissed her, and took the elevator to the third floor.

I was exhausted and starving. The blood from earlier hadn't come back up, which I would have considered a good sign under other circumstances, but it didn't bode well now. I paused to call out sick for the next day and then wobbled down the hall to Liz's bedroom to tell her why she couldn't leave.

EPILOGUE

Thursday, January 13th

I woke the next morning as my alarm sounded. Liz was asleep next to me, lying on her right side, an arm draped over me. I scooted my butt back into her, and she shuffled a little, her arm squeezing me closer. I hit snooze on my phone and lay there for just a little longer. I had love, real love, not the manufactured feelings that Marcella had engendered or the vapid lust of Nastasia's glamour. It was an odd feeling, and I realized something profound. Finding Liz had led me to love her, but it had also taught me to love myself. In turn, that allowed me to love people I'd once believed unloveable, Nastasia and Marcella specifically.

I found feelings of forgiveness I didn't know I could feel. I didn't have to trust someone to love or care for them. My love and care were mine to give as I saw fit, not because someone else bought them somehow. And I didn't need anyone's permission to decide who I loved or why. I smiled at the liberating revelation and drifted off for a bit.

I got up some time later and wandered the house for a while, moving slowly. I pulled a bag of A-negative from the Traulsen and sipped at it as I wandered. It helped with the vampire cravings, but it really did nothing to fill my stomach.

Eventually, I stopped in the media room and watched some

TV. The news wasn't great. Several states, especially in the midwest and south, were already introducing their own preternatural registration laws. One of our state representatives had also introduced a bill to the Massachusetts legislature to make the Boston ordinances a statewide mandate, and that wishy-washy, bitch senator from Maine that I hated but whose name I could never remember put in for a national registry. All I could hope was that the Supreme Court would keep them from turning us into second-class citizens.

TNT was playing *Twilight* again, but I had other options this time, so I flipped around, finally letting *Supernatural* watch me as I snoozed on the couch until sundown.

When I woke, I found Schaeffer in the sitting room thumbing through her phone with Déra looking over her shoulder as they settled on pizza delivery for dinner, which sounded absolutely fantastic. I gave them my order for a small with pepperoni, mushroom, and black olives, then meandered into the kitchen.

"Where's Morgan?" I asked Katie as I scoured the empty refrigerator for the human food that simply wasn't there. I finally pulled out the hunk of blue cheese, then put it back, deciding it needed crackers or something.

"Marcella took her out to feed," she answered as she and Leah played a children's card game at the table.

I spun around as Liz came through the door, saying, "Oh, good. She'll have fun, I suspect." I looked at my watch and back at Liz, eyes alight with hope. "So, are you staying?"

She nodded and smiled a broad, warm, loving smile. "I canceled my flight."

I didn't give her a chance to say anything else as I ran across the kitchen and threw myself into her arms. "I love you," I said and laid one on her.

She kissed me back, then said, "I love you, too."

And at that moment, I knew everything would be alright.

After a few minutes, numerous eyeballs from Katie, and a 'get a room' from Leah, we ended our impromptu make-out session, and Liz scoped the refrigerator. "We need more blood, and we need groceries for you, Leah, and Déra. The fridge is pretty much empty of food. Déra's cleaned us out."

I laughed. "You aren't kidding. God, that woman can eat."

So we left, taking Marcella's electric grocery mover. Our first stop was at the hospital, where we picked up four units of blood in a cooler. That was easy. It seems that if you're willing to pay, blood, like anything else, is easy to come by. At least I finally knew how Marcella had been stocking up all this time. Then we hit the grocery store, and every single employee stared daggers at us as we walked around and stocked up. I didn't blame them. We'd arrived ten minutes before closing. But I didn't care. I was practically dancing on air the entire time in the store, walking hand in hand with Liz and giving her silly little glances that quirked her lips into a shy smile.

When we got back to the car, Liz put her hand on mine before I could push the start button. "I love you, Cait. Let's not break each other's hearts. I want this to last."

"So do I," I said, then I snorted a humorless laugh. "If I survive."

"You will." She let go of my hand and buckled her seatbelt.

I didn't argue with her, but I wasn't optimistic. The most recent round of blood didn't seem to be helping my fatigue as much as I'd have liked.

Liz leaned over, turned my face to hers, and kissed me gently. "We'll sort things out. You'll see. Besides," she said with a cheeky smile and a wink, "Now that you have your fangs back, I know exactly what to do."

Of course, the garage door was still broken, so when we returned, we parked on the frost and ice-strewn winter streets. Thankfully, with a repairman coming tomorrow, this would be the last night of tromping through the frozen air, watching our breath coalesce and glitter first to fog and then to floating gossamer crystals.

I shuddered in the subzero temperatures. "Jesus, Liz, it's so cold I can see your breath, and you're dead."

Liz screwed up her mouth and shook her head in mock disdain. "Cait, love, I'm cursed with un-life, not dead. I do have a minimum body temperature."

I bit back my retort, envious of her ability to walk about in a long wool coat, a dress, and heels without so much as a hint of discomfort. Hopefully, we'd solve that soon before I died from my mangled curse. *Gift, Cait, gift.* I scolded myself.

Behind Liz, I walked with aching arms, hauling six heavy bags of groceries in a less-than-flattering, puffy, fat parka, looking like a bleached version of the big harry monster from bugs bunny.

The tips of my blue-forked tongue stung in the callous wind, and for a split second, I hoped they just broke off so the blasted thing might look a bit more normal. But that would blunt my abnormally heightened sense of smell, and it had been far too handy for me honestly to want that. I'd grown pretty fond of being able to literally smell danger.

I stomped about, trying desperately to get some feeling back into my feet as Liz rummaged around in the mailbox. It only took her a few seconds to remove several envelopes and flyers of wasted paper before she held a neat, flat missive over her shoulder. Given the half dozen bags filling both achingly stiff hands, the weight of which bit painfully into each palm, I could do nothing but stare at the crisp manila sheath. Liz turned and, seeing my predicament, laughed before playfully stuffing the letter between my teeth.

"My God," Liz said with absolute glee. "You look like a little kid stuffed into a giant white monkey suit."

"Hilarious," I mumbled past the paper, tasting the disgusting flavor of chemical adhesive and paper handled by, likely, a dozen people. *Yuck.* Finally, with the squeal and click of metal that had never been designed to work in these temperatures, Liz turned the lock and opened the door. "You want to open that as soon as we get inside," she said, indicating the letter clamped firmly but gently between my semi-chattering incisors.

The blast of humid air that struck me as I crossed the threshold was magical, as was the sweet odor of mulling spices permeating the house from the gently bubbling cider someone had simmering on the stove. *Oh, thank goodness.* I thought as I kicked the door closed, shoving out the last vestiges of frost-bitten wind.

"Damn it, Jabba," I swore as a bundle of orange and white fur shot under my feet, nearly sending me and the groceries spilling across the weird, rune-inlaid circle of marble under the crystal chandelier. The envelope, miraculously, stuck to my bottom lip as I cursed and returned right to my teeth, bringing with it a few new disgusting smells I couldn't, and didn't want to, identify.

"Furry little assassin," I grumbled, pausing to regain my balance and shooting the feline a baleful gaze that should have dropped him dead or at least put him into a deep sleep for a few seconds, had there been any justice in the world. The letter finally slipped from my lips, and I dropped the bags on the kitchen floor. "Fuck. Liz, you're the vampire; you have like ten times my strength. You should have let me carry the blood cooler. I have a terminal illness, remember." I shrugged off my coat and put it on the back of one of the chairs.

Liz rolled her eyes so hard I was positive I heard her neck crack. "Oh, don't be so dramatic, darling; it's not terminal. I had you carry the groceries because they're yours. Also, I don't need to maintain muscle tone. You do. So, truthfully, I'm looking out for you." She placed the cooler on the island and gestured to one of the bags as she sat at the table. "Be careful with that one; it has the eggs." To make matters worse, she scooped the latest' Vanity Fair' and sat at the table, leaving me to put everything away.

"Lazy, sadistic bitch," I muttered crankily under my breath. "I'm just looking out for you, my ass."

Liz laughed. "Well, we can't have you getting all flabby on me. I like buff women; a girl's gotta have her standards."

I shot her the finger as I snatched the letter off the floor and shoved it under a refrigerator magnet that read, 'Vegetarians eat vegetables. I am a humanitarian.'

Liz barked a laugh. "Cait, don't do that. It'll be ten years before you open it."

I glared at her. "Ha, bloody, ha. I'll open it soon enough."

"It's from your sister." Her words jerked me to a halt, and my heart stuttered a step. My chest tightened, and I was gripped by the image of Marcella staring down at me, using her glamour to steal away all memory of my sister. The trauma-induced vision didn't stop there, though. It continued relentlessly to its harrowing conclusion with the last words I ever spoke to Aoife, face to face. 'Wow, she looks like me, Ma.' Then I watched in curiosity as my sister screamed desolately for my help from the back of Marcella's Mercedes and vanished into the distance.

I blinked away tears and put my hand on the refrigerator handle, waiting for the flashback to pass and the maelstrom of conflicting emotions to still.

"Cait?"

"I'm fine," I said finally. "Just give me a minute."

Once free of the paralyzing vision, I took a deep, cleansing breath, blowing it out in a huff, then I pulled the letter from under the magnet and stuffed it into my back pocket. I'd read it later. I tried valiantly to stuff veggies and soy milk into any empty spot in the enormous Traulsen, but blood storage bags nearly filled the damn thing. I paused, celery in hand, searching for an open shelf.

"Honey, do you think we have enough?"

"That's for Katie, love, not me," Liz replied, sounding as if she were explaining it to a small child.

"Don't blame me for your hoarding, Aunt Liz," Katie commented from right behind me, making me jump. She was so quiet. I knew she'd been practicing being stealthy, but now it was just getting creepy—and irritating. She was scaring me on purpose these days.

"Now, girl, I told you to stop sneaking up on me like that— for goodness sake." I whacked her playfully on the shoulder with the celery. Liz howled with laughter while Katie just smiled her most innocent but broad, fang-ridden smile that served as all but a confession of her guilt.

"Sorry, mama," she said, though she didn't look the least bit remorseful as she kissed me on the cheek and snagged a bag of blood from the refrigerator, thankfully giving me just enough room for the celery.

Mama. The way Katie said it made me feel all squishy and warm inside. I returned Katie's hug and then released her as I returned to stuffing groceries into the fridge.

"Ice cream in the freezer, Cait," Liz said from behind her magazine.

"You want to do this?" I called over my shoulder and moved the vanilla-bean gelato to the freezer. *How did Liz see shit like that without looking up, anyway?*

Liz flipped to the next page, a playful smirk on her face.

I gave her the finger. "So, how was your day, Katie?"

She leaned casually against the island of the enormous kitchen, having cut the line on the blood bag, sipping it like a drink box. "Leah and I played cards, but you know that already. Otherwise, it was Fucking boring. I hate these online classes. I want to go to a real school."

I put my hands on my hips. "Cáitlín Briana Reagan! Language! And get a glass." Even as I said it, I could hear my mother's brogue in my voice.

"What? You say fuck all the time," Katie mumbled as she looked at the floor.

Liz grinned. "She's right, sweetheart. You do. Like mother, like daughter. Also, your Irish is showing; you sound like Róisín."

I twisted my face and squinted at Liz in mock irritation. "You keep out of this. You're not helping."

"Yes, I am," Liz replied with a laugh. "I'm just not helping you."

I shook my head as I loaded the last groceries, dug a soda from the refrigerator, and dropped heavily into a chair. It occurred to me that people who watched our family dynamics from the outside might think we didn't get along, but this kind of playful ribbing was one of our languages of love. You had to have a thick skin and a good sense of humor to live in this house. But there was certainly no question that we'd all go to the mat for each other; we already had.

As I sat, I noticed a tightness around Katie's eyes, and her overall expression had turned dark and a little miserable. "You okay, honey?"

Her heartbroken expression was enough to sour my soda if such a thing were possible. "I talked to Anne Fincher today.

She's conscious, but she's not doing well. She doesn't want to sign the adoption papers."

My stomach twisted back up into a tight not. I'd been afraid of this. "Did you explain about your bad times?"

"Yes. I told her, but she can only see her little girl. She doesn't understand that I don't remember her, like, at all. And I don't even like her." Tears began to well in Katie's eyes. "I don't want Leah and me to live with her, mama."

I grabbed a paper towel from a roll sitting on the table and handed it to her. "That's not going to happen again, Katie. I promise."

"There's an easy solution to the problem, Cait," Liz said absently, still reading her magazine.

"Jesus, Liz. I'm a cop! Honestly?" I turned to Katie. "Can you go upstairs, please? Your aunt and I need to have a word in private." Katie sniffed and headed to the elevator. "To the roof, Katie. No eavesdropping." Even from Marcella's bedroom, there was a good chance she might hear what I was about to say. Once I thought Katie was safely out of earshot, I turned on Liz. "Are you out of your mind?"

"Pay her off," Liz said flatly.

I blinked. "I'm sorry? What?" I had expected her to suggest just killing Anne; we could be a vicious lot.

"Pay. Her. Off. Katie was living on the street when we found her. Her mother may be trying to turn over a new leaf, or maybe not. But neither Anne nor Katie's father were interested in finding her until you found them first. And then they were mostly concerned about their welfare check. Now she's a new widow; she needs money."

Liz was probably right. There was just one problem. "I don't have any money, Liz."

"No, but I do," Liz said impassively.

"I can't ask you to do that."

"Who's asking? I'm offering."

"You'd do that for us?" I was floored. I scratched the back of my head, starting to feel a little choked up.

"Oh, don't get all slushy. After I was turned, I never wanted any more kids. But I have come to love her as much as you do.

You know that."

Tears started to well over my lashes. "What do you think she'd take?" I couldn't believe I was seriously considering it; it was crazy illegal.

Liz raised an eyebrow and cracked a mischievous smile. "What do I think she'd take? Or what is Katie worth? Anne will likely take less than six figures. Katie's worth about a tuppence-worth."

"Hey!" Katie's voice filtered down from the second-floor landing. "I heard that."

I hadn't known Katie was listening, but Liz certainly had. Katie returned to the kitchen, looking even more like someone had just ripped the insides out of her favorite stuffed animal. "Do you really think she'd sell me? I mean, isn't that wrong?"

"Katie, I'm sorry. We shouldn't have even discussed it. You're right; it's illegal. And I want you to know that I think you're amazing, not property. It was a stupid idea."

Liz looked at me with her face screwed up, and I was tempted to see if I'd grown horns or another head. I thought that, for a woman who'd actually had children, albeit three hundred years ago, she seemed clueless about how to raise them. But Liz continued to look at me strangely as if waiting for me to speak. I had no idea what she wanted me to say, though.

"That's not what's bothering her, Cait," Liz said finally, setting down the magazine and taking a sip of blood from Katie's discarded bag. "She feels bad because, even though she barely knows Anne, she believes, as do I, that Anne would happily trade her for money. Katie, honey, that's not about you. That's about her. We see how wonderful you are, and we're afraid she'll take you from us. You matter to us. We love you."

Though I had felt for weeks like I had no more tears, my eyes, as always, betrayed me and found some. I had a lot to fucking learn. Katie grabbed my arm, pulling Liz and me into a bone-crushing hug.

I groaned playfully. "Easy, kid, you'll break my ribs." Katie eased up but didn't let go, and Liz laughed without reservation. I knew right then and there that Liz loved us both. And for the first time since Mike died, I felt like I had a real family. And from the way Liz was laughing, it seemed she did too.

The doorbell rang, and I extricated myself from the hug. "I'll get it."

I strode to the door and opened it, wiping the tears of laughter from my eyes. Outside stood a tall man in his late forties with dark hair and a fairly long, unkempt beard. He wore a brown wool trench coat with fraying sleeves and held out an envelope. "Cait Reagan?" His voice sounded familiar, but I couldn't place it immediately.

"Yes?"

He looked like a guy serving court papers. I'd been through this before, so I took the envelope and held out my hand for the pen to sign. My tongue flicked out, catching the scent of stale cigarettes, alcohol, and greasy cheeseburger on his breath. His body odor suggested he hadn't bathed in a while, regardless of how much Old Spice he slathered on. I glanced down at the envelope; it was blank.

"Die, you vampire bitch!" He shouted, and before I could do more than look up, he pulled a shotgun from under his coat and blasted me, point-blank, in the chest. I fell backward to the hard floor, feeling the wind knocked out of me.

"F-f-fuck," I gasped, tasting blood and feeling a warm line trickle down my cheek. No matter how hard I tried to suck in a breath, I couldn't get air. Panic set in, and my vision tunneled at the edges, and I thought I heard tires squeal. I looked left and right, my hands clawing at the marble as I desperately tried to breathe.

Liz appeared over me. "Cait, darling! Hold on. I got you. Just hold on, baby."

"Mama, stay with us." It was Katie's voice, but my vision was spotty, and I couldn't see her. Liz sliced open her throat, and cold drops of her blood fell into my mouth and across my cheeks, but I couldn't swallow.

I coughed. Blood spattered back over Liz's face. I tried to speak, but nothing came out. I squeezed at Liz's hand, and a tear fell down my cheek as I realized this was it. Who would take care of them all if I wasn't there?

Time seemed to slow down as the pain finally burst through the shock, and my body convulsed just once. I flicked my eyes back and forth across them. The family I'd finally found.

I tried to gulp once, then twice. Then the pain fell away as Liz and Katie said something else. But their voices were just faint echoes as the blackness swallowed me.

The last thing I remembered was choking as a hot gush of blood flowed over my lips, into my mouth, and down my savaged throat.

Join Aoife Reagan

In

GREEN RATH: A CAIT REAGAN NOVEL

Coming Soon - Wherever Books are Sold

GLOSSARY

Ánámensí - (os. Ah-nah-men-si) Matron of one of the remaining thirty-seven high houses of the city of Işir on the world of Oşen.

Centrus - (unk. Sen-truss) City that serves as a hub for the currently open inter-dimensional gates, including, most notably, the Kaushkari, Oşeni, and Niatamo gates.

Déra - (os. Day-rah) Uncommon Oşeni female name. Most famously, the appellation of a former guard captain of Işir, who vanished following the defeat of Avra in the Cycle of Our Lady 6998.

дорогая - (ru. Doro-guy-ah) term of endearment (eg. sweetie)

Emisai - (os. Em-is-aye) Construct of Mother Darkness, this creature is bipedal but has no head or obvious sensing organs. Only black-steel as constructed by the Oşeni scholars of Mens-Dhe can harm them. Other metals without magical construction will leave no long-term injury.

Ё-моё - (ru. Yo-my-or) obscene. approx. Fuck your grandmother. Used as an exclamation (eg.Holy Shit!)

Işir - (os. Ish-eer) Primary city of the world of Oşen. The city is ruled by a matriarchal priestess caste. Males are considered second-class citizens having fewer rights.

Koşant - (os. Kō-shant) Bipedal demon-like creature with razor-sharp claws, roughly man-shaped and covered in mottled insectile chitin. It has a triangular, mantis-like face, with a beak-like mouth.

Kylir - (ky. Kī-leer) Single sex, bipedal humanoid species that is the dominant life form of the world known only as the Kylir Plain. They are characterized by iridescent white skin, silver hair, and black eyes. Most notable and interesting is their reproductive cycle. At death, the corpse of the dead Kyliri transforms into a second stage, a worm-like creature that carries a smaller parasitic animal in which the life and memories of the dead Kylir are preserved until introduced to a new host, at which point the parasite consumes the brain of the host, preserving the memories and adding it to its own as it assumes control of the host body.

Oşen - (os. Ō-shen) One of the ten known worlds containing gates to Centrus, the core city of the ancients who constructed the first gates. It is populated by a dioecious species known locally as the Oşeni.

Oşeni - (os. Ō-shen-ee) Bipedal humanoid species populating the world of Oşen. They are concentrated in a single city on the world's surface known as Işir. The species is dioecious (having two sexes, male and female) and typically stands between 2 and 2.1 meters in height. They are characterized by lustrous gray skin, thick silver hair, and muscular frames. It is believed by some scholars that this group may have been the inspiration for certain depictions of elves because of their pointed ears.

Хуй тебе - (ru. Hui-tibyə) obscene. Fuck you or go fuck yourself.

Xharpras - (os. ɦarp-rahs) A stringed instrument of the Oşeni similar to a harp. The black-steel strings and unusual tunings create secondary thematic elements in music, such as the sounds of waves crashing on rocks or wind blowing through trees. It is considered one of the most difficult instruments to play in the ten known worlds.

Umbrá - (os. Um-brah) Uncommon Oşeni female name. Most famously, the appellation of a Kyliri slave who was responsible for the downfall of Avra following the Dark Invasion in the Cycle of Our Lady 6998.

About the Author

Aoibh Wood lives in New England with her wife and their adorable orange tabby, Jabb. . .err. . .Papaya. She enjoys travel, the outdoors, playing guitar, and weightlifting.